IN THE LIGHT OF THE MOON

A LIGHT IN THE DARK
BOOK ONE

NOELLE UPTON

AUTHOR'S NOTE

Dear reader, I hope you enjoy this sweet and paranormal romance book. The characters are very close to my heart, and I hope you love them.

A few notes, this book contains mature themes, including explicit sexual scenes and language, violence, and gore. Feel free to send me an email if you have any further questions/concerns.

Additionally, one of the main characters in this novel is on the autism spectrum. I am in no way an expert on autism and have strived to treat this and my other characters with consideration and care.

I am an independent author, and though this book has been combed through and edited, mistakes happen. If you find any errors, please let me know so that I can do my best to correct them.

With all that being said, I hope you truly enjoy meeting Sylvie and Orion.

To my sister. For everything.

PART ONE
RISE

CHAPTER ONE

SYLVIE

"That'll be thirty dollars and sixty cents." I pasted a pleasant smile on my face, aimed at the two teens that had just ordered, and spun the register's tablet around for them to see their total. They paid me no mind as the taller one tapped a credit card and signed. I noticed that they declined to leave a tip but kept my smile steady. "We'll have that right out." They slunk into one of the dingy booths near the back corner, and I drummed my freshly painted fingernails on the counter.

The Tuesday evening passed by in a dull rhythm that I had grown used to. We were a little busier since it was summer, but weeknights were always a bit slower. And most chose to order online rather than come in at all.

I packed orders after Louis and Evan in the kitchen pulled pizzas out of the ovens, wings out of the fryers. Evan's portable speaker blasted Sweet Leaf by Black Sabbath, and I found myself humming along to it while I wiped down tables, though people mostly sat inside just to wait for their orders.

The hours went by, and I tried to recount my lesson with Granna that morning, testing if I had memorized the newest recipe. I imagined the spicy aroma within the mortar as she instructed me how best to carefully break seed husks so as to not fully pulverize. My fingers still carried a hint of the peppery scent, and I passed the time thinking through her critiques and what I would try to make next. Soon, I was ticking away at my closing duties, the last orders of the night were rolling through, and I heard the guys start to shut things down.

My black combat boots weren't exactly non-slip, but I'd thought it silly to buy new shoes for a job I hadn't intended to stay at for very long. Classes were about to start, and the smell of pepperoni and fryer oil clinging to my hair was beyond unpleasant. I'd asked Josie to let me know if she heard of any openings around, and I planned on taking another walk-through town this weekend to inquire at pretty much any place besides here.

But, for the time being, Vinny's was a simple enough place to work. I could spend most of my time reviewing my notes from Granna's lessons or working on short stories, so it wasn't all bad.

After I mopped behind the register, I stepped carefully and wheeled the bucket where the guys could grab it once they finished cleaning everything else back there. I was in charge of the front of house, so I collected the two half-full bags of garbage from the cans I was responsible for and whistled along to an old country song blaring from the kitchen.

I made my way out the back door and sucked in the humid, but surprisingly cool, night air. Autumn was quietly approaching, and I sucked in a long breath, tasting the impending change of season. I tugged forward the silk bandana I tied around my hair, as it always tended to slip, and heaved the garbage bags up and over into the smelly dumpster. My hands wiped absently at my denim shorts and righted my red work shirt that had Vinny's Pizza stamped across the chest. At least that was all for the required uniform.

Asphalt crunched under my boots as I practically skipped toward the door, excited to be going home in a few minutes, when a choked sound made me pause.

I stilled, cocking my head to try and identify the direction it came from. The old pizza shop was on the edge of the historic downtown, and to my left, there was a grassy area that extended into the dark forest. Though I hadn't lived in town long, I knew that the woods extended for quite aways, part of it even near Granna's house. The moon was bright and almost full overhead, but the trees and brush swallowed most of the light it provided.

There it was again. That noise. I whipped around when I realized that it almost sounded… pained. Like an injured animal? My eyes glanced again to the forest, and when I heard a stuttering exhale coming from somewhere near the dumpster, I walked tentatively away from the door.

Though I didn't know what I would find on the other side, the thought to be afraid never crossed my mind. I'd never been a very fearful person, anxiety about other life circumstances was more my speed, and I only felt a sense of calm concern with the mouth of the woods looming beside me. My chest felt warm, and the branches rustled when a lazy breeze made its way from the forest's depths toward me. It smelled of purest earth, and my gait was almost relaxed as I made my way to the other side of the dumpster.

There was only one light overhead back here, and it appeared almost flickering with all of the moths and flying critters that clustered and fanned around it. Though I was usually worried about insects landing and getting tangled in my hair, I paid them no mind. The sight before me left my body frozen.

It was a man.

Some guy was crumpled and leaning against the dumpster and the brick facade of Vinny's. His chest was rising and falling very quickly, but it was like he was trying to remain as silent as possible.

But then, like the pain was too much, he would make that choked, shuddering sound while his shoulders shook.

I crouched and heard my knee give a hearty crack at the movement. The old leather of my boots shifted, and I pressed my forearms into my thighs. "Hey… are you okay?" The guy stilled at my voice but didn't lift his head.

From where I was, a few good paces between us, I saw that he was probably taller than me, though he was hunched over with arms wrapped around himself. The pale color of his hair made me almost think he was older. But another bout of pain made him twitch, and I saw that his skin was unwrinkled.

I inched forward, still crouched. "Hey? Can I get you some water or something? Do I need to call someone?" He definitely flinched at that, and I sucked in a breath when his head lifted enough for me to see wide, bright green eyes. Like, eerily green.

They were… pretty. Like the almost glowing color of those antique glasses that you'd find at vintage stores. Too dangerous to drink from, but beautiful all the same.

They pulled me in, and then I was within arm's reach of him. His eyes darted to the woods behind me, but he remained silent. I sank down to my haunches and sucked in more air. Now that I was closer, I could smell… blood? I took another big inhale, and the sound of it made him eye me warily. Yeah, that was blood.

I looked over his body again, noting now that he was clutching at his side while his other arm was almost limp against his middle.

"You're hurt. I can call an ambulance or something?" My hand was extended out towards him, wanting to touch and see how bad his wounds were but also wanting for him to remain calm. He kept looking toward the forest, as if something was standing there, and I looked across my shoulder to follow his panicked gaze.

There was nothing but the rustling of trees and the buzzing of the light overhead. I could hear the blaring music the guys played through the door that was propped open, but there was nothing else.

I twisted back around to look at the man, and I marveled at the paleness of him. His skin and hair were about the same, off-white pallor. His lip looked busted, bright red blood contrasting heavily against the plump skin. The blood trailing down from his nose made it even worse. What happened to him?

"Did someone hurt you?" I tried to keep my voice low, soothing, but he flinched again, staring right at me, and bared his teeth.

"Look, I'm not," I raised both palms, "trying to hassle you. But you look like you could use some help." My teeth sank into my bottom lip, trying to decide what to do. His eyes stabbed back toward the forest again.

I crept a little closer, but he ignored me. He didn't seem to have any trouble breathing, but my guess was he hadn't collapsed beside a dumpster at the back of a failing pizza joint because he could just run or drive away. Had someone beat him up back here while the three of us had been right on the other side of the brick wall?

Now that I was just a half-step away, I could see more blood seeping through the fabric of the dark shirt he wore. It was long-sleeved, but I could also see that it was worse for wear. There were scuffs and tears in the fabric, his hair messy and blood-stained. His jeans looked dirty, and I wondered if he had any wounds on his legs, too.

"Let me just see where you're hurt and I—" But I'd been moving too fast. I'd felt lulled into him accepting my company and touch when he let me get closer. But when my left hand reached out to pull some debris away from the injured areas, a grumble made its way to my ears just after he was a flurry of movement. Green eyes and white teeth flashing, my arm was knocked away from him, and so was the rest of my body.

The air whooshed out of my lungs when my back hit the asphalt, and then he was leaning over me. My heart thudded quickly in my chest, and I gasped for breath, to figure out what to do. His hands were planted on either side of my head, but his legs weren't pinning mine down. A drop of blood from his nose dripped onto my cheek, but I didn't dare wipe it away.

Up close, I could see that he didn't look much older than me, and it was like his skin had actually been leeched of color. There were purple bruises forming where someone had undoubtedly hit him, and there were even deep marks that I could see near his collar that looked like... punctures?

I tried to think of something to say, to do, and though he didn't have my arms pinned either, I worried that moving in any way would set him off again.

"I-I'm sorry. That this happened to you," I took a shaky breath, "and that I got too close." My throat actually gulped, and his eerie eyes tracked the movement. I parted my lips to say something else, but then he looked at me again, and my lips slammed shut.

He pressed closer for a moment, just a breath, and I belatedly saw that his hair, though frizzy and standing on end, was made of big, soft looking curls.

The man lurched back, and I was left staring at the darkened sky. I sucked in precious air before carefully sitting up, still afraid to make any sudden movements. He was like an injured animal cornered, attacking anything that got too close.

And, with the way he was crouched, settled closer to the dumpster than before, I supposed he was.

I cleared my throat and gathered my feet beneath me. At some point the music inside had cut off, and I knew that Louis or Evan would be coming out here any second to toss their garbage away before locking up. And for some reason, I didn't want them finding this man.

I wiped at my cheek with the back of my hand and stammered, "I'm going inside to get my things and make sure no one comes back here. Is that... is that okay?" I really hadn't been expecting some sort of answer. He didn't seem drunk or high before, but something in his features seemed more settled, now. There was a little more reasoning in them, and though he wouldn't exactly meet my eyes like he had been, he surprised me by giving a jerky nod.

My lips curled up in a small smile. "Okay, okay, cool. And I can get you some water?" Another nod, and my smile grew. I stood and dusted off my ass and the backs of my thighs but kept my distance as I took a step toward the door. When his shoulders didn't rise in unease, I kept going, even giving a lame little wave.

The guys were grabbing their things when I made my way back inside, and Evan had two full bags of trash in his hands. "I'll grab that for you!" I hurried to get my big, slouchy purse and filled a large to-go cup with ice water. While I waited for the liquid to dispense, I shoved on my old jean jacket and readjusted my bandana once again. I plucked a straw from the restocked drink station before taking the bags from where Evan had left them propped against the wall.

It was a bit awkward gripping the two heavy bags in one fist while I clutched the water cup to me, but I managed not to drop anything. "See you tomorrow," I shouted as they made their way to the front to leave and lock the door from the outside.

The garbage bags were almost dragging on the ground by the time I made it out the back door again, and I kicked in the heavy can of tomatoes that we used to prop it open. The door swung in with a metallic clack, and I lifted my foot to give a good kick behind me to make sure that it was closed all the way.

First things first, I dropped the garbage near the door and held the cup as if it was a priceless treasure or life-saving medicine. My heart picked up again, this time in fear that the man was gone, but when I rounded the dark green dumpster, he was still there, albeit sitting a bit more casually.

His head snapped up when I came into view, but he seemed to relax when recognition flared in his eyes. I crouched again, trying to remember not to get as close as I normally would when speaking with someone.

"Um, here." I extended the water toward him, but then I felt silly because there was too much space between us for him to reach it without us getting closer to one another. I set it on the asphalt and stood. "I'm going to throw some garbage into this dumpster here. There may be a loud noise, but that's all it is, okay?" He looked at the water tentatively then back toward me without meeting my gaze again. He nodded, and I tried to offer another encouraging smile. He ducked his head, fluffy hair bouncing. I wanted to make sure he could get the water himself, but when he reached out with his right hand and promptly hissed in pain before switching to his left, I decided to give him a bit of privacy.

The heavy bags banged the inside of the dumpster as I tossed them in, and I was glad that I warned him about the noise. If I were him, the sound would've made me think I was under attack. And that thought made me wonder again what had happened. He seemed a bit more lucid now, but maybe he didn't know? Had he been mugged?

When I came back, he was taking long pulls from the straw. His right arm was still curled in toward his body, but the left was holding the weight of the water cup easily. One of his legs was cocked up with a knee bent in an almost comfortable pose, and the other was extended and facing me. I could see that it had a darkened mark on the already dark fabric, and I wondered if that was mud or blood. I was guessing the latter. Maybe that's why he hadn't tried to move much more from where he'd probably collapsed in pain.

"Are you sure there isn't someone I should call for you?" I kept my voice low and open so that he didn't feel that I was pressuring him. I wasn't one to jump to calling the police, and ambulances were exorbitantly expensive. That, I knew from experience. What if he didn't have insurance or was too disoriented to really consent to it? What if it ruined whatever rapport we'd built over this time?

His low, husky voice pulled me out of my worried thoughts immediately. "No. Thank you."

My ass met the asphalt once again, and I sat cross-legged, leaning towards him and just managing to not come any closer than that. "Are you sure? I can call you a ride or something?" It felt rude to not offer to drive him somewhere, but I did at least have a little bit of a sense of self preservation.

"No," he said again, still avoiding my eyes every time I tried to meet his, "and I'm sorry… if I scared you." He took another nervous sip, and I heard the desperate pulls of the straw as he emptied the cup completely.

My lips pursed, trying to decide what to do now since Vinny's was closed, and I couldn't get him any more. The ice would certainly melt and provide some more water eventually, but until then, what?

He must have taken my silence, distracted once again by my own thoughts on how best I could help him, for something else, because he cleared his throat and started drawing his extended leg toward himself. When he set the drink down and planted that now-empty palm on the ground, I realized that he was trying to stand.

"Wait!" I couldn't help myself and sprang to my feet. My father would have chastised me, called me too trusting, but I offered my hand out for him to use as leverage to stand.

After a pointed moment of hesitation, wherein his panting was audible and I'd stopped breathing altogether, he relented. His hand was rough with calluses but warm, and thankfully, not slick with blood like his other one.

I kept my arm and hand a steady weight for him to press down on. And though I could feel him holding back, I remained still against the pressure until he was upright. He used the wall to support himself for just a second before pushing up to stand on his own two feet.

He took a long, drawing breath through his nose, and when he exhaled, his shoulders seemed to relax even more. His injured arm was still curled in toward his body, and his face was definitely banged up, but he otherwise looked like he would be okay.

When he slowly looked at me, downwards since he was several inches taller, he met my eyes for a brief moment and then settled somewhere on my forehead. "Thanks. I'll be fine."

My brows drew up at the center. "Are you sure? Do you live near here? Is there… somewhere I can take you to?" Well, looked like all of my good sense had flown out the window. I chewed at my lip again, trying not to let the swell of guilt and worry rise at the prospect of being away from home for longer. Granna probably wouldn't care, but I didn't like leaving her alone for longer than I absolutely needed to.

The man shook his head. "No, I'm fine," he reiterated. "Ah, thank you. For your help." He started to take a slow step forward, and I shuffled to the side to be out of his way.

My mouth kept opening and closing as I watched him take surer and surer steps, not toward the forest or the parking lot, but around the other end of the building. Across a grassy area between establishments, I knew he would come upon more businesses and eventually the main road. Was he going to walk?

"Hey." I jogged to catch up with him, and I saw his shoulders stiffen, though he kept walking. It was like his body was waking up, better able to push past whatever wounds he had with every step. "Are you just going to walk—"

He didn't look at me, but I saw his jaw clenching in the light from the streetlamps and storefronts we walked under. "Please. Leave me alone."

A choked sound left my mouth, and my feet stuttered to a stop. What the hell?

Again, I fought for what to say, but it was like I was stuck in place. He was at least well enough to walk, barely limping, but he couldn't be fine. Right?

In my indecision, he seemed to have picked up speed, and then he was across the empty street. I almost started following after him again, but I then thought better of it. I didn't know this man, and he didn't owe me anything. He was clearly an adult who could make his own decisions, and he was well enough to tell me that he didn't want me to keep talking to or walking with him.

With a confused and frustrated huff, I forced my eyes away from his shrinking form and turned back toward Vinny's where my old red sedan was the only vehicle in the lot.

I got in, closing and locking the door behind me before

cranking the car to life. The twangy R&B music I'd been blaring on the way in made me jump before frantically dialing it almost all the way down.

When I backed out and started up the road, I tried to catch another glimpse of his white body dressed in dark clothing. But it was like he'd disappeared.

I gave up, and while I made my way home, a silly part of me wondered if I'd gotten all worked up trying to save a ghost.

CHAPTER TWO

SYLVIE

The kitchen light was still on when I pulled up to the back of the house. It was after midnight, but I'd quickly learned that older people didn't sleep nearly as much as I thought they would. Though my father had been in his late fifties, twenty plus years younger than Granna, he'd slept way more than she ever seemed to.

I strolled past the bursting flowers and greenery that took on a deeper color under the glow of the porch light above. My hand reached out to caress lush petals of white and red dahlias, and I hopped up the back wooden steps with ease. The screen door on the porch squeaked. Making a mental note to hit the hinges with some WD-40, I entered the kitchen after finding the door unlocked.

Before I could panic, I was met with Granna sitting at the small table under the large bay window with a book in hand and a steaming mug of tea before her.

I locked the door behind me and started to hang my purse on a set of small hooks. "Hey, Granna, how was—"

She cut me off with a short hiss and a finger raised, eyes

darting back and forth on her page. I snickered and busied myself by reaching into the pearl white, retro refrigerator that she'd somehow managed to keep up and running all these years.

The kitchen was a good size and always kept remarkably clean. I often had to shoo the woman away from standing on chairs to dust on top of the high cabinets or getting down on hands and knees to scrub the floors. While she was an active person, and typically sharp as a tack, I'd immediately noticed the passage of time and wear of the years when I moved in just a few months ago.

"Okay, sorry, sweetheart," her soft voice was warm, "how was work?" Granna stuck an old leather bookmark in the center of her latest read and settled it on the table, giving me her full attention.

I poured a glass of lemonade from the half-full pitcher that took up a large amount of space in the fridge. It was lip-puckering tart and mellowly flavored with honey and lavender. I leaned against the counter and faced her. "It was," my head ducked to inspect the floating lavender petals, fingers tapping on the sweating glass, "fine. Typical." I shrugged. Not that Granna would think I was losing it or anything, but I still didn't even know what I thought about the encounter with that strange man. Had he made it to wherever he lived? Or was he lying behind another dumpster somewhere, even more injured—or worse?

Should I have followed him and insisted he accept my help? Or maybe I should have called an ambulance anyway.

"I don't know why you insist on working at that place. You smell like grease, sweetheart." Granna shuddered and took a sip of her tea. Her long, loose hair fell in pretty, gray waves. She'd never adopted the tendency of older folks cutting their hair in shorter styles. Admittedly not as thick as I remember it being when I was little, her hair fell a considerable length down her back, and it shifted against her cotton nightgown.

"Well, it was the first place that was hiring, and I'm trying to find a different job anyway."

"If I knew you were going to be moving in, I wouldn't have sold the shop."

"But if you hadn't, the house wouldn't be paid off. And I wouldn't be able to come back and finish my degree." I stood and leaned over to press a kiss to her head. She smelled like her favorite lavender soap and tart berries, and it further reinforced that I was where I wanted to be. After everything, at least I could call this place home.

I saw that her mug was empty and picked it up, walking over to the sink to rinse it out and place in the dishwasher I'd had to convince her to buy.

"Be that as it may," Granna turned to look out the window, toward the yard and woods that were just a short ways beyond, "you're not getting enough sun working evenings at that place. Sleeping all through the day."

My eyes rolled when I was sure she couldn't see. "Not everyone can spend their days gardening and reading by the creek, fancy lady." Even in the dim light of the kitchen, I could see the darker brown shade her skin had adopted after many hours outside. How this woman didn't have more wrinkles on her face aside from a handful of smile lines and an elegant set of crow's feet was beyond me. She spent enough time in the sun to look twenty years older than she did now.

I looked down at my own hand, and, okay sure, she had a point. My own tawny coloring was a bit light for the summer weather. "Okay, how about we go explore tomorrow? You can keep teaching me your wise witchy ways, and I'll get some vitamin D. Win-win."

Granna chuckled absently with her eyes still somewhere beyond the large bay window, and after she didn't make to turn around, I walked over to see if there was something out there. It was hard to see with the light from inside reflecting in the glass, but as I approached further, I couldn't detect anything besides the small but full yard and the darkened silhouette of dense foliage.

I looked back down at my grandmother and saw that her eyes

were tightened, as if confused or searching. Her slender chest was rising and falling much more quickly than it had been before, but her breaths were silent. Worry started making my hands twitch, and I placed one on her shoulder to try and get her attention. "Granna?"

But she just kept looking with that strange expression on her face, and I watched the empty yard, half expecting for some dark figure to appear.

After an increasingly agonizing amount of time, I gently nudged her. "The wolf will be here for you," she said so quietly that I almost didn't catch it, "and he'll be waiting for me."

Dread. That's what her nonsensical words struck in me. She seemed to shake herself after that, pulling away from her watch of the night outside, and let me lead her out of the kitchen and upstairs to her room as if it hadn't happened.

But these episodes were happening more and more. Her friend next door, Roz, had warned me about it after helping me get settled. She'd pulled me aside while Granna was in the restroom to let me know that while she was usually completely with it, she sometimes had these... slips. Where she seemed to go somewhere else and say things that didn't make sense.

Over the three months that I'd been staying with her, it didn't happen so often that I felt like I had to... call someone. She had regular appointments to her doctor, who was already aware of the occurrence and hadn't found anything alarming. The woman was eighty years old and otherwise healthy.

But this was the second time in the past week. Were they getting worse? I tried to shake away the frantic train of thought my mind was spiraling into as I said goodnight to her and continued to my own room.

It was long ago cleared out after my mother moved out to live with my father and eventually have me, but I felt like I could still detect the faint scent of her.

The furniture in the room now was all that I brought from my old apartment, and I walked to the nightstand that I'd had since I was a teenager to plug in and set my phone down. It was nearly one in the morning now, and if I wanted to be up in time to meet my early rising grandmother, I needed to go to bed.

After scooping up my oversized t-shirt to change into, I made my way to the small bathroom down the hall that I'd claimed as my own. The steam from the shower quickly engulfed the room tiled in shades of green and pink.

I stood before the fogging mirror and began to strip off my jacket when a stinging pain made me hiss. The denim fabric dragged over a tender area on my forearm, and when I finally peeled the jacket off, my breath caught at the long gouge that ran between my elbow and wrist.

The blood was already clotted, but the area was surprisingly tender, especially since I hadn't noticed it at all. My mind ran over what all I had done today, trying to remember how I'd scratched myself this badly. I was no stranger to finding unknown bruises from bumping into things and quickly moving on to whatever I was doing in that moment, but this was far from a stray bruise.

When the hot water of the shower hit my back, I carefully kept my arm out of the scalding spray and gently cleaned it by carefully working in some of the unscented soap I kept in the shower shelf.

I fought pathetic whimpers as I cleaned the wound, and the memory of the man crouched over me, face vicious, made me gasp. How had I forgotten that? Granna's words and his retreating form down the street had been in the forefront of my mind so boldly that I'd quickly forgotten how he reacted when I tried to check his wounds.

After running downstairs to the kitchen for the salve Granna helped me make last week, I continued my nighttime routine of braiding my hair and lotioning my skin. The homemade remedy eased some of the sting from the scratch, and when I laid my head down on my pillow, I couldn't stop staring up at the ceiling, eyes wide open. My head slipped and slid on my silk pillowcase, body unable to settle and find a comfortable position, especially with the image of those bright, green eyes.

Would I ever see him again? Or, I gave a panicked swallow, what if what was happening to Granna… was happening to me? Could that even be possible? As far as I knew, her seeing and saying strange things was a newer occurrence, and I barely remembered my own mother to be able to know if she'd experienced anything like that. The guys at Vinny's hadn't seen him, right?

I turned on my side, keeping my freshly bandaged left arm outstretched so as to not rub it on my sheets. My finger trailed along the length of the cut, careful to only apply enough pressure to feel the existence of it. The answering twinge confirmed—assured—that the man was real. That I'd found him behind my part-time pizza gig and watched him limp down the street into the night like a phantom.

With who my grandmother was, I was certainly open to the possibility of something… otherworldly happening. But, with all that she did and taught me through the years, I'd never had an experience like this one before. Surely at twenty-eight, I wouldn't be seeing my first ghost now, right?

No, I thought to myself before sleep came up behind and swallowed me whole, I'm probably just losing it.

. . . . . ☽ . . . . .

I sat on the boulder, feeling its solid, cool grounding. The air was warm, sticky. But the stream was burbling with cool, clear water, and the trees with their full canopies provided enough cover from the sun. Granna sat aways away, where she was enveloped by the rays of sunshine. Her gray hair shone white under the brightness, but the breeze through the forest coursed past us both. Sweat beaded on my temples, on my lower back, but it was easy to ignore here.

When I lived with my father, the city pressed in on my body and mind so closely that I grew accustomed to the claustrophobic sensation of being closed in and off from this. A wave of sadness threatened to beat against my legs, knock me down and drown me, but I inhaled through it just as another breeze cooled my heated skin. I let images of hospitals and his ashen brown skin and IV drips drift away on my exhale.

My childhood was filled with love from him and his side of my family, but a thread of anxiety always stayed within my grasp, always slipping and cutting through my fingers. Like holding onto it was the only commonality. What reminded me of me. The two weeks each summer, though, when I would visit with Granna, would smack upside my head and leave me drunk on stillness and connection.

As I grew older, where friends and self-image and sneaking out to make out with boys and girls felt more important than anything else, I drifted away from this peace once again. She never admonished me or made me feel selfish for exploring those parts of myself, for being swept up in the excitement of adolescence. And then my father's illness completely swallowed the beginnings of my adulthood. It clouded all of that stage of my growth.

I was free of it now, as fucked up as that sounded.

I opened my eyes, blinking wetly and adjusting to the midmorning light. Granna sprawled on a blanket she'd brought from home, book abandoned and face-down beside her chest while she basked in the sunlight.

When I'd told her I was moving back, I saw her shock, and it made me feel even smaller. Though I had a few extended cousins through my father and a distant aunt I communicated with sporadically, Granna felt like my true family. Who I could exhale with.

The passage of time, the years I saw etched into her elegant wrinkles, worried me. They signaled the time I'd let slip through my fingers like dry sand on the beach. Warm and fleeting.

I closed my eyes again, felt a drop of sweat bead and slide down my chest. The summer heat had just crested, and I felt its descent in the air. As I prepared for the semester to start, for me to finally finish my degree, I'd also committed to learning from Granna.

Which was why I was sitting out here, sweating my ass off, but weirdly contented to keep doing it.

"As much as I enjoy this," my voice broke the spell the nature was lulling us into, "what am I supposed to be listening for, again?"

Without opening her eyes at all, Granna waved a delicate hand in the air. "Listening for any and everything that speaks to you. Between working at that awful place and sitting crumpled on the couch on your laptop, you were in desperate need of some sun."

I passed a hand over the bandage on my arm, trying not to think about the weird tan I'd have when I finally removed it. "Vinny's isn't that bad, Granna." But it felt futile to try and convince her. "And I help you in the garden almost every morning!" Yeah, the spell was definitely interrupted now.

I stretched my arms over my head, and some of my joints gave a resounding crackle. I swung my legs off the boulder, feeling the soft, wild grass between my toes. My lungs filled greedily with the scent of the forest. They said that scent and taste connected most strongly in our memories, and I couldn't help recognizing the pleasant humming I'd been settling into since moving to Antler Pointe. It spoke of hours exploring the land, mixing up potions with no direction but my own imagination, and listening to the whispers.

"Well, as we've established, you're absolutely hopeless when it comes to anything but basic upkeep of the garden," she drawled.

"Hey!" I yelled, but it had no bite, just like her rather blunt assessment was more teasing than anything. Granna basically had a whole jungle of houseplants inside her home, and even more impressive than that was her sprawling garden that remained healthy and growing during all parts of the year. Though she trusted me to water and prune, she just made me sit back and watch while she touched on the flowers to make them unfurl or while she used her powers to rehabilitate anything that needed extra caring.

I very evidently didn't have growing magic. That's okay, I reassured myself. After I killed one of her rose bushes, Granna had redirected my studies to trying out recipes from The Book and exploring other types of magic.

I went over and sat beside her on the blanket, even though the sun felt like it was biting my skin. What I wouldn't give for the crisp breeze of fall.

It wasn't like I didn't appreciate summer and all that came with it, necessarily. The buzzy, sociable energy was nice. The extra daylight hours made me feel productive. But the reprieve of autumn, where the air had a softer bite, made me feel right. The stress of the impending semester would feel a bit lighter once it started getting cooler.

I looked down at Granna, taking in her darkening brown skin and topknot of gray hair. Even though her eyes were still closed, she asked, "What happened to your arm?" The cut had healed substantially while I slept, but I was still weary of exposing it to the sun while we were out here.

"Scratched myself. Just didn't want to get a sunburn while it's still healing." I tried to inject as much nonchalance into my voice as possible.

But Granna, even with her slips, was frighteningly perceptive. She looked up at me from her lounged position. Her deep brown eyes, like the bark of the forest around us, echoed my own. "You scratched yourself. With what, a switchblade? Your fingernails are long, but not that deadly." She gestured to the bandage, and I felt increased heat flood my face.

"Do you believe in ghosts?" I blurted. Though I already knew the answer, it felt like as good a distraction as any.

She scoffed and started to sit up. "Of course, sweetheart. Witches, shifters, Fae, vampires—all of them are a given. Ghosts are a bit more common, though. See them periodically. You know this." I put all the supernatural beings aside and directed my attention to the part about ghosts. It used to scare me as a child, when she would stop in the middle of a shopping trip or stroll in the forest and speak of spirits that she saw.

I busied myself with righting my bikini top, tightening the straps at the back of my neck. "What... do they look like?"

"You don't remember?" When I didn't answer, she sighed and leaned back on her palms.

She was truly a daughter of summer. Her skin seemed to glow underneath the harsh sunlight, and I felt a gnawing regret at not pushing to visit her more often before moving to Antler Pointe this past May. It felt like there wasn't enough time, now.

"For me," she said with her eyes still closed, preening toward the sun, "they look almost as tangible as you and I. But they are also transparent, when you try to look at them square on. You'd probably be able to see them better than me if you open up to it."

And without explaining further, she closed her book, tucking it under her arm, and stood. "What do you mean I'd be able to see them?" A lump was bubbling up in my throat. With her abilities, I'd considered the man from last night being a ghost a possibility... but I realized in that moment that I wanted so desperately for him to be real—alive. Even if I never saw him again.

Granna shrugged, and if I wasn't so experienced in feigning and schooling my expression, I wouldn't have caught her doing that very thing, now. "It's in your blood, after all. You've been closed off to it for a while, but you used to see them all the time as a child."

Another breeze coursed through the forest that would soon be a spectacle of yellows, oranges, and reds.

"Your mother did, too," she continued. "She used to talk to them." I could hear the smile in her voice, and I felt my own lips curl upwards in a grin.

My mother had long ago died in a car accident, so I had very few of my own memories of her. But Granna softened when she spoke of her only child, and I relished the moments where she'd fill in more pieces of my incomplete picture of the woman that gave me life. I wondered if one of the reasons Granna refused to move was because she'd given birth to my mother in her house. It was where she'd raised and taught her about the earth and how to harness its energy.

"Are you ready to head back inside?"

I followed her lead and stood. "Yeah." A cool glass of lemonade was indeed needed after our morning in the heat.

"Well, let's have a snack, and perhaps we can tackle another section of The Book."

We walked silently back to the house, and try as I did to catch the whispers I sometimes heard in my dreams, there was nothing but the crunching of our footsteps and the normal rustling of the brush and wildlife.

When we emerged from the forest and crossed the short grassy distance between it and the small white house, we entered from the side door that led into the kitchen. I immediately sighed at the first blast of air conditioning. How Granna survived without it when she first bought the house, I had no idea. Though the small New England town had fairly mild summers considering, I wouldn't be able to stand sitting in a hot, stuffy house through the entirety of the season.

She stood at the kitchen island and expertly worked a knife over a pineapple, cutting it into perfect chunks for us to snack on. I sat with my feet up on the small bench under the bay window and fanned myself with my hand. Granna sat opposite me, and soon, the two of us were eating fruit and sipping cool lemonade.

Beside the spread was an old, leather tome that was thicker than it had any right to be. Granna just called it The Book, a record and text of spells, recipes, and the members of our family. When she first showed it to me, after I reached adolescence and my father's influence on my outlook of the world lessened substantially, she'd introduced me to the near-ancient text.

She rolled her eyes every time I called it a grimoire, but that's what it was. Spearing a piece of pineapple with a fork, I flipped open the cover of The Book and traced a finger over the list of names that trailed down the first page.

The women in our family who studied and learned from The Book, who were able to read and possess it. When I was sixteen, Granna used a special dagger, one that was as old as The Book, and pricked my finger with it. I stifled a giggle when she'd handed me an honest-to-goddess quill and instructed me to write my name. Signing under my dead mother's name, however, sobered me immediately.

I traced over her name, now, and wondered how much she'd learned before she was killed. She didn't take The Book with her when she moved away with my father, and his trepidation for the subject of witchcraft as a whole made me sad for her. I loved my father, but he wasn't nearly as openminded as myself or Granna.

"This salve seems to be working well for my cut," I said through a full mouth after landing on the page I'd gotten the recipe from. Granna had sat at the table with me while I tried my hand at making the salve from some of the dried and fresh herbs she had on hand. It made me feel like a child, but I wasn't too proud to acknowledge that I was rusty at this.

Granna grunted and took a long drink of her lemonade. Her eyes were fixed on something behind me. "Well, considering your propensity for bumping into corners and scratching yourself, it will come to good use."

I chuckled and flipped toward the end of the book. The spells and incantations increased in difficulty the further you went, and, I squinted, this was a page I hadn't read before.

My head tilted as I considered. "Have you done this one?" I pointed down to the title, Summoning an Elemental Sprit. That seemed like a large jump from making her garden flourish or survive the harsh winters. But if it was in here, I had to imagine that at least someone in our line had tried it.

She didn't answer me for a long time, which I didn't immediately realize since I was focused on reading the strange directions.

I couldn't see myself ever feeling the need to… call on some other-worldly entity. I flipped back to the section that held more simple potions and settled in on one that supposedly calmed the nerves. For a Worried Mind, it read.

"Oh, this is in here for me," I snorted to myself and finally looked up at my grandmother. Her silver brow was furrowed, as if she was figuring out what to say to me. I squirmed a bit under her steady, imposing gaze, but didn't look away. "Uh… is this one okay to focus on today?" We still had a good amount of time before my shift at Vinny's, and with classes starting next week, it would be perfect timing to have an anti-anxiety tonic to help me get my bearings.

Granna passed a strong, slender hand over her chest, trailing it up to her neck and back down. Her skin was a deep brown now after our morning in the sun. "Yes, sweetheart, of course."

My head ducked back down in a nod, and I shoved another piece of pineapple into my mouth. I read through the short list of ingredients and made note of what I needed to grab from the cupboard and what I needed to harvest from the garden.

"And then, maybe you can teach me how to talk to ghosts." I lifted my glass of lemonade and thought of green, sour apples.

CHAPTER THREE

SYLVIE

I hurried up the hallway, flats practically slapping on the tiled floor that could've used a good polishing. But the Department of English and Literature was an old building with fixtures predating me and probably every other student that was walking past.

The cord from my over-ear headphones jostled and bumped against my front, but I ignored it. I was still getting used to figuring out how much time I had between each of my new classes, and I had checked my phone after a pleasant lunch on the grassy area in front of the library to discover that I was most certainly going to be late. But the calming shade of the tree I'd sat beneath made me feel better after a morning stuck inside. My excitement to be back in school made it bearable, but the hour outdoors was a reprieve I got a little too lost in.

Though I'd generally found college courses to be laxer than the ear-shattering bells and detentions of high school, I still felt a gnawing in my chest at the thought of being late, running into the classroom and collapsing into my desk with underarm stains visible for all to see. Or worse, being chastised in front of people that were a good five or six years my junior, at least. I thought about the mind-calming tonic I made. It truly was perfect timing for me to stumble upon that recipe, though I would likely need to increase my dosage.

At least, I'd found after the first week I'd been attending Antler Pointe College that I rather enjoyed my courses and professors. When I'd taken a break from college the first time, Dad had been diagnosed with cancer, and since it was just the two of us, I left to make sure he had someone to take him to his chemotherapy appointments and take care of him at home.

Before his body took a sharp downturn, I got to return for a semester to ultimately have to drop out altogether. It was a hard few years watching him become weaker and weaker. We had never been particularly close, but it was still heartbreaking to see him descend to a state in which he could no longer take care of his basic needs.

The cord on my headphones bumped against my chest again, sliding along the slippery fabric of my sundress as I ran up the steps to the fourth floor. I was fiddling with it, somehow having gotten twisted between the grassy quad area and here, when my shoulder bumped that of the person I'd been unsuccessful in skirting around.

My fingers were working at the tangle, trying to get my mind to focus on anything besides my father's sunken face on those last days, so I absently spun to walk backwards and mutter a hasty, "Sorry!"

And I collided back-to-front with someone else.

Hard hands grasped my elbows to steady us both, and I sank into the touch before jerking away and spinning around again.

My arms fell, and the cord, still knotted, dangled in front of me. I knew that I was staring and that my mouth was agape, but my brain felt like it was short-circuiting.

It was him.

Of course it was. That night had seemed so strange, almost like a dream, so why wouldn't he be standing right in front of me?

When before, he'd been dirty and injured, now, he was clean-cut and standing perfectly upright. His white hair was curly, with the sides and back cut shorter. He was clutching the strap of a leather satchel slung on his shoulder and looking down at me with those eyes like granny smith apples.

I took an involuntary step closer but stopped when his eyes tightened, looking me up and down with suspicion. My mouth opened to ask how he was, but he beat me to it. "What are you doing here?"

I jerked back and pulled my headphones off my ears to hang off of my neck. Maybe I'd misheard that. "Pardon?" The hall was completely empty, now, but my mind was focused in on the man that I'd halfway convinced myself was some sort of apparition or figment of my imagination. Every day that I'd gone to work, I would go back by the dumpster and try to imagine this mystery man who had been so spooked that it was like he couldn't even speak.

Even though there was no one around, he took another glance around before furrowing his brow. "Are you following me?" He didn't sound particularly angry, more astonished. Possibly embarrassed.

My eyes widened, and I sputtered for a moment. "What the hell?" But, it appeared that I had heard him correctly the first time. He was... accusing me of following him? Annoyance flared in my cheeks, no doubt making them a bit red. "Maybe I should ask you the same thing." I crossed my arms and raised my chin.

His expression hardened. "Look—"

I cut him off. "Are you a student here?" He looked older than the usual undergraduate age, but then again, so did I. And maybe he was a graduate student or something?

"No." And then he pushed past me, making sure not to get too close.

But a part of me needed to... prove that what happened behind Vinny's that night hadn't been a dream. "Wait!" I practically yelled down the hall at him. Thankfully, he stopped and, rather reluctantly, turned his head over his shoulder. "A-are you okay? And feeling better?"

I watched his body still, tension evident in his upper back, and something in me deflated. My eyes dropped to my fingers that were beginning to fiddle with the knot of my headphones again.

"Yes," he called just before opening the door to the stairwell and descending before I could catch another glimpse of him.

"What the fuck," I exhaled under my breath.

. . . . . 🌙 . . . . .

Josie lifted one of the rough-cut soaps, holding it to her nose and setting it back down with a shudder. She proceeded to do the same with the rest of those in the section, though I knew she didn't intend to buy any. She was here more for my benefit.

I placed a bundle of sage in one of the store's wicker shopping baskets, along with a new pack of tarot cards. My friend would turn her nose up at all of this stuff, but she would most certainly be the first to ask for a reading as soon as I opened the cards. It was one of the few practices my father hadn't sputtered and gotten anxious over, and I'd grown quite fond of working with the cards in my teenage years. His whole side of the family was wary of anything to do with witchcraft or magic, but it was easy now to flatten the bit of shame that tried to bubble up.

My fingers swept over a delicately crafted bracelet, the beads a mesmerizing swirl of greens and browns. I plucked it off of the display and stuck it in my basket as well.

"So, how are classes going?" Josie spritzed some natural deodorant spray into the air and took a reluctant sniff. She nodded in surprise approval before setting the tester back on the wooden shelf, and I chuckled. Josie was the only friend I had in Antler Pointe, and it was nice to get to spend more time with her since I'd moved back. We met when we were both twelve or so. When while shopping with Granna, a boisterous girl my age bumped into me while running around a clothing store with her friends from school. She quickly complimented me on my cartoon t-shirt and scooped me up to hang out with her little group that day. Never mind that I was a ball of nervous rambles. She just grinned and followed my branching trains of thought easily.

I shrugged. "Pretty good, all things considered. Feels kinda weird being the oldest person in there. Besides the professors, but whatever." It felt good to be in a learning environment again, around creativity and progress. My first year or two of college had been filled with prerequisite courses where many of my classmates couldn't care less besides meeting the requirement.

But now, with my last two semesters, I was in the classes that interested me most. And though it felt like a betrayal of some kind, I couldn't deny that without worrying about my father's ever-fluctuating health, I felt free to fully immerse myself.

Though I was taking care of Granna, she mostly just needed someone to help her around the house. To keep her company and take on the more strenuous tasks that she could no longer do with ease.

"Meet anyone?" And by the tone of Josie's voice and waggle of her bleached brows, I knew what she was implying. "A sexy TA perhaps? Ooh—or you could go for one of your classmates!"

My face pinched in disgust. "Jesus, Josie. Some of them are like children."

"What?" She sputtered, "Vicky was younger than you! And everyone around you is at least an adult. Who cares if you fuck someone that's not 'age appropriate'." She used air quotes on the phrase, and I scoffed. Though I was raised outside of Antler Pointe, I'd kept up with Josie enough over the years to know that meeting and discarding romantic and sexual partners came easily to her. Each time she would text or call and the conversation would inevitably turn to our love lives, I couldn't help often coming up feeling… inadequate. Her enthusiastic and eccentric personality was like a magnet, one that I hadn't been able to resist even when we were too young for her to be doing it on purpose.

At eighteen, when I was reeling from a particularly bad breakup and our Skype call had mostly involved my blubbering recount of what happened, I asked her how she did it. How she moved on so quickly. With softness and comfort in her eyes, she said that she always entered her relationships and trysts knowing that they wouldn't last. That it helped nullify any blow. That sounded so depressing and unattainable, something I knew I'd never be able to do.

And later, with Dad being sick, taking care of our house, and all the funeral and hospital expenses, most of my relationships— platonic and otherwise—went down the proverbial shitter.

I reached the counter and smiled at the person at the register. While they rang up my purchases, I threw my head over my shoulder to tease her. "I did have an interesting encounter with a stranger."

Her eyes went wide. "Oh, you better fucking spill it." She snagged my receipt from the cashier's outstretched hand, hooked her arm in mine, and started to pull us out of the shop. I just managed to grab the paper bag of my purchases before we exited into the summer air.

We continued down the main square, arm-in-arm, and I fiddled with the plastic wrapping on the tarot cards.

"I feel like we should get some coffee," she said absently, and we glanced both ways down the street before jaywalking to our destination.

I tugged down my miniskirt as we entered the blessedly cool building, and there was luckily just one person in front of us. We both stared up at the menu over the front counter, and I leaned my head closer to hers. "Some guy—" But then something stopped me from telling her about the state that I found the man in. Though I was now sure that what happened was real, I still had no clue as to how he'd ended up behind Vinny's. Or what he was doing in the damn English Department if he wasn't a student.

If I hadn't been born with the grandmother I had, I would have written the whole thing off as a coincidence. I would have told Josie everything, used the bizarre situation that night as a bit of a tale to impress her with.

He'd acted so rudely when I saw him earlier today—I certainly didn't owe him anything. But then, I thought about the way he'd curled up between the dumpster and the dirty, sticky wall as if he was hiding. It didn't seem fair to relay that to my friend now.

After we ordered and grabbed our iced coffees, we sat in the corner on a squishy sofa. It was situated between large fiddle leaf figs, and I relaxed into the calm environment.

"Okay, so who is this guy?" Josie asked, straw in her mouth.

My eyes focused on my drink and the swirling ice while I tried to figure out what to say. I rotated my cup to further mix the cream and coffee. "He came to Vinny's, and then I saw him while I was running to one of my classes today. It was weird."

She took an audible suck through her straw before adding in an expectant tone, "And…?"

I shrugged. "Dunno."

Josie scoffed and rolled her hazel eyes. "What did he look like, how tall was he, what did he say, what did his dick taste like, something, Sylvie."

"Goddess, Josie!" I took a deep breath, eyes to the ceiling in exasperation. Why did I open my mouth at all? "He was… pale."

"Pale," she deadpanned.

"Yes, pale. Like albinism pale."

That caught her interest, and again, that feeling of betrayal crept up my throat. Was that an all right thing to say? "And hot?"

My lips turned down, and I tilted my head from side to side. With the stress of the situation when I first encountered him, assessing his looks had been far from my mind. So, I thought back to it now, how his face, though battered and tightened in pain and panic, held strong lines and full, pale pink lips.

Earlier today, I saw those details in clarity under the bright fluorescent hallway lights. The shock of it kept me from really remarking on anything besides how differently he looked when he wasn't… you know, beaten up.

"I don't know about... hot," because I didn't really describe people using that word, "but he's handsome. I guess."

"She guesses." Josie rolled her eyes again while pulling her phone from the front pouch of her overall shorts. "Name?"

My brows wrinkled. "I didn't get his name."

She curled her olive-toned hand in another expectant gesture. "Okay, fine. You said he was on campus? In one of your lit classes or something?"

"Uh, no. I ran into him in the hall, and he said that he wasn't a student when I asked."

Josie nodded and stuck the tip of her tongue out of the side of her mouth in concentration, thumbs flying on the screen of her phone. I sipped my coffee and sniffed one of the soaps I picked up for Granna while I waited for Josie to do her work. She'd surely come up empty soon enough. I didn't even have a na—

"Got him!" She exclaimed so loudly that several people turned towards us. She raised an apologetic hand and said in a much lower pitch, "Sorry." Josie handed her phone over to me, and I struggled to concentrate for a moment. How had she found him that fast? Though I didn't post much on social media apps, I was familiar with them enough to be thoroughly impressed with her quick sleuthing skills.

What I didn't expect to see opened up on her screen was the faculty page at my college.

"What the fuck," I murmured and stared at the headshot of the mystery man. Under the professional lighting, his skin didn't look as ghostly as it had before. His hair looked just like it had earlier today, and the tweed blazer and white shirt brought out the bright green of his eyes. There he was, lips pulled up in a slight, stoic smile, amongst the other faculty members of the Department of English and Literature at Antler Pointe College. Under his name, his title read, Associate Professor.

"Oh, please, please fuck a professor, Sylv." My eyes flitted frantically between her and the screen, unable to fully compute what was going on. He did say that he wasn't a student, but I hadn't expected him to be a fucking professor. In the same department I was getting my degree in. "Cool name."

My eyes shot back down to the screen—I hadn't even really focused on his name.

Orion Gealach.

The mystery man's name was Orion. I read over his last name a few times, trying to decipher how to say it, but I guessed that how it read was not how I was supposed to say it. Why did I have the almost overwhelming urge to look up the pronunciation? What language was that from?

I opened a new tab on Josie's phone and was typing in the strange surname into the internet browser when Josie whispered under her breath, "Holy shit." But I wasn't paying attention. I squinted down at the results that popped up.

Gealach, it turned out, was Gaelic and pronounced like gyalakh. Though I had no experience with that language, I felt a brief surge of satisfaction for guessing that it had a unique pronunciation.

"Orion Gealach," I tested saying it out loud, letting my mouth work around the words. I said it again while I clicked back to the faculty page and followed the link posted with his name. His little individual page listed his areas of study, African American and Irish literature, and I selected his CV while I started to mumble his name again. Something hard hit my shin, and I flinched. "Ow!"

I glared at Josie. She'd kicked me. "What was..." My voice trailed off and died.

Just near the door, coffee in hand and directly in my line of sight, was the mystery man. Orion.

And he was stopped and staring at me with that unidentifiable look in his eyes. My mouth opened then closed in a panic when I realized that I'd been saying his name to myself while I snooped his faculty profile page. And he for sure heard me.

I clicked Josie's phone off and shoved it into her lap, as if that would further hide the evidence of me being a complete creep. He stood rooted there, but I couldn't think of what to say. Was finding his very public profile on my college's website something I should apologize for?

As I opened my mouth again to do just that, someone cleared their throat behind him, and he broke our eye contact and walked out of the shop without saying a word. His eyes were just as bright as I remembered them, even more than in his photo that didn't do them justice.

"Yeah," Josie sighed and took the last slurp of her coffee, "he's fucking hot."

CHAPTER FOUR

SYLVIE

It felt like Orion was haunting me.

The first week of classes, I hadn't seen him at all. And then, after that embarrassing moment in the hallway and the even more embarrassing non-exchange at the coffee shop, I felt like I was seeing him everywhere.

But any excitement I felt about that fact was quickly dashed by the reality of how those meetings went. Because I was an English major, I practically lived in the ancient brick building that housed all of my classes. At first, I just started noticing him in the hallways. Now that I knew who the head of white, gentle-looking curls belonged to, I couldn't help but find him in the crowd and home in on him, even during the bustling moments in between classes.

Luckily, I wasn't taking any of the courses he seemed to teach, but the Monday after Josie discovered that he worked at the college, I was walking toward one of two student lounges in the building. My classmate and I were going together to get some of our required reading done in our free hour. The lounge on the third floor was a large room with old, mismatched couches and armchairs that was dimly lit and smelled like coffee at all times of the day.

When we entered, I felt my feet stutter and stop, as if they'd fused with the scuffed tiled floor. There he was, sitting near the window at the back of the room, sipping from a ceramic mug that appeared handmade. He had a pair of over-ear headphones on, though they were cordless. He was reviewing something on a laptop, but as soon as I came to a pause just across the threshold, his eyes snapped up, immediately meeting mine before darting away a split-second later.

"Oh, hey, one second," my classmate, Kara, said and started walking over. To Orion.

It took a few long moments, wherein Kara had nearly made it all the way to him before I scampered behind her. Why I didn't just slump into one of the couches, perhaps the one that would have had me sitting with my back to the frowning phantom, was beyond me. Because, yes, even without me anxiously sneaking glances at him in the halls or the faculty profile of a certain associate professor pulled up on my phone for days now, Orion had begun to haunt my dreams, too.

I stood a few paces behind Kara, who seemed an easygoing and cheerful person. She stopped a respectful distance from Orion, who took his headphones off with great reluctance.

"Yes?" His voice, deep and husky, sent an embarrassing thrill down my back. I hadn't heard him speak beyond his hoarse whispers that strange night and the accusing grumbles when I'd seen him again the first week of classes.

"I was just wondering if you were offering any additional extra credit assignments this semester? I tried coming by your office hours but it was all blocked off." Kara trailed into a flitter of nervous giggles at the end, and I caught myself giving a small, encouraging smile toward Orion whose blank expression hadn't shifted in the slightest. His hair was slightly mussed from his headphones that were now dangling around his neck. Though it was still unjustifiably warm outside, he wore a full-sleeved, taupe shirt. The muscles in his jaw ticked while he was decidedly not meeting either of our gazes.

"Class?" He started to pull something up on the laptop. Though, if it had anything to do with the extra credit that my classmate was inquiring about, I was unsure.

"Uh," Kara's voice faltered a bit, "Topics in African-American Literature."

Orion sighed and typed something else into the computer, as if it was some great task to do so. After a few seconds of awkward silence, he glanced at her, then flicked his eyes up and down my body before focusing back on his computer screen. "No. Anything else?"

"Ah, no, that's it. Thanks, Dr. Gealach." Though she was still polite, Kara had visibly deflated after the brusque exchange. After fidgeting for a moment in uncertainty, she almost turned into me as she went toward the seating behind us.

Just as I was about to do the same, that deep voice sounded again. "Class?"

"Um…" I felt stuck once again, floundering for an answer. Why wasn't I just turning around?

"Looking for extra credit, too?" He took a sip of his coffee, not even offering me a glance, now. Those bright green eyes were shrouded by long, white eyelashes.

"Ah, I'm not in one of your classes."

"Okay. So, why are you still standing there?" His tone was gruff, dry, and he began to type more on his laptop. He even began lifting his black, expensive-looking headphones toward his ears.

Annoyance flared up in my throat, heating my face that I knew was growing flushed. I could understand that he was maybe still embarrassed about me seeing him injured that night, and then again weirdly mumbling his name in the coffee shop. But I didn't realize that I had been holding out for some sort of… truce. Or do-over with him. There was something alluring about those eyes of his, and I still had no idea how he'd ended up behind Vinny's. But no, I continued to stand there, trying and failing to come up with something that wasn't pathetic or a biting remark.

Before I could find *something*, he settled his headphones over his ears, effectively brushing me off. "Add/drop period has ended, so if you're not already in one of my classes, you won't be for the rest of the semester. There's nothing I can do for you." A beat passed, and he flitted another fleeting glance to my eyes. "Goodbye." *Goodbye*? My head jerked back in disbelief, and that blatant... dismissal.

Finally, I found my voice. "Have I done anything to you?" I tried to keep my words low and steady so as to not draw more eyes over here, as well as maintain a dignified facade against this infuriating man.

He tugged back one side of his headphones to free an ear, though it seemed he heard me just fine, because he answered, "No. But these office hours are reserved for students of mine." Orion's voice was steady, blank. And without a hint of irritation or frustration in it, the words somehow stung worse.

In the face of it, I grasped at the strap of my tote bag to calm the nervous fidgeting that would surely start up in my hands. "Looks to me like you're not in your office, *Orion*. But I'll be on my way now." And just as I was spinning on my heel to finally join Kara like I should have done before this whole disastrous conversation, those piercing eyes met mine and... held them. Just for a stilted, bottomless moment.

That's what I kept seeing in my dreams. The cream-colored skin even with the height of summer, crooked nose that had surely been broken a time or two... maybe even on that night I'd found him. Fuller, pink lips and a square jaw that was clenched tight as he watched me. And those brilliant, green eyes.

Orion broke the contact between us, turning back to whatever he was working on, and I sat down next to Kara in a daze. I pulled out the small book, a translated novel from my Twentieth Century French Literature course, but was scarcely able to retain any of the text that I read. So much so that later that night, after another potion-making lesson from Granna, I had to reread the progress I'd made. But it did little good, because my mind kept returning to that infuriating professor, and, embarrassingly, to how he looked.

There must have been something seriously wrong with me. All my previous partners had been sweeter, more considerate, but, yeah, okay, I had noticed Orion's clean haircut that still left windswept curls. How his shirt was just fitted enough to reveal broad, sturdy shoulders and arms. How his hands looked thick, capable. I groaned, chastising myself all the way while I slunk under my covers, reaching in my bedside table for my vibrator.

And each time after that, when I saw him in the halls, Orion looked at me with various unintelligible glances, as if I was inconveniencing him by just existing.

One morning, when I was packing my notebook and planner into my bag, my back bristled at some pathetic awareness of him, and, sure enough, he was entering the emptying classroom with his own brown leather satchel slung on his shoulder. My professor, Dr. Vanders, was just exiting, but they gave Orion a friendly fist-bump on their way out, their breezy, paisley-patterned pants flowing with their steps.

Orion was in another well-fitted, long-sleeved shirt, though this one was a deep navy blue. His jeans and boots were equally as simple, but that also just—fit him.

I felt his eyes on me while I gathered my bag and pulled away from my seat in the room, and perhaps I did make an effort to exaggerate the swishing of my hips while I walked toward the door. My long dress was a black and slinky number with large white flowers throughout.

"Hey." That voice hit my ears just as I was rounding the large desk near the door. My sandaled feet stopped and pivoted, my body like a magnet to him even if my mind was still irritated. And hurt.

"Yes?" I asked, smiling politely even though he didn't deserve it.

Orion was still standing, though now his satchel was sitting in the wooden chair beside him. He cast a searching look about the room, and I realized then that we were alone. At least for a few moments until his students would start to arrive.

His brows, so close to the color of his skin that they were only visible at closer distances, wrinkled for a moment, as if he was intently thinking through what he was going to say. My arms crossed in front of my chest, and I belatedly realized that the movement just further exaggerated my already full bust when Orion's apple-green eyes caught there for a moment so fast that I wondered if it was real. I quickly brought a hand up to the thick topknot on the crown of my head instead, feeling awkward.

"I just," he cleared his throat and settled his eyes very near my mine but not quite, "wanted to say… thank you. Again." His face was tightened as if he was struggling to even get the words out at all.

My gaze flickered to my left arm before falling back on him. The salve that I concocted truly worked wonders because I didn't even have a mark from the wound he'd given me in his distress.

"Um, you're welcome."

"I am… indebted to you," he said gruffly. Almost like he was bewildered by that fact.

I shifted on my feet, growing more uncomfortable by the second. My heart was fluttering excitedly with having his full attention on me. Speaking with me. And that just made me feel even more pitiful. Wanting to preen with him treating me like a person, now, and not dog shit under his shoe. He was watching me, nostrils flaring a bit.

But, no, I needed to stop this. It was turning into an unhealthy obsession. I moved here to help and spend time with Granna and to finish my degree. I'd already felt more and more disconnected with this… fixation on him. And maybe if he had been kind in return, it might've been worth it.

This was ridiculous. I hitched my bag even higher on my shoulder and forced the words out. "No. You're not. I don't do nice things expecting something in return." And his pupils finally, finally landing on mine gave me a bit more bravado. "Goodbye," I said with a saccharine smile to hide my nervousness.

Before he could utter a word, I left the classroom with my head held high. Even with my stomach sinking.

Twice more I saw Orion while I tried to focus on my courses. Work at Vinny's was tedious, studies with Granna challenging, and though my traitorous mind still drifted to that symmetrical, angular face more than it had any right to, I made a point of avoiding his gaze in the halls. And those two times, he started toward me, surely wanting to cut me or speak more of this *debt* between us.

So, I walked the other way. I kept my head down when I caught sight of him and turned down another path, even with the hairs on the back of my neck prickling with awareness that those eerie eyes were watching me.

CHAPTER FIVE

ORION

"No, Meredith, everything is fine," I drawled while pushing the rickety shopping cart. My thumb swiped across my phone's screen and pulled up the list I'd quickly typed before coming into town. The grocery store was almost, blessedly, empty this early on a weekday. There were six, beautiful minutes where I was able to shop in peace without having to navigate around anyone.

The calming crooning through my headphones was quickly interrupted, however, with her calling. "Why do you sound as though speaking with me is the last thing that you want to do?" I could hear her taking a drawing inhale and, a few seconds later, an exhale. She was certainly sitting on the patio, overlooking the sprawling, manicured yard while having her morning cigarette. Just the sound of it was making my fingers twitch.

"Because I don't like talking on the phone," I said absently while I examined a bag of red grapes before setting them into my cart. We continued in familiar rhythm with her trying to draw out conversation from me, nearly whining when I gave short, simple answers. *First produce, then meat and dairy, then pantry,* my gait wasn't nearly as relaxed as it had been when I'd entered earlier, but it was still unhurried.

I was comparing two brands of peanut butter, as my preferred type was nowhere to be found this morning. After swallowing that flare of annoyance combined with exasperation at the incessant droning in my ears, my head snapped up just as someone rounded the corner and started to head down my aisle.

It was her.

That woman who helped me. The warm pull I'd been feeling toward her started up again, but my mind was unable to think through how to act appropriately. Obviously, what I'd been doing was having the opposite effect I wanted.

And she wasn't alone. There was an older, shorter version of her pushing their half-full cart.

The woman looked almost afraid while they made their way toward me, her companion none the wiser. Her delicate hand reached up to smooth the wild, bountiful ringlets that shot out from her scalp and framed her head and upper back. Her eyes kept cutting to me, then the shelves on either side of us while the old woman stopped just beside me. She struck a line through something on the handwritten list before starting to reach up to the top shelf.

The woman who'd tended to me when I was injured those weeks ago flitted one last glance to me before scolding at the older one and gently maneuvering her out of the way.

"Orion, are you even listening to me? I said that we'll be—" I clicked a button on the left side of my headphones to end the call and started forward without thinking. Though the younger one, who attended the college where I taught, was at least a head taller than her companion, I was a good amount taller than her still. I reached up and snagged the white box of crackers that was up top and shoved back aways.

"Oh, thank you." The older woman gave me a warm smile when I transferred the snack to her slender hand, and a strong scent of lavender and berries wafted off of her skin. She tossed the box unceremoniously amongst the rest of their things. She continued to look at her list, grey brow furrowed, and tapped her pen down the length of the page. "Sweetheart, we need more peanut butter if you want me to make more of those cookies you like. I'll meet you over by the cleaning supplies."

I moved out of the way for the older woman to make her way down and out of the aisle.

And then it was just us two. She had been avoiding me on campus. It became fairly obvious after I couldn't help but memorize the times her schedule intersected with mine. She always took the same route throughout the buildings.

Until she didn't. Until my body couldn't help find her in the sea of students and faculty, only to watch her turn away each time.

Now, though, she didn't leave. We faced each other, only a few steps separating us, and I couldn't help notice her fresh cherry scent. I took another long inhale to try and take in as much of it as I could, and as I did, my eyes went to her face. With large eyes and a round, full mouth, I didn't have to wonder or parse through her facial expression.

I knew that she was uneasy around me.

"Uh, I just need to squeeze behind you." She gestured toward the shelf behind me, but I stayed where I was.

"What's your name?" My mind once again went back to those moments I spoke with her—that night was still too much of a fog —and felt a churn of guilt. In the student lounge, it was evident that I'd offended her, though it wasn't my intention. And when I asked if she was following me, I had just been surprised. And ashamed that she had seen me that way.

But she needed to understand that I appreciated what she'd done for me. Though kindness, like what she'd shown, didn't come naturally to me, my father's voice in my mind wouldn't stop chastising for how I'd acted toward her.

That second time we spoke, I was feeling irritable due to my office being painted and forcing me to hold office hours in the noisy student lounge. Though I enjoyed teaching, at least when the students were engaged and interested in more than just passing the class, my time in my office was a break from the inevitable overstimulation.

Still, I could see now that I'd been irritable and ineffective at hiding it. When I replayed those moments later that day, trying to figure out why her mood had shifted so fast, I realized that I'd acted rudely. Usually, I didn't much care about my lack of social graces, but I recognized hurt when it wafted off of her.

"Why?" She pulled her hand back toward her side, and looked me up and down.

"Because I want to know it. And you know mine." I still didn't know what to make of her saying my name to herself that afternoon. At the time, I'd been more stunned than anything, and the warm curling in my stomach when her smooth voice said my name made me stop in my tracks.

Now, she scoffed and passed a hand over her hair, and I tracked the movement, eyes trailing down her bare arm and then down the curve of her waist. When she finally spoke, though, I felt my whole body snap to attention then shiver with some sort of settling. "Sylvie."

Sylvie, my soul hummed. I inhaled, twining her scent with her name, and tried to steady my mind into one train of coherent thought.

"I owe you a debt, Sylvie. For helping me." Her name felt right on my tongue. I said it over and over in my head, only because some of the sense my mother ingrained into me kept me from doing it aloud. Had that been what Sylvie was doing at the coffee shop? Did she enjoy the sound of my name as much as I did hers?

"Look, dude, I just need to get to the peanut butter. No debt here, but thanks for the sentiment." She spoke with a lightness to her words, and had I not learned to look deeper, I would have been fooled. She was feeling skittish, and I immediately recognized the excitement I felt at that fact.

I was enchanted by her, and I had to breathe through the

dominating instinct. To feel her fluttering pulse beneath my teeth, if only to let her know that within their razor edge, she was safe.

When I didn't move, trying to think of what to say to her with my mind buzzing, she just rolled her eyes and started toward me. I was in a plain black shirt, and when she reached behind me for the shelf, her bare skin touched my sleeve. Then, when she withdrew, her hair brushed my shoulder, narrowly missing my nose, and I had to fight very hard to keep myself still.

Cherries and cool mornings. That's what she smelled like, and I needed more of it.

But Sylvie just edged around me and my shopping cart, heading the way the older woman went, and I was alone again. This time, though, it didn't make me feel relieved. I focused in on the heightened beating of my heart, the flaring of my nostrils as I tried to draw more of her scent into me, and, admittedly, the swelling of my cock. My face felt hot with interest but also frustration.

Of course she wouldn't understand the compulsion to repay this debt. *I* didn't truly understand it, but I kept telling myself that it was what Da would have told me to do. What he would have thought was right. Especially after I... hurt her feelings. After she'd seen me injured and immediately stopped to help me.

And then there was the familiar surge of anger. A psychologist my mother hired during my teenage years, in an attempt to keep me in line, no doubt, taught me a breathing exercise that I begrudgingly found myself still using all these years later. The plundering blows and stinging bites had healed by the next morning, but I still felt them under my skin. I breathed through the rage, trying to focus on my list and getting back home, and rejected another call from Meredith.

The ding of a text message rang in my ears, but instead of an irritated one from Meredith, it was Juno.

JUNO

Wanna get a beer later? I'm already exhausted and the semester's barely started.

I agreed because I felt guilty for canceling on them the last three times. Not because I had anything to do, but because I couldn't fathom being social each time.

I thought again of Sylvie's arm brushing mine. What would her bare skin feel like?

Though I wanted nothing more than to follow that mouthwatering scent of cherry and the melodic tilt of her voice, I kept my distance. Staying just out of sight so that I didn't make that nervousness in her rise again.

But thoughts of that debt and the way her hair tickled my shoulder wouldn't let up. My mind easily went to that instead of the rage while I placed a bag of arborio rice in the cart. How did you repay a debt when the one who helped you didn't want the payment? Da was too long gone to give me guidance on that one, and if I were being honest with myself, that was far from the only thing I wanted from Sylvie.

. . . . 🌙 . . . .

The itch under my skin was already growing. I looked toward the sky, still a bright blue with the setting sun dappling through the treetops.

I took a swig from my bottle while Juno and I walked along the beaten path near my house. *How many times did Da walk this way?* I wondered. The land was passed down through his mother's family for hundreds of years. It all called to me, feeling home at the most minuscule level.

I stepped over a pile of scat, its stench having reached my nose far earlier, and my face screwed in disgust. Instead of running free, I was hiking with Juno. It wasn't unpleasant, but when I looked over at them, clad in a pair of leggings and a cropped shirt,

I caught the slight jerking of their movements. They wanted to run, too.

"I hate this," I said, loud enough for any spies to hear. Though I couldn't smell them, I knew that there would be at least one that would pick up on our walking soon enough.

Juno hummed and took a pull from their own beer. Once the time came for us to go out to some bar they enjoyed, I suggested they come over and we drink at mine instead. Thankfully, my friend was an easygoing type, and they readily agreed. Their high ponytail swished along their back, copper skin flushed from the heat, when they turned to look over at me. I felt their almost black eyes on the side of my face. "I do, too. But I'm planning on going home in a few weeks. You could tag along, and we wouldn't have to do this." They waved around, gesturing to our slow advance around the lake.

The land was indescribably beautiful, lush and bountiful browns and greens that caressed the edges of an idyllic lake that reflected the sky above like a mirror. My home, my father's home, his mother's home, and on and on and on. I deserved to have it in peace, dammit.

I thought over Juno's offer, remembering the kind scents of their family, their encouraging yips while we ran on their land. Though appreciated, the thought of engaging in that now felt hollow. Like I was even more aware of how much I didn't belong.

I was happy to have a friend like Juno, and even happier that they'd been reared with giving people around them. I'd tried to find my own version of that, once I knew that my mother would never provide it and my father seemed content in his forever solitude. And though I very much enjoyed my alone time, craved it more days than not, I still longed for a family.

When I thought I'd found it, eager to please just after my undergraduate studies, it felt like, despite my way of thinking differing from most, I'd fit in seamlessly. Finding my place and even a partner to share my most intimate moments with.

I huffed a sardonic laugh. *Yeah, what a disaster that had been.*

Juno looked over again, unaware where my mind had gone, and I sighed. "No, thank you, though. I'll go just out of the area." When I saw their features fall, and their scent grow sad to match, I added, "You're welcome to come." Even though the words felt sour on my tongue. I tried to tell myself that I wasn't sure why I no longer wanted to run for days on end with Juno. But, that would be a lie.

They eyed me like they sensed this, their black brows pinched while they were probably parsing through the shift in my emotions. I wasn't going to explain myself, though. Especially when I didn't have a very clear idea of what was going on in the first place. "I've already promised my parents that I'll be there. But maybe the next time." Their lips tilted up in a smile. "Unless you figure out a solution by then."

I took another furtive glance around us and stretched my senses. No one besides us and the wildlife that belonged here, thank the gods. Trying to find a solution to reclaiming my land was a constant loop in my brain, always running like a hamster wheel while I planned my lessons, graded papers, did my own research. It was going nowhere, and save for staging an all-out confrontation, there was little else I could attempt. I'd tried negotiating, providing evidence that the land was mine.

But I was outnumbered, and my… less than diplomatic refusal when I first moved back had admittedly put me on poor footing from the beginning.

"I doubt it."

Juno hummed. "Well, enough ruminating. What's new with you, friend?"

I'd caught up to them, now, walking by their side. It was a lucky twist of fate that we'd started at Antler Pointe College in the same semester, two new professors cut from the same cloth. While I'd moved here after my father's death to fix up his house and make a quiet life for myself, Juno took the first job they'd been offered.

"Nothing, really," I started, but the truth was clawing its way up my throat. "I, uh—never mind." I felt my cheeks get hot, and when Juno went all delighted in the face, I moaned at what I knew was coming.

They shoved me with their slender arm that belied the amount of strength they possessed. "What happened, Orion?"

I sighed and took another long drink from my beer, draining it like that would give me courage. My metabolism was far too efficient for me to feel the effects of it, though. "I'm not sure. Exactly. But I've become… intrigued by someone."

"Oh?" They smiled even wider. "And are they intrigued by you as well?"

That was an easier question to answer. "No. I'm afraid I've just been scaring her away—"

"With what? Your usual undeniable charm?"

I rolled my eyes, but their question was in jest, I knew. It'd been a sore spot for all of my childhood. Where I made few friends outside of the books I carried with me everywhere. When a child on the playground had made fun of me for it, I'd quickly learned that listing my father as my best friend was not an adequate retort. There were so many social rules that everyone just seemed to *know*, and it was isolating and exhausting.

Things got better after I learned to look deeper, beyond just the confusing blend of words and facial expressions. The psychologists my mother saddled me with were annoying, but I'd taken some lessons from the collective experience.

To my benefit, in my profession, I mostly needed to be competent and feign friendliness enough so that students continued to sign up for my courses.

"Tell me something about her," Juno suggested, and I wracked my brain to explain. They would just worry if I told them of how she found me, so that was out. And all of their romantic and sexual dalliances sounded easy and plentiful. It made me feel woefully inept. Furthering the feeling that I was always tuned to some channel that wasn't quite on the same frequency of everyone else.

But a physical description I could do. I started by describing the basics. Her approximate height, her skin tone, how her hair looked. Then her scent, down to the specific notes that they wouldn't truly be able to know unless they were in front of her. How even with her exasperation, I could feel her inclination toward kindness. How I ached to scent her.

I felt another flush creep up my cheeks. Or perhaps it'd never left. When I snuck a glance at my friend, they were just continuing to smile. "I'm happy for you, my friend. I know you've longed for a partner."

I scratched the back of my head. "I didn't say anything about a partner." No, I'd just been thinking of another ridiculous word. "But thanks."

Juno gave a tinkling laugh. "Do you at least have the female's name?" Something like pride puffed my chest, and I let her name slip through my lips. It was delightful and more intoxicating than any alcohol could ever be.

But a sharp shift of the air had my face twisting in confusion. Juno was looking down at their near-empty bottle as it swung at their side. Comfortable enough with them, I asked them to explain. Why they seemed unhappy for me now.

"Not unhappy," they rushed, and I tried to catalogue their features, the awkwardness that so rarely wafted from them.

"Is it because..." More heat on my face. While I still had a deep affection for my friend, our sexual encounters had long ago ended. I didn't think that Juno would have any reaction to something like this, especially since they had never reacted to anyone I'd slept with in the past. They had so many sexual partners that I didn't even bother keeping track of them all. Not that I'd reserved remembering names much outside of the classroom, anyway.

Juno, though, shifted quickly to confusion at my question, and then I could see when my meaning dawned on them. They laughed, and my shoulders relaxed. "Oh, no! That was years ago, my sweet friend. I should just tell you now that she is a student of mine. And that we shouldn't discuss anything further about her."

My chest was a mixture of jealousy and relief. Now that I thought about it, I remembered the third time she spoke with me being after I'd seen Juno exiting a classroom I was entering. I hadn't yet thought about the fact that they would get to see and possibly talk to Sylvie multiple times a week. While she all but ran each time she saw me.

I stifled the grumble that threatened to escape my throat, but Juno must have detected it all the same. They looked at me, friendly affection radiating like the rays of sunlight above us. "Doesn't mean I'm not happy for you. I hope it works out."

I didn't have anything to say but gave an agreeing grunt and nod. She was invading my thoughts and dreams enough to the point that I would be a fool if I tried not to pursue her. But I'd have to be careful. To use all my sense to not hurt her again or stare with tongue tied.

"And who knows," Juno shrugged, "maybe you'll get a mate out of it all."

CHAPTER SIX

SYLVIE

Though I'd quickly skimmed the email, my eyes kept returning to the first line. *"We regret to inform you…"* and then it was all more of the same polite words to soften the blow of rejection. With a sigh, I dragged the response to my latest short story submission over to the folder marked 'To Keep Me Humble' and closed the internet browser.

I hadn't added an email to the much emptier folder 'Good News' in a long while, but I fought down the discouragement that threatened to leave my fingers immobile. I leaned back into the purple cushion of the wicker sofa and propped my bare feet on the matching ottoman. The fan in the sunroom did little to cool me down, but I wore as little clothing as possible since it was either this, or subject myself to the two women chatting in the living room.

Not that I couldn't still hear them and the TV that seemed like it was blaring. Roz always turned it on when she came over, and for some reason, Granna didn't mind, even though she barely watched the thing herself.

"Well, from what I've heard, there's been no word at all. And that's what's so strange—" I clamped my headphones over my ears to drown out Roz echoing more of what she'd heard since the last time she'd visited with Granna. Not that I was opposed to gossip, myself. If I weren't determined to get this next story up for submission, I would be sitting in the room with them and absorbing all the tantalizing news and rumors.

But no, instead, I pulled up my latest piece and hunched over to begin another round of edits. My finger twirled the headphone cord as I read over the short story time and time again, finding something to edit, delete, or tweak each round.

Minutes, hours, ticked away, and I refused to admit to myself that I would be done with this already if I hadn't been so distracted. I'd been writing since I was a teenager, and in recent years, started submitting my work to online magazines. After my first rejection, my father, just having been diagnosed with stage three lung cancer, encouraged me to use it like fuel. To inform my next piece and save the evidence of how far I'd come. Well, once he'd rubbed my back through my sobbing and ordered takeout from our favorite restaurant.

At this point, I had eight magazines propped up on my bookshelves that included my stories. And with those eight acceptance emails, I had more than triple the number of denials. I should have known at this point how to edit efficiently, and yet, this zine's deadline had been slowly drawing closer, the days ticking by, while I just stared at my laptop screen. Classes were just beginning to ramp up, and though I was also working part-time, I knew that my responsibilities weren't the reason my writing was stalling out.

It was him. Orion.

Faster, faster, she ran through the darkened wood. All around her, there was only rustling black and the earth beneath her that was soft and cut at the same time. Her bare feet were certainly bleeding, leavign—

I sighed, catching the typo and replacing it with the correct spelling. When I tried to resume editing, the scene I was painting taking shape in my mind, a pale face emerged in the darkness.

One topped with rolling white curls. And then I was back in the grocery store, staring at him blocking the sight of the peanut butter Granna asked me to grab. It was the closest I'd ever gotten to him. It was also the first time I'd touched him since that night.

His arms were lean but roped with muscle, wiry. His chest pulled at the fabric of his black shirt, and he smelled as if he'd spent the morning sitting in a leather chair at a coffee shop after walking around outside. Why would he want to know my name? What difference did it make? *I don't want his money or... anything else from him.*

With a frustrated huff, I jammed the save button just in case and slammed my laptop shut. I hadn't seen him after that—he must've checked out prior to our leaving the store, but I still felt the brush of our arms on my skin.

I looked down to my left forearm, where the graze of his teeth or nails or both was nowhere to be found. Though I'd seen evidence that Granna's words held influence, her concoctions and touch bending things toward her will, I was embarrassed to admit that I didn't think the salve I made would work *this* well. But it stood to reason that I'd inherited at least some of her power. And through my studies, I was beginning to realize just how powerful she was.

It was an exciting, yet unsettling thought. Though I'd been taking that tonic for A Worried Mind, I still felt a hell of a lot of worry. Or... something.

The tugging of my bladder that I'd been denying finally caught up with me and gave a far better excuse to procrastinate further. So, I stood up and stretched my arms overhead before going inside.

When I emerged from the small bathroom, I padded into the living room, where Roz and Granna were still perched and sipping tea. Every surface and free section of wall was filled with varying shades of green. Before she'd retired, my grandmother owned a steady florist shop, where she sold bouquets and rare houseplants. The business was now closed, the space sold, but my grandmother still tended to each and every plant with care. It was in her nature, she told me once. The pull she felt to grow and nurture was one she couldn't ignore if she tried.

"Hey fancy lady," I chirped when Granna smiled over at me. Roz twisted around, her box-dyed red hair just as fluffy and fiery as always, and grinned.

"Ooh, Sylvie it is so *nice* to have you here." She put a hand up to her cheek, like she was going to tell me a secret, but said at the same volume, "I get tired of just talking to this old bat." Granna's trilling laugh made her sound so much younger, and it made me smile even more.

Roz and Granna were about the same age, as far as I knew, but it was evident who was trying to hang on to youth tooth and nail and who had decided to accept age and what came with it.

"What are you two getting up to today? A whole bunch of gossiping?" I sat on the arm of the plush sofa that was also purple, though a deeper shade that was Granna's particular favorite.

Granna waved a hand. "What else is there to do in retirement? Garden, read, and chat. It's what I worked so hard to be able to do."

"All right, ladies, so then what's the latest? I need a break anyway."

Roz cooed and reached over to rub a gentle hand on my arm. Her touch was warm and soft. "You work too hard, Sweetie. But 'fraid there hasn't been too much that would interest you. Just some disgruntled old folks." Then she chuckled darkly and retracted her hand. "And a few people missing or hightailing it out of town without a word."

My head cocked, calling back to something I'd heard when Roz first came over. "Like what they were saying on the news earlier?" Dad and I never really watched local or national news back home, so when I walked downstairs earlier and heard the stereotypical newscaster voice before I'd heard Roz and Granna prattling away, my brain took notice.

Granna nodded and gestured to the smaller flatscreen that I had bought her for Christmas one year. She turned up the volume with the remote, and we all watched in silence as a grim-faced man in a button-down gestured to the Antler Pointe Historic Downtown sign.

"Still no word from Kara Stanton, a lifetime resident of Antler Pointe and undergraduate student at Antler Pointe College. Her family and APPD are asking for anyone with information that may lead to her whereabouts to contact the number or email address below." As soon as her name left the anchor's lips, I felt a chill run down my whole body.

Pleasant, kind-voiced Kara was missing. When had we last gone to the student lounge to study? A week ago? Had she been in class yesterday? I wracked my brain and realized that, no, the seat across from me had been empty that morning, but I'd thought nothing of it. College students skipped class all of the time, and though it seemed like we would become friends, we hadn't been nearly close enough for me to check in on her if I felt something was weird.

Her freckled face flashed on the screen just before another segment began, and I felt my eyes prickle when I thought of her family. Though I didn't know her well, Kara didn't seem like the type to just up and leave. Especially without telling her family, who she'd spoken fondly of once or twice.

"She's probably dead," Granna said dryly and took a sip of her tea.

A choked, incredulous laugh shot out of my throat. Though I'd been thinking it, Granna said it with such a matter-of-fact tone that made me want to blush. I'd certainly gotten my comfort in morbidity from her, but it was different when I could still clearly remember comparing notes with the kind girl.

Roz nodded and puckered her lips that were painted bright enough to match her hair. "Such a shame. That's the third since January."

"What? Like third... disappearance?"

She shrugged. "Disappearance or murder, depending on what state they'll find them in. Whenever they find them, that is. From what I've heard, they still don't have any leads. And do you know that Harriet heard Chief Thompson's wife kicked him out *again*..." And then Roz was off again reporting on the happenings, but my mind stayed stuck on Kara and this news that two others had disappeared this year.

For a moment, I felt guilt for the story I was working on now. What if Kara was in a situation like that? What if she was scared or hurt or *dead*?

Though I had a pretty high tolerance when it came to the things I read or watched, *knowing* someone who may be going through something like that was a very different thing.

Fully tuned out of my grandmother and her friend's chatter, I slunk through the kitchen to fill a glass of water and stuff a handful of chips into my mouth. Maybe she was just... taking some time away. It was a possibility, especially since the newscaster stated that her car had yet to be found.

But the gnawing in the back of my mind kept returning to Granna's blunt prediction. Maybe she'd spoken that way because she could feel it. I thought about walking to class and seeing Kara, but like how Granna described that morning weeks ago. Transparent at the edges—there but not.

And though I'd walked inside to rid myself from memories of Orion and his touch, I came back to my laptop no less distracted than before. My character running through the forest now had Kara's face, to the point that I almost debated her fate at the end of the story. Felt like the blows of the knife were real and not just a product of my imagination.

I fought my way to the end, passing over my writing once more before uploading it to the magazine's website with a sigh. *What if I just sealed her fate?* My mind's anxious voice was one I was all too familiar with, and I imagined it drifting away, like a ribbon caught in the wind.

In its place, though, I saw him. Again. But not the gruff and strong person he'd been on campus. How he'd looked crumpled beside the dumpster. Hiding.

Had Kara gone missing because... Orion was meant to be the third instead of her?

My lungs gave another rough laugh while I tucked my laptop under my arm to finally return inside for the evening. *No, that kind of stuff doesn't happen in real life*, my rational mind reasoned.

Then, that ribbon in my mind's sky swirled and flipped before finally disappearing into the distance, *Like how some say witches don't exist in real life, right?*

CHAPTER SEVEN

The female maneuvered easily within the wood. Her steps were sure, and it would have been so easy to grab her. But something about this stretch of forest felt wrong. Each time I tried to get closer, my hide felt like it was crawling, *burning*, and I had to back away.

It wasn't the right time, anyway. We had a few months, but per his instructions, she was next.

So, tasked with tracking her, I stayed just on the edge of the invisible barrier. I was the strongest I'd ever been—I could run faster and scent better than I ever could before. But I couldn't push past whatever magic they'd put around their house.

My head tilted in curiosity while she crouched near a fallen log. A cluster of mushrooms, bright orange even in the dimming light, were tucked where I could barely see. She seemed to be inspecting it, the female destined for *him*.

I crept along, trying my best to stay just out of the warded area while keeping her in my sights. She kept taking these walks, but there seemed to be no real purpose behind them. Just wandering, observing, and sometimes, she'd turn her ear down like she was trying to listen. I wondered if she heard the earth as we did. The songs and the flavors and the colors. Humans usually didn't notice, and even we hadn't been opened to all of it until recently.

I sat back on my haunches, mind wandering to what I was going to have for dinner. How I could try to get out of this next time. Hunting out here would be no problem, but the energy closest to her house made me wary of letting my guard down enough to eat. And dragging any kill back to safety felt like too much trouble. At that point, I might as well just scrounge for something in the fridge.

The female walked behind a cluster of trees, and though I could smell her, she was no longer visible. Remembering my orders, I adjusted, trying to catch sight of her brown skin and black hair amongst all the brown and black around her.

My body seized, and I couldn't help lowering to the ground, whine escaping out of my nose. I slunk back, away from the direction she'd gone until the sensation subsided. That was another thing he didn't want to listen to me about. That the witches were guarding this part of the land somehow. No one knew enough about them to know how to combat it or how to get around to where we could gather enough information to know when to take her.

But *he* said we were favored. That we were chosen for this land because of the sacrifices we were willing to make. Why our claim to the land superseded all others.

What I'd had enough sense, or fear, to not ask aloud was how we were favored but unable to enter this part of our territory. Why we kept having to prove ourselves. But I wasn't Leader, and everyone was witness to the brutal takeover a few years prior.

He was a good leader, a great, strong one. And if this was what he thought was best, then I would follow.

I still smelled her, and going in the direction I'd memorized now, I could just see the lights from the little white house in the distance. She'd had enough of her evening hike, it seemed, and was going home.

As soon as I heard the door close, I began to head in the direction of my own home. It wasn't too far if I ran through the forest, which I was doing now. To run on this land that was ours was the best feeling in the world. To be free and know that we had the forest on our side, *him* on our side—I'd never felt more pride than I did to be part of this.

CHAPTER EIGHT

SYLVIE

Josie leaned over the bar counter to get the bartender's attention, reaching out her arm but to no avail. The music was a bit too loud for my tastes, and it was crowded for a Wednesday night. But before I could get too irritated, I watched her lift up to kneel on the barstool and nearly climb over the bar herself.

When one of the other cashiers asked to switch shifts with me, I'd felt excited for my extra weeknight off and immediately told Josie. With school and work, I hadn't been able to see her as much as I liked to, and she immediately suggested we go out.

My lower back was starting to ache a little, sitting twisted in the barstool, and more and more people were pressing into the small dive bar. I drummed my fingernails on the sticky counter, happy to let Josie take care of getting our orders in. Though I usually didn't mind a night of drinks and chatting, the noise of the place was pressing a little too close on my nerves. I knew Josie sensed it, having been a bit pointed in her encouraging that she just wanted to stay a little while longer, so I just pressed on. It would feel better once we were tucked into a less busy corner or something.

"Hey!" She shouted over the noise, and the tall woman finally looked our way. Josie put on a wide smile, resting her chin on her fist, and I watched the bartender roll her eyes and smile.

"What can I get you, Josie?"

My friend looked over at me, and I mouthed to her my usual. "Ah, a glass of pinot noir for her, and chardonnay for me," Josie called over and was met with a quick nod.

My leg jumped to the beat of the song playing, and I tried my hardest to not look at my phone. Josie was chatting pleasantly, ass still in the air, with a bespectacled man beside her, and they shared an easy laugh. Now, I was fairly sociable, but Josie made friends practically everywhere she freaking went. It was a little bewildering, but I was used to it by now.

The bartender poured our drinks quickly and heavily, placing them before us on two square napkins.

We both started reaching for our wallets, me digging through my oversized purse and Josie reaching in her pocket, but before we could pull our cards out, a deep voice rumbled softly beside me.

"It's on me."

I knew that voice. The huskiness of it sent an irritating shiver down my back. Like a delectable chill in the way that I felt heat flood my face in reaction. I felt the phantom scrape he gave me that night I found him, healed and invisible now.

"Thanks," Josie said with impressed brows raised and the start of a cheshire grin before she looked at me then back toward him. I didn't want to turn around, but it was as if his presence was pulling at my chest. Not even daring me to swivel in my seat, but demanding it.

His hair was wet. That was the first thing I noticed, especially since the air outside had begun to cool substantially with October almost upon us. But his pale skin wasn't even flushed. The loose curls of his hair hung limply over his brow, and the line of creamy white strands was neat and sharp at the nape of his neck. I fixed an unimpressed look on my face to hide my frustration with myself. I shouldn't notice him enough to spot details like that.

After that irritatingly exciting glimpse of him at the grocery store, I continued my outright avoidance of Orion. Besides the sharp pang when I caught sight of him, it was fairly easy to fill my time with other things. My coursework had ramped up considerably, as had my lessons with Granna.

I made my way into the forest each evening that I didn't have to work. It felt more alive to me, then, with the last rays of the sun just reaching the forest floor. The winding ways between the trees were still carved into my memory from when I traipsed the land as a little girl. Every time, I felt a deep sense of belonging, almost of love, that followed me with every step. And with that comfort and my longstanding familiarity, I searched and listened, knowing how deep to go and where to find the best wild berries and clusters of mushrooms. There were still no whispers, something I still hadn't admitted to Granna. But maybe they would come.

Vinny's was still dull as always, and I'd decided to more seriously look for another job before Josie and I made our way to the bar for the night. Something about it had really grown stale, or stale enough for me to recognize that I wanted something better if I could find it. Josie gave her resounding agreement when I told her, and somehow that gave me the push to stand firm in the decision.

Had I known that I would see *him* tonight, I might not have come. My heart was nearly galloping with him beside me, despite the space I was trying to put in place. His bright green eyes were in stark contrast to his pale coloring, though it also seemed to let them shine brighter, even in the dim light from the dive bar. The bartender plucked his credit card from his grip, and when she asked, he turned back to her. "You can leave it open."

I flicked my dense ponytail over my shoulder, and I begrudgingly admitted that his light appearance seemed to… suit him. Like he was something ethereal or otherworldly. Like an angel.

An angel? I thought incredulously at myself. *Oh, fuck me,* I cringed and lifted my glass for a sip.

My inner dialogue seemed to be showing entirely on my face because he was suddenly scowling down at me, some pink creeping up on his cheeks. "And whatever IPA you have on draft, please," he grumbled over the bar. When he turned back to me, his white eyelashes narrowed. "You wouldn't let me settle the debt between us before. I'd like to settle it."

I nearly choked on the wine I was currently sipping. Settling the debt? "I told you that there was no debt between us. Can't you just let it go?"

His eyes cut to behind me, and I turned my head to see Josie still engrossed in her task of making best friends with the man beside her. Just like most people she interacted with like this, he was being drawn in. Though she was friendly with everyone, I caught the lowering of her voice as she joked back and forth with him. The way she crossed her bare legs underneath her miniskirt.

I turned back around, and he seemed placated by my friend's attention being elsewhere. "You helped me, and I never got to return the favor."

My brows turned up at that, mind spooling back to the first time we'd met. How the dumpster behind him had almost masked the coppery tang of his blood. He never did explain what happened.

I snorted into my glass. "Buying me a glass of wine is repaying a debt? I didn't even do anything." Because he didn't even let me call anyone! After he'd shuffled off into the night, I didn't think we'd even see each other again. But he just kept. Popping. Up.

He clenched his jaw and accepted the frothing glass of beer the bartender wordlessly slid him. "You did. And I've been wanting to thank you." He'd been staring hard somewhere above me, but now he dropped his gaze to take a sip of his drink.

We sat there for a moment. Me with no one to talk to, and him just—standing there. I raised my glass to take a gulp but surreptitiously ran my eyes over the rest of him. He was wearing a dark gray hoodie, and I absolutely did *not* notice the sturdiness and width of his shoulders underneath the fabric. No, of course not.

I almost spilled the rest of my wine when Josie leaned over, placing an unaware hand on my leg, "Hey, you guys wanna go get a booth?"

Before I could squeak a response, she grabbed my arm and started ushering us over to a corner that had just been vacated. I glanced behind me to see that he was... following? Was he interested in Josie? Is that why he was trailing behind us at her command?

When I slid in the old wooden seat, I expected Josie to sit beside me, but she sat across with that man she'd been chatting up settling beside her.

A solid body radiating heat and some cologne that had no right to smell that good sat beside me. I kept my eyes on my best friend, and when she sucked both her lips into her mouth, skin trembling from trying to suppress her laughter, I kicked her under the table. I'd confessed to her about my run-ins with Orion, and she'd quickly seen through my feigned nonchalance. In fact, she'd downright encouraged me to interact with him, arguing that he was probably just nervous around me.

Josie got a rein on herself and grinned over at us all. "So, this is Keith." She gestured to the dopey looking guy beside her. He pushed back his dull brown hair and sat up a bit taller when he ran his gaze up and down my unwanted guest. "And your name is...?" As if she didn't know it. I rolled my eyes as covertly as I could.

"Orion." His voice was almost rough, and I had to hold myself still, given that I had the overwhelming urge to fidget.

"Oh, what an interesting name," she said. Keith seemed to deflate a bit at Josie's compliment as a beat of silence befell our little gathering.

Realizing that my friend was looking at me expectantly, I cleared my throat. "Sylvie." Keith gave a shy nod and mumbled 'nice to meet you'. Josie placed a hand on his shoulder, drawing him into her once again.

My eyes narrowed at her. What was the point of dragging me and Orion over here if she wasn't going to talk to us? At this rate, she was going to be *leaving* with the guy! I loved her, but I internally groaned. I had a sneaking suspicion about how this was going to go. Considering it had happened numerous times throughout our friendship.

Orion coughed briefly, probably to fill the silence on our side of the booth. I was wracking my brain for a snide remark, something to cut him and the awkward moment with, but he mumbled over his drink, "Um, you look nice. Pretty."

My eyes about fell out of their sockets, and my head reared back in shock. A compliment was the last thing I thought I'd receive from the dry, brusque specter that had sidled next to me.

So, why did I feel my face heating again? "Uh, thank you? I mean," I closed my eyes for a moment and shook my head to clear it, "you look nice, too."

He looked down at himself and gave a self-deprecating snort, "Thanks." Before I could stop myself, my face pinched in worry. Did he—did he not think he looked nice? Even though he had bad manners, I wasn't really serious about the ghost thing.

Orion pursed his lips, eyeing me for a while as Josie and Keith laughed together like they'd known each other for years. The music of the bar changed to a more mellow rock song, the guitar's lilting melody settling my shoulders just a bit. I took another pull from my glass, waiting for him to say something. But the two of us just sat there. When I snuck a glance over at him, I would catch his eyes darting away, as if he'd been trying to take me in just before.

He seemed... softer now. I threw back the rest of my drink and set the empty glass on the table. "H-how are you?" I kept my gaze steady on him. If we were sticking in this situation together, I wasn't going to awkwardly sit beside him without speaking.

It was his turn to be surprised. He searched around us, as if the surroundings would give him an answer. "I'm… uh, I'm okay. Good, I mean. And you?" His cheeks started blooming with that dark pink color again, and I felt myself relax even more. He hadn't thrown any rude remarks at me, which was a relief.

He was being sweet. Even though he'd barely said anything, his blush and posture made him seem almost bashful underneath the grumbles. I swallowed, but I couldn't help the lifting of my lips just slightly. He pushed some of the curls away from his forehead, and my smile grew. "I'm fine. Thanks for the drink, by the way."

"You're welcome," he said quickly before gesturing to my empty glass. "Can I get you another?"

"Uh, sure." He nodded and took my empty glass before standing and sauntering fluidly over to the bar. I watched his ass shift back and forth underneath his jeans. I groaned to myself, *It has no right being that perfect.*

He stood for a while at the bar, waiting for his turn, and when I turned back forward, I caught Josie staring at me with a knowing glance. Dammit—had I groaned *out loud*? By the way she was looking at me, it seemed like I had.

I huffed and smoothed my dress. If he was buying, convinced there was a debt between us, I wasn't going to *say no*.

And, he was attractive. *So fucking what?* I dared myself and Josie, who was still looking at me with an amused and encouraging expression while Keith chatted away about some sports team. Yeah, okay, I could admit to myself that I liked the way he looked. The way his voice sounded. If the amount of times I'd thought about his face and voice in the dead of night was any indication, I liked it a lot.

Goddess, even the way he fucking *smelled*. What cologne did he use? It never ceased to hit my senses just right. *Yes*, I was correct, I thought when he came walking back with a full glass in tow, he was fucking haunting me.

But when he slid back in next to me, my lips pulled back into a full grin, the sweet nature my grandmother had always cooed over me for coming to the forefront, and I almost giggled when he reflected it with a hesitant smirk of his own.

The four of us spent the next hour or so in a pleasant rhythm. Though Keith was far more interested in talking to Josie than Orion or me, we had a few threads of common interest to discuss. Then between those, we would retreat to our two distinct sides. Josie laughed and leaned into Keith who looked like a damn giddy fool, surely feeling confident that he was going to get lucky, and Orion and I stumbled our way through decreasingly hesitant conversation.

"Oh, Faust isn't so bad," he assured me over his beer, which I had taken a reluctant sip of to taste before sputtering at the yeasty bitterness. That was the first time I'd heard him laugh. It was low and hoarse, and I realized that I liked it very much.

Though I knew my brazenness was due to the wine, I also knew that my desire to touch him, to test where our boundary now sat, was all me. I gave him a lighthearted shove, and he relented a bit under my touch as I snickered, "Oh, he's an old cantankerous bore."

Orion gave a shrug. "Sure. *But*, he is a wealth of knowledge. I respect him for that." And, after he swept an assessing glance over me, his arm shot out, extending to rest on the back of the booth behind us.

There was a beat between us, where we both were unsure of the step in this direction, but my inhibitions had softened, and I leaned into my seat and closer to his arm. His face relaxed.

We sat and talked like that for a while, and though the alcohol had certainly lubricated the conversation, it felt easy. Once I got past my suspicion at him being funny and kind, it was nothing to lean into it. To let his inner arm bump up against my shoulder. For my hair to brush against the back of his hand. He asked me how I was liking my classes, and I asked about the ones he was teaching this semester and next.

Eventually, Josie ushered all of us across the bar again, this time to the pool tables. Though I assured Orion that I was an absolutely hopeless teammate for this sort of thing, he just shrugged and said he wasn't any good either, so he didn't mind.

We slipped into good-natured insults at each others' skills, and at one point, I had to hold back my laughter when Josie waggled her brows suggestively at me while she requested for Keith to help her position to make a shot. He lightly grasped her waist from behind, and I couldn't help but look conspiratorially to Orion, who looked like he was holding back his own snicker.

Three games later, when Keith and Josie barely claimed victory, I leaned against the pool table, tapping my foot to a nonsensical pattern in my mind and pulled my phone out to check the time. Orion and Keith had taken our cues to put them back up and close out their tabs, and Josie made her way over to throw her arm onto my shoulders.

"I'm going back to Keith's place," she whispered in my ear.

I chuckled. "Oh, yeah, I never would have figured." I'd known from the moment she turned around in her barstool toward him that this was the most likely outcome of the night. When I pulled back and swept my eyes over her, I felt reassured that she seemed to have her wits about her. Her breath smelled only faintly of wine, as she'd switched to water after we left the booth.

I ran a hand over her shaved head, and she glanced at the men coming back toward us. "You'll be okay," she said, and I nodded. We both had an unflinching habit of checking the other's locations at the end of the night. Though he seemed a bit boring, Keith wasn't presenting any major concerns in the few hours we'd spent with him.

"Just call me if you need me to come get you," I muttered before we separated. She gave my arm one last squeeze, assuring me that she'd text throughout the evening and when she'd eventually make her way back home, before she followed him to start walking toward his apartment a few blocks away.

I was left with Orion. Again. We both watched Josie and Keith leave, and some of the awkwardness seeped back between us. Granna's house wasn't far, but my car was at Josie's. I was about to open up my phone to get a car to come pick me up, but before I could pull up the app, Orion mumbled beside me, "I'm going outside to smoke."

My nose wrinkled in mild detest, but I found myself following after him, requesting a car while we walked through the bar and outside. The humid warmth of the crowded place cleared almost immediately when he opened the door. The evening chill of late September was in full swing, and the telltale taste of autumn made my eyelids droop. It wasn't just rising coldness, but a sleepy spice that was only going to grow as the days passed.

I tapped my finger on the back of my phone, holding it down at my side, and Orion pulled a white pack of cigarettes from his back pocket, along with a Zippo lighter. He plucked one from the pack and held it between his lips, and the tinkling flick of the lighter hit my brain in just the right spot. Watching him balance the cigarette at one side of his lips while he held the flame to it was, begrudgingly, one of the most mesmerizing things I'd seen in my life.

"Smoking kills, you know," I said as he made his first exhale toward the moon overhead. But my words didn't break whatever spell I was under like I'd intended them to.

Orion lowered his head, and he looked at me, expression blank and in a way that made the fidgets get the better of me. I pulled at the overly long sleeve of my dress. "And?" He took another drag of his cigarette, cherry on the end flaring for a brief moment that seemed to make his eyes appear even brighter.

A few people stood around us, enjoying their drinks outside in the balmy air or having their own smoke, but they all seemed muffled, not really there, while Orion and I watched each other. We somehow stood in silence the entire time it took for him to finish his cigarette, and my eyes followed as he dropped it to the sidewalk below and crushed it under his boot. My throat clicked with a dry swallow.

I could've blamed the two glasses of wine I'd had this evening, but in reality, I felt as sober as I'd ever been when I dropped my bag to the ground, leaned in, and gripped the front of Orion's sweatshirt. Even through the fabric, I felt the warmth of his skin, and before I could sink all the way into him, he brought his hands to my face.

When his lips pressed to mine, I inhaled the burning scent of cigarette smoke still on his breath, on his fingers. I'd never thought of myself as small, but as we kissed, I felt completely covered and protected by his solid body. My palms rested over his chest, one feeling the beating of his heart, and his hands cupped my jaw in such a way that I felt the tickling of his fingertips at the base of my neck. His thumb softly caressed the tip of my earlobe, and when his tongue gently pressed against my lips, I immediately opened them.

My fingers and toes curled while our tongues slid against each other, learned each other, and I could taste the bitterness from the beer and cigarette he'd had. I'd never thought such a thing could taste so good or make me want to back up against a dirty brick wall and wish I could undress, if only to be as close as possible.

But that was exactly what I was doing. At some point, we'd pushed up against the wall in front of everyone. And now he had a grip on my back, one that I wanted him to trail lower and lower.

My hair was getting caught in the roughness of the brick, my ponytail an uncomfortable knot pushing into the back of my head, but I wanted more.

Orion gentled the kiss and pulled his head back, just enough to be able to suck in deep, calming breaths. I lunged forward while he did and planted a quick kiss on his lips before leaning back fully onto the wall once again. My eyes met his, and I saw that the green was deep, the darkest I'd ever seen it. Probably due to his pupils being blown much wider than they'd been before.

"Sorry," I muttered between us while we caught our breath. His hand was still on my back, mine on his chest, but maybe he didn't want this? I mean, up until now, I thought he'd hated me. Maybe for seeing him in such a vulnerable position the first time we met. Or at the very least, I had been certain he saw me as an annoyance. Someone he'd rather he didn't encounter.

His pale brow furrowed. "Why?" And I felt held by him again.

I swallowed, and another wave of his taste and smoke hit my tongue. "I just—I didn't know if you wanted that. For me to do that, I mean."

I cringed at the breathless, stammering way I spoke, but then he brought his nose to mine and brushed it from side to side. His breath skated over my cheek. "I wanted you to."

"Ah, okay," I took a big inhale, "I mean, good." I cringed again. He'd reduced me to a state where I had no adequate words to say. Nothing to truly convey how much that kiss had affected me. It was almost electrifying, and I was trying really, really hard to not focus on the hard press of him against my lower belly. But my own answering flutter there was becoming harder to ignore.

"Sylvie." His voice was low, probably inaudible to those chatting away around us, but I heard the grumble, the growl in it, and sucked in a quick breath. "I want to..." He pulled back, and I immediately missed the feeling of his face nuzzling mine. I watched his eyes track down my face, then neck, and down my body.

While Orion was warm and comforting, that kiss and the cool night left my nipples sharp against the fabric of my dress. And I knew that they were visible when his gaze seemed to stop there, then on the slight curves of my stomach and thighs before coming back up again to meet my face. He smoothed his thumb along the corner of my jaw and cleared his throat. "Can I... see you? Sometime?"

I'd been chewing on my bottom lip while I waited for him to speak, but I released it quickly, voice incredulous. "Are you asking me on a date?"

"Yes." When I would have usually had the urge to question this, the way he said it brooked no confusion. The steadiness of the way he was looking at me.

But I had to get him a little. With a lopsided smile, I said, "Thought I just got on your nerves more than anything."

He didn't laugh like I'd thought he would. His chuckles and smirks had been flowing consistently throughout the course of the night, but now, the corners of his mouth turned downward. I saw his jaw clench, but before I could apologize again, he exhaled, "I'm sorry. That I made you feel that way."

"Oh, uh, thanks. What would you like to go do?"

His eyes widened for a moment. "You still—" he closed them and shook his head before seeming to gather himself "—um, dinner? I can take you out for dinner."

I tilted my head, hair rasping against the brick, and grinned. "You can?"

Orion nodded a few times, then gave me a knee-buckling kiss before letting his hands fall. "If you'd let me." Headlights swung around and shone from behind his back when a car pulled up to the curb.

Just then, my phone dinged with a notification. I unclenched my fingers from his shirt, smile softening. "That sounds nice. Sure." He was still watching me as I pulled my phone from my bag.

When I told him that my ride was here, the car idling just behind him set to take me home, he walked me over to it and opened the door for me. My eyes shot to my hairline when he asked the driver who they were here to pick up. They seemed barely out of high school, but when they looked at their phone clipped to the dash and said my name, Orion's relaxed a fraction.

I handed my phone to him before stepping into the back seat. "Here, give me your number, and I'll text you." He grunted in acknowledgement and quickly inputted his number before handing it back.

"Night, Sylvie." And I felt heat flood my cheeks when he

dropped a warm kiss onto my cheekbone just before I sat. He eyed the driver with a hard look for so long they began to squirm. After an awkward clearing of my throat, he closed the door for me, and I didn't even attempt to keep my head forward as we pulled away. I sat twisted, watching Orion while the car merged onto the main street. And he was watching me, too, unmoving and with his hands in his pockets until I was out of sight.

CHAPTER NINE

SYLVIE

What are the main branches of the United States Government? How many state senators are allotted to each state? I rolled my eyes and clicked through the exemption study quiz. Though I could somewhat understand why such courses were graduation requirements, I was irritated for having to waste my time when I had papers to write.

I leaned my head into my hand, clicking and scrolling, clicking and scrolling while barely reading the questions. There was no way in hell I was going to take the actual course that was required, but studying for the exemption test also felt like torture.

The little bell above the coffee shop's door was giving a steady jingling with people coming and going, and my foot tapped absently to the old rock song playing quietly from the speakers overhead. I took a sip of my caramel latte, gone lukewarm now with how long I'd been sitting.

Seventy-five percent correct, the results flashed across my screen, and I groaned aloud, collapsing my arms on the table and burying my head atop them. I needed an eighty-percent or higher to exempt the class and finally graduate. There was a graduate program application I had to finish, papers I needed to write, and I could *not* afford to be bested by a freshmen-level course that I should have been able to pass in my sleep.

"Bit early to start the finals-time despair, I think." My heart immediately started to pick up at the sound of that low, steady voice.

I rotated my head, peeking one eye out to look at Orion. He held his own to-go cup, satchel slung on his other shoulder. What kind of coffee did he drink? I'd bet it was black drip or a triple espresso or something.

"Not finals. Civics exemption," I grumbled dramatically and hid my face once again.

His huffing chuckle made my stomach tighten, and we lapsed into another silence with the ambient sounds of the coffee shop filled the space between us. Eventually, Orion cleared his throat. "Ah. Do you mind if I sit?"

My head flew up, and I quickly blinked to adjust to the light around me. I smoothed my hand over my head to attempt to tame the flyaways and situate my frizzy ponytail. Somehow that night and that kiss seemed far away and just an hour ago at the same time.

When I'd gotten back home, I'd checked that Granna was all right, then done the same with Josie by texting her and checking her location.

After showering and getting in bed with a book, I'd sent a text to Orion, telling him I got home okay and thanking him again for the drinks. Well, I sent the text right before setting my phone to do-not-disturb and focusing all of my energy on the assigned reading I had to finish before Monday's class.

I couldn't resist, though. By the time I'd finished the reading, assuredly not retaining much because my mind kept wondering whether he'd texted me back, I clicked off my bedside lamp and almost frantically checked my messages.

ORION

No thanks necessary. I had fun, Sylvie.

His message was short, but it left me smiling as I laid my head on my pillow and drifted off.

I nodded now, inviting him to sit, and pushed aside my laptop and study packet to give him room. My latte was downright cold at this point, but I threw the rest back and crumpled my napkin into the empty mug.

Then, I shrugged off my sweater, though the air wasn't exactly warm enough for a sleeveless shirt. I just couldn't figure out what to do with my hands with him in front of me again. And I normally wasn't this nervous, but with his woodsy cologne wafting toward me, I couldn't sit still.

Orion's bright green eyes seemed soft today, like they'd been at the bar four nights ago, and I wondered if he still wanted to go on a date. "You look nice," he said before taking a sip from his cup.

I grasped my thigh to keep my hand from running over my hair again. "Thank you. So do you." His small smile was warm, and the skin around his eyes crinkled a little with the movement. There was another pause, an awkward silence, and my mind raced to desperately decide what to say to fill it. Not that I didn't like silence, but… I felt like I *had* to say something to him.

But what would be the right thing? Every other interaction with him felt like a dream, and that kiss, though I could still feel it on my lips and his hands still on my body, was almost too amazing to be real.

"Uh, busy today?" And then I winced at the lame question, but he didn't seem to blanch, nor did he laugh.

He shook his head, and I watched one of the bigger curls atop his head bounce and sway. "No, I got most of my grading done this morning before I left the house. Just needed to swing by my office and run some errands today. You?"

I relaxed in my seat, thankful that he'd picked up my pathetic attempt at conversation. "A bit. I was able to get out of the house some to study. As you can see," I gestured at my laptop, "it hasn't been the most successful venture."

Orion's chuckle was husky, and it made me lean a bit closer. "I'm sure you'll do fine on the exam."

"Oh, I don't know. Papers, I could write all day long. But I get *horrible* test anxiety. I could very easily choke." I shrugged and shifted until I sat on my hands. The pressure on my fingers calmed the urge to fidget just a bit.

"Well... do you need someone to help you study? Quiz you, maybe?" His voice was gruffly hesitant, as if we hadn't had our tongues down the other's throat a few days ago.

"Um." I chewed on my lip for a moment not wanting to seem too eager, but I *was* eager. He was waiting patiently for my answer, but I noticed the nervous twist of his fingers against the cardboard sleeve around his coffee cup. "If you aren't too busy. That would be helpful." His immediate exhale made me feel lighter.

And with that opening, I directed Orion to the study packet that had bulleted lists of definitions and information that I had only halfway memorized. Most of it *seemed* like it should be ingrained in my brain from growing up in this country and being a good student all these years. But, for some reason, the information wasn't really sticking.

"Which of these states were included in the original thirteen colonies of the United States..." Orion created his own questions based on what was included in the packet I bought from the campus bookstore, and we went back and forth for a long while. When I groaned in misery at each incorrect answer, Orion would give me a small smile and ask me to take another guess.

We worked through each page in the packet, ordering more coffee at the halfway point, and when he asked his last question, I almost rejoiced in triumph when I guessed the correct president. "Well, done, Sylvie. That was..." Orion looked to the napkin he'd been jotting down a tally of my correct responses and the number of questions. "Forty-one correct out of fifty, so eighty-two percent."

"Oh, thank goddess," I muttered and passed relieved hands over my hair to pat it down. Orion gave another low chuckle and closed my packet to hand back to me.

While I stuffed it and my laptop back in my bag, he cleared his throat and started, "I've been thinking about… our date."

I sunk my hands into my lap and gave a tentative smile. "Yeah?"

His brow was furrowed now as he stared at some space between us, "I was wondering if you'd be available tomorrow?"

I had to temper my smile. Vinny's was closed on Mondays, so work wouldn't be an issue. "Sure. Where were you thinking?"

He shrugged self-consciously but said, "Thai food? There is a nice place just a block from here, actually."

"That sounds great." I grinned. "I love Thai food."

Orion ducked his head as he took the last gulp from his coffee. "Me too." But I also saw the pleasant tilting of his lips in a smaller version of my smile. "I've only gotten takeout from there, but the food is great." I noticed the pink color flushing his cheeks and the tops of his ears.

I nodded, and my smile grew even more at the realization that the feeling I got at the bar was correct. Orion *was* bashful. But then my mind went back to that knee-wobbling kiss. In those moments between us, after he'd relaxed and joked with me over our poor billiard skills, he seemed anything but. He was more sure of himself while he smoked in front of me in silence.

His hand reached up to ruffle the back of his head and the curls that looked extra bouncy today. He shifted in his seat, not looking at me, but it only made me soften more toward him. "Orion?"

He looked down at his empty coffee cup but dropped his arms to rest on the table. "Yes?"

"What changed?"

His brow wrinkled and so did his nose, just slightly. After a long silence where he seemed to be turning over my question again and again, he finally asked, "What do you mean?"

Though I wasn't upset anymore—far from it, really—my lingering anxiety couldn't let go of this unknown shift in the way he talked to me. "Until four nights ago, you acted quite cold. What changed?"

The skin on his forehead crinkled even deeper before his eyes lifted to meet mine underneath his long lashes. He held my gaze, and I felt myself leaning in. But I remained quiet, giving him time. Orion's attention flitted somewhere beneath my eyes before settling on them once again a moment later. "I was bewildered. And… uncomfortable that you'd seen me that way. That I scared you."

I said nothing, sensing that he was still working out what he wanted to say. His gaze was swimming across my face, as if he was struggling to find the words. When I gave him an encouraging tilt of my lips, he homed in on the change in my expression, and with a relaxing of his shoulders, he continued, "I'm not… *great* at social interaction. After I hurt your feelings, I realized my mistake. I'm sorry."

My head tilted, picking up that there was more to be said about that. But, who was I to judge? We both seemed to lean toward being more anxious, and I realized that I felt comfortable holding space for the awkwardness that sometimes crept up between us. Maybe I was too soft. Or a fool. But after the bar and him helping me study, I knew that I had forgiven Orion. For hurting me physically and emotionally, and I was more than willing to give him a chance. Even more than that, I was burningly curious to see where this could go with him.

"It's okay. I forgive you."

He let loose a bigger sigh than I would've thought he was holding, but before he could share what he'd been about to say, someone stopped before our table and stole the conversation. "Long time, no see, Sylvie."

My mind took a moment to catch up, having been so absorbed

by Orion's presence. I looked up to see a familiar but unexpected face. "Uh, hi. How's it going?" Jasper had been among the group of kids running around with Josie the day we met. His mop of sandy brown hair was still present after all this time, though he'd grown taller and broader over the years.

"Pretty good. Nice to see you back in town." His smile at me seemed to harden like crystalized sugar when he focused on Orion beside me. And Orion, having been soft and shy with me earlier, shut down. His pink lip was curled back, nearly in a snarl.

"So... how are things at the store?" Jasper's father owned the mom-and-pop hardware store that was still hanging on down-town, and both had been nice enough to me throughout my visits with Granna.

"Fine, same as always. See you've met this bookworm, here." Even after this short amount of time, I'd worked out the fact that Orion struggled with keeping eye contact, but he and Jasper were locked into an intense stare down that felt out of place for the commercialized chill of the coffee shop. They clearly knew each other, and *very* clearly disliked each other.

And though we hadn't even gone on a date yet, I felt oddly protective over Orion. His shoulders held a new tension, his eyes hard and sharp gems. Perhaps it was a bit forward, but I put a hand on his forearm. I looked at Jasper. "Yeah, Orion's great and was helping me study. It was nice to see you." Kindness was my default, but my tone now chilled significantly. Jasper's friendly smile toward me took on a knowing glint, and Orion's arm beneath me tensed even more.

He stood, nearly toppling over his chair. If I thought the night Orion lashed out at me in fear was frightening, I now had a new standard for that side of him. His back, though already framed with wide shoulders, seemed to broaden or thicken, like he was making himself bigger to both cover me from Jasper's view but also tower over him.

I craned my neck to better see around Orion's body. They weren't saying anything. Just staring at one another with faces pulled tight in barely-contained rage. Jasper looked as if he were rearing to make a move, but then his eyes widened, seeing something on Orion's face that I couldn't from where I sat. Jasper broke first, expression and posture wilting in submission.

"Hey, what's goin' on?" I almost groaned in exasperation at yet another interruption, this time with the swaggering nonchalance of Chief Thompson's son. He was stereotypically handsome with chocolate brown waves tousled in that way that was supposed to look unintentional.

"Nothin'." Jasper made one last effort to puff up, but Orion was still standing just as tall and imposing as before. In fact, by the way his hands and jaw were clenching, I was anticipating a physical fight to break out.

Graham gave a shit-eating grin to Orion while palming the back of Jasper's jacket and started shoving him toward the exit. Some nonverbal comment passed between Orion and Graham, and I had to assume that it was about me. Because Graham's cocky stare landed on me and gave a wink.

I watched Graham and Jasper leave, the first sauntering, the second scuttling, and I wondered what the hell that had all been about.

"Sorry." Orion's voice was deeper and strained, as if he was trying to rein himself back in from that disquieting display. Now that he was eye-level with me, I got a better view of how tensed for an attack he really was. A full pink flush was slowly receding but still visible, and the muscles in his neck were tightly clenched.

"Are you okay?" I reached for Orion's arm again, squeezing the soft fabric of his flannel shirt.

Before turning back fully to me, he closed his eyes and took a deep inhale. His chest stilled then fell with an even longer exhale. He did this rhythm a few more times, always inhale, hold, then exhale, and I watched his whole body relax. My hand remained, and he didn't shove it off.

I sat and observed, the coffee shop noises slowly trickling back into my awareness, and then Orion opened his eyes. He still wasn't as relaxed as he'd been before Jasper's and Graham's interruptions, but it was far from how he'd been just a few moments ago.

"Yeah, I'm fine." The weak smile he gave was little reassurance, but I decided not to press him on it. Aside from growing up with my father, my circles of family and friends mostly consisted of women. Even with the men I'd dated in the past, I had never been privy to such a primal display of... whatever that was.

"Okay. Well, I should get going," I felt his arm tense all over again, "but we're still on for dinner tomorrow?"

His brow pulled low as he took a long blink. "Yes. Please. I can pick you up?"

My hand smoothed over his sleeve. "Sure. I'm looking forward to it."

Orion nodded and stood, although this time, the motion was smooth and controlled. I followed and shoved my things into my bag. We took our dirty dishes and tray to the designated area near the door, and the air between Orion and I had nearly cleared by the time we parted ways outside.

I walked toward my car, parked a few spots away, and tried to make sense of what had unfolded back there. Since moving to Antler Pointe, I barely saw Jasper or Graham, and never spared either of them any thought. I made a mental note to ask Josie to see if she would know any reason why the two of them seemed so at odds with Orion, who, from what I could tell, was a quiet and solitary sort of guy.

The air wasn't nearly as scorching as it'd been a few weeks prior, and with my stomach swooping with excitement about my date with Orion tomorrow, I felt a prickling on my back, like I was being watched.

Expecting for it to be Orion or a stranger giving me a passing glance, my fingers fumbled to fit my keys in the ignition when I saw, across the street and down aways, was Graham. Jasper's attention was on his father, who was leaned up against his shopfront and talking to his son. A rush of something hot and sharp filled my chest, and I returned Graham's stare, all urge for pleasantness completely evaporated.

Even from this distance, I saw his thick brows and grin rise. If it weren't for Jasper nudging Graham's shoulder, stealing his attention, I would have stomped across the street and—

Done what? My rational mind pushed forward, and I placed a calming hand at my chest, where my heart had begun to race. My lips puckered with a conscious, forceful exhale, and I pulled away, headed home.

Those surges of rage weren't new for me. I turned up the volume on my speakers, letting the heavy metal music and the jumping of my left leg take my excess energy. Images of marching up to Graham and grabbing him by the throat for how he'd looked at me and Orion were harder to dispel, but I'd nearly done just that by the time I pulled up at Granna's.

It would *not* bode well for my new life in Antler Pointe for me to attack the police chief's son. No matter how satisfying the fantasy was.

CHAPTER TEN

ORION

I pulled up to Sylvie's grandmother's home, fingers flicking along to the steady bass guitar rhythm trailing from my car's speakers. They lived just outside of the historic downtown, and though I was a ball of nerves—a state I hadn't experienced to this extent in a long time—the proximity to the forest mollified me just enough to stop from stimming any more than I already was.

The gravel of the drive resembled my own, and that was another moment of familiarity that made me feel on steadier footing.

It was almost ridiculous how much this woman was making me feel like a pup with uncoordinated limbs, all gangly with excited flailing. Even with my missteps and the blatant display of territoriality yesterday, she'd agreed to let me court her.

The boors who followed that arrogant jackass were getting too bold. But the beginnings of capitulation in the first one's scent was so satisfying, I had to strain even harder to keep my dominating instinct in check.

His leader, coming to his rescue, obviously knew that the boy was outmatched, and before I could rip his throat out for making eyes at Sylvie, they were gone. They both seemed to know her, but I had a feeling that they would have acted differently if I hadn't been sitting beside her. If she wasn't already starting to bear my scent. I still hadn't decided whether this served to protect her or paint a target on her back.

I shook my head, trying to clear the baser thoughts that were washing my mind with physical needs to dominate and protect and avenge. The situation with Graham and his followers wasn't one I'd found a solution for yet, and I certainly wasn't going to find it tonight. Even after seeing that side of me, Sylvie hadn't rebuffed my courting. For that, I was grateful. She kept giving me chance after chance, and I was determined to make her effort worth it.

While I'd showered and dressed earlier, I tried my best to settle my insecurities. Though it was to be a casual dinner at the Thai restaurant downtown, I was going to do everything in my power to ensure a successful first date. When I'd texted Juno, asking their opinion on the whole thing since they dated and fucked humans far more than I did, they'd cooed over me for 'Trusting and being vulnerable with them.'

They luckily didn't push me into a phone conversation or, I shuddered to think, a video call. But they suggested I dress as comfortably as possible since the restaurant was going to be a sensory nightmare for me to begin with.

When I'd caught Sylvie's scent leading to the bar that night, I hadn't even consciously considered where I was going until the cacophony of music and bar patron scent and chatter slammed into me. Above it, though, was the smell of cool cherries, and I abandoned all plan to pick up my dinner for the evening. It would have been far easier to fare if I'd had my headphones to cancel out some of the noise, but I found that being around her was enough. To breathe through the overstimulation was completely worth it when I got to spend time with her.

I pictured Juno's dangly earrings tinkling as they sent me text after text, encouraging me to not feel pressured to act any differently. As it was 'best to present my realest self' if I was hopeful for this to go anywhere.

Why did this all make me feel like a lanky teenager again?

I did, following their advice, take off the new and untested jeans I'd bought for the occasion and went with my favorite, worn-in pair. I had no problem admitting when Juno was right.

I checked my hair in the rearview mirror after I finally pulled up beside a red car that was sitting in front of the house. My mind went back to sitting at the bar with Sylvie, stumbling through conversation until it flowed between us. Part of this was the over-stimulation of the setting, another was my treading carefully due to my mucking up our first encounters. And another part, larger than I wanted to admit, was holding back my urge to have her right then and there.

My hands scrubbed at my face, trying to calm the heating of my body being this close to her again. While maneuvering socially was a labyrinthine task I'd only slightly gotten better at in my adulthood, sex was far easier to navigate. It called to both sides of me, and there was far less room for second-guessing and having to covertly rely on scents when words and facial cues made little sense.

With Sylvie, though, it wasn't just my longing to learn her in that way. No, it wasn't just sex, but I would've been naive to ignore the desire she brought out in me. Was it overly confident that I'd stuffed a few condoms in my wallet for the first time in months? Maybe, but judging how Sylvie initiated the first kiss between us and my body's already revved engine, I wanted to be prepared for all possibilities.

Since moving to Antler Pointe, my romantic relationships had been purely sexual—scratching the itch without committing to anyone that would spoil my own peacefully solitary life.

Well, as peaceful as I could manage, considering. Hell, I hadn't even courted anyone since—

My phone rang with an incoming call, and I immediately

rejected it when I saw Meredith's name splashed across the screen. I shook my head sharply and allowed myself one minute of breathing. In through my nose, hold, out through my mouth in a rhythm that was my old and faithful. Though it didn't work every time, it worked now, and I was able to calm my thoughts enough to climb out of the car. I made unfaltering steps to the front door and knocked.

Sylvie's perfume was potent even here, and when the front door opened, an avalanche that carried her chilly air and cherry smell made me want to find the source and throw myself on her.

Jesus. Was this a good idea? Tempting my self-control like this?

I took a cooling breath and smiled down at the older woman standing in the doorway. She was dressed in soft looking pants and a sweater, despite it being a fairly warm evening. Her long, nearly-white hair hung loose down her back, and despite her age, I felt flayed open by her keen eyes. They were the same color as Sylvie's.

"Hello," I stuck out my hand a beat late but managed to remember my manners, "my name is Orion. I'm here to take Sylvie to dinner."

She gave a smile and shook my hand. While Sylvie smelled like the best part of autumn, this woman, her grandmother, smelled of citrus and lavender and summer days. And… *fuck.*

I started to wonder how I'd missed it, but I knew exactly how. Sylvie's presence and all it triggered within me clouded my noticing this important detail. But faced with this woman and all of her attention, I knew partly why their scents made my body thrum in recognition. I was familiar with the world around us enough to recognize the pair of witches, now.

"I know you." Sylvie's grandmother's words were loaded, and I worried that she was going to refuse my entry. For, if I recognized her, she certainly knew what I was. Did Sylvie? She hadn't said anything, and by her reaction yesterday, she didn't understand the significance of what I'd communicated to the two oafs. I refocused on her grandmother, and her smile brightened in the way that Sylvie's did. "Please, come in."

I fought to keep my gait calm and still my fingers down at my side. I nodded in thanks and crossed the threshold. While she closed the door behind me, I took in their home. It was warm and done in calming colors of cream and purple. There was also an aroma of a multitude of herbs and spices that seemed almost baked into the floorboards and sunk into the walls.

Sylvie's grandmother gestured toward the room to my right, and I gave a longing glance to the staircase in front us before making my way into the living room. It was absolutely dominated by plants in a variety of pots and vases. Though the colors of the furniture and decor were more understated, there was an explosion of green in almost every corner and on absolutely every windowsill.

"Please, sit." Her tone was welcoming but also firm, and I obeyed, taking a seat on the sofa. I rested my hands in my lap and kept my back straight.

Impressing the family of the one you courted was incredibly important and something I'd anticipated for tonight. However, where the woman had been distracted but kind in the grocery store, she was sharp in more ways than one tonight. I fought like hell to make myself meet her assessing eyes.

"Thank you," I said.

"So, *faoladh*," I flinched, but she perched nonchalantly on a rattan armchair, "what are your intentions with my granddaughter?" We weren't going for any of the pleasantries, then.

Sylvie's grandmother held my worried stare, not in challenging or dominance, but with a knowing that made me feel relieved and unnerved at the same time. Was her question intended for a male with amorous intentions toward her granddaughter or for the faoladh, as she identified me, who she'd permitted in her home?

I cleared my throat, swallowed. But when I opened my mouth

to give her a response, an exasperated voice preceded loud stomping down the staircase.

"Goddess, Granna, I'm almost thirty. Stop treating him like he's taking me to the prom."

My mouth went dry, and I had to take another round of breaths while Sylvie made her way into the room. Her usually bouncing hair was tied into a knot on the crown of her head, and there were meticulously styled waves ending in perfect little curls beside her ears.

The dress she wore was sleeveless and long, but the way it clung to every dip and swell of her curves was a sight to see. Her long, sharp fingernails were tipped in a deep red color that complimented the soft green of her dress. She didn't wear much makeup from what I could tell, but her doe-like eyes were darkened and accentuated. Her plump lips, reddened.

My heart was beating hard in my chest, my mind reeling from the sight of her, and, embarrassingly, my dick was rapidly growing hard. *Fuck,* I cursed and tried to clear my thoughts to say something. Luckily, Sylvie and her grandmother commenced to go back and forth.

"Well, he's come here to the house to pick you up. Why am I not allowed to ask the important questions?"

"*Because*, you could scare him away," Sylvie pointed a finger, "and I know how you are. Your size makes you a wolf in sheep's clothing, and I have seen you in action. Tearing men apart is like a pastime for you."

Her grandmother threw up her hands and scoffed. "Oh, please. I wasn't going to say anything offensive. And, it's not my fault that all men are disappointing at best." She added, "No offense."

By then, I'd gathered myself a bit. "None taken." I looked back toward Sylvie, tightening the leash on all of my instincts that were bucking against my control. "And, you look breathtaking, Sylvie. Beautiful."

She gifted me with one of her smiles, and if her grandmother weren't there with her watchful eyes on me, I would have fallen to my knees. Or commanded that Sylvie get on hers. I'd take either.

Instead, I stood, and took two steps to be closer to her. She was a few inches taller than when I'd last seen her, the heeled sandals giving her a bit more height, and my instincts spilled over in the form of a kiss I gave to her cheek.

The grin was still on her face when I pulled back, and I offered her my arm. "Shall we?" I ran a questioning glance at her grandmother, who just returned it with a minute incline of her head.

Sylvie nodded and looked to me sweetly. "Let's go."

· · · · · · 🌙 · · · · · ·

SYLVIE

Orion looked so handsome in his simple jacket and shirt, the dark, earthy colors bringing out the green of his eyes. We both handed our menus to the server, and I stopped myself from running a nervous hand over my hair. I really didn't want to ruin the bun that'd taken me longer to get right than my makeup and dressing combined. While video chatting with Josie, I'd bemoaned my hair for refusing to be tamed without brute force after she helped me settle on my outfit for the evening.

"Well, that one I think checks all the boxes, so I'd go with it over the top and skirt. Plus your ass looks great in it." She'd been clicking away at her screen between giving input on the outfit options I modeled for her.

"While I do want to look nice, I'm not trying to give off 'fuck me on the first date' vibes."

Instead of making a snarky comment, Josie turned her full attention to me, eyes uncharacteristically serious. "Is there a reason why not?"

"Well... it's just been a while, and I don't want to rush into anything."

"But you like him." She framed it as fact, and I nodded. "Why not just let it be known?"

I groaned toward the ceiling. "I don't know! I'm just nervous. And my dry spell immediately after two unsuccessful relationships has me feeling all off."

"Take your time if you need. But he's here to stay, Sylvie."

I whined. "How can you even be so sure? He's been an ass for the majority of our interactions. Even if he's been sweet most recently."

Josie just shrugged and focused back on whatever she was working on. "Not sure. Just have a hunch."

Orion had been nothing but a gentleman when he'd picked me up. Granna was acting weird, well more strange than she sometimes did around people that weren't me or Roz, but she seemed to like Orion enough.

The lighting above us now was pleasantly soft, and though I could tell that Orion was more nervous than our last two encounters, I was, too. Getting drinks and helping me study, while slower to navigate in the beginning, didn't have the stakes that this date did.

A moment of silence passed, but it wasn't awkward. It was like just letting the newness of this fill the space, and I felt my nervous buzzing slow. The server came back to deposit a daintily poured cocktail in front of me and a bottle of beer before Orion.

"I can't believe I've never been here before," I commented after taking a sip of my drink. It was delicious. "And you said that you've ordered food from here often?"

He nodded. "Yes, the green curry is my favorite."

"Your favorite food ever or just here?"

Orion met my eyes then lowered them as he took a sip of his beer. "Just here. I'm not sure I can narrow down my favorite food to one dish. What about you?"

I hummed in contemplation then smirked. "I have to agree. I'm also not very picky, so as long as it's fairly good, I'll enjoy just about anything."

A small smile crept up Orion's face, and I couldn't help but zero in on his lips. They were so much softer than I thought they'd be when we kissed. And when he gave me that peck on the cheek that I could still feel on my face. I wondered if he was going to kiss me again tonight. "My father used to tease me about how picky of an eater I was. Still am, somewhat."

"Oh, yeah? And do you get to see him often?"

Though Orion's smile didn't fall completely, it dimmed in sadness. "He was from here but died a few years ago."

It was a strange camaraderie I felt in that moment, but his palpable grief made me feel closer to him. "I'm sorry to hear that. Mine passed away earlier this year. It's why I moved in with Granna."

"And where did you live before?" Orion started to shrug out of his jacket, and I felt my tongue trip up on my response when I took in his exposed arms for the first time. His right one was enveloped by tattoos that ended just at the line of his wrist.

"Ah, I'm sorry, what?" My voice had taken on a breathiness that I tried to sate with another sip of my cocktail.

When I chanced my glance back to Orion, he was wearing a curious expression. The muscles at his jaw were jumping, and his eyes met mine in an intense lock that lasted a few breathless moments.

He leaned forward, pressing his arms into the wooden table between us, and I tried to, very covertly, take in the tone of his muscles and the various art pieces on his skin. "I was asking where you lived before moving here." His voice seemed deeper, now, and all the nervous air around him vanished. It was the Orion that I saw when I'd watched him smoke, completely entranced. It was the Orion who pressed me up against the side of the bar and kissed me like he needed it more than air.

Though he dressed simply, the dark t-shirt and jeans didn't look cheap, and I'd definitely noticed how they pulled at the flexing of his muscles in all of the right ways. *Taking it slow, taking it slow*, I chanted at myself, even though I was finding it very difficult to not imagine that tattooed arm pulling me close and holding me tightly.

The silence between us this time was charged, the noises of the restaurant around us seeming to disappear. It was like a vacuum, feeling as though we were the only two in the room, and it reminded me of the first time we met. How mesmerized I was by him.

"Order of satay chicken." A food runner came round and placed our appetizer on the table before flitting away, and the spell between us lifted.

Orion blinked a few times, white lashes fluttering, and directed his attention to the food in front of us. I cleared my throat again. "I was raised just outside of Hartford. My mother died when I was a baby, so my father and I lived in his hometown near my family on his side." The chicken skewers were hot and spicy, the peanut sauce perfectly seasoned. I nodded in appreciation for the food while we both chewed.

"How are you liking your classes so far?" Orion asked after the last fizzles of tension between us faded.

"I'm really enjoying them. My advanced creative writing class is my favorite, obviously." He tilted his head in question, and I realized that it wasn't necessarily obvious to him. "I enjoy writing. Short stories mostly, but I hope to be a novelist one day." I continued, "Do you enjoy teaching?"

"Yes, generally."

"Was that always what you wanted to do?"

Orion tilted his head from side to side. "Not entirely. Though, I don't think there was a clear path before I decided on pursuing my doctorate. Like you, I took a break during my schooling."

That comment made me feel far better than expected. There was always a bit of shame in the back of my throat when I told people that I was still finishing my undergraduate degree ten years after starting it. "Oh? And what did you do during that time?"

At that point, our entrees arrived, and we took some time to situate with our meals. Orion's green curry did smell divine, and my pad see ew was spicy and flavorful. "I worked under a master carpenter for a while, then decided to go to graduate school a few years later." A pink flush started on Orion's cheeks and went all the way to his ears, but I didn't understand why he would be embarrassed by that path. The way his lips thinned after he said it made me too reluctant to find out.

So instead, I asked him about the carpentry. I'd noticed that his hands looked stronger and more callused than someone who spent all their time reading books or typing up papers. They were long and sculpted in their own way, but there was a roughness there.

"My father was self-taught and built his home during my childhood. I suppose my interest came from helping when I would stay with him. I got a job at the college after he died and just finished fixing up the cabin a few months ago."

"A cabin?" My plate was only half-gone, but my stomach was beginning to protest any more bites of food.

Orion, on the other hand, had nearly licked his bowl clean and finished off the last of our appetizer when I made no move to eat more. He took another pull from his drink, and I noticed one of the designs on the inside of his forearm was what looked like an animal woven into elements of delicately curving lines. "Yeah, it's about fifteen minutes outside of town."

While my food was boxed up and Orion paid the bill—he'd flinched incredulously when I volunteered to pay—he told me more of his home that was surrounded by the Antler Pointe forest on all sides. Where he'd frolicked and explored as a boy, then wandered and relaxed as a man.

And he asked me about my writing and settling into town, how I was managing school while working and taking care of Granna.

After Orion opened the door for me and got into the driver's seat, I amended, "Well, it's not like she needs a whole lot of assistance. It's more her teaching and me lending an extra pair of hands around the house." I decided to leave out Granna's slips, which hadn't occurred in a few weeks. Afraid that speaking of them would cause a new one, I tried to banish the worry from my mind.

"What's she teaching you? Are you training to be a florist?" I'd mentioned earlier Granna's business and felt another wave of warmth toward him when he frowned in recollection, stating that his father used to buy his grandmother flowers from Granna's shop.

I chuckled. "In a way. Though, I'm hopeless at taking care of most of Granna's flowers. She's teaching me our family's traditions, which is a bigger task than I anticipated. I'm understanding more and how much I don't know. But she's patient with me."

Orion hummed and tapped his finger on the steering wheel.

Far sooner than I wanted, we were pulling back up at the house. Though I'd only had one cocktail, I felt drunk on Orion's presence.

He put the car in park, unbuckled his seatbelt, but didn't make to open his door just yet. I heard him shift in his seat, and I turned to find him looking at me steadily. "I had a very nice time with you, Sylvie. Thank you for allowing me to take you out."

I smiled at his formal words and unbuckled my seatbelt, too. My dress slid easily against the leather seat as I faced him beside me. "I had a great time, too. Thank you for dinner."

His skin and hair were still very pale in the low light of the evening, but I remarked at how it just fit him so well. Like the light in the darkness, like the moon and stars in the sky.

Orion's brow knitted for a long moment, and I sat patiently, knowing now that he got this expression when he was trying to choose his words carefully. "May I take you out again? Sometime soon."

My heart skipped, and I realized how much my anxiety had started to creep up as our date was drawing to a close. To not have to go through the usual 'will he text me first' or 'should I and how long should I wait' that often came after first dates was a sharp relief. "Sure!" And for once, I didn't feel ashamed for my eagerness. "I have another day off on Saturday, if that works for you?"

His shoulders relaxed a fraction. "Yes. That's perfect." That wrinkle in his forehead was still present, and I gave him some more time. Eventually, he opened his mouth again and met my gaze. "I'd like to kiss you."

And without another word, he leaned over the console, lips stopping just before meeting mine, and I didn't even think about pulling away.

A warm, callused hand met my jaw the same time he eliminated the last inch between us. My fingers rested on his chest, letting his body heat seep into my skin while his kiss was like fire. Want and need grew rapidly within me like a swarm of butterflies. The wet glide of our tongues together drew a small moan from my throat, but it sounded so loud in the quiet of the car.

Orion's hand tightened around my face, the kiss growing harder, more passionate.

The flare of desire was taking me over, and by the time I was crawling over to his side of the car, I was lost to it. The hand on my face drew away just before his seat pushed back to give us room.

Though Orion's car wasn't large, I was able to fit on his lap, especially as he reclined the seat to a nearly horizontal position.

Making out with him like a teenager hadn't been expected, necessarily, but his large hands holding me closer felt right. My dress was hiked up to my thighs to give me enough slack to straddle Orion's lap, and I could feel that his cock was a steel bar between us.

He palmed my ass, encouraging me to keep pressing into him, and I caught his bottom lip gently between my teeth. Orion gave an honest-to-goddess growl and moved his mouth to my neck. His nose tickled my skin while he inhaled, and my eyes rolled back when he dragged the flat of his tongue over the curve under my jaw.

"Oh shit," I cried, and the sound of it was like a smack to my senses. My pulse leapt under Orion's tongue while he gave more kisses and licks, his body sturdy and warm underneath me. The anxiety of if this was too fast, of Granna just a few feet and certainly still awake inside the house, and of unknown uncertainties that made my body start to stiffen crept over like clouds rolling in over a bright, blue sky.

Orion's body stilled, and his mouth stopped moving. He pulled back, resting his head on the seat to look up at me. "Do you want to stop, Sylvie?"

Hot, embarrassed tears prickled in my eyes, and I wavered on the edge of giving in to the lust that was still coursing through my body or succumbing to the wall I had erected around myself. It wasn't that I *didn't* want this. But it was...

"Hey." Orion's low, husky voice sounded above the racing of my breaths that'd started to quicken without my notice. His thumb caressed my bottom lip with a tenderness that made one of my tears spill down my hot cheek. "We'll stop. I'm in no rush, Sylvie."

I clenched my eyes closed, trying my best to not let the familiar voice of self-loathing make its way to the forefront. My mascara was no doubt running down my face, and with our kissing, my hair and dress were a certain mess. But when I peeked my eyes open, Orion was staring up at me with a soft patience. Like he understood the overwhelm that left me feeling paralyzed.

"Can," it felt like I had a frog in my throat, but I swallowed thickly to make my pathetic request, "can you just hold me for a little while?"

Orion's smile wasn't a light in the darkness like his white hair or bright eyes. The skin around them crinkled, and his face broke in a way that made another tear fall down my cheek in awe. It was like the grounding embrace of the forest, where I felt the most at peace. His arms opened for me to settle on his chest, and it was a primal calm that I felt nuzzled into the fabric of his t-shirt.

We laid like that, in the front seat of his car, for what felt like a lifetime, but neither of us fell asleep. It was strange to be there with this man that I'd met while he was battered and bloodied, then curt and stinging. But now, Orion was brushing kisses into my hair, drawing deep breaths while he rubbed his hands on my back. It felt far more intimate than what we'd been doing before, but the hot tar of anxiety within me never boiled or stirred.

Maybe Josie's hunch was right.

I waited for the simmering of fear to start, but it remained still as I let the hope settle that this would last. And when we reluctantly emerged, Orion walked me to the front door, kissed my cheek, and wished me a good night. I muttered the same to him and all but floated back to my room, with the butterflies returning at full force and carrying me to bed.

CHAPTER ELEVEN

SYLVIE

The wicker of my basket was digging into my arm, so I switched to carrying it in my hand while Granna and I walked further in the forest. My pocket knife was a steady weight in my pocket that I felt with every step. With her own basket in tow, Granna got to plucking at a cluster of juniper berries just off our usual path.

I grabbed a few as well and added them my spoils of our afternoon. We set off again, and I held my fingers up to my nose, inhaling the scent of the berries and the woods around us. The last waves of heat were dying, and under the cover of the trees, it felt even cooler.

I'd been coming out here on my own, trying to reconnect with the frolicking and wandering I'd engaged in for endless hours when I was a child. Each time, I felt more connected, more grounded, but there was still something missing. There was still a haze, almost, but with each walk out here, it was clearing, bit by bit.

After more silent walking, Granna and I stopped at another tree and started on harvesting some oyster mushrooms. I ran a reverent hand over the gills and felt the buzzing of more fog dissipating. They were my favorite, and we almost had enough between us for the pasta Granna promised to make for dinner tonight. Her long, slender fingers deftly pulled the mushrooms from where they grew, and when her basket became too full, she began handing them to me.

I imagined her doing this, foraging in the stretch of forest by her house, for years with my mother, then by herself after she died. Granna's eighty years on this earth hadn't worn her down but built her into a wizened fixture. One that I could easily imagine in the peak of youth as looking not far from how she did now. Sharp, knowing eyes, nimble hands for working with plants and flowers, and a mouth that was as quick to cut as it was to joke.

"Have you quit that awful job yet, sweetheart?" Granna was crouched and turned a particularly large mushroom this way and that, examining it, before tossing it with the others in my basket.

I blinked up above, watching a squirrel hop across a series of branches like they were an obstacle course. "Not yet, still looking for a better job to replace it."

She stood with an audible crack of her knees, but started back to walking as quickly as I did. "You don't need to work at all, Sylvie. We have enough."

It was an argument she continuously brought up. Not that I didn't disagree, but Vinny's wasn't that bad. The pay wasn't great, but as far as part-time jobs went, there were few that didn't mind me writing or working on schoolwork while at the register.

And I didn't feel right pulling money from Granna's savings. She'd received quite a sum for selling her florist shop, but it made me feel better to use my own money when I went out shopping or to lunch with Josie. Orion hadn't let me pay for anything on our past two dates, so I was planning on finding some sort of gift for him soon.

I just shrugged off Granna's assurances, so she pressed more. "And that boy?"

It was like she could read my mind sometimes. "Great, actually. Though, he's thirty-three, Granna. Hardly a boy."

She waved my comment away. "He's a boy in my eyes. A nice boy, I will admit." And then she scoffed when she saw the wide grin on my face.

"Yeah? He managed to even soften your icy heart, fancy lady?"

"Oh, calm yourself. I didn't meet any of your dates in the past, but I know the stories. I have a good feeling about this one."

I pulled my water bottle from the basket and took a swig. The droplets that clung to my lips were still cold, and I wiped them away with the back of my hand. "Now you sound like Josie."

Granna cut her eyes to me with a brow lifted. "And what did she say?"

My face mimicked her expression, and she rolled her eyes. "That she had a hunch that he was here to stay. Why?"

Now it was Granna's turn to shrug. "She knows you well. And I agree."

"Well, I'm glad that you both approve. But it's only been two dates and texts between us. Hardly a marriage proposal."

"Just wait and see."

I sent my eyes skyward and took a deep breath. "While I like him very much, it's too soon to tell. Especially with everything else going on." I gave her a suspicious once-over, but she was still focused on the path before us. "What's turned you into a romantic all of a sudden? You've always been rather prickly when it comes to love."

"Oh, you love this boy now?" I just sighed at her deflection, but the little pitter patter in my chest was more difficult to ignore.

"Maybe you need to go on a few dates, Granna. I know there are some men in town that would be honored to take you out." Well, that might be a little bit of an assumption. But there were a handful of older men that obviously flirted with her when we were out and about. Now, and even when I used to visit during the summers, it wasn't uncommon for some man to admit a crush they had on her back in the day. As far as I knew, though, my grandmother never dated. During my childhood, I'd quickly gotten the hint that questions about my grandfather would go unanswered.

Granna just stopped in her tracks and gave me the longest side-eye I'd seen from her yet. I stood, palms facing upward in an expectant gesture. She had friends in town, primarily Roz, but she mostly just tended to her gardens and wandered the forest. I never outright expressed my worry that she was lonely, but by the way she was looking at me, she caught my underlining meaning all the same. "Sweetheart, no. And I'm not prickly."

"Yes, you are! Come *on*, have you ever even been in love? Acted a fool for someone?"

"Of course I have. Are you ready to go? Let's go."

She spun and started walking back toward the house, leaves and twigs flying up from her quick footsteps, but even she couldn't hide from me the reddening of her cheeks. Because I lived to keep her on her toes, I giggled and exclaimed, "Oh my goddess, you're blushing! Who are you thinking about? Is it Jeff Newton from the grocery store? He's pretty dapper."

Granna made another choked noise. "Knock it off, Sylvie. None of these men are worth my time. And we were talking about *you*."

I clutched my basket tighter while I leapt over a fallen log to catch up with her. "But you're thinking about *someone*. My grand-father, maybe? Were you in love?" She'd never even told me his name. As far as I knew, he got her pregnant and left, but even that was a mystery. Dad couldn't ever give me answers on it, and I wondered if my mother even knew the truth of her paternity.

I expected another attempt to shut me down, another scathing look to force me to drop it. So, when her steps slowed, and my grandmother heaved a long sigh, I instantly deflated. I caught up with her, ready to apologize and change the subject, but her face wasn't sunken in grief. There was a hint of that in the twist of her mouth, but her eyes looked almost... dreamy. Like she was thinking about pleasant memories and just waiting for the chance to make new ones. "I've always been in love with him." Her whisper was met with a rustling of trees, and she tilted her head toward the forest canopy above, soft smile making her look decades younger.

It was an expression she'd worn before during our time out here, but it'd never come with mention of the man she refused to speak of or name. Through years of asking sporadic questions when she was in a good mood, all I knew about my grandfather was that he was tall, had black hair like mine, and was kind. "And... you can't be with him now?" I hedged, keeping my voice as gentle as possible.

"Not yet." And then she just started walking again. I followed, trying to comb over the moment and wait for her to say more. She didn't, of course, and we continued wordlessly through the woods until we were in the backyard once more. Her garden was still thriving, from little to no help from me. The sight of it was beautiful and comforting, but I still felt heavy.

I guessed that my grandfather was dead, which would make sense with her being so reluctant to talk about him. My grandmother had lost so much, but she just kept on like she did now. Back straight with her eyes on what was ahead. Only in these little moments did I see her taking a deep breath to look back.

A ding rang from my back pocket while I climbed the steps behind Granna. After placing my basket on the counter next to hers, I pulled out my phone to find a text from Orion.

ORION

You are a talented writer, Sylvie.

I let Granna know that I was going to shower after our day outdoors, and she waved me away while she got to sorting all that we brought back.

Not until I closed my bathroom door behind me did I respond to him. After he'd inquired more about my short stories, I hesitantly asked Orion if he'd like to read my latest one. He quickly agreed, thanking me for letting him see my work, and I fought the panic in my stomach at his possible judgement. He didn't teach creative writing classes, but he obviously had a sharp eye for literature. My fingernails tapped quickly on the screen.

ME

You have to say that since we're dating. But thank you.

Those three little dots appeared immediately and then his text came through.

ORION

If I didn't like the story, I would tell you.

I gnawed on my thumb nail and sputtered when a chip of polish came off in my mouth. Just as I was about to respond, he sent another text.

ORION

Thank you for letting me read it.

ME

You really liked it?

ORION

Yes. Especially when everyone died at the end.

I laughed out loud while I stood to turn on the shower. It felt like a risky choice to kill off the protagonist at the end, but reading that he enjoyed that little twist made me feel more confident in it. Now, if I could only get others to feel the same.

I cranked the shower on, putting the water almost as hot as it would go. Before stepping inside, I shot off another text to Orion.

ME

Tell me more about how much you like my writing while I hop in the shower real quick.

It wasn't until I was under the spray that I realized the suggestiveness of my text. But instead of regret, I just felt excited. Orion had kissed me after our second date, dinner at my favorite Italian restaurant this time, and I could tell that he was letting me direct the intensity of it. In the cage of his arms, my fingers in his hair, I wanted so badly to be able to ask him up to my room. Or suggest we go to his house. But the words choked in my throat.

Leaned against the passenger door of his car, Orion planted petal-soft kisses on my bare shoulders while his hand gently caressed my loose hair. I'd noticed he particularly enjoyed doing that and inhaling just under my jaw. I never put perfume on, but you'd think I had with the way he all but latched on to the area.

I was starting to get frustrated with myself for holding back from him, and with my spine to the shower tiles, foot propped up on the lip of the tub, I thought about what it would be like for me to let go. For me to let myself continue to that next step. My fingers were slippery while they worked between my legs, and I imagined they were his. How his kisses would make me melt while his touching me would make my heart race faster than it was now.

Steam filled the room, and I rolled my nipple between my fingers while I plunged two inside myself. My hips rocked against the heel of my hand, and I moaned at the thought of it being his cock instead. I'd only felt it pressed against me while we kissed, but even then, it felt long, bigger than I'd had in a while.

I fantasized him spreading my legs atop his office desk, with students bustling outside of his locked door, none the wiser to him fucking me amongst the books and papers he surely had neatly stacked on the surface. Would he give me tender, deep strokes or fuck into me and rattle the drawers of his desk? I alternated my fingers with pulling out to swirl and diving inside, release barreling towards me. Because I somehow knew the answer to that—while he'd so far handled me with care, I knew that when I finally gave him permission, he'd absolutely devour me.

With the thought of Orion turning me over and shattering me

from behind, my back arched and brows turned up in ecstasy. I whined through clenched teeth while it flowed and settled, and my mind floated back to the warmth of the shower and tile behind me.

With shaky arms, I finished washing and climbed out. My towel was fluffy, and I wrapped it around my body. After biting at my lip and hyping myself up, I picked up my phone to find another two texts from Orion.

ORION

> Your handle of setting and voice is quite masterful. The images you paint are unique in the depth of fear and foreboding they invoke in your reader. As someone that doesn't read horror, I felt just as engrossed in the story. And I left the world you built still pondering the gruesome fate of all those involved. Well done.

> I'm also having a hard time not imagining you in the shower. Are you available for coffee tomorrow?

I grinned and typed out my reply while I walked back to my bedroom.

ME

> Thank you for your totally unbiased review, Dr. Gealach. And for being an honorable gentleman in the face of my relentless teasing. Coffee tomorrow sounds great.

He took a moment to respond, and my mind whirled with the implications of why.

ORION

> It is unbiased. If it wasn't good, I would tell you.

> And I'm happy to be teased. I told you, I'm in no rush.

CHAPTER TWELVE

SYLVIE

"Okay, so, the card you chose is the High Priestess." I held it up to Josie, who craned her neck from her reclined position. She squinted from behind her sunglasses and peered up at the card.

"All right, so what's she got to tell me?" Josie took the card and continued to examine the intricately colored illustration.

"Well, based on your question of 'What's holding me back in life?', the High Priestess can symbolize a reminder to look inward and trust your own intuition. Do you feel like you've been ignoring that lately?"

"Hm. Not really. I tend to be pretty go-with-the-flow." It was a fairly cloudy day, and though Josie had long ago graduated from Antler Pointe, she suggested we have lunch together on campus. In addition to the pair of perfectly greasy burgers, she'd also shown up with a blanket to spread out on the grass.

"Take what resonates with you." I shrugged and took the card back from her. "But I think your question may be indication enough that you're not being as intuitive as you think."

Josie snorted and popped a handful of french fries into her mouth. She worked from home most days, her job as a graphic designer at a small local firm flexible enough to where she could meet up with me in the middle of the day. "Okay," she wiped her hands together to clear off the salt and crumbs, "I wanna try."

"All right, but really wipe your hands and put sanitizer on. I don't want you getting them dirty." Josie sat up with a scoff but commenced to do just what I told her. I shuffled the still-stiff cards and took a deep breath to ground myself again after the single-card pull for my friend.

Legs crossed, she held out her hand, and I gave her the deck. "All right, so you'll want to knock on the cards three times, then shuffle while speaking your intention for this reading. We'll just do a single card like I did for you. And my question'll be, 'What's one thing I can still expect to come this year?'"

With her fingernails chewed nearly to the quick, Josie moved the cards back and forth between her hands in a moment of hesitation before she did as I instructed. I was honestly surprised that she'd even asked at all. Most of the time, when I talked about anything I'd been learning from Granna, Josie seemed amused at best, frightened at worst.

But today, her curiosity seemed to be getting the best of her, and she knocked on the cards with her knuckles like I told her to. "I'm, uh, doing this reading for Sylvie who wants to know one thing she should still expect this year." She shuffled quickly and spread the cards as I'd done for her. After I picked one toward the middle, Josie pulled the card. Instead of presenting it to me, though, she held it up to herself and shielded me from seeing what it was. "Okay, I'm going to guess, and you tell me if I get the meaning right."

"Ah… okay."

"All right," she cleared her throat, "so, when I look at this card, I get the sense that something big is brewing. Some kind of change that you might be apprehensive about, but it's inevitable.

It'll, like, completely shift how you view the world around you, but you'll be able to find your footing."

I frowned towards her. "Wow. That's pretty in-depth for someone that doesn't believe in this stuff."

Josie pushed her sunglasses to rest on the top of her buzzed head that was the color of creamsicles today. "Well, you told me to trust my intuition, and that's what my intuition's telling me. Who knows if it's even remotely what this card means. It looks ominous enough, though."

She unceremoniously placed it upright before my legs, and when she retracted her hand, I sucked in a breath, releasing it in an impressed, slightly uneasy chuckle. "Actually, you were spot on."

Josie picked the card up again, though she held it lowered so I could still see the dark tower facing me with all its lightning and chaos. "I was?"

"Yeah," I said before launching into the meaning of the card and its significance in the upright position. She didn't ask any questions, but when I looked up to check that she was still paying attention to my lengthy explanation, her eyes were still on the card. I watched her take a nervous swallow and look at the rest of the deck with even more trepidation than I was used to her showing around my cards. "We can be done, if you want?" She nodded gratefully and reached beside her for another bite of her burger.

I gathered my cards together and placed them back in the slim, wooden box I typically kept them in. Josie was still acting a bit skittish, as if she was the one that got the ominous reading, not me, but I did my best to steer the conversation in a lighter direction.

Munching on the rest of our food, we continued on in the same way as Granna and Roz. We gossiped, since talking of work and school soon grew too dull to keep on, and I let Josie finish my fries in exchange for the last bite of her burger.

"We stopped hanging around with him after that summer. His dad's cool, but Jasper got really weird. Gave me a bad feeling even back then, ya know?" Josie explained when I inquired about what happened between them. He'd seemed as much a part of her group of friends as everyone else, but I did recall him being absent when I came back to visit the next summer.

"What about Graham Thompson?" I asked. Josie's lips turned down, and her expression spurred on the bubbling enmity I'd felt toward Graham since I caught him staring at me. He'd always had a punchable face, but when I thought about the way he'd looked at Orion then me, it made my hackles raise.

"Unpleasantly pleasant. Acts like he's untouchable because of who his father is. Even the chief's wife doesn't say anything bad about him. And he's the evidence of his old man's infidelity. Might feel bad for him if he didn't seem like such an asshole." Josie lifted up her thumb to chew on a nonexistent nail. I was still disconnected from the town in a way that Josie and Granna weren't. But it made me feel better that she wasn't susceptible to Graham's looks or confidence. Hopefully I'd never have to deal with him again.

"Hey, isn't that your professor over there?" Josie actually pointed, rarely one for subtlety, and I was about to argue with her that since we were on campus, parked right beside the English building, seeing one of my professors walking around was a given.

But when I turned over my shoulder, I saw white curls and light green eyes that met mine as soon as I found them. He'd been heading into the building, walking beside Dr. Vanders who was chatting animatedly and waving their arms about while Orion listened silently and smoked.

As they'd drawn closer, Orion's eyes had casually passed over the quad, but as soon as he found me, he returned my grin with a soft smirk of his own. He jostled Dr. Vanders to get their attention, and when he must've mentioned me, Dr. Vanders looked over in my and Josie's direction. It felt a bit weird, since I was dating Orion, and Dr. Vanders was one of my teachers, but they gave a kind enough wave and peeled away toward the English Department building. Orion was still smiling while he walked over to our little picnic.

Making literal kissing noises, Josie started gathering our trash together and stuffing it all into one big, grease-stained bag.

Orion's pale face was lightly flushed, and he wore another plain, nicely cut shirt. It was a dark brown today, and his boots thudded softly on the dead grass of the quad. After waving him down to sit, Orion crouched beside me with his ever-present satchel slung over his shoulder. "I have a meeting in a few minutes, but I'm happy to see you."

I refrained from kissing him, unsure of what the protocols were but certain it would be pushing past some boundary we hadn't quite established yet. Instead, I just placed a hand on his arm for a second, hoping the growing affection I felt for him transferred within the touch. "I'm happy to see you, too. How's your day?"

Orion's eyes were crinkled in good spirits. Talking of Graham and Jasper and the tense tarot card reading melted away, and my mood brightened. So much so that I was barely bothered when Orion took a drag of his lit cigarette, blowing the smoke over his shoulder so as to not trail in Josie's or my face. "It's better now that I'm seeing you. But fine. Yours?"

"It was good before, and it's great now." Josie scoffed in mock offense, so I gestured toward her. "Josie was sweet enough to have lunch with me today. We were just finishing getting up to some witchy things and gossiping." Despite Orion's appearance and loose posture remaining unchanged at my dropping of that little detail, I braced myself for him to express displeasure in the same way my father had whenever I mentioned Granna's craft.

Orion's head tilted while he took another inhale from his cigarette. After the moment of silence, wherein I was becoming enchanted all over again, his face softened even more, reassurance shining in his eyes. "That sounds fun."

I was melting. Orion's words were simple, but the whoosh of comfort and delight under my skin whenever he was around threatened to reduce me to a pile of longing looks and stammering words.

Before I could say anything, Josie brought her legs beneath her, gearing to stand, and snickered. "Didn't they ban smoking on campus a few years ago?"

Orion just took another puff and shrugged, though the break in our eye contact helped me gather more of my wits from the puddle they'd been. I was delighted to also notice that, while he answered her question with an air of defiance, something in him seemed more closed off when he looked at Josie. Not in rudeness or fear, but it was as if however he acted around me was reserved for the moments between us and never somewhere else.

"They did, but no one has said anything to me. And if they did, I wouldn't care."

"Touché," Josie muttered and finally stood. Orion and I followed, and after I folded the blanket for her and gathered my things as well, Josie brought me in for a hug. In my ear, she whispered, "Remember my hunch. Don't be afraid, Sylvie." And then she waved at Orion before walking toward the parking deck, heavy combat boots flattening the brown grass.

When I turned back to Orion by my side, his translucent brow was raised, matching the questioning tilt of his head.

"What?" I asked. Remembering that he'd mentioned having a meeting, I started us toward the English building. I would be a bit early for my next class, which in of itself was a fucking miracle, and Orion's presence was a heavy grounding. Like my weighted blanket that I kept at the foot of my bed.

Orion hummed as he took the final pull from his cigarette and tossed it into the outdated receptacle that stood outside of the entrance. He seemed entirely unconcerned that his was the only cigarette butt, and he smoothly bounded up the steps and held the large, heavy door open for me.

It was an undergraduate faculty meeting he was now almost late for, apparently, and I followed Orion to the second floor to see him off before I would have to sit in the student lounge to bide my time before my Multicultural Feminist Literature class.

When we stood outside of one of the meeting rooms, he didn't kiss me, but I thought I caught the slight dip of his head like he'd started to. Instead, we exchanged simple goodbyes that held lingering excitement for the next time we'd see each other again. Another professor arrived, heading inside for the same meeting Orion was to attend, and I began my short walk further down to the student lounge. And, if I again made an effort to swish my hips in an exaggerated sequence, that was my business.

Trying best to ignore the mustiness of the old spongy sofa I perched in, I retrieved the novel we would be continuing to discuss in my next class. My phone chimed a minute or so later, and when I pulled it out, there were two texts. Clicking my phone to silent, I read the one from Josie that had assured me she'd made it the short drive to her apartment safely.

The other, was from Orion.

ORION

I think you've put a spell on me. I miss you already.

Biting my lip to keep from smiling, and ultimately failing, I put my book down to text him back.

ME

You've caught me. I am a witch, after all.

He texted back immediately.

ORION

I knew it. Lucky for you, I'm quite partial to being enchanted by you. Do your worst, my little witch.

Maybe he was joking, but his words made my heart soar all the same. Josie told me to be unafraid, to trust the hopeful prediction she'd given me the night of my and Orion's first date. Maybe this was the change, the upheaval that the cards predicted. That I'd be able to have all things—a future with Orion where he knew of and accepted all parts of me. Because I was also starting to feel that, no matter what he had in store for me, I liked him enough to do the same for him.

CHAPTER THIRTEEN

SYLVIE

I once again lamented my failure at making more advanced mixtures to keep some of Granna's flowers blooming past their season, but she just snickered. "Safe to say you've not got a strong proficiency for potion craft, sweetheart. And I wouldn't say your thumb is black, necessarily..." But she didn't need to. She really only let me go near the plants when I gave the most basic maintenance. Which, by non-witch standards, was what everyone did. But my retired florist grandmother had the greenest of green thumbs, and it felt like I was letting her down.

I drummed my fingers on the counter while I waited for the old and reliable coffee maker to bubble and dispense while child-like shame crept up my back. She never said it outright, but I knew that I would be further along if I'd made it more of a priority to spend time learning from Granna. And though I wished that I could blame it on my father's disdain for witchcraft, I'd had the autonomy to take my studies seriously for a long time now.

But I felt *something* swirling with me. Each passing day, it was like some urge wanted to release, but I had no idea what. Basic poultices and tonics were fine. Little spells to give me confidence for my exams and writing were only marginally useful. The Book held a wide variety of information—for a line of witches with varying abilities, Granna informed me time and time again when I got frustrated.

"Not everything is going to work for you. And that's okay. Your mother was also completely hopeless when it came to creating and nurturing life besides yours. You are doing a fine job with basic spells and incantations," she comforted me while she swept a very tiny collection of debris into a pile.

"Yeah, well, nothing else seems to be working for me," I muttered sullenly while I mixed cream and sweetener into my travel mug.

Granna just shrugged, directing her eyes back to her meticulous sweeping of the tiled floor, and I left her a steaming mug on the counter for whenever she'd take a break. "Well, you've been focused on trying to learn the basics and those that *I* have an affinity for. At this point, I would encourage you to follow the natural pull your being is drawn toward."

Why did I feel like she was speaking in riddles to me? Ones that she already knew the answers to. I took an irritated seat at the bay window and tucked into my quick breakfast of bacon and toast. While I ate, I added to and crossed lines in my pocket-sized notebook. It mostly served to record my anxious ramblings. Not journaling, but giving external space so that my mind didn't get too overwhelmed. Next to my ongoing list of part-time jobs to apply for so that I could leave Vinny's, I started drafting ideas of where I could take my studies, trying to look inward for this 'pull' Granna mentioned. This wasn't the first time she'd given me the directive, but she also wasn't offering much help in illuminating the path.

"Granna, can you just tell me what path is for me? You sound like you know it already," I whined and frustratingly shoved my journal in my bag.

She sighed. "Sweetheart, some of the benefit is the journey."

"But some guidance, *please*. I promise I'll do the real work on my own!"

I was about to take hold of the dustpan for her, but Granna beat me to it and disposed of all she'd cleaned from the floors. "Well, Sylvie, you already know that you have an affinity for nature, as do I. I could barely get you to come back inside from wandering the forest when you were a girl." Granna waved a hand in the direction of the woods. "I'd find you crouched behind a log, whispering to the mushrooms or the spiders that made home in the decay." She knew that I'd been taking walks out there on my own, but I kept my fruitless attempts to myself. It felt so embarrassing to bend down and try to listen for fucking mush-rooms to speak to me, only to hear nothing. To continue on until I reached the marking etched into the bark of a large oak tree. As a girl, it'd been the barrier that warned I was about to go too far away from home. Even now, I still never went past it.

I huffed. "So, what? You're saying I should direct my attention toward darkness and death?"

She rolled her eyes and took my set of keys off the hook by the door. She held them out to me on extended finger. "There is more to manipulating the natural elements than growing and blooming. That's just one part of the life cycle." And before I could say much more, Granna gave me a hearty shove out of the door.

My jeans swished between my legs as I made my way to my car, the red color matching my nails, and in my usual routine, I looked to the forest that was the ever-present backdrop of Antler Pointe. My father's home was much more urban, the city life constricting and gray. Here, however, I felt still. Relaxed. The subdued buzzing of anxiety that I felt here was a far cry from the panic attacks and indigestion-inducing sort that colored much of my teenage and early adulthood years.

The forest was now awash with reds, oranges, and yellows. It was beautiful, even more than the vibrant and dark greens of spring and summer.

Granna's words played in my mind on repeat, memories of

doing just what she'd said—rolling around in dirt, talking with fungi and spiders and believing wholeheartedly that they spoke back—percolated like our old coffee maker. When I'd gotten used to that sort of playing after a few weeks at Granna's, my father would go through the lengthy process of discouraging the messy behavior once I came back home. To the point that, as I grew, I almost forgot that part of me entirely.

I thought back to what Granna said about my mother and I. I'd yet to see any ghosts, but the darkening and wilting of Granna's flowers under my hand when I tried to exert any power or influence always made me feel as deflated as the brown, curling petals. I rolled down my windows, letting the spiced air of autumn flow through my car while I drove to school.

With the sweet warmth opening up in my chest, I let my hand roll in the current of wind as I drove and focused in on that feeling and where I'd experienced it before. Always this time of year, when I frolicked as a child, and while exploring the wood now. Even if the whispers never came.

And I felt it when I was with Orion. I knew that Josie was the one to pull the High Priestess the other day, but maybe it was time I take that piece of guidance, too.

· · · · · 🌙 · · · · ·

I felt like a teenager breaking house rules, but I supposed that added to the thrill of having Orion sprawled on top of me. His hand was gripped tightly on my hip, and I couldn't keep mine off of him. From running over his arms that were soft and rippling with lean muscle, to feeling the prickle of emerging stubble on his square jaw, I wanted him to feel how much I enjoyed this.

And just like in high school, the music playing over the small bluetooth speaker on my bookshelf was just barely drowning out the sounds of our kissing and heavy breathing. I couldn't keep the little sounds of pleasure from escaping when he nibbled at my neck. Never lingering in one place long enough to leave a hickey, but it sent tingles down my spine all the same.

Suffice to say, our evening had been going quite well. When I suggested we go to one of the more quiet bars in town to grab some food, Orion agreed, and the conversations between us now ebbed and flowed easily. Even the moments where our chatter died down felt natural. To pick up talking again was no hardship, and no awkwardness came.

With an encouraging touch, I took Orion's hand in mine and directed it between my legs that were spread wide to accommodate his narrow hips. Even though we'd had drinks already, I invited him inside for another while showing him around the house. He'd agreed and walked quietly behind me while I showed him Granna's little old house with its jungle of plants. Though I was hopeless at making them truly flourish, I was able to list them all out and describe the additional uses for each one.

After babbling about the care routine of Granna's giant monstera deliciosa, I caught myself and turned, worried that I was boring him. But Orion was absorbed by the plant and touched one of the deep fenestrations on a leaf that was twice the size of his head. After a moment, he briefly met my eyes, and his were crinkled in contentment.

I then asked him upstairs to see my room and show him my growing book collection. And yeah, after a few minutes, we ended up on my bed, kissing in a rhythm that never ceased to make my heart race. His mouth tasted like whiskey and cigarettes, his cologne slightly earthy, and I felt another chunk of the barriers in my mind crumble and fall away. When his long fingers met the warmth coming from beneath my jeans, he slowed his kisses and pulled up to look at me.

"Sylvie, we don't have to." Though his pupils were dilated wide with lust, and I could feel his heart thudding in his chest, his voice was steady and ringing with sincerity.

"I know. But I want to." I offered a reassuring smile, but he was still looking over me with that mixture of arousal and concern. With a huff, I moved his hand up to my breast. I went out braless more often than not, and I knew that the thin barrier of my top would drive him wild. My fingers squeezed over his, letting him know that I really was okay with him touching me like this.

Orion's face scrunched, and I watched his Adam's apple bob with a deep swallow. I pulled my hand back to let him touch me as he saw fit, or pull away if he so chose, but after a moment, he let his brow fall to touch mine. His hand, large with long fingers, was able to fit most of my breast in his palm. Orion softly kneaded and teased my hardened nipple with his thumb.

I'd always been particularly sensitive there, and my hips pressed up into his, ramping up and chasing any and all pleasure we could have together.

His lips crashed into mine again, our tongues exploring each other deeply. With a gasp, I arched back when the movement between our bodies made his dick press against my clit. Even with the layers of clothes between us, it forced a lightning bolt of pleasure that mixed with that of him still caressing and pinching me.

A deep rumbling sound came from his mouth and went into mine when I ground into him again, needing more. Slowly, Orion trailed his hand down my front, sending goosebumps across my stomach, and I panted into our kiss.

His fingers pressed between my legs, surer than they had just a second ago, and immediately found where it felt like my heartbeat was throbbing out of my skin.

Orion kissed his way to my ear and lightly pulled at the shell of it with his teeth. "Can I make you come like this, Sylvie?" Again, it was the juxtaposition within Orion that I was growing used to and excited by. He was shy and dry at times, then sure and commanding at others, primarily when he was kissing me.

"Fuck," I cried as he kept pressing. My body continued to push back, intensifying the sensation even more and rapidly bringing me closer and closer to the edge.

"Mm, I think I can. You're already so wet." Like he did after our first date, Orion gave the side of my neck a long drag with his tongue. Although this time, he paired it with even more pressure on my clit, and my vision whited out completely. Distantly, I felt Orion kiss me sweetly while my body went taut with the orgasm that wracked my entire system.

When I came back down, feeling the bed beneath me once again, he was caressing my jaw. "I think I almost passed out," I exhaled and grinned at him.

Orion leaned down to pass his nose back and forth over mine. "Truly a sight to behold."

"Oh, *right*. I bet I looked fucking ridiculous."

He held my jaw still and pressed two more quick kisses on my mouth. "Breathtaking, actually. I could watch you come all night."

I pushed my head further back onto the pillow and found his eyes already looking at mine. They didn't move away as they so often did, and I took advantage of the connection. There were little gold flecks hidden in the field of light green, and I wondered if that was why they looked so bright when the light caught them a certain way.

"Well, what about you? I wanna see your come face." I tapped my finger on his lips and then squealed when he snapped his teeth at it. A bout of giggles bubbled up my throat, and his arms tightened around me.

"I doubt it's as nice as yours," he said with his eyes all crinkled in amusement.

"Let's see, then." I tentatively reached down and trailed my touch along the length of Orion's erection that was still very much present. It flinched under my fingers, and I flattened my palm against him, moving back and forth to explore the shape.

"Sylvie, you're killing me." He was holding himself back, having kept his attentions all on me and my pleasure. But, in a renewed commitment to being as unafraid with Orion as I was with other aspects of my life, I wanted this. Continuing to watch him for any resistance, I kept one hand caressing his jaw and the other starting to unbuckle his belt.

Orion groaned but made no move to stop me, and I peppered his cheek with kisses while he buried his face into the pillow beneath me.

Even with the louder music playing from my speaker, the *zzst* of his zipper felt like a harbinger of some new level between us. Before I released him, though, I moved Orion's hand beneath the fabric of my off-the-shoulder top. He sucked in a breath and let loose another grumble, his warm touch circling my bare nipple and rolling the stiff nub between his fingers.

"*Ah.*" Orion took my moans for the encouragement they were and kept on. His lips found mine again, and I swirled my tongue around his.

I barely needed to reach into Orion's boxers before his cock flicked free. It felt even longer and thicker now that it was bare, and my mouth watered even more at the thought of tasting the precum that was slicking my fingers.

"*Sylvie,*" he moaned into my mouth just as I began to wrap my hand around him. My fingers barely closed around his shaft, and I felt another flood start within me down below. Orion's hips began fucking into my fist, and the sound of my hand jerking his cock was delightfully obscene.

I began to sit up, taking Orion and his nimble hands with me. I broke our kiss and touch for just a moment to pull my shirt off my head and toss it aside. His eyes were almost fully black now, roving over my body, running his touch over my waist and breasts while I set back to making him come.

He was uncut, something I didn't have much experience with, but I found myself just as mesmerized by the way his skin looked and felt beneath my touch. His cock was pinker, slightly darker than the rest of him, and the head was even more flushed than his shaft. Moisture flowed in a steady stream, and his cock kicked again, getting even harder than I'd thought it could.

"Are you going to come for me, baby?" I gasped, enraptured by the sight.

He seemed to have gone completely nonverbal now, only giving a stuttering nod at my question.

While pushing on his chest to keep him above me, I collapsed back down to the bed and shimmied into position. My breaths heaved as I gave just three more pumps. Hot cum splattered my bare skin, painting the peaks of my breasts, and some spurts reaching the base of my throat. The translucent white was stark against my brown skin and even darker nipples, and Orion and I groaned in unison while we both waited for his release to run its course.

"That's it. I've died and gone to heaven, I think," Orion mumbled, voice gravelly and nearly silent. I huffed a laugh, looking at the mess we made. Following my intuition unquestioningly, I swept a hand through the ropes of Orion's cum that splattered my chest. I brought my two fingers to my mouth, filling it with the salty flavor of Orion.

"*Fuck*, there you go casting spells again." He sounded a bit more conscious now, and we descended into a pattern of me scooping his cum into my mouth just before he dropped down to give me a tonguing kiss to taste the mixture of us.

Eventually, I was crusty but clean, and we lounged beside each other, staring up at the ceiling. Orion hadn't bothered to fasten his jeans just yet, and I could see the patch of almost white hair behind the opening in his boxers. My tits were still out, and Orion had a proprietary hand over one of them. He didn't squeeze or pinch but just kept it still, like a dog keeping his hand on his favorite toy.

"I really like your come face, Orion." I blew my loose hair out of my face so that I could see him beside me. The vibration of Orion tapping the bed was like the undercurrent of a lullaby, and by the small, contented smile spread across his beautiful face, I hoped that it signaled his happiness. With me.

He blew a raspberry toward the white ceiling above us. "I'm

positive that it isn't as beautiful as yours. I look forward to the next time I'm blessed to see it."

I traced a nonsensical pattern on the leg of his jeans. "What about this weekend?" What we'd done was still sex, but I was excited to explore more of my lowered boundaries. To see if I'd be able to let him into me. To feel how we joined together in the closest of ways.

His touch tightened on my breast, and I turned slightly to get a better look at his face. Orion's eyes met mine, brows drawn in disappointment. "I'll be going out of town this weekend. I'm sorry."

Despite the high of our orgasms, I deflated. "Oh. Where?"

"I'll be about two hours away. Camping." Orion's tapping picked up, and so did my heart, but I did my best to temper it. We'd only been dating for a few weeks. And in that time, we'd been lucky to have our schedules match up enough so that we hadn't gone more than a few days without seeing each other. In the time between, there was a thread of cheeky texts to tide over until the next meeting.

"That's okay. I'll be extra happy to see you when you get back." I painted a wide smile on my face, pulling my cheeks back and fighting past the disappointment when he didn't offer for me to come with him. "And you can send me photos or something."

Orion's pink lips twisted before relaxing. "I'll try to take some. But I'll be racing back to you. I promise."

"It's all right, baby." I flicked the tip of his nose, causing him to give a breathy chuff.

More color bloomed on his cheeks, though it wasn't the beautiful flush when he came. Instead, it was more of that bashful pink and was such a charming contrast with the low raspiness of his voice. "I like it when you call me that."

It took a moment for me to realize that I'd started to use the pet name, but once I did, my smile became less brittle, softer. "Well, I'll keep doing it. So, you better stay safe during your trip and not get mauled by a pack of wolves or something. Make sure you come back okay."

He got another curious look on his face before he leaned over to press a kiss on my brow. He promised to come back in one piece, and, spurred on by the noise of Granna arriving through the kitchen door, we dressed.

With our legs tangled, Orion and I changed the subject to the newest story I was working on and what Granna had told me earlier today. Though he didn't have any concrete advice on the latter, having his unflinching support made me feel closer to him all the same.

Hours passed, wherein I'd noted Granna's quiet pattern through the house before going to bed. I learned more about Orion's life and childhood split between two homes. After his parents' divorce, he explained, his mother retained primary custody and went from living with her parents to marrying a wealthy man who she was still with to this day.

"She shipped me off to boarding school before Ramona was born, so I lived there mostly. I'd visit with them but preferred to stay with Da when I wasn't at school." Orion's speech took on that flattened cadence when he spoke of his family, and I found myself giving his chest slow, circling caresses while he explained the dynamic. When he mentioned his father's passing just after he finished college, he fell silent, and I didn't push him to say more.

I spoke instead of experience with my own deceased father, how our different breeds of anxieties fed each other but also fostered a sort of understanding I didn't have with anyone else. How he'd encouraged my writing and soothed me when I grew sad after witnessing other children with their mothers. Not wanting to continue to pull the mood into a somber place, I mentioned how Josie had scooped me up during one of my particularly awkward and insecure phases, making us inseparable—despite the distance—ever since.

When I asked Orion what his circle of friends looked like, he cracked a wry snort. "Do I seem like a person who attracts many friends?"

"Well, you managed to wear me down with your unique sort of charm." I flicked a loop of his hair that was hanging over his forehead.

He gave another little huff and shrugged. "One or two of my colleagues, maybe. Juno—Dr. Vanders—and I hang out some-times." That made sense, considering the handful of times I'd seen the two of them chatting. Well, Dr. Vanders talking while Orion listened.

"They're one of my favorite professors! I'm in their Multicul-tural Feminist Lit class, and it's actually a joy to write my analysis papers." I gave his shoulder a weak shove, but he didn't budge an inch, "Makes sense my two favorite teachers would be friends." He blushed again at that, and with a kiss to his temple, I set out to pull up a movie on my laptop since I could sense that he was done talking. After Orion stated that he hadn't seen one of the classic horror films that popped up on the home screen of the streaming website, I declared that I now had a new commitment to expose him fully to my favorite genre. Halfway through the movie, though, I found myself straddled over his hips and pinning him with my kiss.

At nearly two in the morning, Orion and I made our way down the stairs. Throughout the night, I'd again felt nothing but tender, passionate care from him, with his touches and his words. I didn't even hesitate to grasp his jaw and bring him down for a goodnight kiss.

"I'll text you when I get home."

I nodded against his chest, held close by his long arms. "Sounds good, baby."

He gave another kiss to my hair, and I watched him walk to and climb into his car. In the light of the porch, Orion's eyes glowed just for a second, and I waved as I watched him back out and drive away.

CHAPTER FOURTEEN

ORION

The trees whipped past as I ran, my lungs filling with the crisp, spiced air before emptying in even breaths from my mouth. The leaves and growth brushing against my body sent ripples of pleasure through my entire being, and my muscles were singing with the sweet exertion.

Days in the forest and sleeping under the stars, would never, ever grow old. Feeling this close to the earth, to the life around me. The patterns of the animals and the steady humming of the trees made sense. The way my body fit into this framework of nature, of the *world* as it was meant to be, felt right. It was only until recently that I started to feel this way around anything besides my time in the forest.

But only here, I could be myself. Truly.

I let out an annoyed huff, feeling the air whoosh out of my mouth. *And I had to drive almost two hours to get it.*

Juno wasn't with me this time, which was a relief. I knew that it wasn't very rational, but sharing this time with anyone besides Sylvie felt wrong. Especially with someone I'd hooked up with before. Even if after the haze of lust, Juno and I quickly decided that we didn't want to engage sexually again.

Luckily, I didn't have to reject any offers for Juno to come out of town with me since they'd decided to return to their hometown, a few hours south of Antler Pointe, and spend the weekend with their family instead.

Even if I'd have to make these trips by myself for the rest of my life, I'd do it. Even if I felt a clench of longing in my chest when I remembered a time when I ran the forest, not with my father or mother or Juno, but a group that, at the time, felt like my true family. I didn't miss *them* particularly, but there was something about racing amongst the trees with them that made me feel like I'd truly *found* somewhere that I belonged.

That had obviously gone to absolute shit. But. Maybe one day.

My legs pushed even faster, harder, as I bounded up a hill. Creatures scattered out of my way, and if I could have, my lips would have pulled back into a wild grin. Up I went with only the desire to feel the breaking of the sun through the canopy of the trees. This wasn't my land, not my father's, but it would do.

Golden and warm, the sun was on its descent, but that made it all the richer. I stood on the grassy area, panting but more energized than I'd felt in, well, weeks.

This was what I needed. What I should've been able to do at my home. I sat back, sinking into the cushion of the lush clearing. The familiar flare of rage surged again when I remembered the last time I'd been forced to come out here. The urge had grown too strong for me to take cautious jaunts through the territory that was *mine*. They claimed it not so, but I felt it down to my bones. Who were they to kick me out? When my very home sat upon it?

But I wouldn't have this freedom there. Not yet, at least. Where I could spend days without looking over my shoulder, listening for *them*. I'd been too confident that last time. Too cocky to realize the true depth of their blind greed. And then they ambushed me while I was walking through town.

I took a deep breath, sucking in the symphony of scents. There was no one for miles and miles, just as it should be. Everything was clearer here, the scents cleaner. My land used to feel like this. When I'd lived there with Da and then when I moved back after he'd gone. When I could see those memories etched in the ground, on the bark of the trees. Though he didn't have much, my father made me feel like the entire world was open for me. To take only what I needed so that I could bask in the glory of it, be part of it when the rest of my life made me want to shut it all out.

My head shook quickly, as if I was clearing the Etch-A-Sketch my father bought me on my sixth birthday. The ache of Da's death was usually dull but ever-present. However, whenever I did this, it was harder to ignore.

I sat on the hill, feeling the wind race over me, and I breathed. My lungs took up the familiar pattern, one where I didn't even really need to count anymore.

And the sun continued to set, giving way for the moon to start lighting up the night in a different but equally brilliant way. The drive back to Antler Pointe last time had felt hollow. Where I had to tear myself away to go back to my life and responsibilities. But this time, as I went briskly back down the hill and toward my car, I had something else to look forward to besides the creature comforts I'd insulated my life with.

Sitting at home with a cigarette, a book, and a cup of coffee were what I had before. What would make the transition back bearable.

But now, my mind cautiously hoped, I had her.

Sylvie.

Just the sight of her kind smile would make this worth it. The feeling of her lips on mine, her body melting into my arms, would convince me to never come back out here if my body didn't need it to survive. And when she laughed? Her nose wrinkling and her eyes lighting from within? I'd wanted to fall to my knees in worship the first time I'd heard it.

Was that normal? To feel this burning inside my chest each

time I was away from her and then this deep, deep settling when I was finally around her again?

When I'd felt I found a mate, who ended up being the furthest from it, I thought we were meant for each other. To be fair, she did an excellent job lulling me into that sense of security, only to rip it away when someone better came along. Someone with an equal drive for power, who was charismatic and had others gravitating toward them like the pull of the earth.

For a while, that betrayal and exile was like a hot blade in my back. Shame, heartbreak, and rejection all melded together in the worst weapon imaginable. One that eventually pushed me to finally return to my father's land that had been left to me. To clean up his home and make it my own once more. I took to cleaning out the abandoned cabin with my own hands, now much bigger than when I'd helped him build it as a child.

Da used to play his records while we hammered and sanded and constructed his home with our own labor alone. And it hadn't felt like work then. Even when he had to progress more slowly because he had to explain and teach me at the same time. He was always patient and never made me feel like a burden.

So, when I took to adding onto the cabin, making it a home for myself as an adult, it was almost meditative. Letting the honeyed melody of Da's soulful music collection carry me through renovating the kitchen, adding a back porch and my bedroom, putting down new floors, and updating all the appliances.

The major projects were done, but working on the house was something else that made sense to me in the way that a lot of things in my life didn't. When I'd returned to Antler Pointe, I just wanted to carve out a sanctuary for myself. That was still certainly my intention, stupid overly territorial imbeciles be damned, but now I carefully opened myself up to the possibility that… maybe the home would one day not be just for me.

My black car came into view, and I still sensed that no one was around. My steps were relaxed as I went to the tree I'd buried my keys under and quickly dug them up. It was the easiest way I'd found to keep them safe without tying them to my neck.

With unspoken command, the air around me grew charged, warm, and I packed this version of myself—that was free—within. It took seconds for my fur to shrink back into my skin, to be replaced with the curls atop my head and the finer strands on my arms and legs.

My front legs lengthened and snapped into place to become arms once again. My hind legs grew and strengthened until they could comfortably and easily handle my weight. The claws retracted, and my fingers and toes emerged.

It didn't hurt, necessarily, but it was a sensation that I couldn't describe to anyone that wouldn't ever have the experience. Both versions were me, but the human skin had far more restrictions than my wolf form ever would.

Not to mention that I always missed my tail. To anyone else, it might have seemed like a small thing, but to have it shrink and disappear made this feel almost final. My muzzle shrunk to give way for my longer and weaker human nose at the same time my sharp teeth and fangs shrank and became blunt.

I shook out my arms and legs, ridding the last few pinpricks that always chased the ends of the shift. My smooth skin flushed, body now feeling the chill in the air.

It was hard to fully resent this form like I used to when I thought of returning to the female waiting for me. Showing her my wolf form was out of the question. Right? I'd convinced myself of that before, but her grandmother certainly knew what I was. So was there reason to believe Sylvie would accept me, too?

First things first, clothes. I bent down to pick up my keys and dusted the soil off the fob and house key. I walked barefoot to my trunk that contained my change of clothes, wallet, and phone. The long weekend was just what I'd needed. Three whole days spent in the forest on four legs had me feeling energized and ready to go back with a calmer head.

Though I normally hated talking to others, as it involved

parsing through confusing expressions and unspoken intentions that often warred with everything else my senses were telling me, I was very eager to talk to her. Sylvie.

"Sylvie, Sylvie, Sylvie…" I hummed her name to myself, since I was alone and free to do it. It just felt so curling and delightful to say, and my thumbs tapped against my fingers in time with the syllables. *Syl-vie, Syl-vie, Syl-vie.*

While my phone was turning back on, I shoved my legs into my jeans and my arms into my shirt. Still bobbing my head to the rhythm of her name, I put on and laced up my boots. Would she like for me to cook for her? Was this the right time to ask her to come over to my house? Would she *like* my house?

My left hand continued its tapping when I finally picked up my phone. I had just enough time to make it to the event on campus I was obligated to attend, and then I would see her. Maybe I could suggest some things I was confident in cooking and see how she'd feel about it. That was what couples did, right? Were we a couple?

I shook my head again. Two minutes back in human form and the uncertainties were already in full force. Though it was all tinged with excitement, I felt a pang of longing in my chest for the ability to be what felt like my true self with her. So that I could have both forms of peace.

"Fuck," the air left my lungs and my heart began hammering in my chest. I felt hot and cold all at the same time.

Six missed calls, and under that, multiple text messages from Sylvie.

SYLVIE

Orion?

Are you okay?

Hello?

I launched myself into my car and called Sylvie while I drove toward the main road. My hands were clenching the steering wheel so hard that the leather squeaked loudly in protest. When I told her that I was going out of town, I didn't think she'd... do whatever this meant.

The phone rang for a moment then went to voicemail the first time. Then just straight to voicemail the next.

This was not good. "Fuck, fuck, fuck, fuck." I smacked my palm on the steering wheel, needing to put my anger at myself *somewhere*. I messed up. I could see that now. And I had two hours before I could rectify it.

I pressed my foot further on the gas. Make it an hour and a half.

CHAPTER FIFTEEN

SYLVIE

"I can't believe this," I mumbled over the damning page pulled up on my phone. Just as I was about to hop out of the car to inquire about a part-time position at the small boutique shop where I'd purchased my last set of tarot cards, the sound of the new email was like a gunshot.

After taking the civics exemption exam earlier this week, I knew it was only a matter of time to get my results. From what I could tell, I didn't have any seer abilities, but by the pit in my stomach, I already knew what I would read.

I clutched my phone tightly in my hand and almost tripped getting out of the car. Sweat immediately started beading on my forehead while I stomped up the sidewalk. An unexpected death rattle of summer was upon us, and I was irritatingly dressed for much cooler weather. With another submission rejection just below the evidence of my most recent failure in my inbox, I hyped myself up to get this done before I could retreat home.

The smell of lavender and sage helped me feel a bit better, at least, and the employee at the register was kind enough when I asked about any job openings. They handed me a little card with an email address to send my resume to, and I painted a broad grin on my face before scuttling out of the door.

I didn't even feel like hopping across the street for a coffee—that's how abysmal my mood was. My lids furiously blinked back the prickling of tears while I committed to putting one foot in front of the other to get back to my car and wallow at home. While I loved my grandmother and was grateful to spend time with her now, she was a bit shit at comforting anyone besides her plants. Her method was a few hesitant rubs on the back and steering us both to spend some time outdoors amongst the flowers or the wood.

But, I wanted to bask in a pile of my own self-pity. Without thinking about it, I pulled my phone from my pocket and began to text Orion. He'd sent a brief message that he was on his way out of town, and then I hadn't heard anything else. He did warn me that he wouldn't have signal where he was going, and maybe I would have had a more positive attitude about it if I were in a better place.

I had to force myself to close out the text message app. No, I wouldn't be that sort of person.

My sneakers gritted on the sidewalk, and my loose hair was making a full on sweat break out on the back of my neck. Thankfully, my car was just half a block away now, and I wove around everyone else that was out and about on this Friday afternoon, heart perking at the thought of crawling in bed, drawing the curtains, and burrowing under the covers with a slasher movie. Yes, that sounded divine.

However, the universe had other plans for me, and they weren't good. My thoughts had been spiraling with having to make plans for a make-up exam, wondering what Orion was up to, adding the job application to my to-do list, and figuring out what to order for dinner tonight when an arrogant body stepped right in my way.

I almost ran into the person, side stepping at the last moment, but then they flinched that way, too, and committed to blocking my path.

Irritation and that familiar bubbling of rage hit me square in the chest, but I tried to outrun it by stepping quickly in the other direction. My pursuer, however, anticipated and blocked that, too.

I took a step back, my hands raising and readying for something, and finally lifted my gaze. Graham Thompson stood before me, mouth quivering with a barely suppressed smile, and I wanted to claw it right off of his face while I cried stinging, angry tears. With his windswept hair and t-shirt and jeans, he exuded an air of calm and cool, but I could smell what was underneath. His green eyes were nothing like Orion's. They were mixed with a golden brown that would've been pretty on anyone else. Because he was looking at me the way he had a few weeks ago. Like I was nothing but a piece of... something. Not a person, and definitely not someone that deserved respect. It was similar to how Jasper had all but leered. But I had never been afraid of him.

Graham's head tilted in contemplation, stare running down my body brazenly. I wasn't really even scared, now. More so startled with the realization of what it felt like to be prey.

"What's goin' on Sylvie?"

"What do you want? And how do you know my name?" I seethed, trying to make my way around him, but he kept blocking my way. I wasn't a small woman at five foot eight, but, like Orion, Graham was quite a bit taller than me still. And where my boyfriend was all lean and strong, Graham was stockier, broader. He crossed his arms at his chest, and I saw the size of his fists. No, I would need to avoid those if the time came.

Head cocked like a cat playing with its dinner, Graham's lips pulled wide to show all of his white, straight teeth. "How could I not know the name of the newest witch in town? Beautiful one at that."

It wasn't a secret, necessarily, that Granna practiced witchcraft. And, I figured, most just assumed I was a witch by association.

Whatever. "Well, you better let me pass if you don't want me to put a hex on you," I seethed.

"Whoa," he said loudly, "no need for threats. Just wanted to extend my warmest welcome and see if you'd want to hang out sometime?" Some people passing were turning their heads, not-so-covertly eavesdropping but doing nothing to intervene.

Perhaps I was more like Granna than I'd previously realized, because my first reaction was to stand back, look him up and down with a cutting eye, and scoff. "Please. There's nothing you can do for me. Leave me the hell alone." And when he made to block the path to my car once again, I shoved my body forward with all of my might. Like I'd hoped, it took him by surprise enough, and he staggered backward, nearly falling on his ass. His descent was caught on a set of bicycles chained to a rack that fell to the sidewalk instead.

When he glared up at me, handsome facade cracking, I spat at his feet, lest I give way to the fiery urge I had to truly claw his flesh from his face now that we were nearly eye-level.

The eyes of passersby were wide, but I was much more focused on the hot tears falling down my cheeks to feel embarrassed by the scene that'd just unfolded. Throwing myself in the car and merging into traffic, I waited until I passed the historic downtown's sign, where the road widened, to scream.

I yelled until my throat felt raw to keep from crying any more, but my eyes were still puffy and red when I pulled up back home. With a miserable glance at the rearview mirror, seeing the absolute pitiful state of myself, I gave in to the urge to call Orion. Just to hear his husky voice, to hear his reassuring words. If I couldn't have his arms around me, that would do. Just to tide me over.

No answer. Straight to voicemail, in fact.

It was insane and needy, but I called again. And then again. He didn't even have a personal voicemail to placate my spiraling state. My fingers were shaking as I resorted to a text message.

ME

Orion?

With phone in hand, convinced I would miss his call if I put it down, I set out to do just what I'd planned. Granna wasn't home, probably out with Roz again, and I thanked the universe and goddess and whoever had decided to take mercy on me with this small blessing. Even when they'd given me this hellacious day in the first place.

I changed into my favorite Freddy Krueger t-shirt, stripped down to my underwear, and dove under my comforter. I texted Orion again.

Are you okay?

The movie began to play in my darkened bedroom, overhead fan on full blast to cool me down. But I could hardly concentrate on even the opening scenes, the wrath I'd been riding now tanked into my familiar companion—anxiety. He'd warned me about the reception, but surely he would've sent a message stating he'd arrived okay? Right? Or maybe he had, but it wasn't able to deliver?

Or... was it a lie? Had he even said who he'd be camping *with?*

I replayed our conversations about it and, no. No, he hadn't.

I made another two calls to his phone, fully accepting my crazy girlfriend status, now. Why would he turn his phone off, knowing that I'd be worried? *Did* I have a reason to worry? Instead of letting the comforting gore settle my mind and emotions, I let my worries flood my being. *Trust my intuition, my ass.*

CHAPTER SIXTEEN

SYLVIE

I tucked my loose hair behind my ears and clapped my palms together. The respectful applause echoed softly in the student lounge after the final reading of the event. I'd barely been able to focus, but my own stubbornness kept me planted, faced forward, and ignoring the man behind me.

The normally cozy and haphazard student lounge had been rearranged so that the couches and chairs and beanbags were all facing a space up front that made a stage. The lights were low and mostly concentrated where the ten or so performers stood before the crowd and read their various poems and excerpts.

Orion had arrived just before the performances began, forced to not sit with me, even though the intensity in his gold and green told of his desire to. His hair was standing in all directions, the curls messy and delicious, and I just wanted to massage my nails against his scalp and watch the goosebumps appear on the back of his neck.

But, I was still hurt, so I'd pointedly lifted my chin and looked away.

After sitting in my room for three days, glaring at the phone

I'd turned off in retaliation, I reluctantly dressed and drove to campus to attend the extra credit event. A few of my classmates, some I barely talked to and some I considered acquaintances, had performed, and, as Granna so lovingly put it, I needed to 'get the hell out of the house and stop pining like a lovesick thirteen-year-old.' To her credit, I'd only taken breaks from burning my eyes with movie and TV binging to choke down some food or go to the bathroom.

But showering made me feel a little better. And then sitting at my vanity mirror to apply mascara and lipstick kept my mind from worrying and letting my anger at Orion completely burst into flames. That was reduced to a hot smoldering, now, especially after I put on my favorite skirt and boots.

When I arrived on campus, anxiety won out again, and I turned my phone back on. *In case Granna needs something*, I tried to convince myself. But she hadn't had a slip in a long while. To the point that I almost couldn't quite picture the faraway look she got when she said those strange things.

10 missed calls

Orion's texts filled my screen.

ORION

Sylvie, I'm sorry, my phone was turned off since I didn't have reception anyway. Is everything all right?

I just spoke to your grandmother, and she said you're heading to the reading on campus. I will be there and want to talk to you.

Sylvie, answer the phone.

I clucked my tongue at those last two, the commanding text specifically sending an annoying flittering across my chest. Oh, now he wanted to speak with me.

"If you'd be so inclined, please join us now for a reception hour with the writers who you listened to tonight. Refreshments are in the back, please help yourselves." The head of undergraduate studies for the English department stood from their seat and announced to the rest of the room.

Those beside me on the ugly plaid couch stood, so I followed. It took a moment for the makeshift aisle to clear, but I made sure to keep my gaze anywhere but where I knew Orion was sitting amongst some of the other professors that were present.

Now, everyone was either congratulating their friends that had participated in the reading or made their way to the tables at the back of the room for hors d'oeuvres. Out of my periphery, I caught him watching me, not even paying attention to the TA from one of my classes who was talking to him.

I walked in the opposite direction and struck up a conversation with one of the presenters, expressing my admiration for his poetry piece that chronicled the seasons of his life and the ebbing of his mental health. It was one of those that I happened to pay attention for, and I inquired about his inspiration, anything to keep from becoming cornered into forgiving Orion.

Things had been going so well, and then radio silence. My gut reaction was to reason that there was surely an explanation. That he was very obviously interested in me.

But I was hurt, all right? I thought I deserved to feel that way. And to inflict a little bit of that pain onto him.

Not to mention, that, though he wasn't *my* teacher, I was an undergraduate student. And he was a professor. It wasn't a secret that we had been dating, but it felt improper to flaunt it here.

Are we even dating anymore? I scoffed internally at myself and grinned wider at the guy that had no trouble going on and on about his work to me and a few others that had gathered around to speak with him.

"Sylvie." Orion's low voice made a shiver go down my spine, and I had to bite the inside of my cheek to keep myself centered in the moment. To not sink into a puddle of longing.

A few people's eyes flickered to where Orion was standing behind me, and the social pressure to turn to him grew too much to resist. I flipped my hair over my shoulder while I turned to gaze up at him over my back. "Yes?" His pale jaw was clenched, and he didn't look at the few who were still giving the two of us curious glances while our classmate prattled on.

"Can I speak to you for a moment?" He put his hands in his pockets, eyes not flinching once from mine.

Dammit, dammit, dammit. "Sure," I croaked and followed him away from the group. I crossed my arms and pinched the skin of my biceps through my cropped sweater. There was no harm in talking, fine. But I was *not* going to give in. To let him get out of this.

At least, not too easily or without explanation, I amended.

We stopped just before the back corner of the room. We'd talked between my classes some, but having a conversation about our relationship during a department event felt like some… declaration or something.

"Sylvie. I'm sorry that I haven't been communicating with you. I turned off my phone since I wouldn't be able to contact you while I was camping." His hands were still in his pockets, but he looked down at me, eyes pleading. The aroma of cigarettes trailed off of his breath, but mixed with the spice and musk of his cologne, it smelled like what I imagined an expensive cigar would be like. Or that, but combined with the deepest, coziest autumn evening.

But, no, I was *not* going to get reeled in with just a breadcrumb that wasn't even that. When he told me that he would be away, I hadn't realized it would feel like he dropped off the face of the earth. I lifted a sardonic brow, and I saw that the expression took him aback. His full lips flattened into a tight line. "Camping. Where."

He ran a hand up the back of his head, ruffling some of the curls that were longer on the top. My eyes narrowed at the movement, trying to decide if it was just a nervous tic or a tell of a lie. "About two hours north of here." He cleared his throat and dropped the hand.

Though my heart was beating frantically at being near him again, speaking to him again after what felt like such a long time and none at all, dread clenched in my stomach. The whole thing was hurtful no matter which way I looked at it, the worst part being that it all didn't feel like the truth in the first place.

I sighed through the ache and smoothed a hand over my skirt. "That sounds like bullshit, Orion."

"It's not—" A round of laughter behind me made its way over to us, and I saw his eyes harden. His voice grew about ten degrees colder, and he jutted his chin over my head. "I didn't have any signal, and I like to go pretty frequently. Seems like you've been fine, though."

I whirled my head around to see what the hell he was even talking about, but it was just that guy still talking to some of our classmates.

Realization burned my face, flushing my cheeks and sending my mind reeling. I'd barely even been paying attention to what I was saying before. Just letting the laughs and conversation come to keep from letting my body drift over to Orion.

I turned to look back up at him. "Are you kidding me? I called and texted, and you didn't respond *once*. What the fuck is your problem?"

He actually flinched, but he gathered himself quickly and spoke low and in opposition to my rising pitch. "Sylvie, I'm sorry," he said through his teeth. "I didn't—I didn't mean for you to worry."

But I'd heard enough. I gave him a moment, to see if he'd say anything else. Offer any kind of truth or detail to explain where he'd gone.

Before I could give him a cutting remark and put him further into his place, someone sidled up beside me, clearly unaware of what they were interrupting. "Dr. Gealach." The student butchered his name, but I knew that wasn't why Orion stood tense, nearly snarling at the interruption.

"Yes?" He reluctantly tore his eyes away from me and was

soon swept into the student making their case for an extension on an analysis paper for his class.

I slipped away just as Orion interrupted the unprepared man to state that he wouldn't be offering an extension unless he could provide a more solid excuse as to why he couldn't finish his work on time.

I managed to smile and greet a few familiar faces on my way toward the door, signing my name on the sheet for extra credit before leaving all together. There was no way I'd be able to continue standing there, making small talk while Orion was in the room. And if he didn't want to be honest with me, there was really nothing more we had to talk about.

We haven't even—I shook my head and cleared the invalidating thought bubbling up. No, we'd shared enough moments together for this to sting. I wouldn't take the fault for it.

My heeled boots clicked as I hurried up the hall, and I mentally began separating myself from Orion. Though it hadn't been that long, only a month, I'd grown quite attached to his witty messages. His encouragement and sweet kisses and just feeling… like I could let go. Not worry.

I straightened my spine as I rounded the corner that led toward the stairwell. No matter. I'd been alone enough where the familiarity of it would soon drown out the hurt of this. And I had Granna and Josie. My studies both in and out of school. I'd be fine.

I'd been lost in my thoughts, mindlessly stomping through the halls. My face was flushed and pinched with my frantic musings, trying to pull myself together, when warm hands spun me around.

My own flew up onto a strong, solid chest and felt the fast beating beneath. His lips were soft and warm, and my body relaxed into Orion while my mind melted all together. He clutched his long fingers at the base of my skull and pawed my lower back with frantic intensity as he kissed me.

He pulled back just enough to separate our lips with a delicate smack and nuzzled his nose against mine. "I'm sorry, Sylvie. Please believe me. I only just got back. But I know that I hurt you. I'm so sorry." His lips met mine, and I couldn't form any words, anything articulate to respond to his apology with. Because it felt too good to have him in my arms again. To hear the fervent words leaving his mouth that was opening to meet my prodding tongue.

I deepened the kiss between us, and maybe it was because I was weak or too trusting, but I believed him. It'd been a long while since I'd seen that harder version of him, but as I molded my body against his, head craning up to meet his kiss, I remembered how good things felt with him.

But he tried to deflect his frustration onto me, my brain couldn't help conjuring, and then I was pushing him back, breaking our kiss that was heating to a place that was threatening to make me lose all sense. His arms dropped from my body, and I panted, "And yet you insinuated that I was—what? Cheating on you? You really believe that?" My voice was strained, but it had enough venom to underline the seriousness of my words.

I could tell that he was grinding his teeth together, but I didn't care. He deserved it, even if I... ultimately forgave him. After a moment's tense silence, he stepped closer to me again, though this time, he didn't try to kiss me. Orion gripped my forearms, firm but delicate, and leaned into my ear. "No. But I can't stand to watch you smile like that at someone else." My eyelids drooped at the commanding intensity that'd taken over him.

I somehow managed to scoff into the air, but my navel quivered at the tone of his voice and his breath skating down my neck. "You've let me in, Sylvie. Don't be surprised when I see you as mine and only mine." His stubbled cheek rasped against my face, and I felt his lips brush against the curve of my ear. "When you look at me the way you do, kiss me the way you do. You should know that I will always come back." Something in him was different. It was similar to the Orion I knew who was more unabashedly confident, but it was also more. His face looked...

wilder, his touch rougher. But instead of making me bristle in trepidation, I was even further soothed.

And then his teeth closed in on my throat, just under my earlobe, and I couldn't suppress my moan or keep my eyes from rolling back in my head. The pressure he applied with his teeth wasn't nearly enough to break the skin, but I knew that it was something. Something that made my skin feel like it was on fire and my soul feel like it was unfurling and settling into him.

Then there were voices growing louder, more than one person threatening to round the corner and see us both like this. "Orion," I croaked after trying and failing twice to get my voice to work. But he was already pushing me backwards, almost lifting my feet off of the ground completely, and we were suddenly out from under the bright overhead lights of the hallway.

A door closed with a thud, and I hardly had time to take in the office we were in before I felt his hands grip just under my ass and hoist me fully into the air. Something hit the ground with a clatter as I squirmed on the top of the desk set adjacent to the windows on the far wall. Above the lingering smell of coffee and cigarettes, the room smelled overwhelmingly of *him*.

Orion gripped my face, the heels of his hands against my neck, and his kiss was more untamed this time. His tongue fought with mine, teeth nibbling my lips and striking against my own while I fisted the front of his shirt. His hands wandered down my body, thumbs flicking my nipples through my sweater before trailing down my sides and palming the fullest part of my hips.

"Swear to me," I breathed into the dark room, "swear to me that you're not lying to me. That you're sorry."

I felt his teeth close again on that spot at my throat, and I moaned at the pleasure it sent through my whole body. I'd surely bruise there, but I didn't care. I wanted him to mark me, claim me.

Just before the bite turned painful, he pulled back to swipe the flat of his tongue over it, and I couldn't help but imagine how his tongue would feel over the rest of me.

Between long swipes, he spoke gravelly, almost like a growl. "I had to go away, but I was alone. I won't hurt you again. I'm sorry." In the back of my mind, I recognized that he hadn't quite sworn that all of what he was saying was the truth. That he wasn't hiding anything.

But his hand moved again, and this time it was under my skirt. My legs responded immediately, opening wider for him. He moved up to my ear again, the sensation of his face against mine warring with that of his fingers pushing aside my panties. "You're too precious, too important. But do *not* think that I won't rip someone's throat out for touching you." He emphasized his words by dipping into the wetness that'd been pooling since I first caught sight of him. This was the first time he'd touched me like this, and I immediately knew I wasn't going to survive it or keep up my anger toward him.

I scrambled to get the last bit of it out before I truly melted. "Are you still stuck on this? I was just talking to that guy to avoid you. Make you jeal—" My words cut off into a desperate cry when Orion started to circle his fingers, sending a lighting jolt of pleasure up my entire body. My back arched, which only pressed my chest more firmly into his.

"I know," he gritted before pressing his forehead to mine. His lids were lowered under brows drawn in lust while he watched his hand work between us. "And I deserve it. But make no mistake," he slowly pushed a finger into me, and my eyes rolled back again as he pumped and circled at the same time, "I am possessive by nature and do not make idle threats. You walk in looking like this, smelling like this, and then gift your smiles and laughs to someone else? It took everything in me not to throttle him."

I smirked, the proprietorial words doing nothing but making me feel more ramped up, more turned on. "You like the way I look, huh?"

His fingers picked up speed, and I sunk my own in his hair, holding him to me. He grabbed a fistful of my curls while my body started shaking uncontrollably, the inevitable orgasm almost taking me by surprise. At first he didn't answer, breathing heavily through his nose while he fingered me in his office, and my boots were scrabbling against the sides of his legs, trying to find purchase.

My vision blanked out, mouth dropped open, but before the boom of my climax could make me groan loudly enough for someone to certainly hear, Orion dropped his mouth onto mine. He took every morsel of sound from my lungs, giving me his own ragged groan in kind.

It took a few moments for my brain to come back online, but when it did, I was already deeply kissing him back. We'd been taking this part of our relationship slow, but now that he'd given me a taste of it, I wanted it all. He withdrew his touch from between my legs, only to replace his tongue with his fingers.

He watched me, bright eyes wild, and I held them while I sucked and licked, working over his fingers to show him what I would do if I could drop to my knees.

But I'd do that another time. Because I had another need burning in my gut, and when I moved to palm the front of his crotch, I knew that the same was true for him.

I moaned around his fingers, and though it was nothing to take the entire length of them in my mouth, I began to bob my head, moving back and forth while I undid the buckle of his belt. He watched me with rapt attention, and his mouth opened in pleasured panting when I unzipped and pulled his stiff cock out.

He was so hard, I wouldn't be surprised if it ached, and I closed my fist around his shaft. Orion's brows lowered, almost looking like he was in pain, and I brushed my thumb against him, feeling a tick vein winding up toward the head. As I began to pump the cage of my hand up and down, I moaned at the length of him.

He withdrew his fingers from my mouth to palm my ass, and his head bowed again to watch. I traced the slit at the tip, feeling the moisture beading there and trailed it back down to the base.

"Sylvie," he groaned and tightened his hold on me.

"Please tell me you have a condom," I breathed and let my hand move faster, marveling at how he grew even harder.

He reached into his back pocket, fumbling for a second since his pants were now loose around his waist. He retrieved one from his wallet before throwing it carelessly to the floor and ripping into the gold foil with his teeth. Orion let the wrapper fall, too, and then he was setting the condom against his tip. I watched as he quickly rolled it on.

I raised my hands to twine around his neck, and while I scooted to the very edge of the desk, Orion held his cock at the base and guided it between my legs.

His name escaped from my lips in a long, low moan once he began to push inside. Both of us were panting, and I felt the muscles of his shoulders and neck strain as he forced himself to go slowly and let me adjust. But my body made quick work of taking him, in total agreement with my desperation and primed from his fingers.

And Orion's need rivaled mine, his thrusts quickly growing deep and teeth-chattering. His eyes were still bright in the darkness, and they met mine with a hard, imposing look. "You feel perfect. So sweet and soft and fucking *good.*"

Just then, he gave a particularly desk-rattling pulse, and I cried out despite trying to silence the noises he was thrusting out of me. He thumbed my bottom lip, watching the skin pull and my tongue that licked at him with a mind of its own. "That's it. I want to hear your cries while I fuck you."

I wrapped my legs around his waist, boots crossed at the small of his back and my nails digging through his jacket. "Fuck, baby. *Fuck.*" I'd shifted my hips to take him even deeper, let him fill me even more to the point that it almost felt like too much. He gave an approving grumble each time I moaned, and his smell of tobacco and wood sang to me on the basest of levels. Wherein I felt reduced to a primal version of myself. One that matched the almost brutish grunts and growls Orion was giving me that were only growing in intensity and becoming more unsteady. His fingers dug into my skirt, gripping my ass for leverage against his fucking that was cracking my heart wide open.

I started falling first, body going absolutely liquid with the deep rush of release. And the feel of it, my body constricting and going limp at the same time while I couldn't make any noise anymore, sent him pounding just before letting loose an inhuman growl and biting me for the third time.

Orion pulled out just before his release took him over, resting his throbbing dick along my inner thigh. I clutched him closer while he came, teeth embedded in my skin. I rubbed his back through it, and all the reasons why I'd been so upset seeming far away and over with.

Orion dropped his hand from my mouth and reluctantly pulled away from my neck after placing a few kisses on the now very tender area. But I loved it. I'd never had someone do that before, the biting and the desperate fucking. It was also just him, though. Our eyes met, and I traced my touch over the corner of his jaw, down to the little dip in his chin, and then back up.

He still looked a bit out of it, and I was sure I did, too. "Well," I gave him a wry smile, "I'm glad you're back, I guess."

Orion chuckled and then slowly pulled his hips away from me. Riding the high and still a little loopy, I didn't comment on his not coming in me, even with the condom on. I just watched happily sated as he removed the condom, tied its end, and stuffed it and the wrapper at the bottom of a waste basket. My boots shifted against the wood of the desk, body leaned back on my hands. It was pretty dark in his office, but my eyes had adjusted a bit at some point. His milky skin and hair seemed to almost glow in the faint light filtering through the windows at the other side of the room. I could see a comfy looking armchair set beside the glass, and there were two bookshelves full with neat rows of books.

And even I could see the intensity within his gaze that was flipping between my face and just slightly lower.

After zipping up his pants and buckling his belt, Orion stood before me again. My thighs framed his legs, and I rubbed the side of my foot against his calf. He traced a long finger on my neck, and the mark from his teeth tingled.

"You are so wonderful, Sylvie. I'm sorry I hurt you," he whispered.

Though my heart clenched at the vulnerable tone in his voice, I tsked and brought my hand to cup his wrist. I grasped it gingerly. "As you should be. But I forgive you."

His eyes flicked away from my neck to meet mine. "Because of what we just did?"

I shrugged and ran a hand up his front, feeling the dips and ridges of his muscles. "Might have made me forgive you a bit faster. But I was going to regardless." Because I knew I didn't have it in me to continue being upset with him the way I had been. Not with the sincerity of his apology.

And maybe I was just naive, because when he held my face again to nuzzle our noses together, there was a strange tone to his voice. One that I couldn't quite pinpoint, but it filled my lungs with a sense of foreboding, even with his words making a grin spread on my face. "I don't know what I did to be fortunate enough to cross paths with you, Sylvie, but know that you are special, precious, to me. No matter what."

CHAPTER SEVENTEEN

SYLVIE

My last shift at Vinny's was dragging on miserably. At one point, I even debated faking a slip and fall or not-so-accidentally cutting my finger on one of the knives in the kitchen for an indisputable reason to go home early. Granna told me before I left the house this afternoon that I should just call out, given that I was already leaving anyway. But Josie somehow convinced me that I would regret it if I didn't follow through with my promise to work tonight before leaving the pizza joint for good.

I was somehow too bored to even jot down ideas for a new story, and the scribbles of lists in my journal were mocking me.

I could be with Orion right now or working on that new spell with Granna. But, no. My lower back was aching dully while I leaned over the front counter for perhaps the slowest night in all my months working at Vinny's.

Evan and Louis were working again tonight, but every time I tuned in to what they were doing, they were either making dirty jokes back and forth or talking about some shooter video game that I didn't understand or care to know about.

Mid-terms were now in my rearview, giving me a few solid weeks of reprieve before I needed to work on my final assignments in earnest. Not to even mention finalizing my MFA program application. What I didn't realize, however, was that for Orion, this time of the semester meant that he had many, many papers to grade. Though he said he was content to sit at the coffee shop, him grading and me working on whatever, I knew that I was interrupting his flow. He just looked so cute with his headphones on, face still and focused on what he was reading.

We still hadn't quite worked out the boundaries between us when we were both on campus, and though I wanted to post up in his office or have him join me in the student lounge, it seemed inappropriate. Especially since I was still often replaying his taking me on his desk. It would most certainly happen again if we were left alone in there for longer than five minutes.

"I should be done with this last push by the weekend," he'd dragged a hand over his face while we packed to leave after hours of working away on our laptops this morning, "then I'd like for you to come over to my house. If you'd be interested?" I could tell that sitting in those public spaces tired him out. His shoulders were drawn and tight the entire time, but he never complained and always agreed to spending time together.

Even still, things had gotten even more comfortable between us. Hell, for most of our outing today, he'd held a hand on my thigh or I'd reclined with my feet propped up on his lap. The dark, slightly purple bruise on my neck was still present, and every time Orion's eyes landed on it, I could see the blatant hunger in the flaring of his nostrils.

But, as I told him after the reading on campus, he was still in the doghouse for a while. Once I returned home and came down from the near mind-altering sex, I felt the lingerings of hurt still in my throat. Which I told him, wanting no more secrets between us. And instead of fighting me on it or asking more questions, Orion just accepted it and vowed that he would make it up to me.

I was very close to ending his little probation early, though.

Especially if it involved him whisking me away from the pepperoni-scented purgatory. Based on his last text an hour ago, though, I knew that he was powering through his last class's papers.

"I'm going outside to take my fifteen," I hollered toward the kitchen. It was met with sounds of acknowledgement from the guys, and I took my styrofoam cup of water out back to stand in the fresh air. It was nearly six, and if business was going to pick up, it would be soon.

I heaved a sigh of relief when the autumn air kissed my skin. The days were rapidly growing shorter, and the sun was already nearly set. I leaned against the brick, not too far from where I discovered Orion crumpled in pain all those weeks ago. He still hadn't explained what happened, and I'd been too hesitant to ask.

The forest in front of me was a calming force, and instead of remembering how worried and confused I was that night, I just remarked on how far we'd come. What did it look like around his house? Orion tried to describe it to me, but all the photos of his cabin on his phone were reference images he'd snapped when needing to run to the hardware store for supplies.

My to-go cup squeaked, the straw shifting against the lid in a squeal of plastic-on-plastic, and I breathed deeply through my nose. There it was, that warm glow at the base of my chest. *The pull*, Granna called it. She said she felt that way every time she cared for her houseplants or garden outside. It'd made her decades of being a florist not just worth it, but a joy. A contentment and energizing she never felt with other forms of magic.

That *was* how I felt as a child when I plucked ripened wild strawberries and sat with the sweet tang while listening to the whispers of the vibrant chicken of the woods. Granna used to sit out there with me, never letting me wander too far but allowing me to explore while she basked in the dapples of sunlight or read.

A rustling of leaves, shuddering more fervently than they had before, drew my attention. My eyes searched the direction it came from, to the right and deeper into the wood than I'd been staring unseeingly.

My water slipped from my hand, bouncing, toppling, and lid bursting from the impact. Ice-cold water splashed on my boots, but I barely noticed it.

Kara was stumbling into the forest, eyes wide and looking over her shoulder as if something was chasing her.

I pushed off of the brick and began walking toward where she was retreating into the dark. "Kara?" I shouted, confused when I saw that no one else was out here. Downtown was still bustling, but the noise quickly retreated the further I went.

There was no clear path here, no beaten earth that'd regularly been tread, and I had to climb over and through thickets, pulling back branches to make my way after her. The further I went, I kept my eyes on her red hair that was pulled back in a messy bun. She was wearing a cropped tank top and shorts, and I couldn't help worrying that she must be freezing. It was cool outside but even colder out here. Even with my jeans and boots, my bare arms were almost threatening to break out in goosebumps. And I tended to run hotter than most.

"Kara! Stop—do you need help?" Her family must've been losing hope by now, but at least she was safe.

If she'd just stop for a second, then I'll be able to take her inside where we could call someone for her. But she wouldn't slow down, and I picked up to a jog that overtook her pace.

That blooming in my chest was growing, pushing and pulsing against the heaving of my lungs, and when she stumbled over nothing but a clear patch of leaves, I yelped in surprise. I fell to my knees, immediately feeling the damp earth begin to seep into my jeans.

The acrid smell of her fear wasn't in my nostrils but clear in my mind, and I wanted to draw her into me. She just looked so afraid, lips trembling and tears falling from her eyes, when I felt nothing but frantic concern for her.

"Hey, hey, it's okay, it's okay." I'd had more than my fair share of panic attacks before, and I could see that this was what was plaguing her, clouding her rational mind until she was a shivering mess.

She wasn't looking at me, cowering from something that wasn't here, and I reached out to comfort her, despite how badly the action had turned out when I did the same to Orion when he'd been panicking.

Instead of her lashing out at me, though, my fingers just met with chilled air. I nearly fell on top of her, the action taking me physically and mentally off balance.

"What..." I whispered, astonished but with knowing creeping up the back of my neck. I pulled my hand back and... through her shoulder.

Kara shivered, and it was only then that I noticed the slight shimmering on the edges of her skin. Her whole body, really.

"Oh, honey." My voice was raw, tears springing and collecting on the edges of my lids. She looked at me then, really looked at me, and her expression shifted from the frenzied panic to one of quiet despair. Kara sat up and pulled her knees to her chest. I tried again to touch her, but it was just as fruitless.

"Can you talk to me? Hear me?" I whispered.

She nodded into her knees, and when our eyes met, I saw echoes of pain and anguish in what used to be vibrant amber. "I can," she whispered even more softly than I had. Her voice sounded no different aside from the utter lack of hope that was never there before.

"What happened, Kara? How can I help you?" I sat on the ground beside her. Our feet would've been touching had she been alive, and the lack of contact made me want to give her a hug that could never be. She'd never be embraced again.

"I don't know," she said with thick melancholy. "I can't remember."

"Did—" I took a deep breath "—did someone hurt you?" Because it felt insensitive to ask if she'd been murdered.

Her lips crumpled, and she rubbed at her nose. She seemed to be working through her thoughts, gaze darting on the ground beside us until finally looking up at me and nodding again.

"Okay. Are you hurting any more? Now? Or has it stopped?"

"It's stopped. I'm just... I feel stuck."

My teeth gnawed at my bottom lip, debating on asking, but ultimately deciding I had to. "Did it happen out here? Them hurting you?"

Her chest started rising and falling more rapidly, her nod stiff, and then she turned her body to where she'd been heading. There was just more trees, more brush, but I had a clear idea of what she was trying to convey to me.

"All right." I managed to keep my own voice steady. "Okay. Would you mind taking me there, Kara? Or telling me how much further to go so that I can take a look?"

She gasped a few times, like the surprising tremors that came after a good, long cry, before rising to stand. She dusted off her butt and the back of her legs, as if dirt and debris clung to her body. They didn't, of course, which made my heart crack for her even more. It was too dark to see very clearly, but I noticed then the little cuts and bruises on the illusion of her arms and legs. I sucked my lips into my mouth, trying to stay as calm as possible for her while we continued toward where I expected to find her body.

When she finally came to a stop, though, I found nothing but a hair clip. Though I vaguely remembered her wearing it to class sometimes, it was hardly a corpse. She wrapped her arms around herself, and I stared down at the crunch of dead leaves and branches that covered part of the clearing we stood in. Was she buried here?

Before I could ask the question, Kara pointed to a cluster of detritus a few steps to the left of us. She kept her finger directed at that spot until I crept over, chest pounding at the knowledge that whatever I was going to find wouldn't be good. And there was definitely no bringing her back.

I crouched down, but I didn't need to pull out my phone's flashlight to see the peek of white underneath the browns and black.

The bone was large and thick, though not as big as a femur. I reached out to pick it up but held myself back at the last moment. Curiosity and pull had to be ignored now. This was a crime scene.

My knee creaked when I stood. "Okay, Kara. Thank you for showing me. I'm going to call the police now. And then they'll probably let your family know. I'll stay out here to help them find you. Okay?"

She held herself again, looking so out of place and dressed for a warm, summer hike. She was looking down at the bone that I was fairly certain had scrapes of teeth from whatever scavenging animals had cleaned her flesh from it. "I want to see my sister." I could hear the watery tears in her voice, and it made my own fall in sympathy. I didn't have any sisters, no close family alive besides Granna, but I knew that darkness of grief I heard in her tone.

"I'm sorry, Kara," I said instead of holding her. I called the police station, informing them that I knew where the body of Kara Stanton was located. There was a stilted pause from the 911 operator, then they asked me a series of questions to determine where I was and what I saw. Knowing that I couldn't explain that I was standing here with Kara's ghost who'd led me to where she'd been killed, I explained that I recognized the blue hair clip as one she wore to class, and though I wasn't certain, I believed that the accessory and bone were evidence enough to call.

While I waited for officers to arrive, I decided not to accost Kara with any more questions, and she didn't offer anything else. Hopefully it was enough for me to bear witness to this for her. I'd want someone else to do the same for me.

Soon, the whoop of sirens sounded far in the distance, and I found myself running a nervous hand on the bark of a fallen tree. There was a cluster of oyster mushrooms thriving on the dying oak, and I ran the pad of my finger on an area of rippling gills. The pull in my chest tugged again, and I leaned my ear toward the fungus. What I didn't expect, though, was to actually, finally, hear the whispers.

CHAPTER EIGHTEEN

ORION

When I picked up the phone, happy to have a call from Sylvie distract me from the disastrous paper that I was reading, my heart dropped all the way into my stomach. Police sirens were blaring in the background, footsteps and frantic voices warring with the soft sound of hers. She found a dead body, she said. Could I let her grandmother know and then come pick her up at that the police station, she asked.

I wasn't even sure I'd locked my front door when I raced out of my house. I burned through two cigarettes on the way, though everything in me wanted to get to Sylvie now. Her grandmother didn't have a cell phone, and no one was answering the house phone, so I promised to stop by to see if her grandmother was home.

My knocking was met with a grimace that would have put my tail between my legs if I weren't already vibrating with the agitating need to find and protect my Sylvie.

When I'd gritted an explanation to the witch, she shoved me back out of the door while grabbing her purse.

So, that's how I found myself bursting into the police station with Sylvie's grandmother. I was struggling to gather my words, animalistic needs and instincts crashing through my thoughts like turbulent waves. The bright lights and chatter and ringing phones were like clacking marbles in my brain and were only making me more agitated. It was almost all I could muster to not shift in front of all of these humans. Though, with the way Sylvie's grandmother was doling cold commands and indignation at her granddaughter being driven to the station in the back of a cruiser like a criminal, I wasn't the main one they should've feared.

"… when she's done nothing but help you *useless* pigs." She somehow looked down upon everyone from her truly tiny stature. After enough people tried to placate us, they soon realized that we wouldn't just *sit in the lobby and wait a moment*. I was all but snapping my teeth at any who approached us, and I felt the itch of my fangs and claws wanting to descend so that I could tear down all who separated me from my mate.

We were left to stand and pace under the harsh fluorescent lights, officers and staff watching us with wary eyes. I felt like the snapping wolf at the feet of a battle queen with how Sylvie's grandmother's glare made even the biggest and most heavily armed shrink and dart away from us.

"This is fucking ridiculous," she muttered and looked up at me, "can't you just rip them all apart?"

Her encouragement was not helping when I was trying to halt my fantasies about doing just that. I probably could do what she asked, but I would end up riddled with bullets before we even made it out of here. "Yes, but that wouldn't help." I had enough of my rational mind about me to know that, at least.

She huffed. "No, but it would make me feel better. When are you going to tell her, anyway?"

I looked away, trying to calm down. Did Sylvie even know about shifters? Would she see me any differently because of what I was? *No*, my heart said, *she wouldn't*. But I had no good model for what our relationship would look like if she knew I wasn't human. Sean *still* didn't know about my mother, and they had been married for nearly twenty years. And Da didn't seriously date any humans as far as I knew. Juno never revealed themself a Wolf to any of their trysts, but maybe I'd revisit the topic with them just to be sure.

"Orion." My hackles raised, and I lunged forward. Sylvie's grandmother's hand was surprisingly strong when she held me back, and, for good measure, she gave me a zap that made me back down. Wasn't she the one who was just asking me to kill everybody?

"You two are making quite the scene," he mocked us, and I launched forward again. I grabbed the front of his shirt, bringing our faces just an inch from each other. The repellent on his scent was strong, and it made my territorial instinct surge even higher.

"You hold my mate here a minute longer, and I will fucking end you." The growl was evident in my threat, and Graham growled back. If I hadn't been caught in the riptide of my own rage, I would have startled at the admission that'd just slipped out.

Mate. When had I begun to think of her as my mate? Before the night in my office, but when I closed my teeth around her throat, it felt like a confirmation. Usually, my days shifted into wolf form left me more clearheaded, but seeing Sylvie laugh and smile at that boy left me wild with the need to claim what was mine. I'd retained enough sense to not pierce her skin, but it'd been enough. My mark and scent were on her, and they'd only need to take one sniff or one glance to know that she was mine.

Graham didn't back down or begin to submit like the other one had. He shoved back on my chest, but I didn't let go. "*I'm* not holding the witch for anything. *Back down.*" The air around us began to tingle and warm, but I couldn't give a single fuck at this point. My anger was egging on his defensiveness, and the shifts were ramping up to tear through us. His eyes were yellowing, starting to deepen in color, and I felt my fingernails start to give way to my claws.

"… acting like a pair of rabid *dogs*." A larger zap shocked my side, and my hands dropped from Graham's shirt. There were little holes where my claws pierced through the fabric. His chest was heaving like mine, fists clenching and unclenching while he tried to keep from half-shifting.

"Now, *what* is going on here?" The deeper voice of Chief Thompson boomed across the lobby, but that was all it did. He may have had authority with this town and the humans, but his scent told of who between him and Graham was the Pack Leader.

Graham lifted his chin, seemingly more in control of his Wolf now, "The White One and this witch say you've got his mate here unjustly." Graham looked to his father, who lowered his eyes in deference. His back was turned to the rest of the room, and his shoulders stayed straight, but his scent was laced with submission.

I knew what it felt like to battle for Leader and be beaten. But at least I was given the decency to be exiled and leave the territory. Graham won and kept his father in the pack. So that he could be reminded every day of how he welcomed his estranged son, only for him to take over a few years later. If I weren't so angry, I would have felt bad for the male.

But to the eyes around us, Chief Thompson was the authority figure, here. "We aren't holding her unjustly. She's being questioned as a witness at this point. She is free to go at any time."

"Then release Sylvie at this moment. I don't want to hear anything else from you. She helped you find that girl when even your heightened senses couldn't do the job. You should be thanking her and nothing more." Sylvie's grandmother cut her hand through the air to emphasize her point, and the two Other Pack Wolves flinched. She was certainly powerful—I was still feeling the tingling from her chastising blow—and these two knew it.

How powerful would Sylvie be in a few years' time?

"Now, Ms. Johnson, I understand that you're upset. And our officers should be finishing up with her soon, but this is a delicate matter—"

"Unless you want to watch my granddaughter's mate exact his rightful retribution, you will let her go. Unless you want me to blast you and your wretched son and singe off every stitch of fur you have and may ever hope to grow, you will release her. *Now*."

Chief Thompson looked aghast and afraid at the same time, while his son's eyes started shifting again. I held them, absolutely unmoved by his growing posture of dominance. I'd already made it clear that he would never be my leader.

Graham wasn't backing down, and his father seemed resigned to the chaos that was going to break out. He wouldn't go against his pack leader, after all.

"Orion? Granna?" Her melodic voice was scratchy, but her scent was still that cool cherry. With it, too, were hints of my own. The other Wolves took a step back from her, detecting that she belonged to me and me to her.

Her grandmother and I ran forward, and I crushed Sylvie into my chest. I scented at her neck, filling my nose with her and snuffling in her hair while her grandmother ran a hand in circles on her back. Though it was already there, I planted more of my scent onto her with my face running up and down her throat and my hands doing the same on her spine.

She began to squirm a little, so I pulled back, now satisfied that she was physically unharmed and covered in my scent. The mark on her neck was just peeking over the collar of her work t-shirt, and my chest rumbled in satisfaction.

I had a mate. She was everything, and I was going to protect her.

Sylvie leaned back her head, and I descended, giving her a strong kiss to further remind everyone in this gods-forsaken precinct that she was *mine*.

When I pulled back, she twisted to put her arm around her grandmother. They embraced, and I took the moment to glance back at the other Wolves. Chief Thompson was conversing with the plain-clothed officers that brought Sylvie out to the lobby, and Graham was eyeing Sylvie's mark, jaw working.

My body hummed when Sylvie brought her hand to my chest, stealing my attention that was always half on her anyway. Her little nose was wrinkled like she'd caught a whiff of something that stunk, so I brought mine to hers, passing it over in the show of affection she so easily accepted from me.

"All right, son, drive us home." I could smell the exasperation under Sylvie's grandmother's words, and I turned to guide us out of the precinct. When we made it to my car, I opened the doors for both Sylvie and her grandmother and pulled us away from the police station as quickly as I could. My muscles were still trembling, and I breathed, attempting to ground myself and rid the lingering tension. She was safe. My mate was with me, and she was safe.

"'Son,' huh?" Sylvie grinned over her shoulder to look in the backseat.

Her grandmother scoffed. "Shut up, sweetheart. You've had my nerves completely shot, and I had to stop your boyfriend from throttling that boy *and* the Chief *twice*."

"At one point, you were telling me to," I deadpanned. If I had a temper, Sylvie's grandmother had one just as bad.

"Be that as it may, explain to me, granddaughter of mine, how you came to find the missing girl."

Sylvie turned back to face front and grabbed my forearm. I released my hand from the wheel, steering now with just one, and twined my fingers with hers. "She showed me," Sylvie whispered.

My fingers tightened, but I made myself relax them. I took a deep inhale to calm myself further, and I detected that under her natural cherry and connection to me, the electric warmth of her power felt stronger. It had grown since the last time I saw her.

"You saw the girl's ghost?" Sylvie's grandmother didn't sound surprised. In fact, she smelled as if she were delighted. Proud.

She'd mentioned her witchcraft more and more in the past weeks, but she hadn't spoken of anything to this extent. I tried to keep the fear and anxiety at bay.

Sylvie's hair shuddered against the leather seat with her nod.

"And talked to her. She said she was murdered." She swallowed. "And..." her shoulders drew higher, and I brought her hand to my lips. Her tart anxiety was filling the car, and it churned my stomach to know she was feeling unease.

"And?"

"While I was waiting for the police to show up, I... I heard the whispers again."

"From the fungi? Well, that's splendid, sweetheart. Seems like your power is blossoming again. What did they say?" I caught her grandmother's gaze in the rearview mirror, and her question from earlier plagued my mind. Yes, when was I going to tell my mate? One, that she even *was* my mate. And two, that I wasn't human. If she was able to speak to ghosts and hear whispers from... mushrooms? She was going to be able to detect that I wasn't human soon enough.

Sylvie turned back to look at her grandmother, and her words made my heart drop into my stomach all over again. "They said that the wolves killed her."

CHAPTER NINETEEN

SYLVIE

The witch raised her dagger, hilt to the dark sky above. Her eyes rolled back in ecstasy at the screaming offering at her feet. A surge of power, just a taste of what was to come, made tears fall from her eyes. Yes, she was blessed.

She brought the blade down, piercing skin, muscle, bone. The heart of the one who thought themselves innocent pumped hot, thick blood, and it began to pool around the shining steel of her dagger.

I paused, trying to think of the facial expression of the dying man, and rubbed a knuckle between my brows. I'd been sitting in the sun room all morning, but the words weren't flowing.

Granna padded into the room, two mugs held in one hand while her other arm was wrapped around her middle. She wore a sweater *and* held a blanket around her body in addition to the fuzzy slippers on her feet. Autumn was fully upon us, and it felt delightful with the cooler air and bright sun streaming through the windows.

I gladly took the proffered tea and the opportunity at distraction.

"How's it coming, sweetheart?" She took a sip from her mug

after sitting at the other end of the sofa. She shivered as the tea warmed her.

I snapped my laptop shut and placed it on the coffee table. Tucking my knees to my chest, I took a drink. "Difficult today. So maybe I just need a break." The new story centered around a witch and her coven, which I thought would be an interesting direction. But the events of earlier this week were still leaving me off-kilter. After the police arrived, Kara's ghost had followed me into the cruiser and to the station. But, when she saw her family, she quickly left my side, and I hadn't seen her since. I hoped that she was able to move on.

I went out to the mushrooms every morning since, and when I bent down to listen, they continued to speak. It wasn't any language that I could consciously respond with, but when I asked them questions, they answered with words that made sense to my mind. They told of the early frost that would come. Where I could find wild fruits before the harvesting season ended.

When I asked about the wolves, they said that only one wolf came close to the house. A white wolf.

But I'd never heard any howling, never saw droppings or evidence of a wolf marking the stretch of woods around our house as their territory. That particular message from the fungi caused an anxiety and caffeine driven research dive into the behavior of wolves. I was surprised to find that they generally steered clear of humans, and if I was correct in assuming that Kara was reliving her final moments when she was running in terror before my presence reminded her that she was already dead, then something vicious had been chasing her.

Could she have provoked a pack somehow? Threatened their young? *That* theory took me down another rabbit hole of wolf mating and breeding habits, only to find that wolves generally gave birth in the spring.

And then I thought again of what Granna mentioned offhandedly before school started. "Um… Granna. Do werewolves exist?"

Her body stiffened for a blink, and then she schooled her

expression. So, that was a yes, then. "Sure they do, sweetheart. Though, I've been told by several that they hate that title." She paused to put her mug on the coffee table. "Why do you ask?"

"Well, when the mushrooms—"I scrubbed a hand over my face "—I feel so ridiculous saying that. Anyway, when they said that wolves killed Kara, I thought they meant, you know, *wolf* wolves. But what if they just saw…" I waved my free hand around helplessly.

"Wolf shifters."

"Okay, yeah, wolf shifters. What if they were just shifted into wolves when they killed her? Right? That would explain why she was running and so scared. And," I swallowed, "it might explain the bone I saw. It had teethmarks."

Granna nodded, and the bun on her head began to come loose. While she released and began twisting it back up again, her tone took on that of when she was teaching me. "Well, that's certainly possible. And based on what you've seen and heard, it seems like the clearest explanation. Wolf shifter packs are generally very tight-knit and insular groups. They have their own leader—"

"The alpha?"

She waved my guess away with a bobby pin in her grip. "No. That's a word humans attached to wolves for some reason. Most just say Pack Leader. Or their specific group has a word that has roots for them. Anyway, they have their own traditions and rules and manner of governing themselves. And their own ways of doling out justice. I'm wondering if your classmate disrespected or angered the pack in some way."

"So there *is* a pack here. A group of wolf shifters?"

Granna shrugged like this wasn't the most interesting lesson she'd ever given me. "Yes. They call themselves the Antler Pointe Pack, which is highly original." She rolled her eyes.

"And who's in it? Anyone I know?" I tried to think back to all the people I'd met, but I didn't even know where to begin to identify someone that could just casually change into a wolf.

She pursed her lips and patted her bun to make sure it was secure. "I can't tell you that, sweetheart."

My head jerked backward, tea sloshing in my mug and spilling down the side. "Why the hell not? Shouldn't I be informed to help find the ones that did this to Kara? She didn't deserve to be chased down and eaten Granna, be serious."

"Well, one," she lifted a spindly finger, "we don't know that. Like I just told you, packs have their own rules. To them, her death may have been completely justified. Two," she lifted another finger, "it is not my place to disclose the identities of shifters. Though wolf shifters are family-oriented and generally have the protection of their pack to back them up, shifters as a whole do *not* take kindly to those who reveal their nature without their consent. It is a risk to their safety. And I love you, but I have already revealed enough."

My back curved, shrinking into myself. Guilt flamed on my cheeks. "Okay, I'm sorry. I didn't realize."

She patted my bare foot. "That's all right, sweetheart. I know this is all new and exciting information. The good news is, with your powers unfurling and growing these past weeks, you should be more open to what has been hidden before. With that should come the ability to detect supernatural creatures. Wolf shifters have a distinctly earthy smell. Some I find neutral enough, some just smell like wet dog."

I snorted. "And how kindly do they take to you telling them that? Because I know you have."

She waved her hand and reached over to pick up her mug again. "Oh, they chuckle or bare their teeth, but what else are they going to do? Shifters are naturally hesitant around witches."

I heaved a big sigh. Of course, something else she'd held from me in the name of waiting for the right time to dispense the information. "And why is that, oh wise witch?"

"Well, some of us have the power to influence their shifts. Not to mention that we're some of the few non-shifters that can see through their human forms."

"*Okay*, I suppose you aren't going to tell me how to influence shifts right now," her raised brow confirmed as much, "so, is there anything else you can tell me? That might help me help Kara?"

She huffed. "Well, I'll reiterate that your powers are growing. I can sense it. So, The Book will become more of a reference to you. Humans can learn witchcraft, utilizing the recipes and spells in tomes such as The Book and sometimes even develop their own powers. However, you and I are born witches. You have your own innate power, such as understanding the language of fungi, speaking with ghosts—"

"So, anything to do with death." It was comical, really. Maybe that was why I'd been entranced by horror movies from such a young age.

"Don't interrupt me sweetheart. I told you. There are multiple stages in the life cycle. There is bringing life, there is nurturing it, there is resting, and there is reaping. If we're being reductive. You touch the tomato plant, trying to make it grow, but you are focusing on the wrong thing."

"Well, they just shrivel and die when I concentrate too much!"

Granna rolled her eyes. "Yes, the reaping comes more easily since it's the final stage. But I believe you'll be able to toe the line of rest, of *harvest*. Especially as you hone your powers."

I narrowed my eyes. "Harvest? Like get the fruit to ripen?"

"*Yes*, Sylvie. Took you long enough."

I sputtered, "Wha—I'm *sorry* that I didn't realize that my powers would differ so much from yours! You could have just told me!"

"Well, it is better when you are already feeling it. If I'd told you the first day you arrived that you would be able to do these things, you'd just grow anxious or incredibly frustrated when it didn't happen right away. Am I wrong?"

"Okay, *fine*. That's possible."

"Now, why don't you go practice toeing that line. I'm willing to sacrifice the tomato plants for your training." Granna began to stand from the sofa, apparently done with giving me the earth-shattering lesson for now.

I picked up my laptop to make sure that my work from this morning was saved as she began to walk back into the rest of the house. My witch story was pulled up right where I left it, which made another question bubble up. Before she got too far, I hollered, "Wait! Granna. Are there other witches in town, too?"

Granna stopped her advance toward the kitchen, probably, and turned to lean on the doorframe. "Well, yes, we're not the only ones. But some don't realize they have any sort of inclination toward witchcraft. Some enjoy practicing alone, such as myself."

But maybe that meant I didn't have to be a novice on my own. "I know you won't out any shifters to me," I raised my palms hastily, "and I don't want you to! But, it would be nice to learn alongside other witches that aren't, you know, experts like you."

Her face softened. "Oh, sweetheart, I know this is a lot of information. But you're doing exceptionally well."

Her tone made me feel like a child, which made me both comforted and embarrassed. "Even still. Maybe it'd be nice to have some sisters. Or a coven!"

She shrugged nonchalantly, but the corner of her mouth tilted upward in a smirk. "Well, why don't you ask your seer friend?" My mind blanked out, racing to figure out who she was talking about. But, really, who else could she mean besides Josie? When I continued to gape, Granna chuckled. "Why do you think you were such fast friends? And why she barely comes over here? That girl uses fear to try to keep her visions at bay. I can smell it on her. Maybe it's time you help her accept what she is."

I just have a hunch… I feel like we should… Could Josie's offhanded remarks not be so offhanded at all? She did seem genuinely trepidatious when it came to all things involving witchcraft, but there were also moments her curiosity got in the way of her own fear.

"Granna, I think you've fried my brain today," I groused into my hands. Was this the reason Josie was able to deduce the meaning of the Tower so accurately? I'd thought it was luck and her being able to use the context of the illustration. But, maybe not.

"Well, sweetheart, I think you'll be able to find your footing. What else would you do?" And with that, Granna left me to pick up the pieces and reconstruct my view of the world around me. Shifters, ghosts, my own powers, and a best friend that could apparently peer into the future.

I stood, and instead of following my grandmother into the house, I left through the screen door. The purple and yellow mosaic tiles that led to the garden were ice-cold under my feet, but no chill ran up my legs. The unevenness felt like a massage, and once again, I focused on the pull within my body.

The caged trellises that housed the tomato plants stood straight and tall against the side of the house. With Granna's care throughout all seasons, the tomatoes were still thriving, producing plump and juicy fruits every day. How she managed to keep her home garden and business running at the same time for so many years was beyond me. Managing this alone seemed like a full-time job.

With no plan besides touching the plants and trying to influence the red and green fruits to ripen, I plopped down in front of the wooden trellises. The first premature tomato I touched began to immediately grow and darken. The plumping fruit pushed back on my finger while it rapidly fattened, and an excited yelp shot out of my throat. *I'm doing it!*

I looked to the kitchen window above and yelled for my grandmother to come and see, ecstatic that this was going so well on my first try.

Until a wet, squelching thud turned me back to the plant to find my ripening fruit brown and oozing into the soil below.

"Well, fuck." I shouted back up at the window, "Never mind!" Frustration bubbled and threatened to come out in more curses, and maybe tears, but I fought the battle to swallow it down and eventually won.

I tried again, this time getting the green tomato to stay full and ripe, but as soon as I removed my touch, it over-ripened and died like the last one. Again, and again, I worked through fruit after fruit, stalk after stalk, until I was able to dial the spigot of my power so that I could give just enough for the plant to mature and then leave it in that state.

Sweat trickled down my temples and collected on my lower back, even after I tossed my sweatshirt to the side. Over and over, I worked until all the tomato plants that were still alive stood mature and full.

It must have taken hours, because Granna came round the side of the house to check on me. With an impressed frown, she crossed her arms, inspected the plants, and nodded. "Finding your footing, indeed."

CHAPTER TWENTY

SYLVIE

My thoughts were still a jumble from Granna's lessons, but now, my stomach was all aflutter with the prospect of my first overnight with Orion. The volume of my heavy metal music was turned low as I tried to calm myself for whatever was about to happen. The GPS got a little wonky the closer I got to his house, just as he said it would, and I called to mind the directions he'd texted me. Just as Google blanked out completely, I spotted the mouth of the gravel turnoff. I left the paved road, driving slowly with my tires crunching further away from town.

In all my years of visiting Antler Pointe, I'd never really left the downtown or immediately surrounding area. Besides traipsing around the forest, of course.

The road to Orion's house cut through a thin layer of trees, with the wood darkening to my left and right. The days were getting shorter, and though it was only just five in the evening, the sun was already almost set. The sky was a deep, pretty pink that matched the dress I'd chosen for tonight, and as I spotted lights in the distance, my stomach lurched again with excited nerves.

Was the overnight bag in my trunk too optimistic? Maybe, but it also represented the possibility that this night would go in the direction I hoped. To hear Josie say it, my spending the night with Orion was an inevitability. When I called her for input on what to wear, it was difficult to not immediately vomit all about the assertion Granna made about her abilities. And when I tried to focus the conversation on my anxieties about tonight, her predictions just made it worse.

"He's already in love with you, Sylv. It's almost painful how I can already see you living in a cozy wooden cabin with him and your two kids."

"J-Jesus, Josie, two kids? We only just had sex. I don't think you have to worry about kids for a long while. If we even get to that point."

I followed the curve of the road, coming around the bend toward a clearing up ahead, and replayed her words over and over. I'd never told Josie that Orion said he lived in a cabin. If her seeing, as Granna called it, had any merit, this date felt like a preordained step toward the future Josie saw for us. I made a mental note to ask Granna about the extent of seer abilities and to figure out a way to approach Josie about her powers that she may not even realize she had. And then ask her if she wanted to start a coven. Easy.

My brow wrinkled as I began to second-guess myself on that one, but the sight of... the most breathtaking home I'd ever seen quickly took up all my attention.

This is where he lives?

The narrow road led right to what was indeed a cabin, but instead of the logs I'd pictured, the facade was made of smooth wood painted a deep, almost black, green.

The porch lights were on, and as I pulled up beside the black car I recognized as his, I had to consciously force my mouth closed. It wasn't a big house necessarily, but it was a lot larger than I thought it would be. A stone chimney stood on the left side of the house, and when I stepped out of my car I—*is that a* lake?

Petrified. The flutters in my stomach had turned to a gnawing sensation, though there really was no reason for me to be terrified. But... if *this* was where Orion lived, I couldn't just ignore anymore the fact that he was just so well put together. For goddess's sake, he was a fucking professor who lived in a paradise in the woods that he somehow *built*, and he wanted to date *me*? A two time college dropout that just quit working at a failing pizza place?

Just before my panicking made me do something stupid like cry or get in my car to turn around, the front door opened, releasing a wash of warm light. And stepping out of that light, in a simple gray shirt and dark jeans was Orion.

Though he didn't smile much, I could see the flush bleeding into the tops of his white cheeks, and the panic left me like a gust of wind.

With his hands still stuffed in his pockets, Orion bounced down the wooden steps and headed toward me. As he drew nearer, I saw the light in his green eyes, the upward tilt of his lips, and all my energy released in a big, relieved grin.

He stopped advancing, face dropping to an expression that made my insecurities flare. His hands drew from his pockets, thumbs tapping on his fingers, and his stare was almost... reverent?

"Um, hi." *Hi?* This was the same man that fucked me with abandon just one hallway down from a department event. Steeling my spine, I pushed forward, my chunky heels wobbling on the stones. My walking seemed to jerk Orion out of whatever trance he was in, because he lurched forward, catching my elbows to steady me.

"Sylvie." Orion's low, husky voice soothed the rest of the unease that had been creeping up, and it was as simple as breathing to let him pull me in. His solid arms twined around my back. My face smooshed into his shirt, his chest warming me immediately. This was perfect—he was perfect.

"I'm sorry I'm a little late." My words were muffled against his body, but he didn't seem to mind about either thing.

"I don't care. You're right on time." Orion's usual grumble was turning into a freaking lullaby, the reassurance smoothing over my anxiety and insecurities once again. It was something I felt self-conscious about—the frazzled-ness. But he never seemed to mind.

I took the opportunity to explore his torso a bit, tentatively running one hand up his side, the other up his spine. A low, contented noise vibrated my ears, and I fought back a giggle when I realized that *he* didn't realize he was doing it. I put my fingernails into the movement, giving him light scratches that left trails of goosebumps in their wake. His thin shirt could've been painted on, and my mind warred not with my desire to rip it off of him but with what I wanted to do with him afterward.

His body was leanly muscled, his shoulders deliciously broad, and I was already aching with wanting him inside me again. But I also wanted more of this—curling up into him. Maybe with him holding me as we slept.

Judging by the hard press against my lower belly, his mind was going in those directions, too. Perhaps it was more of a plausibility than I'd thought.

With a clearing of his throat, Orion's arms began to loosen around me, and I reluctantly leaned back to put space between us. When I looked up at him, I found his gaze soft, the green color calm like blades of grass in the rain.

"Would you like a tour? Of my home." He said it in an adorably formal tone, brow furrowing like it was a very serious task.

I nodded and bobbed excitedly on my feet. "Yes, of course! It's so beautiful—I want to see more."

Pink flushed his cheeks and the tops of his ears, and when he turned toward the front door, grabbing my hand on the way, I noticed that his hair looked freshly cut. He'd never really let it grow out since we met, but after seeing him yesterday, I realized that he must've got it cut between now and then.

It could have just been his routine, but the thought of him

getting it cut for this occasion made *me* start to blush while he led me toward the house.

Now that we were closer, and I didn't have my panic flaring or his body pressed to mine, I registered the soulful crooning coming from inside.

Orion walked us slowly, which I was thankful for as I stepped carefully on the gravel and up the short stack of wooden stairs. There was no furniture on the front porch, but I noticed a ceramic ashtray on the railing that was empty. Was it new or freshly dumped out?

That question was quickly wiped from my brain, though, as we stepped into the foyer of Orion's cabin.

I saw from the outside that it was all one level, and the small entrance area held an artisan-looking rug in a deep red color with an angular, geometric pattern. Orion closed the door behind us, and I tried to keep my eyes from bugging out and looking over every inch that I could see. I quickly slipped out of my shoes, and once he'd removed his boots, he set them both under a wooden bench.

Orion's home was warm. Cozy. The walls and floor were both made of the same wood, and the ceilings were higher than I expected. He started us to the left, where the foyer gave way to a large, open living room. The leather sectional sofa sat before a large fireplace that was set in the same stone as the outside. Two armchairs in a dark green fabric were positioned perpendicular to the sofa, and I could just see him curled up there, reading before the fire.

He didn't speak as we padded further into the room, and I recognized the Bill Withers song that played softly from the impressive looking record player and speakers set within a sprawling shelving unit that must've held… *hundreds* of records.

I glanced around, trying to find a television, but stopped when my eyes landed on the fireplace's mantle. A large, abstract painting stood behind a row of photographs with mismatched frames.

My body acted almost on its own accord when I zeroed in on the little boy in one of the photos. I wanted to pick up the small frame for a closer look, but I suppressed the urge by grabbing onto the wooden shelf to lean in as closely as I could.

The little boy was obviously Orion, his pale skin and green eyes round and sweet-looking. His short curls were a bright white, not the pale, cream color that they were now. And his sweatshirt and jeans looked like an adorable version of what he still elected to wear most days.

Orion's lips were pulled back in a wide smile that didn't meet his eyes, almost as if he didn't understand the expression but tried to mimic whoever was behind the camera when they commanded, 'Say cheese!'

"Who's that?" I asked and pointed to the man standing next to him. His brown hand was on Orion's shoulder, and his smile lit up his entire face. They both stood before metal siding that looked like the facade of a shed or trailer.

"My father," Orion said, and my brow lowered in more confusion. When I inspected the man's face more closely, okay, yes, I did see that he and Orion had the same nose. They had the slight tilting of their eyes in common as well. But the man's tighter curls were a dark brown, and there was the obvious difference in his skin tone.

I turned to my... boyfriend? The man I was dating? And looked at him more closely. We usually had a sixth sense about this sort of thing, so how did I not know that Orion wasn't white? Well, in race, not necessarily color of his skin.

"You never told me that you were..." My voice trailed off when I caught the little wrinkle between Orion's eyebrows and the flaring of his nose. *Had* he told me?

"That I was what?"

My eyelids fluttered for a moment, trying to find words that wouldn't come off accusatory or offensive. I'd heard that biracial children often felt alienated from both sides of their heritage, so I certainly didn't want to add to that. "Ah... that your dad wasn't white?" But then I cringed at the awkward way I'd phrased it.

Orion's brow crinkled more, but I saw his shoulders relax. "Oh," he muttered with an inflection like he was relieved by what I said. He looked back at the photo. "No, he wasn't. My mother is."

I nodded, but then, of course, I blurted another question without thinking, "But your last name?"

This time, Orion let out a raspy snort. "My grandfather was white, Irish. Da always complained about being a black man with a last name like Gealach." He gestured his hand in a lazy wave at himself, "My mother has albinism, and Da must've carried the gene, so that's why I look like this."

He said the words in that matter-of-fact way of his, but it made me feel bad that I'd brought it up all the same. I placed my palm on his chest and felt the calm beat of his heart. "I love the way you look. I hope my questions didn't offend you."

When I chanced a glance to his face, Orion looked anything but. He reached up to hold my hand on his chest, almost covering it completely. The contrast on the skin of his tattooed arm looked even sharper in the mellow light of his home. He spoke softly, eyes hidden beneath lowered lashes. "They didn't. I hadn't mentioned this before." He peeled my hand off of his chest but kept it clasped within his grip. "Shall I show you the rest of the house? Or are you getting hungry?"

My excitement bubbled up again. "Tour, please."

Orion pointed out the rest of the photos quickly, and all of them featured him and his father. Down the line, both grew older until the last one showed a softly smiling Orion in black cap and gown, and his father, with salt-and-pepper hair this time, looking as proud as could be.

We made our way out of the living room to a hallway at the back of the house that held two spare bedrooms. With each, he pushed the doors open and gestured quickly to the interiors that held neatly made beds and cozily mismatched furniture. I wondered how often he had guests or if the rooms had just been his father's idea.

At the end of the hall, he pushed open the last door to reveal a sight that had my jaw hitting the floor.

This bedroom was certainly his. Not only by the fact that it smelled most like him and his cologne.

The room was made almost entirely of windows. Wooden beams separated the panes of glass that extended all the way to the vaulted ceiling, and my hand slipped from his as I advanced forward.

His large bed was pushed up to the left wall, as neatly made as the others, and his nightstand held a neat stack of books beneath the lamp that was emitting dim, yellow light. To the right was another lamp, this one standing on the floor, right beside a leather recliner. And beside *that* was a long, low bookshelf that took up the rest of the wall. Though absolutely stuffed with books, it was organized neatly, and, I guessed, arranged with some system that only made sense to him.

I kept walking until I was almost pressed against the glass of the far wall. There *was* a lake back there. No more than two hundred feet from where I stood, was a sizable lake bordered by the forest I'd driven through on the way here.

And this was the view Orion saw as he was falling asleep and waking every day. What he looked upon when he read in that chair, which I assumed he did often.

After a long, long time, I turned around to see him watching me warily and mussing the curls at the back of his head.

I opened my mouth to speak, but he beat me to it. "You look beautiful. I should have—" he shook his head "—I should have said that when you first got here. I was just… nervous."

My lips tilted downward, and I immediately made my way back toward where he was standing near the door. "Thank you, baby," I chuckled, "and I was nervous, too."

Orion looked truly confused, now. His eyes searched this space that I imagined was where he felt most at home. If I lived here, this would certainly be my favorite room. "Why would you be nervous? Do you," he took a bracing breath, face hardening as if steeling himself for criticism, "do you not like it?"

My head jerked back on that one, and I blamed my desire to make him laugh on what I said next. "Oh goddess, Orion, I *love* it. It's the most beautiful house I've ever seen! And I was nervous because I'd been worrying about being too presumptuous when I packed an overnight bag in my car and *then* started to think you are so completely out of my league."

There was a long stretch of silence where Orion met my gaze for the first time since his greeting me outside. But before I could start fidgeting and try to retract my embarrassing honesty, he held my face and brought his nose to mine. He brushed it against mine in that way I'd instantly loved the first time he'd done it, and his breath tasted like coffee and cigarettes in the best way. "If anyone is out of the other's league, it's you, Sylvie." He kissed me for the first time tonight, soft and deep, and I nearly whimpered in protest when he pulled back to speak over my lips. "And, if you'll allow it, I was hoping you'd spend the night."

I couldn't hold back my grin. "You were?"

It only climbed higher when the timbre of his voice went even lower, "Yes. I've been wanting you in my home, sleeping in my bed, for a long while now."

My breathing picked up. "Oh?"

And then he almost made my knees buckle when he took the flesh of my bottom lip between his teeth, all uncertainty leaving him as he turned into what I thought of as Sexy Orion. Where it felt like he was able to tune out all insecurity in the name of revealing his true desires. He released my lip, now swollen and throbbing in time to that between my legs and pressed a chaste kiss to my cheek before leaning into my ear. "That and taking my time with you. Savoring you like I should have the first time."

"Shit." My brain must have short-circuited because that was supposed to stay an inside-thought.

His thumbs caressed my face in gentle passes. "Mm. But first, I'll finish making dinner. Are you ready to eat?"

I had been spending way too much time with Josie, because my first thought was an immediate yes, followed by what I was eager to taste that was not food. That, luckily, stayed in my mind while I nodded.

Orion gave me another kiss on my cheek before leading us back out toward the rest of the house. "Then I'll cook for you, my little witch."

CHAPTER TWENTY-ONE

ORION

Sylvie sat on one of the barstools and watched me cook. It was an activity I discovered that I quite enjoyed in the years before graduate school. Da was a terrible cook, and the chefs at my mother's and Sean's home took care of all of our meals when I stayed there. Boarding and undergraduate school held dining halls, so it wasn't until I had my first apartment that I discovered the satisfaction that came from turning ingredients into something totally different and delicious.

I supposed in that way, it was similar to carpentry, which I was already familiar with. After a two-year-long fixation with learning to cook Italian cuisine, my fingers were quick and comfortable as I flattened the pasta dough and set the bolognese sauce on the stove. As soon as Sylvie texted her agreement to come over the next day, I'd set out to the store to purchase and begin prepping everything. The sauce was best when it was given the chance to cook low and slow, and even better when the flavors had been mellowing overnight.

She sipped from her glass, bopping her head along to the music coming from the record player that I kept on more often than not. "Is the wine okay?" I remembered that she liked pinot noir from the night she first kissed me, but I'd had to take a guess on which one when she couldn't tell me a specific brand she enjoyed.

"Mhm," she smiled over the counter at me, "this is all so wonderful, Orion. Thank you." Though her skin was that beautiful, warm brown, I could still see the flush that was blooming on her cheeks. I surreptitiously took a drawing inhale, happy to find that her scent read as pleasant, content.

"Of course. I'm happy you're here. I don't ever get to cook for anyone besides myself. I hope you like it."

"I'm sure it'll be delicious based on how it smells! And you know that I'm not picky. You could've put a frozen pizza in the oven, and I would've been happy."

My lips turned down. "I wouldn't ever subject you to that, Sylvie. And I want to take care of you." Though I'd loved my time with my father, the cardboard taste of frozen pizzas was one I wanted to erase from my memory forever.

"Well, thank you," her voice lowered, "and next time, I can take care of you. Maybe cook for us?"

I began feeding the rectangle of dough through my pasta roller, slowly cranking the handle to flatten it to a uniform sheet. "No."

"No?"

"I enjoy doing this. Just let me take care of you without feeling like you need to reciprocate. You give me more than enough by just being you." She'd told me about how she spent years taking care of her father. And I knew that she saw it as enjoying time and learning with her grandmother, but Sylvie spent enough time worrying about others. I'd never had someone I wanted to do this for—be this way for—until her. And even she wasn't going to keep me from doing it. She deserved to rest.

"Ugh, why are you so perfect?" Her words sounded frustrated, but her contented scent just deepened.

I didn't know what to say to her besides, "I'm not perfect," because it was the only thing about her words that I knew for certain.

"Yes, you are. With your wonderful house, your impressive career, your sweet and tender words. How cute you look barefoot with an apron on while making me pasta. People write romance novels about men like you, Orion."

Well, I wasn't a man, but I wasn't ready to say that to her. So again, I responded with the words I knew for certain. "I'm not barefoot." I waggled my socked foot for emphasis while I finished running the pasta through the machine once more and flowered the clean counter.

Sylvie snickered and pressed forward on arms folded in front of her. "What are you doing, now?" The movement pressed her breasts up against the neckline of her dress, their pillowy softness almost spilling out. I'd meant what I said earlier, about my intentions tonight. It was a wonder that I hadn't fully mated her that night on campus. Even though the recent days shifted should have left my mind in a calmer state, the sight of her smiling at someone else and then her cherry scented flesh yielding and so soft under my teeth almost snapped my resolve.

Because I wanted to mate her. Breed her. My teeth itched with my fangs threatening to emerge at the thought. Of locking myself to her while I buried my fangs into her neck, truly breaking the skin.

But that could never be. She was human, and I wouldn't bind her to me in that way when she didn't know what it meant. When it could turn her. I'd already gone too far with the half-mark on her neck.

So, I shook my head and set my knife to the folded layers of dough. "The sauce is almost done reheating, so I just need to shape and boil the tagliatelle. But that shouldn't take long. The salad is already assembled and in the fridge." I gestured my knife toward the refrigerator behind me and continued to cut into the yellow dough.

Sylvie watched me and hummed while I stored half of the

noodles for freezing and brought the rest to the boiling water on the stove. I dropped the little bundles of tagliatelle into the pot.

"Are you all right if we eat outside?"

"Ooh, yes, it feels nice out there." Sylvie's enthusiasm was rubbing off on me. An easy smile stayed on my face while I finished making our meal. After plating the bolognese and salad, I put everything on a tray and led us out of the kitchen.

Sylvie followed me silently, her scent identifying her as curious but excited, and when we reached the entrance to the back porch, she pushed the door open for me.

"Orion, this is too much." Her voice was almost choked, and I fought the urge to whirl around to see her face with our dinner still in my hands. I'd purchased some of those twinkle lights my sister loved and set them up to illuminate the little area. Ramona said it made for a cozy ambiance when I asked her why she'd had them set up in her room a few years ago. Now that the sun had set, and I took in the sight of my backyard, lake and all, I agreed that it did add something to the view. Normally, when I sat out here in the evenings, I needed little light. The thought of setting these up had never occurred to me until I imagined sitting out here with Sylvie, thinking about what might make her feel comfortable and welcome. I realized that I enjoyed it as well.

Once I set the food down on the iron patio table I thrifted earlier this year, I turned to her.

She had tears in her eyes.

Without thought, I crossed the distance between us and brought her into my arms. My nose settled at her neck, unable to stifle the urge, and I took a deep inhale. She shivered but wrapped her arms around me. There was sadness there, but it was underneath the layers of sweetness and excitement that were still present. It was confusing.

"What's wrong?" My voice was harsher than I intended, but I was frustrated that I didn't understand.

I pulled myself back so that I could look at her face, to memorize the expression that paired with this particular aroma of hers.

"This is just… so nice. I hadn't," her breath was shaky, "I hadn't expected anything like this."

Despite the usual discomfort, I met her eyes, trying to find clarity in them. It was becoming easier and easier to do with her— the color reminded me of running through the forest, something that never failed to calm me. "It's… overwhelming?"

A wobbly smile started to spread on her face. "Maybe. But in a good way."

Like how her kindness makes me feel, I related in that practiced way I'd been instructed to as a child. Through the years, it got easier to do. And then, at a certain point, I didn't much feel like extending myself to understand the way other people felt. Not when it required all of this.

But I wanted to do that for her, my little witch. And when I thought of what she said in this way, I understood.

I pressed my lips to hers, offering that unspoken reassurance, and by the way hers molded to mine, she accepted.

After a few moments, we sat at the table, side-by-side, and began to eat. The sight of the lake and forest beyond was so familiar, I probably could have painted it from memory with great accuracy. But looking out upon it with Sylvie made it feel new. I always acknowledged its beauty, but the way the moon and stars reflected on the dark surface of the water was magical. We didn't talk, but where I normally would have felt a nagging obligation to fill the silence, I relaxed. Sylvie's satisfied 'Mmm's' while she ate and my hand resting on her thigh was just the right amount of communication between us.

She'd used the word 'perfect' to describe me, when I felt anything but. However, I would have used that word to describe this, with her.

After we finished eating, we lingered on the porch, eyes still on the land before us with the music from inside trickling out of the open back door.

Sylvie had her feet propped up in my lap, now, and I ran my hand over her smooth calf. "Are you ready for dessert?" I asked.

She shifted with confusion. "Did you make some?"

I shrugged and began to gather our empty plates back onto the tray. "In a way." She stood at the same time I did, and we went back into the cabin. If things were different, I would have kept us out there. Done this under the stars with the land I loved so much surrounding us.

But there was always chance of one of them lurking. And though they knew that she was mine and that we were together, I would not expose her to them in this way.

Instead, after placing the dishes in the deep, porcelain sink, I gestured toward the dining table. "Sit."

Sylvie eyed me curiously but did as I said. Well, she sat at one of the chairs, back to the kitchen, and watched me over her shoulder.

I couldn't hide my smirk, now, and her brows rose expectantly. I was banking on her enjoying this slight deception, and by her surprised but excited yelp when I pulled her chair back from the table, I was on the right track. My instincts flared, the ones that wanted to pin her down to draw out more of those little sounds, but I pushed them to the back of my mind.

Instead, I picked her up, hands palming her ass, and placed her where I'd intended. I settled myself into the chair and spread her legs while I scooted closer to her.

"Wha—" She began to ask but cut off her question with a gasp when I shoved the hem of her dress up to the middle of her thighs.

"Lie back, Sylvie."

Again, she did as she was told, and her obedience made my cock twitch. "This is my dessert?" Her blunt teeth bit at her bottom lip, and I wanted to take it in my mouth again, to feel the plush weight of it yield beneath my much sharper ones. But, there would be more time for that later.

I pulled her dress up further, so that the hem settled around her waist. Her panties were black and lacy, and I trailed a reverent finger on the edge that ran along her inner thigh.

Her arousal was one of the sweetest scents I'd ever beheld, and it was almost unbearable this close. That was part of the reason I didn't mind when she needed to take it slow at first. When I broke our kiss outside of the bar instead of turning her around and pounding her into the brick like I really wanted to do. When I kissed her and touched her over her clothes instead of tackling her to the ground and tearing off every shred of fabric that separated us.

My skin felt like it was on fire with the held-back urge. But it was a sacrifice I was more than willing to make. For her.

I shrugged while pulling her panties down and off her legs. My fingertips brushed against her all the way to her delicately arched feet, and I marveled at how different our skin was. Pale and deep, hard and soft. "Dessert, appetizer, whatever you want to call it."

She huffed a little chuckle, just before I palmed the underside of her thighs and placed them on my shoulders. I leaned in, letting the sight and aroma intoxicate me. My mouth was already watering before I took my first taste of her, and once my tongue made a long, wet drag over her entrance and clit, I knew that I was in deep, deep trouble. But, as I suppressed the urge for my claws to come out to pin her down on the table, I couldn't bring myself to care.

CHAPTER TWENTY-TWO

SYLVIE

Orion was insatiable. When he'd lifted and sat me down on the table, exposed me from the waist down, I didn't even have time to be self-conscious before my mind turned to a lust-fogged mess. Though we'd already had sex, this was an entirely new experience.

I writhed and arched while Orion's tongue worked in swirls and swipes that left me whimpering. The noises I was making were obscene and pathetic, but I could tell that he loved it. The way he would hold me tighter after a particular pass of his tongue made me moan.

My fingers pinched and plucked my nipples while he brought me through one, two, then three orgasms on his dining table. I'd told him that I wasn't much of a dessert person, but if this was his idea of a final course, I would certainly be a convert.

I was riding his face by the end, blinded by the pleasure he was drawing out of my body, and after that third time, he released my legs and stood over me.

I pried my eyes open, body still twitching with aftershocks, and I watched Orion's eyes rove over me. His chest heaved, fists and jaw clenching, while he took in my form that was certainly a complete mess. The glint in his spring green eyes and flaring of his nostrils was so far from the shy sweetness he'd shown me earlier tonight. It was a switch he flipped, and my navel fluttered again, excited and readying for when his control finally snapped.

Maybe that was why I said what I did. I raised my feet to rest on the surface of the table, brazenly presenting myself for his hungry eyes. It was as if I was under a spell. Or some new part of me had become unlocked, and now there was no turning her away.

"What are you going to do with me now, Orion?"

His eyes locked with mine as he planted his hands on either side of my hips. Orion leaned over me, his face taking on a heated expression that I'd never seen from him, even when we'd fumbled in the dark after he gave me his teeth. His mouth and chin were glistening, nearly dripping, with me, but he didn't even try to wipe himself clean.

"That all depends on you." He reached out a finger to trace the corner of my jaw. "I said I wanted to savor you, and I meant it. Are you going to be good for me? Let me take care of you?"

I nodded frantically, body aching for him to touch me again. "I'll be good for you, baby, please."

A low sound rumbled from him just before he lunged forward, crashing his lips onto mine. My fingers sunk into his soft hair while our mouths joined in a desperate symphony. I wrapped my legs around his waist to hold him close, and Orion responded by hoisting us up off of the table. My body bobbed in the air along with his steps, but I was too lost in the kiss, exploring every bit of his soft lips, to realize where we were until he dropped down to take a seat.

My stomach dipped in surprise, and I lifted my head to find we were in his bedroom, where the only light was that coming from the moon outside. With the wall of glass to my right, it felt like we were in our own world with nature surrounding us.

When I looked back down at him, this man that had come into

my life that I now didn't think I could live without, I felt those three words bubble up in my throat before being forced back by barriers of anxiety.

I ran a hand from his brow to his scalp, carding my fingers through his curls and clutching at his shirt with the other. Orion's hands were holding my hips until he brought his thumb to my mouth.

I sucked it in without command, without question, and swirled around the pad of his finger with my tongue.

"So beautiful. My little witch."

I shot a breath through my nose, still sucking on his thumb, and ground my naked hips into his clothed ones. He sat us on the end of his bed, and I was growing impatient. I'd already had a taste of what it felt like to have him inside of me, and I needed it. Now.

Orion made a sympathetic noise, brows turning upward. "Tell me what you want, Sylvie."

I released his thumb, letting a trail of my saliva fall down my face. Even in the dark, I was able to see Orion's pale face clearly, and again, it was like he was another person. Another version of himself that wasn't shy, wasn't grumbling. One that was… ravenous. "I want you to fuck me. Pl—"

My pleading ended on a startled yelp when Orion pulled down the neckline of my dress, exposing both of my breasts to the air heating between us. I gave another whimper as I watched him, without preamble, bend down to take my left nipple into his mouth. I untangled my feet from behind his back and shifted to kneel over his lap. I pressed up, feet tucked beneath me and on either side of his legs, to get even closer to him.

And he delivered, flicking his tongue while he nipped gently with his teeth. My hands pressed on the back of his head, holding him to me as I arched, groaning into the spacious room.

After nearly working me out of my mind, Orion switched to the other breast and pressed down on my waist. I relented, bending to sit down on his lap, and my eyes rolled all the way back when I felt the hard, warm press of his naked cock.

"Oh fuck, oh shit," I gritted through my teeth as my body moved over him like an animal in heat. The crown of his dick gave just the right amount of friction and pressure against my clit, and I shook while chasing the release that was so close, just out of my reach.

My nails nearly shred his shirt with how hard I clung to him, but he seemed to like that too, and a deep growl from Orion vibrating against my skin sent me over the edge. I went limp as the waves of pleasure thundered through me, my breathing almost pained with how good it felt. If he could do this to me now, I was almost scared of what was to come.

Orion gentled his kisses and licks and trailed them up my chest then settled at the mark that was always tender, always throbbing, when he was near.

"So sweet when you come for me. So good," he praised into my skin.

I scratched his back in answer while my mind was slowly pulling itself together from the pile of goop he'd left it in.

"Are you sleepy now, mo ghrá?"

I shook my head, kissed his brow. "Not yet." He smelled earthy and strong, like he belonged in the forest just beside us. It calmed something within me, made me feel like I could truly exhale.

My hips wriggled, body apparently revving up to go again, and Orion's dick was still hard between my legs. "I want you inside of me."

Instead of responding, Orion took the bottom of my dress and pulled it over my head. I reached my arms upward and finished what he started by throwing the dress across the room.

Then, it was only a matter of seconds before we were both pulling at his shirt, shoving down his jeans and boxers. My back met the firm mattress of his bed just before his body settled over mine.

We'd never been naked with each other before, never had so much contact between us. I felt greedy to touch and explore his strong shoulders and arms and the firm round ass that I'd ogled many, many times.

I opened my legs wider and wiggled until I felt him just a faint thrust away from finally giving me what I craved. His body was trembling over me, as if he was just a breath away from succumbing, and I took his jaw in my hands.

We'd talked about it briefly, and a bit awkwardly, but I felt like I needed to confirm this for him. "Please, Orion." I ran my finger over his brow that was pulled low over his eyes.

"You're sure?" he asked, and I just nodded, smiling up at this man that I was already so in love with. Did he feel that way about me, too? By the way he nodded along with me, face pained while he hooked a hand under my knee, I guessed that he did. He pressed my thigh to my chest, but I kept my eyes on his.

I let loose a helpless cry as he finally gave himself to me. Just an inch, and then another, Orion slowly entered me, and I knew. I knew that there was no going back. He was it—*this* was it. We savored each other, joining in this moment that erased all others before.

He was mine, and I was his. And when his hips finally met mine again, his cock buried and stretching me completely, I was truly home. With no barriers between us, I kissed Orion, letting him feel all the love I had in that moment where I was truly without words.

And I felt it from him, with the way his lips molded to mine, with the way his warmth became mine.

And when we started moving, his thrusts gradually becoming deeper, harder, I just held on and met him. Orion tucked his head into my neck, panting and kissing and groaning, and where before he'd fucked me like he couldn't take being apart for another second, I realized now what it meant to truly be made love to.

He turned me on my side, still holding my thigh, and entered again from behind. The trees and lake watched as we took each other, and the pressure built again.

I craned my neck and found him staring down at where our bodies joined, watching his cock thrust in, out, in, out.

"Don't stop, baby." My voice was breathy, desperate, and his chest rumbled into my back. It was already starting, my muscles going taut, when he looked back at me.

"*Fuck*. Come for me, Sylvie. Now," Orion groaned, and when his eyes met mine, they almost seemed to glow.

With his name on my lips, I did just that. The noises between our bodies were obscene and delicious, and I couldn't help myself from grinding my hips, chasing more, more, more.

He gave it to me, mouth dropped open until I claimed it with mine. I sucked on his tongue like I'd done his thumb earlier, and he answered by taking me in earth-shattering pulses.

My whole world felt like it was this, us, and soon, Orion broke our kiss to pant that he was close. We'd discussed that too, and though I was at the dangerous point of beyond caring, Orion pulled out just in time. With my leg hooked back around his hip, he fisted his cock while chanting my name like it was a prayer.

I clutched his head to my neck once again, this time while he painted my back and side. My nails scratched encouragingly on his scalp, holding him through his release.

A long time passed before our breaths calmed and Orion was able to speak. He passed his tongue along the bruises from his teeth. "*You* are perfect, Sylvie." And I couldn't help but blearily preen while wrapped in his arms.

Orion kissed me repeatedly on my neck and my cheek before gingerly untangling himself to grab a cloth to clean me with. I lay on my side, eyes still on the beautiful sight just beyond his windows, and felt content down to my bones. Once he returned, Orion wiped my skin clean, and after he disposed of the cloth in a laundry hamper that was hidden in the depths of a closet, he joined me on the bed.

He settled behind me and encircled my body in his arms once

again. My hair had nearly come loose from the tight topknot I'd secured it in before coming over, but I couldn't bring myself to fix it. Not with the drowsy peace that I felt in Orion's arms. Not to mention that my body felt absolutely spent.

"Thank you for making me dinner, baby," I grinned into the dark, "and my dessert."

He planted a kiss just behind my ear. "You're welcome. Though, that was a dessert for me, too."

"True," I teased, "you came very hard."

Orion nipped my earlobe and gave another low rumble. "And who was the one who came… was it four times?"

My smile grew, and I twisted around to look at him. "Five, I think. Well done, Dr. Gealach." My finger bopped him softly on the nose, and he huffed, shaking his head to clear my tickling. "So, what's next?"

"Next?"

I shrugged my shoulders as much as I could in this position. "I mean, it's probably only like eight o'clock. Don't tell me you're so much of a grandpa that you go to bed this early."

Orion turned me onto my back and caged me in between his arms. Despite thinking my body was done for the night, I felt my navel flutter again in anticipation. Though it was a far cry from when he pinned me down outside of Vinny's, I could acknowledge that both times, I felt excited at the thought of being under his mercy.

Instead of baring his teeth at me, Orion smirked and placed a kiss on my forehead. "No, I usually grade papers or read far later than I should. What would you like to do?"

"Hm…" I contemplated then had a devious idea. If he was so set on treating me, taking care of me, maybe he'd give me my way on this, too. "We could watch a movie?"

He took a deep breath and narrowed his eyes. "What kind of movie, Sylvie."

I ran my finger in little swirls on his chest, feeling the thin patch of translucent hair there. "Well, we could do that slasher film I told you about... unless you're finally ready to watch *Twi*—"

Orion groaned like I'd punched him in the gut. "Oh, please, anything but that."

"Okay, great! Slasher film it is." And I gave him my most winning smile before smacking a kiss on his lips.

CHAPTER TWENTY-THREE

ORION

Sylvie's eyes were wide with rapt attention at the killer chasing the female protagonist through the graveyard. I was reluctant to admit that the film was quite entertaining, but what drew my focus more was the way Sylvie reacted to it.

She hyped the film up to me as one of the best horror movies to come out in recent years. I had little to no frame of reference for that, but, despite her sweet exterior, my little witch loved all things scary.

Though she'd already seen the movie in theaters, I watched curiously as she flinched at the first stab in the character's back. More gore and blood painted the screen, and though she had the urge to look away, Sylvie's heart rate and scent picked up in the way she normally did when she was excited.

"You're going to miss details if you keep watching me like that, baby," she droned without taking her eyes off of the carnage. I huffed and tried my best to refocus on being frightened. About halfway through the movie, my phone began buzzing on the coffee table. That was the second time this week Meredith had called me, and I promptly ignored the call, as I had done all the others.

Sylvie was tucked into my side with a mug of hot chocolate in her hands, though it had long gone cold. I balanced a bowl of popcorn on my lap, but it seemed I was the only one that remembered to eat any. She was sucked in, my Sylvie, and I had to admit that the movie wasn't terrible. Though, I was able to quickly deduce the identity of the killer, which I whispered to Sylvie fifteen minutes into the film. Much to her chagrin.

Once the credits began to roll, we turned off the television—it was one that mimicked a painting when turned off, and Sylvie marveled at it for at least ten minutes when I'd shown her the deception—and began to get ready for bed.

The pleasant pattering of Sylvie and I walking about the house was a rhythm I didn't realize I would welcome or love as much as I did. We worked with a familiar ease while she helped me put mugs and the popcorn bowl in the dishwasher, fold the blanket we'd sat under while sitting on the couch, and turn off all the lights inside and outside. It was a lengthy and pleasant routine as I put things back just so, making sure my appliances and kitchen utensils were lined up and in their proper places, that the blanket was placed in its particular perch on the couch. But Sylvie followed my direction without question, just with sweet enthusiasm.

I watched curiously while she spread creams and serums on her face while I brushed my teeth, the large bathroom feeling less cavernous with both of us standing before the mirror. It had been nearly a decade since I'd spent the night with someone, and, though I had been excitedly anticipating tonight, I'd worried that I wouldn't enjoy sharing my space with someone. But it was Sylvie, and her sweet, calming scents, and her acceptance of when I didn't have words to say. She would fill the silence or just let it lie, and the only one I'd ever felt peace like this was with my father when I was a child.

I reached a hand to organize the glass bottles and hair cream jars she'd brought, only to pull back at the last second. Instead of chastising or ignoring my urge, she encouraged me to put them wherever, and I breathed a sigh of relief when I restored order to the counter. I organized her things by type and size, and the knot in my chest loosened.

I couldn't contain my smile as I watched her braid her hair and secure a silk scarf over it for the night. Though my father's mother died when I was quite young, the action reminded me of her.

We settled in bed with more than a few yawns erupted between us. It was another first for us, but our bodies found and fit together seamlessly. And when her lips snagged mine with an urgency that was only emphasized by her scent, I found myself staring up at Sylvie as she rode my dick with languid waves of her hips. The oversized *Nightmare on Elm Street* t-shirt was falling off her shoulder so that I had a perfect view of my mark while she threw her head back as she came.

I was in love with her. It was so clear with the way I yearned for her, with how my mind, so set in its ways, opened willingly and eagerly to let her in. Now that her scent was mixed with mine in this house, I wanted it to stay. To go to bed with her every night, to watch all the violent films she wanted, to cook her every meal.

Sylvie's body constricted around me, and I felt my release race down my spine. Her needy little sounds were almost cruel in how my instincts delighted in them. But it also made me want to lose control so badly. To pin her down and rut into her until she screamed. To truly lose ourselves and make her body lock onto mine.

But I couldn't. It was difficult to maintain the dual awareness, but I managed. After she came, I flipped Sylvie on her back and knelt over her. I hiked up her shirt and came over her belly instead of inside her.

The look on her face was still sweet, though, and having her in my arms as we eventually fell asleep made it so, so worth it.

When we woke in the morning, I inhaled her sleep-warm scent

like it was a drug. To watch the sunrise reflect in her deep brown eyes was another spell she'd put on me. Because I was now addicted to this. To her passing caresses and kisses while we dressed for our respective classes that morning and while I made us breakfast.

Though I knew it bothered her, Sylvie sat with me on the back porch again, munching on her avocado toast, while I smoked my first cigarette of the day.

I packed us travel mugs of coffee, and I offered to drive us both to campus since we were going to the same place, anyway. And if she saw my attempt at her returning to my home later today, perhaps for her to spend the night again, she didn't comment on it. She just agreed and gave me another generous grin.

We'd been driving in relative silence, with my melodic commute playlist soft between us, when she turned to me and spoke. "Um, Orion?"

My attention zeroed in on the shift in her ease. It may have been because we were nearing the college, but she'd repeatedly spoken of how much she enjoyed her classes. My hands squeezed on the steering wheel, and I tried my best to concentrate on her scent, her words, and the road before us at the same time.

"Yeah?"

She took a bracing breath which just made my anxiety spike even more. If anything, Sylvie often shortened her breaths when she was upset. "Will you… get in trouble for being with me?"

We were stopped at a light just a few streets from the Department of English, and I took the opportunity to turn to her. My brow knit low over my eyes, but I forced my hands to relax on the wheel. "What do you mean?" The thought of anyone taking her away from me was making rage flare underneath my skin.

"Well," she ran a hand over her hair to smooth it, but I knew she did this repeatedly when she was nervous, "since you're a professor, and I'm a student in your department. Even with me not being a student of *yours*."

The light before us turned green, and I pointedly turned back to face forward. My shoulders relaxed. "I doubt it, but I was going to disclose our relationship to the head of the department once they get back in town next week."

"Oh." She deflated.

"As long as you're all right with that? With people knowing."

And then I felt the soft press of her lips on my cheek. When she sat back in her seat, Sylvie smelled back to her normal state. "Of course, baby. I just didn't want to jeopardize your position or anything."

I scoffed. "If they ended up having a problem with it, I wouldn't care."

I felt her wide eyes on me while I pulled into a faculty spot behind the building. "Are you sure? I couldn't ask you to possibly—"

"You are more important to me than all of this." I waved one hand at the building in front of us while turning my car off with the other. I pivoted in my seat to see her eyes shimmering, a blush creeping up on her cheeks, and a soft smile playing at her lips.

"Okay, baby. Thank you."

I leaned over the console and pressed my lips to hers quickly but firmly. Everything I told her was the truth. Before we'd gone on our first date, I'd looked into the department and college policies on such matters. And if it somehow backfired on me... oh well.

My studies and my career were important to me, of course. After my disastrous attempt at having the pack life, they'd been my only companion. But now, as I looked to Sylvie—'girlfriend' felt too flippant of a word for what I felt for her—I knew that I would give up everything if it meant she was safe and happy.

Based on what I felt in my soul, and on all the accounts I'd read, that was love.

Maybe it was too soon—it'd only been a month and a half of dating. Perhaps it was an inappropriate time. One where I should have constructed a private, intimate moment to share my feelings towards her. But being around Sylvie helped me feel free of second-guessing my lack of social graces. She understood.

I kissed her one more time, and when our lips pulled back, I couldn't hold the words to myself any longer. Telling her that she was my mate would come later. This, though, I could do. It felt as natural as shifting to tell her, "I love you."

She gave a little gasp, a sharp inhale of air, but I didn't have time to grow worried because the deepest, sweetest aroma flooded my senses. Sylvie brought both of her hands to my face, and she passed her nose over mine back and forth. If I hadn't been in my human form, my tail would have been wagging ferociously.

"I love you too, Orion." When she pulled back, her smile was brighter than any sun or moon rise. "Thank you for being so amazing. I'm so happy with you." And then she laughed merrily, like being mine was as much a gift as being hers was to me.

I kissed the round tip of her nose and tucked a stray lock of her hair behind her ear, "I'm ridiculously happy with you, too. Happier than I've ever been."

And when we exited my car and entered the building for the day, I remarked on how that night we met now felt like such a blessing. Even with the troubles I still faced, having Sylvie in my life made it feel brighter, worth living.

CHAPTER TWENTY-FOUR

JASPER

The knot in my stomach didn't seem to loosen anymore these days. Not when I was running, not when I was working, and I just ended up tossing and turning when I was trying to sleep.

Our Pack Leader's pacing was not helping. He got on edge between every solstice and equinox, but this was the worst I'd seen him since we started all of this. The relief after the last one was short-lived, and I knew that my hours of scouting the witches was for nothing at this point.

"What do we do now? They're mated." I complained and picked under my fingernails. The four of us were gathered at his house, trying to think through our options and coming up with too many that weren't as attractive as the one we'd been working toward for a while.

He grunted and continued to pace. I was his best scout and still hadn't come up with someone that was a good enough replacement. *He* wanted her specifically. The winter solstice was the most important one, he said, and we'd all been feeling the pressure to get this right. Snow still hadn't fallen this year, but I could feel it coming. The weeks were ticking by, and while I worked long hours at Dad's store, my mind just kept running around and around with nothing to show for it.

I went to the kitchen and grabbed two beers, knowing that he would want one, too. Just like I thought, he reached for the proffered bottle immediately. When he thanked me with a tight nod, I felt my chest puff up with pride. I was the Leader's right hand, even rising further than Dad who'd been a member of the pack since he moved to town in his early twenties.

Graham muttered something under his breath before taking a long gulp from the bottle. I took a sip myself before daring to ask him to repeat what he just said.

"Not claimed," he muttered again, eyes gazing forward but not focused on his audience. After Graham challenged our old Leader and took over, he'd changed his inner circle to us. No one left the pack, but there was a definite divide between all of us. But they just didn't understand. We were moving the pack forward, cementing our ownership of the territory and us as the guardians of Antler Pointe Forest.

It took me a few minutes to digest what Graham was saying, but while I was blinking at him, trying to understand those two words, Ana uncrossed her legs and leaned forward beside me. "She's his mate but isn't claimed?" Her face was twisted in the same confusion that I felt, but the knot in my gut was moving and flexing. Growing.

When he refocused on the three of us on the sunken leather couch, he still looked half a world away. "He says that she's his mate, but there's no true claiming bite. Can't you smell it?" His lips started curling up, and he took another sip from his bottle, nodding to himself.

Graham began spouting off more explanation, but I still couldn't move past the first thing. The most important detail. "But —" I interrupted "—she's not shifter. Not Wolf. She *can't* be bitten unless he wants to risk turning her. So..." I opened my free hand in a helpless gesture. Two of us here had parents in the same boat.

Mom wasn't a shifter, and neither was Declan's dad. Though some shifters didn't fully recognize it, they were still our parents' mates, claiming bite or not.

Instead of pausing, seeing my reasoning, and turning to other options, Graham stopped before me, looming and narrowing his eyes. Mine automatically dropped to the beaten wood floor, and my cheeks blazed with what was to come.

"Are you questioning my leadership, Jasper?" His Leader scent was raining down on me, hot and suffocating, and I swallowed back the whine that tried to erupt from my throat. This was the third time since the coffee shop that he'd accused me of doing such, but this was the first time that... I realized I actually was.

But Graham was a good Pack Leader, bringing in more members, strengthening our foothold on the land, and aligning us with beings more powerful than we'd ever imagined. We were stronger and more connected to the forest. If—if this was the way to do it, I could understand. I had to.

"No, Leader. I'm behind you. We are behind you." I spoke to the floor, and the others muttered their agreement. We bowed to and would follow our Pack Leader to the end. We were the most loyal, and if taking her was what needed to be done—what *he* would want—then we would do it.

There was a tense moment where I wondered if he'd try to make an example of me, but eventually, the onslaught of the dominant scent receded, and so did the sight of his pristine Air Force One's. I let out a large, silent exhale.

Graham and the others began discussing plans, solstice and otherwise, and I nodded along, trying to ignore the knot that had just doubled in size instead of shrinking. We were still moving forward with our original solstice plan.

Another hunt, another kill, another blessing. Because we *were* blessed. And she would be the most important one yet. My mouth watered, remembering how the surge of power felt. When *he* would bless us and further our connection to the land.

Memories of hanging out with her and my old crew from

middle school flitted through my mind, but I shoved them back. Just like I had to do for Kara, Wes, and River.

Not claimed, the glint in Graham's eye when he came to that conclusion stayed stamped behind my eyes long after I left his place and drove home. Orion wasn't pack but he was Wolf, and he'd marked her as his mate. Just like Dad had done Mom. Would we admit this to the others? Though they all consented to Graham's ruling that all Other Wolves were forbidden to run on our land, I could tell that most didn't harbor any ill will toward Orion. In fact, some spoke of him and his family fondly when they thought the four of us weren't listening.

But surely Graham had already thought of that, because he thought of everything. I just couldn't remember. I'd been too preoccupied—all of this was stressful, but once this was over, we'd be able to relax.

Unless it was gonna start back the next equinox. When... when were we blessed enough?

I shook that thought away while I climbed out of the car and headed up the stairs to my apartment. Graham solved our problem, and I was grateful. Scouting was what I was best at, and I would continue to do it so that we could plan the right time. And we would feel *his* power and all its healing, and all of this would be worth it.

"Yeah." I nodded to myself while I unlocked my door and stepped inside my place. Yeah, we would be good.

CHAPTER TWENTY-FIVE

SYLVIE

The music from the record player was as buttery as the dim light in the room. The fire Orion had set was a pleasant crackling that seemed to be in tune with the increasing bubbling of the kettle he set on the stove.

I hugged my arms tighter to myself as I padded into the main area of Orion's home, and I tried to imagine a younger version of him. With the mop of white curls like in the childhood photos, maybe nose buried in a book while sitting hunched but relaxed on the old leather sofa. I ran my fingers over the back cushion, picturing him tinkering away with his father, working on this house that he'd told me they built with their two hands.

He palmed my waist from behind, and I melted. Orion's arms circled around my torso, his warmth evident even through his thick flannel shirt that I'd thrown on after waking up from my doze. After Orion drove us both to campus, I'd called home to ask Granna if she'd mind me being away for another night. When she'd scoffed and chastised me for even entertaining the notion that she wouldn't, I called Roz and asked her to check up on

Granna tonight, maybe feigning a spontaneous desire to have dinner.

Before I could text Orion or find him in the building to ask if it would be all right if I spent the night again, he texted me during my second class that morning.

ORION

I'll be done around 4 today and have no plans tonight. Would you want to stay over again?

Though his directness had been off-putting during our first encounters, I was now grateful for this quality. It lessened my anxiety substantially, and having his declaration of love also didn't hurt. One night of having the explicit realization and subsequent agonizing over whether I should tell him was enough for me. It was like he couldn't bear to be any other way besides honest, and it was one of the things I loved most about him.

Now, Orion kissed the curve of my neck, where the mark of his teeth still hadn't faded even though he'd never broken the skin.

Maybe it was barbaric, but I liked having that signal that he had been there. That I'd let him close enough to do that. "You should let me mark *you*," I snickered aloud, but Orion's answering grumble vibrated both of our bodies.

I worried that I said the wrong thing until he answered, voice low for reasons other than sleepiness, "Don't make promises you don't intend to keep, Sylvie."

I spun around in his arms and wrapped mine over his neck. My cheek pressed into the hollow of his throat. "Who says I don't?"

He stilled, and I noticed his breaths quickened just slightly. "You would... want to do that?"

My lips pulled back, and I knew he could feel my smile on his bare skin. "Sure, if you'd let me." It felt a bit ridiculous, to want to give each other what were a lot like hickeys but not. Something about it felt right, though.

Orion lifted his hands to my face and pulled it back. I gazed up at him, and his brows were drawn in an expression I couldn't decipher. "I never… asked you whether this was okay."

I suppressed the shiver his fingertip trailing the mark of his teeth drew out of me. His green apple eyes flickered with longing and shame, so I tapped the pad of my finger against his lips to get his attention. "I like it."

"Why?" His lips turned down beneath my touch.

I shrugged. "I don't know. Feels right. Don't worry about it." I wasn't going to start distrusting my intuition now that I was determined to follow it.

Orion pursed his lips as I brought my hand back to clasp with the other behind his neck. I took the time to take him in, this man whose eyelashes were so white that it looked like he'd been standing in the snow, flakes collecting and tips freezing.

"If you did that, Sylvie, you'd never be rid of me."

It took me a moment to turn over his words. His face was serious, but I wasn't being flippant. Not at all—I just couldn't understand why it felt like he was constantly warning me. "Is that a bad thing?" Was this his way of telling me that he didn't want *me* in that way? But, no, he'd just told me this morning that he loved me.

Had it really only been this morning? It felt as easy as breathing to imagine Orion being by my side for the foreseeable future and beyond. Even without Josie's prediction.

He brought his hand to my chest and rested it over the beating of my heart. "Be careful what you say to me, Sylvie. I already see you as mine. If you did the same to me, that would make it true."

"Oh, goodness, Orion." I smacked a quick kiss on his lips before dropping my hands. "If you don't want me to, just say that."

His finger made one more circle around the mark. "Sylvie, if you marked me, I wouldn't be able to drop to my knees fast enough. You'd have me crawling behind you for the rest of both of our lives and after."

I shuddered with pleasure, with another surge of that sense of rightness. We hadn't been together that long, but the thought of Orion with me forever was one I wanted to make real.

I lifted his hand off my chest, kissed his knuckles, and then rubbed my cheek over them. "Be sure that *you* are ready for that."

A low grumbly sound emanating from his throat was the only warning I had before my back flopped onto the supple leather sofa, nearly knocking the air out of me. Orion looked down on me with eyes wilder than I'd ever seen them. He swept his nose around mine over and over, and I spread my naked thighs for him to settle between them. Before I could run my hands over his chiseled arms, his chest, he brought my wrists together in the cage of one hand and held them above my head. My heart picked up excitedly, and I couldn't stop my hips from writhing and trying to meet the tenting of his pajama pants.

"I've been ready for you to claim me since the night we met, Sylvie." And then his mouth was on mine in a staggering, smashing kiss that was a mess of tongue and teeth. I moaned, taking it all and still demanding more. My heels pressed against the backs of his thighs, pulling him closer.

I felt the back of his other hand fumble against my inner thigh, and then it was the unmistakable steel rod of his cock. His hips were making small thrusts already, and the moisture already dripping from him swept across my leg. He was holding himself back, arms straining with tension, but I was already nodding, squirming. Anything to get him closer.

So when he finally seated himself in one, long, breathtaking thrust, I did nothing but flex my own hips to make sure he got as deep as possible.

He arched upward when our bodies met in a resounding, confirming, thud. The veins of his neck were bulging, the muscles above his shoulders straining with his ragged moan. And what I did next felt again like the most primal version of myself. Someone that had been resting in the depths of my soul, suddenly out of their slumber to confirm that this was what I needed.

My back strained with my hands still held against the cushions, and my teeth clamped around the soft skin around his collarbone. Coppery blood met my tongue. Maybe if I weren't already overcome with lust, I would have worried that I was doing this wrong. That his mark hadn't drawn blood, so maybe mine wasn't supposed to.

But Orion let loose a deep, inhuman noise while I stayed latched onto him, and his body started up a pounding that would've sent me slipping across the couch if he weren't holding me down.

The sweet, slow lovemaking we'd had earlier was nowhere to be found as I pushed back against Orion's hips, making the savage connection between us even deeper.

He flipped me over in one swift movement and released my hands so that I could prop up on them and my knees. Some of his blood was trailing down my chin, but I wanted it there. To have the confirmation of my mark.

Sharp nails scraped against one of my hips, and when I felt the prickling of more against the nape of my neck, I didn't have any time to question it before he was back inside me.

The smack of Orion's skin against mine was almost as loud as the whistling of the tea kettle. I didn't know when it'd started, but we both continued to ignore it. "Sylvie." His voice wasn't just low anymore. It was an impossible bass, like the distortion of a recording, but it just deepened the burning I felt for him. For not just this rutting that would leave me with beautiful bruises, but for everything he was. For everything I felt allowed to be with him.

My mouth tried to function enough to say his name, but it just came out in choked grunts while I continued to push back to make us fuck as hard as we could. To chase the height of the ecstasy that was ramping higher and higher.

Until it crashed into me on the tail of a shattering thrust. My arms gave, and I cried out, face pressed into the leather. It was like a crack of lightning with the following roll of thunder, and distantly, I heard Orion give his own, anguished groan. His rhythm descended into short, stuttering pulses just before I felt him brush my hair back and away from my neck. His shirt was rucked up toward my shoulders, and he pulled out just before I felt him come on my exposed skin.

"Mmm," I mumbled once he finished spilling over me. My legs were trembling, but I also felt like there was no way I'd be able to steadily get up from the couch. Instead, I flattened completely onto my stomach with a contented sigh.

Orion rubbed his fingers over my sides, scraping sensation now gone, and if I could've started purring, I would have.

I felt him shift behind me just before he wiped me up and pulled the shirt back down.

"Would you get the kettle, please?" I grumbled into the couch. The screeching of it was cutting into the afterglow, an annoying pitch that I now couldn't help but notice. My eyes were closed, but the glowing of the fire brightened the inside of my eyelids. Under the melodic singing from the record player, I heard Orion's feet padding quietly across the space.

The whistling cut off, and I sighed in relief. It took the entire length of time of him retreating into his bedroom once again then clinking away in the kitchen for me to sit myself up. I smoothed my hair down as best I could, but I knew it was still a mess.

Giving up, I pulled it into a thick bun at the crown of my head that would surely fall out at the first quick movement.

Orion rounded the couch, and the aroma of hot chocolate preceded him by just a few seconds before he sat carefully beside me. With his pickiness and deft making of pasta from scratch, I was surprised that he'd elected to make the powdered stuff, but I wasn't mad in the slightest to have the hot, sweet drink.

Orion's hair was significantly messier too, and it made me smile. I briefly noticed that he had changed into different pajamas, but the deep bruising on his shoulder completely stole my attention.

I absently grasped the drink he offered me and brought a tentative finger to hover over where my teeth had sunk into his flesh. The white skin on his chest was marred by the purple and red mark—*did I truly bite him* that *hard?* It looked like it hurt tremendously, and my eyes started to burn at the thought that I'd inflicted pain onto him.

He was sitting perfectly still, but when I hesitantly touched the corner of the bite, he shuddered. My hand flew back, and I almost spilled the hot chocolate all over my lap. "I'm sorry." I bit my lip and tried to blink away the tears that were rising.

Orion set his mug on the thick, wooden coffee table in front of us and placed a warm hand on my cheek. I avoided looking in his eyes, and he didn't force me to. But he didn't let me go. "Don't be, Sylvie. You've given me a gift."

A tear escaped the corner of my eye, and I shook my head as much as I could with him holding me. "But I did it too hard. I hurt you. And you didn't make this one bleed." I waved to gesture at my neck. "I'm sorry." The first time he'd bitten and scratched me, when he was injured and visibly shaken, I hadn't felt the sting until I got home. And by the next week, all evidence of it was gone. The one that remained on my skin would get tender, more than anything. But, still.

The bite I'd given him looked particularly violent against his pale skin.

Orion plucked the mug from my grip and set it down next to his. When he turned back around to face me again, he brought his lips to my brow, and another tear trailed down my cheek. "I know you don't fully understand, but it doesn't hurt. At all. I told you that if you marked me that it would make you mine. It makes me yours, too." He took a deep inhale. "I've never belonged to anyone before."

My mouth twisted in sympathy at his words, even with the confused turn of my eyes. I bumped his nose with mine, which he returned. "As long as it isn't painful."

He smiled almost self-consciously. "No… ah, it feels good."

I huffed. "Now you know how I feel." I wondered if Granna would be able to tell me why that was. It almost felt ritualistic.

Surely it must have meant something? Or maybe we both just liked being bitten. Josie would have a field day with that one if I told her.

He flicked his pinky finger over the edge of the mark on my neck, and of course, my body vibrated with the shiver that raced down my spine. Orion kissed me deeply, but it wasn't like before. It felt like a nonverbal confirmation of all his feelings toward me, and I tried my best to communicate the same. His tongue swiped at my lips and the skin around them, wiping up his blood that'd dripped down my face.

"You can mark me any time you want, Sylvie. Bite me as hard as you—" his eyes went a little distant, searching but unseeing until he blurted "—what did you mean I didn't make *this one* bleed?"

Something in his tone made my heart pick up. When his eyes refocused and met mine, he looked almost... panicked? "Um..."

I didn't want him to feel bad, because it wasn't a big deal *at all*. It really wasn't anything. You couldn't even tell where it had happened. "Sylvie," his hold on my face tightened a little, and I returned my gaze back to his, "what are you talking about?"

My teeth worried at my bottom lip, and now his eyes were widening, mouth parted slightly in horror. "I—well," I took a steadying breath, "when I found you behind Vinny's. I was trying to ch-check you for wounds and help you, but, but, you..."

"*Where, Sylvie.*" He was almost shouting now, and I couldn't help but cringe.

"Um," I waggled my left elbow, "just on the inside of my arm —" He dropped my face and tore the sleeve of his shirt, right up the seam. Though the air in the cabin was warm, goosebumps raised on my skin almost immediately.

Orion ran his frantic touch over the skin, examining it. He turned my arm over again and again, and his chest was rising with quick, worried breaths. This was why I didn't want to tell him. It made me feel incredibly silly—there wasn't a scar to be seen.

My words came out rushed. "It's nothing, baby, okay? You can't even tell. And you were hurt and panicking. I didn't really even notice until I got home."

He gave a miserable whimper and lowered his brow to my arm. The sound made my heart crack, and fat tears welled and fell down my cheeks. Today had been perfect, so, so perfect, and now it had fully shifted into this.

"I'm so sorry, Sylvie. I never," his voice was trembling, "thought…"

"Orion," I rubbed my hand over his back in a slow, soothing pattern, "please don't feel bad. I didn't mention it because I didn't want you to get upset over something you hadn't even realized you'd done. Especially when I'm perfectly fine."

His pained, horrified eyes raised to look at me, and more tears fell from mine at the sight of his threatening to spill over. "It's not nothing, Sylvie. I—I—"

"Baby, it's been months. I'm fine, and I just want to drink our hot chocolate—"

He frowned, eyes almost narrowing while they raced between my face, my neck, and my arm. "It… *has* been months. H-have you been feeling any differently? Strange?"

Now I was confused. "No… should I be?" Something was nudging at the back of my mind, but Orion's distress was taking all of my attention.

Orion lurched up to my neck again, and I automatically arched, making room for him. He took a long, deep inhale through his nose. His exhale was almost impatient before he took another whiff of my skin, now clutching me as closely as possible. A new sense of foreboding crept over me. Had I been so blind?

"Um… is everything okay?"

"You—you're sure that you feel all right?" He spoke into my neck, but his breaths seemed to be calming. I kept rubbing his back.

"Of course. Just kind of worried that you're not okay. Or that, um, we're not okay?"

He kissed my neck again until he was trailing up to my lips. After many sweet, reassuring pecks, my own trepidation had fallen away almost completely. Orion pulled me into an embrace and leaned back into the couch, taking me with him.

I rested curled into his warm body and closed my eyes. "We're better than okay, Sylvie. I'm sorry I scared you. I love you," he whispered over me.

My body relaxed into him even more. "I love you too. And it's fine." I chuckled. "You just had me panicking that you were a vampire or something." I couldn't bring myself to mention the other words that were growing in my mind. I did, however, notice Orion stilling around me for a moment, but then he took up caressing with reverent tenderness. Maybe he didn't understand my joke. *Yeah, that was it*, I lied to myself. The alternative meant that the bite marks were surely more than just glorified hickeys.

The alternative meant that he didn't trust me.

But, he'd said we were good, better than okay, and that was all I needed to hear.

PART TWO
SET

CHAPTER TWENTY-SIX

SYLVIE

I poked my finger at the tender flesh of my arm, gently prodding the bandage over the incision.

"You're gonna mess it up if you keep doing that." Josie eyed me warily over the metal table between us.

I quickly dropped my hand, eyes going wide. "Are you sure?" Granna had reminded me thrice now that nothing a seer saw was set in stone, but I wasn't about to take any chances. Even when the birth control implant felt weird and foreign under my skin.

Josie snorted and dipped a french fry into the extra aioli she'd ordered with her panini. Luckily, my new doctor's office was close to her apartment, so the appointment gave me an excuse to ask her to lunch afterward. Not that I needed one, per se, but I'd been avoiding broaching the topic of witchcraft with my best friend. Each time I tried to hint at my wish for a fellow student or for her to try reading my cards again, she got all fidgety and changed the subject.

But, as I felt my own abilities growing, I started to notice them in others as well. Just a few people in town, one in my creative writing class, carried the whiff of witchcraft. To me, it smelled like berries and sage.

Josie smelled, *very* much, like berries and sage.

She snorted. "Uh, *no*, I was just joking. What's with you?" She dropped her fry back on her plate. "Are you feeling funny from the appointment? Should I take you home?"

I took a worried sip of my water. "No, nothing like that. I... I've got a lot on my mind."

"Like...?" she drawled.

Like not knowing how to approach you about your super cool powers or the fact that there is a wolf shifter pack that most likely has something to do with Kara's death—not to mention the two others that were missing (probably dead)—or that the man I love is probably a wolf shifter, too.

Because, yeah, I'd figured that much out as well.

The territorial nature, the sounds he sometimes made, especially in the throws of ecstasy. How when he took me from behind, he seemed to let go even more, to the point that I could feel prickles of what felt like claws on my back. The marks and how mine warmed every time he was around. How Orion shivered every time I touched his that had now healed to a dark scar. Among his organizing and tapping, I noticed him rubbing over the mark for comfort when he was stressed.

I'd be foolish to write them off as a meaningless gesture—the bond I felt in my chest appeared the night he'd let me mark him. It was different from the pull, like it was always seeking him out, pointing me to him. And when we were together? It felt like my soul was singing. Over the weeks, I'd caught Orion purring in his sleep while he had his arms wrapped around me, and my own chest rumbled in kind. If I weren't who I was, it would've been strange.

But, I was still whispering with the mushrooms who told me about a gray wolf that walked around near the house, though it never got too close. They spoke of snow coming. They mentioned the white wolf visiting the house.

Unlike Josie's berry and sage, Orion was a wildly good scent of earth and wind and warmth. Last Monday, after spending the previous evening at his place, Orion watched me dress with smug satisfaction and helped me pull one of his sweatshirts over my head. Did I complain about the cold that didn't really bother me to justify my stealing his sweatshirt for the day? Maybe.

When I argued that it was because whatever cologne he used smelled too damn good, he gave me a funny look, brows upturned in confusion, and stated that he didn't wear cologne because it was too overstimulating. Even with what Granna told me, I asserted that he was joking with me. I even chuckled while rifling through his bathroom to find the hidden bottle of whatever expensive scent he wore. However, I really did find nothing, and when I emerged from the bathroom to admit defeat, he wasn't meeting my eyes again. As if doing so would allow me to see too much.

But, I'd already been starting to suspect. And I would bet good money that Orion didn't spend his camping trips sleeping in tents. Really—how had I not thought about it before? Maybe because I was so in love with him that his hypothetical ability to shift into a wolf didn't matter.

What mattered was his lack of trust in me to say anything. What was I doing wrong? What had I said to make him hesitate? I would never try to wrestle the secret from him, but dammit, I was going to show him that he could trust in me.

Over the past few weeks, I'd opened up to him more about my writing and studies. I asked his advice on my works in progress, and I showed him my practice in Granna's garden. That, too, was more evidence. When I demonstrated my growing powers, Orion didn't sputter or run away. He just kissed me silly, smile wide and praising after he watched me ripen and mature the okra and peppers Granna had growing in her vegetable garden. Two days ago, I'd even shown up with a basket of all my harvest spoils, and he'd made it into a delicious meal before fucking me into oblivion before his fireplace.

That time, while my legs were on his shoulders, I begged him to come in me, so far gone that I couldn't hold back my desire to feel even closer to him. The request made him arch his neck and groan while he pounded into me even harder, but when the time came for him to finish, he pulled out and spilled over my labia and inner thighs. Before I could initiate a conversation about it, let him know that I could always just get on birth control so that it wouldn't be an issue, he bent forward, started lapping at his own cum on my clit, and then proceeded to eat me out until I came twice more.

The next morning, though, I was determined. I made an appointment to get the implant. To eliminate another barrier between us.

I tried not to think about the thing under my skin, rationalizing that there was no way I'd be able to keep up with a pill or stomach something being lodged inside my uterus. There were other options, I knew, but I'd been too anxious to weigh them all.

I shoved a forkful of salad into my mouth and forced myself to chew, swallow. "Well," I took a deep breath and let it rush out, "I've been working on my craft with Granna, and I've been learning a lot, and I kind of, um, have reason to believe that you'd be good at it, too, and it would be so, so cool to have someone learning with me..." I looked up, and, though Josie's shoulders were drawn in trepidation, her eyes were still with me. So, I continued, "*And*, okay, please don't freak out, but," I lowered my voice in case the near-vacant restaurant had listening ears, "I think you might... be like me."

After a long, long pause, wherein she started to nervously swirl her french fry in ketchup, she answered. Her shaved hair was a neon, tennis ball green, and it seemed even brighter under the restaurant lights. She lifted a glance toward me. "Like, bisexual?" Josie tried at a lame joke, and I felt my shoulders relax. Okay, so she wasn't mad.

"You know what I mean."

Josie worried at her top lip, then abandoned her fries

completely and dropped her hand to rest beside her plate. Her heavily lined eyes searched mine, and I caught the shimmering of emerging tears. I took her hand, and, following the pull I felt in my chest, I focused on Josie's calm. On her rest.

Her features softened, bleached brows no longer pinching. "I... Sylvie, I," she shook her head but then pressed on, "do you remember that summer where I went... M.I.A.?"

We'd been sixteen at the time. After daily texts or phone calls, Josie's end suddenly went dark just a week before I was set to visit with Granna. Neither she nor her mother answered the phone when I tried to call, and when I'd driven to her house, no one answered the doorbell. It clouded the rest of my visit with Granna and incited not one, but two panic attacks.

I didn't say that, though. I'd never told her how worried I'd been. Now, with her hand in mine, I just nodded. "My mom, she... I've always... seen stuff. Sometimes known about things before they happen. It scared her, and so it scared me, too. To the point that she checked me into a hospital."

I sucked in a breath, calming energy stuttering for a moment until I regained my composure. How could she not have said anything? "And when *that* didn't work, she tried priests and homemade remedies, and then..." Josie sniffed and rubbed at her nose. "I just couldn't take it anymore. So I pretended it went away."

My thumb rubbed gentle passes on the back of her hand, and she held me tighter. "Oh, honey," I whispered softly. How could I not have seen this? Josie had moved back to Antler Pointe and cared for her mother through her sudden stint with breast cancer.

I'd always wondered why she stayed after her mother passed away.

"Josie, I don't want to bring up traumatic memories for you. I'm so sorry."

She fully looked up at me, now, and I exhaled, seeing the small smile on her face. There was a hint of fear still in her eyes, but there was something else there, too. Maybe hope. Maybe excitement. "Don't be. I've been trying to avoid it, but... maybe it would help. To learn about all this. To maybe not feel crazy for once?" She gave a tinkling little laugh, and my face split into a grin.

"You're already my sister, but maybe we could be coven sisters?"

She raised a brow, looking me up and down, but her smile just grew, "Sounds real kooky, but I guess I'm down. Beats worrying that I have schizophrenia, right?"

Not wanting to give her another moment to start reconsidering, I leaned toward her excitedly. "Okay, so, we'll have to start with—"

"What's up ladies?" My blood drained then began to boil. No, no, *no*.

"Hey Graham." Josie rolled her eyes and looked over to where he'd stopped beside our table. He held a bag, presumably of takeout, in one fist and the other in his pocket. Though Josie had been the one to respond, his eyes were on me when I finally looked up and over.

The smell, my nose wrinkled, face screwing in repulsion. It was like...

Wet dog.

Wet dog and something else that had my body screaming to back away. To move.

Instead, though, my hand relented to another instinct that reared its wrathful head. The steak knife that'd been brought out with my grilled chicken felt like a good enough weapon, and I was suddenly clutching it in my fist. The heat coursing through me was almost exactly the same as during the incident that got me sent to counseling in the first place. When I'd snapped a ruler and held it to the bully's throat before I realized what I was doing.

Back then, all that was in danger was my emotional wellbeing, my pride. Something about Graham, though, made my self-preservation alarms blare. Something about him made me believe he intended to harm me. I stood, holding the knife at my side.

Graham was almost a full head taller than me, but I would bet he'd crumple in pain if I decided to strike.

Granna really needed to teach me some offensive magic if this man was going to keep coming around when I'd already made it known that I wanted him to leave me alone. And if what I saw between Orion and him at the police station was any indication, Graham already knew that I was Orion's.

"What're you gonna do with that, witch?" Graham's deep voice made my stomach turn, but before I could show him exactly what I'd been fantasizing about, Josie shot up from her seat and stood between us.

"Hey, okay, how about you leave us alone, Graham? Before she cuts your balls off or something."

He just chuckled, and I wondered what his wolf form looked like. Was it grotesque or large and imposing? Both? Was the taunting green of his eyes, so different from my Orion's, the last thing Kara saw before she died?

"Your runt of a mate can make all the threats that he wants, and you can draw all the blades that *you* want. But you both should recognize who's really in charge here. Be glad I haven't whipped both of you into line yet." And then he sauntered away, head and shoulders thrown back in cool, arrogant calm.

I wanted to kill him.

Not shove, not slap. After the incident at school, the counseling helped for a while. The breathing, the processing, the strategies to remove myself from stressful situations. But the heat never went away. Sometimes it would take me completely off guard—a snide comment from a classmate could send me into planning how to smash their head into the concrete block wall until it split and oozed. But then they would walk away, and the guilt for my murderous thoughts would crush me. So I cowered and tried to smother it. When my tendency to succumb to the swell of rage subsided, they'd all seen it as a resounding success.

Admittedly, it just made me more aware of the need to bottle it up. To stuff it down to the point that it exacerbated my anxiety.

My father was gone, though, and I doubted Granna would care. I seemed to get the urges from her, anyway.

No, if I weren't brandishing a knife in front of the few lunch-goers that watched our interaction with wide eyes, and Josie hadn't stopped me, I might have truly lunged at him. Because, while I was sure that Orion had nothing to do with Kara's death, Graham very well may have.

"Okay, girl, let's drop the knife." Josie more so just pried it out of my hand. After tossing it back onto the table, she stood in front of me, searching my eyes. "Will it help if I say I'll join your coven?"

Though my face was still flushed with white-hot rage, I was able to see through it enough to tear my gaze away from the door Graham disappeared through. "Yes."

She ran her hands over my arms in a soothing gesture, but then her eyes went distant. Far away. Was this seeing? I remained silent, anger draining out of me while I watched her undoubtedly have a vision.

When her eyes focused on me once again, I was far too scared to ask what she saw. And she didn't offer. Instead, we sat back down to pay our bill, and we stumbled into our usual rhythm. She asked me how many pregnancy scares I'd had to convince me to '*finally* get on birth control,' and I asked her how long she'd with-stand that horrendous hair color before she'd change it again.

After we paid, we left and opted to walk for a while and take in the Halloween decorations. The brisk air cooled my heated skin, and the clouds calmed my anger that was still flaring each time my thoughts were idle enough to think of Graham. Josie prattled away, talking about her work projects and possibly seeing Keith again, and whichever else, and I tried to keep my father's disappointed face from popping up.

When I'd had my few years of trouble at school, he hadn't met my behavior with anger. Just disappointment that felt gray and sludgy, and, at thirteen, I promised to keep it in check. Even though the breathing and the reasoning just felt like a flimsy, damp band aid that I tried to reinforce with layers and layers of anxiety. Worry about the repercussions had been a powerful enough motivator as a child, and as the years rolled on, I had many more things to be worried about to keep the lashing out at bay. *Until now, I guess.*

Josie and I rounded a corner, and I caught sight of white, bouncy curls. My neck heated, my shoulders dropped, and my smile appeared without any coaxing. The last time we'd spoken, Orion had acted a bit funny when I mentioned that I was starting birth control, but all that was wiped away when I saw him tilt his head, wrinkle his nose, and began to search the passersby.

I wondered what his wolf form looked like. Would he want to show me? Would he ever tell me?

The anxiety that threatened to roll in like dark, thunderous clouds cleared with the sunshine of Orion's smile. Just from seeing me.

No, he would tell me when he was ready. I'd asked Granna more questions on the nature of shifters, wolf ones specifically, and with each conversation, I understood more and more how personal their other form was to them. Sacred.

So, I wouldn't pry. I trusted him, and I hoped that he was understanding that he could trust me, too.

CHAPTER TWENTY-SEVEN

ORION

Juno was sitting at a table outside with me so I could chain-smoke. The morning after Sylvie spent the night at my house, I'd made the decision to quit. Though she still smiled pleasantly every time she sat with me while I smoked, I sensed whispers of disgust and unease when she eyed the cigarettes when I pulled them out.

But after she'd admitted that I hurt her—*bit her*—in a fit of mindless, raging defense the night we met, I'd been smoking more than a pack a day.

With her no longer working at Vinny's and taking a few weeks' break before her new job started, she'd been spending more and more time at my house. I rubbed a reverent hand over my shoulder, feeling the mark she'd given me, even under the fabric of my sweatshirt. *Mate, mate, mate,* my mind chanted.

And she didn't even know it yet. Even without that knowledge, she could *feel* my claim on her, as technically unfinished as it was, and she'd asked to claim me, unprompted. I didn't deserve her. She needed better than a coward like me.

"What's got you down, my friend?"

Juno wasn't a habit smoker, but they bummed a cigarette from my proffered pack. Though the act usually made me feel less alone, it wasn't doing anything for me now. Their look of concern and brightly colored blouse and coat were hurting my eyes.

"I fucked up. Still am fucking up." I eyed the passersby, though there were fewer of them since it was a fairly cold day today. November was nearly upon us, and gaudy Halloween decorations littered every shopfront downtown. Juno and I, though, ran exceptionally warm, so we were both comfortable to smoke under the cloudy skies.

My travel mug kept my caramel latte, a drink I'd started ordering at the recommendation of Sylvie, and I took a nervous sip of it. Though my metabolism was faster than a human's, the caffeine couldn't be good for the churn of anxiety that I was feeling.

"How so?" Juno took a sip of their tea and then a drag of their cigarette. Talking to them about Sylvie was awkward. It was a frustrating set of boundaries we had to maintain, especially now that the head of the department was aware of my relationship with her. Like I'd predicted, I received no reprimand for being with her, but I was reminded in a lengthy lunch meeting about my responsibilities as a professor and the need to retain said boundaries when interacting with my colleagues. I'd also been tasked with relaying these guidelines with Sylvie.

Though it made no sense to me, Juno still prohibited me from using Sylvie's name during these conversations, as if that would somehow make it easier for them to remain impartial.

I stubbed out the spent cigarette and immediately picked out a new one. Juno's expression didn't shift as they watched me, but my free fingers still tapped where I had them propped on the table.

As had been the case for the past few weeks, the smoking and stimming did little to soothe me. The only thing that worked was being around Sylvie, which made sense given our bond, now. She'd broken my skin, drawn blood, and... without realizing, I'd done the same to her. Every time I reminded myself of this, a renewed wave of guilt washed over me. Her scent still hadn't changed in the way that would signal an impending shift, but she deserved to know that my feelings for her went past love.

I relayed all of this to Juno, professional boundaries cracking with my need for advice. I never wanted others in my personal life, but it wasn't like I had other Wolves I could ask. Besides my mother, at least, who was probably the reason I felt so hesitant to tell Sylvie the truth in the first place. I'd had enough therapists growing up to realize that.

"Without asking for more details, I know that *you* know you should tell her. Especially given your concern about her changing. Though, it does sound like it didn't take."

"But what if it happens again? What if I accidentally…"

They lifted both hands. "I don't want details. At least until the semester is over. But, she deserves to know, Orion. You're doing your mate a disservice by keeping this from her. And only prolonging your agony."

My eyes met and then slid away from theirs. I took another drag from my cigarette.

Juno clucked their tongue and made a comforting noise like how I'd heard my mother do for my younger sister. "What's she doing now? Maybe you should just tell her today. Rip the band-aid off?"

I turned my head over my shoulder, exhaled smoke. "She had a doctor's appointment, then lunch with her friend." Last Monday, while we sat outside reading together, Sylvie mentioned her intention of getting a birth control implant later in the week. That fact alone didn't make me startle in the slightest—I'd remembered my mother's frantic call when she realized Ramona was sexually active and then Ramona's subsequent texts complaining about our mother and asking me how to tell her that she wanted to get on the pill. My dry responses to both of them swiftly ended both conversations, but I was well aware that it was something females had to consider. Not that I had any intentions of coming in Sylvie.

Oh, but *she* did, I realized when her scent shifted and revealed an unspoken meaning beneath her words.

Juno shook their head while they stubbed out their spent cigarette in the ashtray between us. "I said I didn't want details, Orion."

"How are you going to give me advice if you don't know what's going on? I trust you to maintain professionalism with my mate. And I don't have anyone else to talk about this with."

They heaved a heavy sigh. "You can't expect to be with her long-term and not ever have to tell her why you won't… finish in her."

I rubbed the heel of my palm over my eye. "Fuck. Fuck, fuck, fuck."

"You're thinking too hard on this, Orion. It isn't like you to hold secrets, which is probably why you feel so conflicted. But, even *I* can smell the power within her. She knows about and is developing her abilities, which means that she will scent it on you if she doesn't realize what it is already." They twined their finger around a long, black strand that'd come loose from the messy bun at the back of their head. "Do you want her to find out for herself? Or have someone else tell her?"

"Her grandmother seems to be granting me the courtesy of telling Sylvie myself." I'd been invited over for dinner twice at Sylvie's so far. Though I could tell she much preferred having dinner at mine so that we didn't have to fight the inevitable urge to tear each other's clothes off, her grandmother had insisted. And both times, I'd been nearly vibrating with anxiety, wondering when her grandmother would stand from the table and announce me a Wolf, only to push Sylvie to sever our bond completely.

But that moment never came. The last dinner we'd had, while Sylvie was in the bathroom, her grandmother asked me when I was going to tell her. When I didn't have an answer, only nervous sputters, halfway fearful that she'd force me to shift right then and there, she just sighed and stated that Sylvie wouldn't mind. That she just deserved to know.

Which was what Juno kept saying, bugging the shit out of me. Really, they sometimes seemed both a witch and shifter. Their ability to retain infuriating calm through every situation was more supernatural than their wolf form could ever be to me.

"I wasn't referring to her grandmother." Juno's voice turned low, guarded, and they cut their eyes to their left. I did the same to my right, only to lock eyes with the weak one. The pup that'd saw fit to challenge me in front of my mate. His eyes immediately dropped in submission, and while I did feel a surge of satisfaction, it was swiftly followed by more guilt, more fear.

The Antler Pointe Pack had been keeping eyes on me ever since I declined their demand that I join. To them, it was either submit to Graham or be forbidden to run on their land. Including that of my home.

To hear Juno tell it, I'd actually spat at their feet.

I didn't regret rejecting them, but it was its own kind of insult to smell them on my land. To sneak my own shifting and have to go out of town to spend more than a few hours in my other form.

"This can't go on, friend," Juno drawled once the pup was out of earshot.

"I know. I know that I need to tell her."

"Well, that, yes. But I was referring to them." They waved a hand toward the direction the Other Wolf went. "I do *not* have a good feeling about this pack or their leader. From the moment I met them, I sensed something sinister. They aren't all family, not *pack*. It almost feels like a cult. And it isn't right how they've treated you, especially." Instead of going about rejecting the pack in the manner I had, Juno had elected to take a different approach. Before we met, when they moved to Antler Pointe for work, they politely declined Graham's offer, stating that they wished to keep their ties to their family pack, and they still held the scent to back them up. They'd agreed not to run on Antler Pointe land, and that was that.

It was an excuse that I would never be able to use. My own scent gave the distinct *No Pack* indication. One that left me more vulnerable to parasites like Graham. And I'd given it to Sylvie.

But I just shrugged at Juno's words. My friend rested their head in their palm, and I wasn't too proud to admit that I envied them. Not just for the lack of trouble Graham and his subordinates gave them but for their multitude of siblings and pair of loving parents and a whole pack that they still ran with more often than not. When I'd visited and been granted permission to run with them in the past, it made my own lack of ties painfully obvious. Though they invited me to become pack every time, I hadn't been able to bring myself to accept.

It was too painful after what happened with my former one.

And I was *not* going to challenge Graham for Leader, which was the only way I'd bring my line back to the pack that my ancestors started. I'd escaped death last time I'd challenged, but I was sure Graham wouldn't be so generous if I lost. And I wouldn't leave Sylvie.

At least when Chief Thompson was Leader, he'd let my father live and run on our land as Unpacked in peace. It was a decision made by my great-great-grandmother when a new pack leader deviated from the values my family had tried to instill since its inception. If Graham weren't leader, and I hadn't been burned so badly a few years prior, I might have heard out Chief Thompson or literally anyone else about joining. But when Graham came to my house, not two days after I moved in and started working on renovating, and demanded I join or agree to not run on what he claimed as their land, maybe I did spit at his feet. After being pursued and attacked each time I tried to enjoy my land in wolf form, I had to resort to running elsewhere. Where I could at least be Wolf in peace.

"And how do you suppose I fix this situation, Juno? I am one, and they are at least twenty at this point." I was strong but not that strong.

"I'm not sure. But you know that I will back you one hundred percent. And if everything goes to shit, you are always welcome with mine." Their smile was mushed against the heel of their hand, and I grunted and nodded along with their reassurance.

Welcome and belonging were two very separate things.

"And your mate as well. Any pups you may have in the future, too." My brows tightened at the endearing words. I managed to hold their eyes, so similar in color to Sylvie's but vastly different. Juno gave a deep incline of their head, managing it somehow with their face still in hand, and I returned the gesture, emotion clogging my throat. Yes, this wasn't just about me anymore.

I had to keep reminding myself that, by human standards, this relationship was in its early days. Pups were a conversation for further down the line, but I wasn't human. And Sylvie barely was. In fact, she seemed further from it with each passing day.

Not a turned shifter, but something else. When I was around her and her grandmother, there was still a difference there that wasn't just the tart witch smell. It made me want to scent her all over, bow at her feet, rip the world to shreds, and tear myself apart, all at the same time.

My head snapped up, catching a thread of that very scent, now. And then, the melodic trill of her voice. My muscles hummed, and I searched the street around us in the direction my body turned to without thought. *Mate, mate, mate,* my Wolf rejoiced, and then I saw her.

Her black hair bouncing, as if it was almost weightless, the flushed warmth of her brown skin. The loneliness and despair I'd been feeling evaporated in an instant.

"Good lord, your tail is wagging." Juno snickered, but I ignored them. Because her eyes just met mine, and she was grinning.

I would tell her. And I would make our land safe for us, somehow. And if I couldn't do that, we would go somewhere that was. I would never let them harm her the way they had me.

Sylvie's friend had been gesturing wildly but dropped their

arms like their strings had been cut. Sylvie, though, rushed forward and rounded the little fence that enclosed the patio seating. I stood and met her kiss, cradling her face and feeling her warmth under mine. She initiated our noses brushing, and it made my heart gallop.

"What a lucky coincidence." She giggled, and I kissed her again, swallowing the joy she was granting me.

"Indeed," I said.

A throat clearing made Sylvie stiffen and shift, so I settled to wrapping an arm around her waist.

"I'm sorry, that was rude of me." She laughed self-consciously, and my lips pursed in confusion. What was rude about being excited to see each other? "Oh! Hey, Dr. Vanders." Sylvie gave them a pleasant smile in greeting. Before Juno could say anything, though, Sylvie's scent popped with curiosity, and I saw her head was tilted and nose wrinkled.

Juno gave me a loaded glance before standing. "Hi, Sylvie, it's good to see you." Then, much more stiffly, they greeted Sylvie's friend who had stopped a few paces away from our table, "And you, Josie."

Confusion and discomfort were a swirl all around us, and Juno quickly said their goodbyes and left.

"I hope we didn't intrude, baby," Sylvie said.

I bent to kiss her forehead, smoothing the wrinkle that'd appeared. "You didn't. How was lunch? And your appointment?"

"Oh, all good!" Sylvie proceeded to hold out her arm and direct me to feeling the implant she'd gotten inserted. It made my gut clench to think of it stuck there under her skin, but I tried my best to smile at her in return.

I would have to tell her soon that the potential of pups wasn't my immediate concern.

Her friend's wry snort cut through my anxious thoughts. "Yeah, and then you almost gutted someone at lunch, Sylv."

Sylvie's scent immediately shifted, not matching her friend's faintly concerned joking at all. I looked down at my mate and lifted her chin so that I could see her face fully. Often, people were able to craft their expression to one different from what they truly felt. My Sylvie, though, seemed to struggle with this or reject the notion altogether. She ran her teeth over her plush lip, but beneath the nerves, I smelled wrath, saw it brewing in her eyes.

It was a living, breathing part of her that I'd caught glimpses of. It would swell and crash just as quickly, often followed by a roll of guilt and shame. But it was ever-present, always simmering. When I took her and her grandmother to the grocery store over the weekend, when someone brushed past her grandmother without so much as an 'excuse me,' I didn't even have time to get angry before the scorching spice startled me still. In reality, her grandmother needed no extra defenses, as she went after the oblivious teenager who grumbled an embarrassed apology.

I kissed Sylvie now, caressed her cheek and waist. When she confessed one night that she'd had to get counseling for anger issues in the past, as if it were some great sin to want to protect herself and those she cared about, I'd drawn her into my arms.

Her tears had soaked my shirt after I told her what seemed to me like the simplest truth and shared my own experience being put in therapy. Being made to think there was something wrong with me by my mother and taking years to unravel and accept what just *was*.

"He just keeps fucking with me. I know it's on purpose," Sylvie groused and shot her friend a look.

"Who?" My hackles raised, but I tried to keep myself in check. Until I had all of the details.

Josie was on her phone now, scrolling and digging her pinky finger in her ear. "Graham Thompson, the police chief's son."

I couldn't contain my growl, my own rising wave of fury. I took Sylvie's face in my hands again, eyes frantically searching for any injury, any sign that he'd harmed her. I sniffed, searching for his scent on hers, but it seemed he hadn't touched her. Why hadn't she told me that he'd come near her? Even after he had verbal and scent confirmation of my claim. My nose planted in

Sylvie's neck, rubbing and inhaling. It was that comfort that kept me from actually shifting, and I felt her body relax into mine.

"I'll kill him. I'm so sorry, Sylvie."

Instead of shrugging off my promise, she just curled further into me. Whether she knew I was serious or not, she accepted my vow to keep her safe, even though I'd already broken it. Leaving my mate to face the fraud of a Pack Leader's accosting on her own.

Her friend was the one to pipe up, though. If she thought my reaction to Sylvie strange, she neither smelled of nor verbalized wariness.

Witch, my Wolf recognized not just by her scent but by the distant yet pinning look in her eyes. "Might not be such a bad idea."

CHAPTER TWENTY-EIGHT

SYLVIE

"Ugh, I'm just hopeless at this." Josie thew up her hands before collapsing and burying her face in her arms. I rubbed a reassuring hand on her back, and Granna snickered while she stirred our dinner that was simmering on the stove.

It'd been a few weeks since our conversation over lunch, and just as she'd promised, Josie had begun to hone her craft with me.

The first night, Samhain, Granna and I introduced her to one of our most sacred rituals. The meal and decorations and fire felt heavier and lighter at the same time. Before moving in with her, I at least made an effort to spend every Samhain in Antler Pointe. Dad never wanted to partake, but that was okay.

We would decorate the house with dried flowers and pinecones and set up my mother's altar in the sunroom. We would set her place at the table, serve her food, and after dinner, we would walk into the forest and build a fire in the clearing near her favorite stream. Every year, it was a tradition where Granna told me stories of my mother, and we honored the woman that I barely remembered but thought of every day. When we'd stand before the fire with the black sky above, I would feel my mother's arms around my shoulders. The wood on those evenings buzzed with something *else*, and while my friends trick-or-treated or attended parties, I was absorbed by the thinness of the veil.

This year, with Josie joining us, we made altars for her mother and Dad, too. We moved dinner to the formal dining table to make space for all the deceased that we were honoring, and the three of us held hands before the fire. The tears were joyful, and the love was palpable.

Unfortunately, studying was a little rockier.

While Granna had begun instructing Josie on how to handle her visions, and I continued my work in the gardens and in the forest, we carried on with learning from The Book. And while I knew I could get frustrated quite easily, Josie, I was finding, was even worse.

Simple rituals for protection and positivity were integral for any witch, Granna told us time and time again, but it was especially important for Josie given the nature of her seeing gift. She joined me in incorporating many into her daily routine. Even with her frustrated groans, the amulet I showed her how to make hung around her neck.

Skills like lighting a candle without a flame, though, were not something she was able to do yet.

She raised her purple-dyed head that matched the amethyst around her throat. "This is fucking hopeless, dude. You make it look so easy!"

Now I was realizing how Granna felt. When I'd shown her the little trick, it had been to entice her to keep going. For her to have something to look forward to. "Well, I *have* been working at all this for a long time. And even if you can't light candles, you can literally see into the future. If you don't have any other powers, I would count your seeing as pretty fucking cool. All I can do is talk to mushrooms and sometimes spiders."

Josie pouted and pushed the candle across the table, as if she couldn't stand it being close to her anymore. "I guess. Though, you're talking like that's *all* you can do, Sylv."

"You're both right. Seeing is a very rare gift, Josie. And don't you feel much better now that you have multiple measures to safeguard your mind?" Josie grunted and glared at the white candle that stood unburned in the brass candleholder. "And you are far too powerful to reduce your abilities in such a way, sweetheart." I blew a raspberry in response and stood to check on the bread in the oven.

I gently nudged Granna with my hip, and she stepped away while holding a steaming spoon to her lips. I peered into the little window to see inside the oven, and, satisfied with the dough's rise so far, I straightened and leaned against the counter.

Granna was adding more salt and pepper to the stew that already smelled of garlic and thyme, and I fished my own spoon out of a drawer so that I could taste. My teeth sank into a tender chunk of potato, and my mouth watered even more at subtle hit of acid amongst the savory and hearty.

"This is good, Granna."

"Not good enough yet," she murmured while hunting through the army of tiny spice jars she had on the counter.

Josie came over to test the stew for herself, and after a series of downright filthy moans at the taste, she retired back by the bay window to read through more of The Book. "See, it's great! And the bread will be ready in just a few minutes. Stop messing with it."

"No, I want it to be perfect for him, and it's not there yet."

"Gah, fine, keep fussing." I pulled out the oven mitts and put them on. "But, there's no one here to—" What Granna said made me stop, and my face screwed up in confusion. "Orion's not coming over, Granna."

She waved a hand while adding a pinch of cayenne pepper. "I know that, sweetheart. Though I'm surprised you tore yourself away from the boy for a whole evening."

Josie snickered from the corner of the room, but sparks of

dread were prickling on the back of my neck. Before I could say anything, Granna muttered under her breath, "Only have a few weeks, and not anywhere near prepared. So much to do, so much to do."

My throat clicked with a swallow that felt like a rock tumbling down my dry throat. Among all the good and exciting that'd happened after Samhain, Granna's slips were popping up more and more. "Who are you talking about then, Granna?" I lowered my voice, tried to make it calm and soothing. I snuck a glance over at Josie whose attention was still directed at the book in front of her.

Granna tsked after another taste of the stew was deemed unsatisfactory. "Of course I'm—" She stilled with her hand hovering over the little bowl of salt. Her eyes darted up to me, and they weren't glazed or faraway. They were sharp and present.

At first, her lips pressed into a firm line, but I watched her gaze swim over my face, and my stomach dropped with the glistening of tears in her eyes. Her gray brows turned up just before she clenched everything shut. Granna's thin chest heaved with a deep inhale, and when she opened her eyes, her face was smoothed. She pushed back from the stove and began rifling through a cabinet for bowls. "It's ready, girls."

The somberness that'd come over her seemed to linger, though. We dished up the bowls, I cut the bread, and Roz arrived in a trail of crimson, chatty fire. She wasn't a witch, but she was Granna's oldest friend, and we drank the wine she brought while eating the stew and bread I baked at the kitchen table.

"… and I am still spittin' mad at Chief Thompson for treating you the way he did, sweetie. I saw him in town today and gave him a piece of my mind. You should've seen his face!" Roz cackled, her southern accent spilling into her words. She smacked a playful hand on Granna's shoulder for good measure.

Granna glanced at Josie and I above her glass of wine. "What they should do is focus on catching who—or what—killed that girl. Matter of fact, the bodies of the other two that are probably dead, too. I'm sure you've heard about the dressing down I gave both him and his stupid son. He'll be staying away from Sylvie if I have anything to do about it."

Roz nodded, and the fluffy spikes of her short hair bobbed. "That *and* your boyfriend almost beating the boy in front of his father. Ha! I wish I could've been there." That got Josie cracking up with her, and Granna and I both joined in with snickers of our own. I still hadn't seen Kara again, but I tried to hope that it meant she had moved on and was no longer stuck.

Every day, Orion checked in with me about Graham bothering me. I could tell that it was tearing him up that Graham confronted me during moments I was without Orion by my side. Each time we'd reunite after time apart, he would look over me with worry and settle at my neck for a long time, breathing and rubbing his face into my skin. Whoever killed Kara still hadn't been caught, and if it was indeed a group of wolf shifters that'd done it, I didn't think they'd ever be brought to justice. As far as I knew, the Chief could've been in on it.

The fungi hadn't given me anything else of note about the Wolves in regard to Kara's murder. Just that the White Wolf was around. That others walked the forest further away from our house.

I hadn't said anything about wolf shifters to Orion, not wanting him to feel like I was pressuring him, but he was still acting more overprotective than usual. Every night I spent at his place, he'd set me up on the couch or in his bedroom and refuse my offers for help with… anything.

Granna and I went to a thrift store one Sunday, and when I showed up in Roz's pickup truck with two rocking chairs in the back, he'd been frantic. They were too good of a deal to pass up, and my new job paid better than Vinny's. I had money saved up and noticed he didn't have any furniture on his front porch. The chairs were painted black, and as soon as I saw them, I knew they'd be perfect for his house. When he hefted them out of the truck bed with no issue, he gently chastised me for getting him anything and going to all the trouble. But I saw the way he carefully placed them on the porch, stepping back and positioning, then stepping back again to make sure that they were perfectly centered.

That night, we drank beer and rocked in the new chairs with the cold air whipping through our hair. It didn't bother either of us, and when we switched to hot chocolate, I kept waiting for Orion to bring out a pack of cigarettes and smoke. But, he never did, and my exasperation for him worrying over me and the large secret sitting between us fell away with the setting of the sun.

I shoveled another bite of stew into my mouth and shrugged a shoulder. "He's protective, and Graham thinks he's untouchable."

Roz clicked her tongue while dipping a piece of crusty, golden bread into the dish of olive oil and balsamic vinegar. "Don't understand why Chief doesn't rein that boy in. Lets him walk all over him *and* his wife. It's downright shameful." She took a bite and continued talking with her mouth full, though she placed a well-manicured hand in front of her chewing. "Come to think of it, there're quite a few who treat Graham like that. At first, people eyed him with pity for moving in with his philandering father, but then it just flipped! One day, I went in for a new screwdriver and caught Bill Ferrows talking to the boy and acting like the Chief wasn't even there! And they used to be as thick as thieves, you remember that?" She looked to Granna who nodded.

What Granna couldn't say, however, was that all the people she was mentioning were shifters in the same pack. Since I'd started noticing the scent of wildness that clung to Graham, the Chief, Jasper, Juno, *and* Orion, I started to parse through the different notes each time I saw one of them or any of the others in town. I hadn't seen Graham or the Chief in a long time, but Jasper, his father, and Ana who worked at the library all had some note that I remembered being on Graham and his father. It made my nose wrinkle in a way that Juno's and Orion's didn't.

"Okay," Josie stuck her arms out and almost knocked over my glass of wine, "can we talk about something else? Preferably something that passes the Bechdel test?" Did it count as passing the Bechdel test if you were talking about men to explain the Bechdel test? Either way, the conversation turned into Josie explaining what it was to a surprisingly delighted Roz who asserted that she would make an effort to apply it to more of her interactions with friends, even after we explained that it started as a way to examine things like film and writing.

She waved that away, though. "Still, couldn't hurt. Only conversations I can think of that *might* pass the test are mine with this one," she jutted a thumb at Granna, "but that's because she's refused to date the entire time we've been friends! And spurned any advance that's come her way! Time and time again, she's turned heads or attracted some fella's attention, and—" If Granna's eye rolling and grumbling wasn't funny enough, Roz's almost comical slapping a hand over her mouth for immediately failing the test tipped Josie and me into near hysterics.

The rest of the dinner and the hours we spent even after we were too full to keep eating made me feel recharged. It was different than when I was with Orion, but it felt like something else I was missing had finally slid into place. Josie had been my best friend for over half of our lives, but to have her relate to and be part of my life in *this way* was better than anything I could have expected.

While Roz cracked open a box of chocolate truffles she brought from a shop downtown, I slung an arm around my friend and rubbed my hand over the bristles of her shaved head. We weren't a full coven just yet, but to have a sister in this way was one of the best feelings in the world.

I bit into a chocolate that oozed teeth-achingly sweet caramel and caught Granna's eyes on me. It was like she was turning over what to say to me, deciding whether or not to confess something. But I didn't need her to explain the slips, and I didn't want her to feel self-conscious for them. So I gave her my most winning smile, but the one she returned was brittle at the edges. Once again, silver shined around the corners of her eyes just before she shook herself and tuned back into the conversation at hand.

Granna had done so much for me, and I knew that she also mourned the years lost between us. She never said it, but I felt it in the way she guided and encouraged me in that dry way of hers. In the way she cared for me.

The slips were out of her control, just a signal that she'd lived a long life. *And, besides*, I talked down the panic scaling up my throat, *we have so much more time left.*

CHAPTER TWENTY-NINE

ORION

Sylvie's heart was a consistent beat that seemed almost in sync with the Otis Redding record I had playing. Though I'd made updates to the cabin, brought in my own furniture and decorations, Da's and my record collection was prominently displayed for all to see, and I played from it constantly. Sylvie didn't seem to mind, often humming or tapping her feet without really noticing she was doing it.

Her big, soft eyes closed in pleasure as she tasted what I'd cooked for us tonight. She slurped a long noodle again after the first time had drawn a little chuckle from my anxious throat. It wasn't the action in of itself but the dimples that appeared when she did it.

She'd said that she vaguely remembered that her mother used to make spaghetti, and though she nor her grandmother knew exactly how to tell me how to make it, she seemed content enough with my rendition. Sylvie picked up the basket of bread I'd laid between us on the table, putting it back down closer to the edge than it had been before.

I didn't even try to stop myself from lining everything back up just so. The dish of grated Parmesan, the salt and pepper in ceramic shakers my father had bought at a garage sale when I was a boy, then the bread. My mind focused on making them equidistant and centered.

When I drew my hand back to stab a meatball and shove it into my mouth, I realized that I'd stopped engaging completely to reorganize the table. But when I glanced at Sylvie, she didn't seem to mind. She smiled warmly at me and continued eating and picked up humming with the bridge of the song that was nearly over.

She was so sweet, so precious. My instinct to protect her had only grown with each day we spent together, and when she said that she wanted to mark *me*, without even knowing what it meant, I'd almost fallen on my knees right then. I looked to her neck now, at the darkened impression of my teeth on her perfect, brown skin, and I felt a rumble try to start in my chest. I rubbed at my own mark, where she'd pierced me with her blunt teeth, and nearly closed my eyes at the deep sense of belonging washing over me.

I'd told her that I'd never belonged to anyone before, and it was true. Would she rebuke me if she knew the truth and how long I'd been keeping it from her? My mouth went dry at the thought, and I gulped down more of the expensive wine I'd bought for the occasion.

Ever since she'd told me I'd bitten her that first night, something I didn't remember, I had been fussing and fawning over her. Every day, I nestled into the crook of her neck, trying to smell as deeply as possible to detect any sort of transformation. There never was, but I couldn't get rid of this deep, deep fear that things would suddenly change. That her body would decide now was the time to try and shift.

Bile threatened to rise in my throat at the image of it. Not because I wouldn't want Sylvie to be like me. But from what Da and others told me, for those bitten, the first few shifts were painful and distressing. And the many whose bodies rejected it completely…

My teeth ground as I fought down the nauseating fear at her body just—giving up. Her not being here anymore because of me.

I needed a fucking cigarette, but I'd also taken up trying to quit for her again. I downed the rest of my wine.

"Are you okay, baby?" she asked over her now empty bowl. Her thick brows were drawn in concern, and I couldn't help but shiver when she called me that. I didn't think she even really noticed, but I held the moment in my mind each time.

I cleared my throat and rose to clear our bowls. "I'm fine, Sylvie. Are you full, or would you like more?"

Her groan made my body shiver. "Ugh, no, I wish. Too full." Her sweet, sleepy smile forced a small one from my lips. I bent to kiss her forehead as I padded on socked feet to the kitchen.

My meal was mostly uneaten, but I realized now that I wouldn't have enough of an appetite to finish. I began settling into the routine of putting the leftover food into containers, lining the dishes up beside the sink for washing, and wiping down the stove and adjacent counters.

At the sound of the faucet starting and the clatter of dishes, I called over, "I'll wash those. Go relax." I jutted my chin toward the direction of the living area while I scrubbed a particularly tough splatter of sauce.

She scoffed and started to drizzle soap over the brand new sponge I'd set out the night before. "You cooked. I can at least do the dishes."

"No, Sylvie, I've got it," I said through my teeth. I didn't want her to do anything. She already took care of her grandmother, and I just wanted to take care of *her*. What if the change was just taking place very slowly—that would certainly be exhausting, right?

And if she'd somehow avoided it, I knew that she was stressed about her final papers and exams she had coming up. She'd already given me so much. I could easily wash some pots and pans.

But she was insisting, stubbornly planted in front of the sink and already working on the pot I'd simmered the sauce in. "Orion, shut up. It's fine." Though there was a lightness to her words, mind raced at the exasperation I detected in her words.

"Okay, I'm sorry." I could scent it now, how her sweet smell shifted in the air. I was fucking this up. *Stupid, stupid, stupid*, I chastised as I finished wiping down all the surfaces aside from the one beside her, now clear of dirty dishes. Sylvie was making quick work, her shoulders drawn higher than normal, and I took a nervous swallow.

She made me jump when she whirled around to face me. Her hands were still soapy, and some of the suds dripped down onto the floor by her feet. I dug my nails into my palm, trying to resist the urge to wipe them up. Because she was biting her lip while eyeing me up and down as if she was trying to decide what to say to me.

We faced each other in silence with only the rich ballad playing from the living room. "Rion, what's going on?"

That was a new one. Well, for Sylvie. She didn't know that my da used to call me that. "What do you mean?"

"I don't know!" Her hands shook, and my eyes watched another splash of suds hit a counter near her calf. "You've been acting funny since the first night I spent here. Like… I'm made of glass or you're dancing around me. It makes me feel like something's wrong."

My throat gave a dry click as I swallowed. I didn't… I didn't know that she had noticed anything amiss. With her easy smiles and reassurances, I'd thought my worries were my own. Had I missed a sign? I thought I'd gotten better at reading the cues. Scents were always easier, but her cherry sweetness had always remained present. If anything else came up, it was so fleeting that I had just attributed it to the regular fluctuation of emotions. Now, though, her scent turned into a torrent of different notes, and I was losing track.

"I—I." I clenched the rag in my hand as I tried to fight for the words to say. I'd been rehearsing them in my head for days, but they seemed to fly out of my brain, now.

"Are you upset with me about something? Did I do something wrong?"

I lurched forward, careful to not step in the wet spots on the floor, and grabbed her arms. She was in another one of my sweatshirts, and my own scent mixed with hers relaxed me enough to find something, anything, to reassure her. "*No*, Sylvie. You've done *nothing* wrong. I just…" Was I really about to do this? "I… there is—something."

She sucked in a breath but remained silent, and I was doing this, wasn't I? She deserved to know. Especially if she could be affected in the way I was afraid of. But also because I knew that I couldn't be like my mother. Hiding this large part of herself to placate her so-called partner.

"I'm, uh…"

She clenched her eyes closed and seemed to be bracing herself. I'd never had to tell a human before, never having gotten close enough to one where it was needed. My past relationships with other Wolves, though, had gone just as terribly as I feared my revelation would push this one.

I took a long breath, drawing in as much of her scent as I could in case this was the last time. When I finished, I exhaled, "I'm not human. I can… change. Shift. Into a wolf." Because calling myself a werewolf sounded fucking ridiculous.

Sylvie's eyes flew open, and her shoulders sagged. "Oh." And the word had a slight upward inflection.

What does that *mean?* I was staring at her, eyes tracing frantically over her face, and when I focused on the furrowed wrinkle of her brow, my stomach began to plummet. My hands slid off of her arms, and I started to take a despairing step back.

She followed after me, pulling my hands into her own. "No,

Orion, I just—" she let out a wobbly laugh, and I stared back, confused at the quick shift of her emotions "—I thought you were about to break up with me. I'm relieved."

I flinched in her grasp, head shaking. "Gods, Sylvie, of course not."

She took a deep breath, squeezing my hands on her inhale then relaxing her palms on the exhale. "Okay." And then she smiled. She lifted her chin, face warm and loving, and I felt all of my worries leave in a rush.

Sylvie reached up to run a thumb over my lip, and I sniffed the air, sensing nothing now other than relief and love from her. In that moment, I felt so absurd for worrying about this. Just like everything, my mate understood.

I bent down, lips nearing hers for a kiss, but the hair on the back of my neck reacted before my other senses caught up. My head lurched to the side, toward the noise that had startled me, and Sylvie froze at my reaction.

A growl started at the base of my chest, and I couldn't hide it from her. I let my senses fully slip to the forefront, scent and hearing picking up on a group walking right up to *my* house. On *my* territory.

Just because they saw the entire town, the entire forest, as theirs, it didn't make it so. Their thinly veiled threats were one thing, even attacking me to the point that I limped to the first place I could find. The night Sylvie found me was still a foggy blur, but her soft, kind eyes and fresh cherry scent had made me calm. The tartness of her fear was what completely snapped me out of it.

She was starting to smell like that now, and it made me take a deep breath, remembering what I must've looked like to her. I unclenched my jaw, relaxing my bared teeth, and tried to parse through the possible reasons they'd be coming here.

My father's cabin was surrounded by the trees, and for a moment, I hoped that they were just passing through.

But then their voices continued growing nearer, and there were steps coming up the stone pathway leading to my door.

The instinct to protect my home and the female that was mine was like white hot fire in my chest. I turned back to Sylvie and took her face in my hands. Her round, beautiful eyes were wide with concern, and the fear in her scent rose.

I kissed her hard, and she let me. Her hands grasped my forearms. "Stay here, Sylvie. Don't come outside," I said once I pulled away, holding her stare so I was sure she saw the seriousness in my face.

She didn't speak, but she twitched a nod, wild hair swaying.

They would certainly smell her, but I wanted to eliminate any other chance of them being around her.

I stalked to the door and flung it open before he could knock. "*Leave*," I demanded.

There were four, two of which I recognized as the ones who attacked me. The third, I knew all too well.

I closed the door behind me and walked to the top of the short stack of wooden steps that led to their little posse. Graham's dominant scent of Pack Leader had already made me half-shift, claws and fangs drawing to protect what was mine.

He stood at the center of the group, shoulders back and tall, and bigger than his pack members in every way. "We just wanted to talk, Orion. See if you'd changed your mind." Graham smirked when I gave another snarl. I'd barely suppressed the urge to hunt him down and rip his throat out after Sylvie told me that he'd been accosting her, even after I'd claimed her. Now he wanted to posture and antagonize me?

I moved forward and descended a step. The arrogant pup that stood on Graham's left shot him a look, but none of them moved otherwise. It was one thing to have the evidence of their entitlement all over my land, and it was quite another to have them nearly knocking at my door. My self-preserving reasons for not attacking the Antler Pointe Pack were starting to make less and less sense. My Wolf instincts were already taking me over.

"This land is mine. Leave."

One of the members, shorter and thicker than the others, piped up, "Bullshit. We're the rightful guardians of this land."

I barked a humorless laugh. "If it were yours, you wouldn't have to fight so hard to convince me. My line stretches back to the first who became pack on this land. No matter what you say, it is mine."

Graham scoffed, but I felt the wave of his Leader pheromones wafting toward me. They just made my body ready further for an attack. "I do you a courtesy, Unpacked. You and your fe—"

"*You don't speak of her,*" I roared and felt the prickles of fur sprouting on my arms, my face. "You harass my mate, the one I have claimed. You are no respectable Leader. Your pack has allowed themselves to be fooled. But *I* am no fool. Leave or I *will* kill you."

That got the others going, and in a blink, we all were half shifted and crouched. My eyes began to dart over the group, calculating whether I'd be able to lunge at Graham successfully and without being too injured. When I'd refused those years ago, I was assured that I'd be left alone as long as I didn't run on pack land. I shouldn't have been surprised that Graham wasn't keeping his promise.

His voice was as twisted as his face, now somewhere between a wolf and a man's. His deep brown fur was beginning to cover his body, and I knew that we were just a flinch away from clothes ripping and Wolves lunging. "You have not *claimed*. She is no mate. Become pack or leave this land, White One."

My shirt began to rip, growing and shifting muscles flexing too large for the fabric. One of Graham's Wolves, a male with blond hair and pale brown fur, shifted completely, and the rest were nearly there. The air around us was thrumming with snapping energy, and I was barely holding on. The shifted Wolf was baring his teeth along with the others, and Graham was letting it happen. What changed, I didn't know, but I wouldn't let them get to Sylvie, and they certainly weren't leaving now.

I drew a breath, about to settle into the shift when an onslaught of rage overtook my senses. But instead of coming from myself or the group before me, it rushed from the house, then continued forward. I watched in horror, shift stalled completely, as my mate charged between us.

She wore my sweatshirt, hem reaching the middle of her thighs, and brandished a large kitchen knife. But her scent, gods, it was wrath and fiery power. She stalked, legs and feet bare, until she stopped right in front of Graham. "Get the *fuck* out of here, or I won't hesitate again." Another Wolf shifted, leaving just Graham and the pup on two feet. Sylvie didn't even flinch with the snarls around her, nor did she when I tried to pull her back. Her skin was hot to the touch, and her little body didn't budge.

"Get your bitch, Unpa—"

"We said to *leave*," Sylvie screamed and shoved Graham at his chest. The Pack Leader actually yelped, falling back a step, and I watched, eyes wide and body shaking, as his claws sunk back, and his fur disappeared. Doubled over and panting, he looked up with hate in his eyes, but the other pack members retreated a few paces. They were still growling, but their wariness flooded the space between us.

The pup made to take a step forward, but the snarl let loose from my mouth made him freeze. My mate's power was dripping off her, and with it beside me, I felt even sharper.

Sylvie lifted the knife in her fist. "Jasper. Take your leader and your pack and get off my mate's land. You are not welcome here." She lowered her gaze to the leader in question. "And if you come near me or my mate again, I will gut you. Don't fucking test me."

We stood silent and ready while the pack members darted their eyes around, trying to assess what to do. Graham straightened himself and looked to me, but before he could open his mouth, I growled in warning. His nostrils flared, and for a moment, I thought he would shift and attack anyway. But another wave radiated from Sylvie, her power dark and burning and unlike anything I'd ever felt before. For all I knew, he wasn't able to shift right now with what Sylvie had done to him.

Graham resorted to spitting at our feet and turning on his heel. The others followed suit and stalked behind him on two or four legs. They walked into the trees in the direction of town, and I refused to look away, to let my guard down, until their scent trail was lost to the forest.

The air was bitingly cold, something I hadn't noticed until my rage began to subside. "Baby?" Sylvie's voice was soft again, so far from how she sounded when she faced down the Pack Leader. I hesitated for a moment, not wanting to look away from the darkness of the wood, but there was only the soft rustling of bare tree branches and scuttling of peaceful animals.

Soft skin cupped my jaw, and I nuzzled into the touch. "You're so beautiful," she whispered, and I met her gaze. Her eyes roved over my face, my body, and I realized that I was still half-shifted, the tatters of my shirt barely clinging to my body.

My lids clenched shut, and I pulled her into my chest. I scented at her mark, feeling that she was here with me, and a small, pitiful noise escaped my throat. "You were supposed to stay inside, mo ghrá."

"I know, but I couldn't." I gave another grumble, and she clung to my back, pulling me tighter.

CHAPTER THIRTY

SYLVIE

Orion had insisted on nearly carrying me back into his house, and now, he thrust a steaming mug of cider into my hands. I accepted and reclined back on his couch.

Whatever I'd done to Graham had sapped a lot of my energy, or maybe that was just the adrenaline rush I'd had when I decided I couldn't listen to what they were saying any longer. It almost hadn't felt like me when I grabbed the knife and flung open the front door. The only thing I'd been afraid of was them hurting Orion. Nothing else mattered, but something in me must've known what to do, because, not only had I stopped Graham from shifting, but I'd reversed the partway shift entirely.

I took a sip from the mug, and the tart warmth made me shiver. Orion sat on the coffee table in front of me, arms resting on his legs, and he looked more relaxed and tenser all at once. He seemed looser, maybe? Now that I knew what he was.

And he was still a bit upset with me for inserting myself in the middle of a Wolf fight.

"That was very dangerous, Sylvie," he said for the third time. After his immediate relief that Graham and his pack left, and that we were all right, Orion soon turned grumbly over me being caught in the crossfire. When I argued that it had been my decision, he gave me an exasperated harumph like an annoyed hound.

If I weren't coming down from the rush and a little irritated with him, I would have laughed. "I *know*, baby, but it's over now. And I feel like we have more important things to talk about."

He sighed and ran a hand over his messy hair. Instead of changing into a new shirt, Orion just threw away the remnants of his ripped one, and his skin looked warm and inviting in the dim light of the living room. His black tattoos almost eclipsed the pale skin of his arm. "Sylvie. They have already killed at least one person, that we are sure of. I need you to understand that when I tell you to stay in the house, it's to keep you safe. I know that you're powerful, but it worries me when you're in danger."

"Why were they saying that this is their land?"

Orion gave me a long look at my change in subject, but he relented. "Because they feel as though they can. Since Graham has been Pack Leader, he tries to assert that those not in his pack are prohibited from running on the land they claim is theirs."

"And by running, I'm assuming you mean in your wolf form." Orion nodded warily, like he was preparing himself for me to have something negative to say about it. But I was just relieved he'd finally told me. I hadn't even been surprised to see Jasper with Graham's little group. What happened in the coffee shop now took on a whole new meaning. "What were they saying about me not being your mate?"

Orion winced, and he dropped his gaze to his lap. "I should have told you sooner. Let you know what this meant." He waved a despondent hand at the darkened mark on his shoulder. I reached up to touch mine and felt it warm under my touch. I'd guessed it had something to do with claiming a partner, even before I'd figured out what Orion was. Through the wall between us, when I heard him call me his mate, my heart leapt at the word that encompassed how I felt for him.

"That we're mated you mean?"

His brow was drawn low over his eyes, and he wasn't even attempting to look at me. He nodded. "Yes. Though, I understand if I've broken your trust and you don't want that. I just..." Orion chuckled to himself, shook his head. "I've been selfish. I wanted to have you and not have it tainted by all that comes with who I really am. And I've put you in danger. I am so sorry, Sylvie." His voice was rough, trembling at the end, and I just couldn't take it.

I put the mug on the floor beside my feet and knelt between Orion's legs. I ducked my head to catch the soft, miserable green, and took both his hands in mine. "Orion. I forgive you. And, while I don't know everything, obviously, I already guessed you were a... a wolf shifter. So please don't be upset. I love you."

He sucked in a gasp, and I waited. I rubbed my thumbs on the backs of his hands and watched while he inched closer to me, nose sniffing intently. He didn't even have to ask, my head just turned to the side, offering my neck for him. Orion took to the area again, inhaling and exhaling in quick succession.

After a while, he reached some sort of conclusion, and he pressed his brow against mine. His voice cracked as he whispered, "I love you, Sylvie. So much. I don't deserve you, but I will be by your side for as long as you'll allow."

I kissed him quickly, just a brush of our lips, and nuzzled my nose against his. He grunted, lashes tickling my cheeks, and I couldn't stop the smile on my face. How many times had Orion held himself back from making these little sounds? From being his true self? It still hurt a bit that he'd feared I'd reject him, but my joy in another barrier fallen between us eclipsed it.

"I've already claimed you, remember?" I poked gently at my mark on his skin. But what Graham said immediately started niggling again at the back of my mind. "Wait," I pulled back to look at him, "when he said I wasn't claimed, what did he mean, I thought—"

The sound Orion made this time was more menacing, angry. His lip curled back away from his teeth. "I *have* claimed you."

"But why doesn't he think so?"

Orion's hands landed on my neck, cupping my jaw, and my pulse beat steadily under his fingers. I waited while he fought with himself about something, jaw working, but I saw when he decided how to explain. "I… For Wolf mates, the bite is the claim. Piercing flesh with the intent to mate." His finger tickled where his teeth bruised but never broke my skin.

The difference dawned on me after a moment of furrowed confusion. "But I broke your skin. Does that not count?"

He gave a weak shrug. "You aren't Wolf. To them, it doesn't hold weight."

"Okay, but why does it matter?"

"To me, it doesn't. But I think he's trying to find a reason to provoke me. Matehood is sacred to all shifters, and for those of us that tend to group in packs, mates—shifter or not—are extended protection and special consideration." Orion's body went rigid, and in the dim light of the room, it looked like his teeth sharpened. "Harassing you as my mate is a special kind of disrespect. Unforgivable. To state my claim incomplete is an attempt to justify his actions."

I nodded, but I was annoyed. These rules seemed primitive, but I had to remind myself that it was most likely Graham manipulating their customs to his benefit. Because he'd only tried to ruffle my feathers when Orion wasn't around. That couldn't have been a coincidence. "Okay, well," I exposed my neck once again, "bite me properly, so he at least won't have that to hold over our heads." At least this had a simple solution. I fought to keep my expression serious, even when the prospect of Orion sinking his fangs into my neck made me more excited than seemed appropriate to admit.

I sat there, neck craned to the side for a long time. The anticipation had been distracting enough that it took a while for me to realize that Orion hadn't moved at all. I turned back to him. "Baby?"

Orion scrubbed a hand over his face, and I saw a flash of the black wolf illustrated on his inner arm. On our first date, I hadn't realized what it was, but after hours spent with him, I'd catalogued the old Irish art style that made up the majority of his tattoos. The animal leapt across the length of his forearm, its form incorporated in a series of swirls and Celtic knots.

When he finally spoke, his tone was firm. Almost so much so that it disguised something blue—sadness or regret. "No, Sylvie. As much as some of the legends about my kind have been wrong, if I break the skin, you could turn. Something that is very painful if it doesn't… end your life."

I searched his face, lips turned down in a decided frown that matched my confused one. "But, you've already bitten me once." Well, bitten and scratched, if I was remembering correctly. It'd happened so fast, but I was fairly certain. "And nothing happened. Maybe my being a witch rejects it somehow? Either way, I'm willing to take the risk."

Orion looked at me as if I'd said something horrific. He shook his head vehemently, and he took my head in his hands again. "*No*, Sylvie. I won't budge on this. There's no way to be sure—"

"Orion, you aren't listening to me. Let *me* decide. I'd rather not give that pack any reason to doubt us."

He gnawed at his lip, gem green eyes swimming in the middle space between us. He whispered, more to himself than me, "I can't lose you."

I leaned into his left palm and bent to kiss his wrist. "Oh, baby, you're not. I know it. None of this scares me. *You* don't scare me."

Orion just chuckled and shook his head. "My little witch, facing down five shifted Wolves. You may not have been afraid, but I guarantee the rest of us were."

"Pfft, they had it coming. And I meant what I said. You *are* beautiful."

His brow quirked. "I'm not sure anyone's called my half-shift beautiful. I've certainly never thought of myself that way."

I gave his wrist another kiss. "Well, you are. And…" Orion's head tilted to the side, waiting and also a bit like when a dog hears a strange noise. It was extremely cute, almost as much as he was when he blushed. It made me dredge up enough courage to ask, "Can... can I see?" I cleared my throat. "Unless you're uncomfortable, because in that case, I would never—"

My words cut off abruptly, and my eyes went wide in wonder. Orion was still holding my face, but his grip loosened. To give room for claws that prickled gently on my skin. He took a deep breath, closing his eyes on the inhale, and I felt my own lungs stop to watch in awe. Orion's eyes already had a slight upward tilt at the ends, but my mouth dropped open while they shifted to a very definite slanted almond shape. The round curves of his ears lengthened until they came to pointed ends.

When Orion exhaled, his pink lips parted to reveal long fangs on the top and bottom rows of his teeth. His eyes opened, and the bright green reflected in the light, glowing.

They weren't meeting mine, but that was okay. He gave a little, self-conscious smirk, and I rested my hands on his chest. His heart was hammering beneath his skin, and in reflex, I lightly scratched, giving him goosebumps.

"My mate." I grinned.

Orion nodded, brows turning up and crumpling at the same time. I thought about the kiss he'd given me before storming out of the house to confront Graham and his pack. It felt almost like a goodbye, and it'd left a hollow drop in my chest. I'd known before that I loved him, but in that moment, when I realized he thought there was a chance he wouldn't come back, I almost panicked. And then hearing Graham's slimy words turned the panic into anger. Orion was mine, and I would protect what was mine.

I would do everything to keep him and his heart safe. He said those weeks ago that he'd never belonged to anyone before, but that wasn't true. Looking at him now, baring this vulnerable part of himself, I knew that he'd always been mine. We just hadn't found each other yet.

"Do you..." Orion spoke slowly, but his words were somehow unencumbered by his lengthened teeth. "Would you like to see me? Fully shifted." He met my eyes now, and I nodded with an encouraging smile. Orion leaned in, then hesitated.

I closed the distance between us and crashed my lips into his. He needed to know that I wasn't afraid, that I meant it when I said he was beautiful, so I followed what my body was already screaming for anyway.

My tongue licked along the seam of his lips, and his grip on my jaw tightened a fraction before he let me in. Orion's tongue had changed with his half-shift as well. It felt flatter than before, and when he slid it tentatively against mine, it was noticeably rougher.

Carefully, I tickled the edge of his sharp canines, and I shuddered with something that was far from apprehension. I wondered what I smelled like to him, if he could tell that, if anything, seeing him like this made me feel even more connected.

I trailed my kiss to his cheek, down the length of his jaw, to his neck. "You're amazing, Orion." A growl reverberated against the muscles of his throat, and I latched myself onto a patch of skin, placing open-mouthed kisses that just made him growl more.

"Sylvie." Orion's voice was deeper, lower like how it'd been the night I bit him.

My thighs squeezed in reaction. "Tell me what you need, baby."

He pulled me off of his neck, and I moaned in protest before I was caught in the spell of his stare. He searched my face for something, breaths coming heavy through his nose, and I felt at risk of becoming a puddle at his feet.

He brought a palm to my throat, claws pressing into my skin but nowhere near breaking it. I couldn't tell whether I was relieved by that fact or not. "I want you." And the groan I gave was nearly a whine. Before I could suck my bottom lip into my mouth to stifle the noise, Orion caught it between his teeth. He licked and nibbled, pulling on the flesh, and I continued to melt.

When he released me, I breathed, "You have me." I scooted forward and began fiddling with Orion's sweatpants. He leaned back on the table, the wood creaking beneath him, and I ran a hand over the trail of soft, white fur that had appeared on his muscled lower belly.

His growl when I lapped at the bead of precum was louder than the others. My hand worked over his pale pink shaft, and Orion's delicious taste flooded my awareness. He gripped my hair and thrust his hips, and I worked to get him all the way in my throat. I eventually rested my hands on his thighs and let him fuck into me while my eyes rolled back.

His rhythm grew erratic, and the wild noises he was making warned of him being a breath away from spilling down my throat. Though he groaned in frustration, Orion immediately released me when I pressed up off of him.

He was otherworldly, between man and wolf and something unique entirely. My mate, my Wolf.

Orion caressed a clawed thumb on my cheek, and I leaned into the sharp edge. I didn't miss the wave of desire that crossed his eyes that were now shaped like a wolf's, and he did it again. I wanted him to be uninhibited like this with me. Finally.

"*I* want you, baby. To take me and come in me." Even after getting my implant, he'd still refused to stop pulling out without explanation.

"You know what happens when a Wolf takes his mate, Sylvie? If I come in you… we'll be stuck together. Knotted." I recalled something I'd read about when I looked up wolves before. Was that truly it? I'd been fixating on that detail, on what I saw as a lack of trust in me, but if it came with him being a shifter, I understood why he hadn't been able to explain to me before.

But I already loved and accepted all parts of him. Just to rile him up further, I raised a brow. "And?"

He willingly took the bait, maybe even realizing that I was mimicking him from the night we first kissed. His claw scraped over my lip, and I opened my mouth, welcoming the danger of it against my tongue. Even with all his worrying, I knew that Orion would never hurt me. Anxiety made it hard to submit and give up control in all other areas of my life, my father's sudden illness still making me feel the need to cling onto whatever little bits I could.

Giving it all up to my mate, though, was an entirely different story. It made me feel safe and cared for, and through our time together, I'd learned that he especially enjoyed it. Craved it, even. To care and support and lead when I was willing to be led.

"Are you going to behave for me? Be good?" His husky voice was downright gravelly, his teeth menacing and sharp. I nodded with the pad of his finger still pressing on my tongue, and it was no time at all before I found myself bent over the couch and my knees pressing into the supple leather. I arched and moaned at the first scrape of his claws on my hips, but when he thrust into me with one long, fast motion, I cried out before immediately begging for more.

While he fucked me, Orion nipped at my earlobe. "I love you, and I love you on my cock. You always smell so sweet when I fuck you."

I couldn't think of anything to respond with—it all just came out as more desperate moans until his relentless pulses made me muffle my scream into the couch. He growled behind me, and if anything, he started fucking me harder. His clawed hand found my throat again and arched my head off of the cushion. I sucked in air and pushed back against his hips. The intensity was almost too much, and I kept moving, chasing more. "Don't you *ever* try to hide your precious little noises from me, Sylvie. I want to hear how well-fucked my mate is. Do you understand?"

My fists tightened, leather shuddering between my fingers, and I nodded while arching my back even more.

"Say it, Sylvie." Orion snarled behind me, and the back of my head found the strong, hard slope of his shoulder just as my eyes rolled while I rushed toward another release.

On the way, I babbled, pleaded, "I understand, please. Please, oh fuck, please baby come in me, please." I floated high above us, swept up in an orgasm that ended with my body already on its way to another. "Do it, please, baby, I want it." I clutched one of his hands, squeezing to encourage him to stay, to keep going.

As if that was all he needed, Orion's thrusts grew more erratic, and I felt a new pressure in me. It stretched me in a way that was further than I thought possible, and I tightened my hand over his even more. My muscles clung around him, our movements shortening until he couldn't move any more, and then he let loose a long, deep groan that was laced with a growl.

I followed him over the edge, stuffed fuller than I'd ever thought possible. It felt foreign, strange, but also right. To let him into me this way.

I giggled in surprise when Orion's nose tickled my neck, sniffing along the curve of my throat. "I'm sorry... I should have explained more thoroughly before. I—"

"Shh, baby. Let's get more comfortable, I think you turned my body to jelly."

Orion didn't try to apologize anymore, and I heard the rustling of fabric before he carefully pulled us both onto our sides on the couch. Though he tried his best to keep our hips steady, his movements still jostled his dick inside me, causing involuntary whimpers from the waves of pleasure.

His arm pulled my back firmly into his chest, and our naked legs were tangled along the length of the cushions. I yawned. "How long are we... knotted? Is that what you called it?"

Orion shifted behind me, and I felt his eyes on the side of my face, though my eyes were closed. The ecstasy of having Orion finally finishing inside of me was settling to a humming bliss that I felt in my bones.

"You are taking all of this very well, Sylvie. Are you okay?"

I shrugged. "Yeah, why wouldn't I be?"

He scoffed. "Because you're currently trapped on my dick, and if the claws and fangs weren't indication enough of my not being human, *this*," he wiggled his hips a bit for emphasis, and I moaned, pressing back on him since it felt nice, "is—further evidence of that."

"Mm. Well, I suspected for a while that you weren't human. That you were a wolf shifter. So I had time to wrap my mind around it. Though, it wasn't hard. Maybe if I were *just* human it'd be different, but," I waved a hand in the air, "it's who you are. And I love everything about you."

He huffed and kissed me on my cheek. "Well. To answer your question, we'll be able to move in about thirty minutes or so."

I hummed and held his arm tighter around my middle. Now Orion's commitment to pulling out made complete sense. When I'd skimmed over wolf mating habits in fear that Kara had startled a wolf pack and their newly born pups, the description of how wolves locked together during mating didn't seem at all pleasant for both parties. But lying here with my own Wolf made me feel warm and goopy. Content.

"Is the rest of your family like you?" I found myself asking after some time of lying in silence. I still felt the knotted base of Orion's cock in me and was relieved to have this for a little while longer.

His claws were still out, and he tapped his first two fingers in a steady rhythm on the crest of my hip. "My parents, yes. Ramona and her father, no."

"Oh, well how do they feel about all this? Your sister and mom's husband, I mean. I'm assuming they're human."

He gave a snort that wasn't quite a chuckle. "Well, Sean doesn't know about any of this."

I turned my head as far as I could, peripheries catching the long, pale slope of his nose. His fangs were gone, and I wondered if it was easier to speak without them. Even though he sounded the same whether they were present or not. "My mother has kept our nature secret from her husband for their entire relationship. Ramona knows, because while she's human, she's also... different."

"Different how?"

"Heightened senses, mostly. Sean just thinks we all have really great hearing. She also can't be turned. Something about having a shifter parent makes children like her immune."

I nodded along, though his step-father's cluelessness made me frown. How could he be so unaware? "Isn't that hard on your mom? And you guys?"

"Well, my mother is going to do what she wants to do. And I was away with Da or at school most of the time. Sean was away working more often than not. I'd imagine it's hardest on my mother, but it was her decision. She never explained her reasons to me, so I stopped asking long ago."

I puckered my lips in silent request, and Orion pecked the side of my mouth in answer. "Well, I'm glad we won't have that secret between us. I want you to be yourself around me."

Orion chuffed and snuffled in my hair. "I am so lucky. Thank you, my wonderful mate."

I grinned toward the fireplace, wishing that we'd thought to start a fire before we committed to being stuck on the couch for a while. It was sweet, easy, and Orion let me ask all my questions about his life as a wolf shifter. His answers flowed out of him, and I swallowed down every story, like how his father had guided him through his first shift at age twelve, or when at fourteen, he spent an entire week in his wolf form so that he wouldn't have to talk to anyone.

"I just ran and hunted and slept under the stars. After a while, I'd started to feel more Wolf than anything else. It was like the land here spoke to me. I even convinced myself that there were creatures besides animals out there. Ones that ran with me through the snow and helped me find food."

"So, have you never been in a pack then?" I remembered what Graham had called him but hesitated to use the word in case it was some sort of insult or slur.

Orion stiffened behind me, and it was then that I noticed the pressure inside me had lessened. Orion slid out but remained at my back. I waited, not wanting to push him to saying anything while he was still clearly thinking it through. I missed him inside of me, though.

He pressed up, bracing on a palm, and he ran the other hand up the back of his head. I watched and waited, and when he finally opened his mouth, I held my breath for what was to come.

"I... when I was in college. I started running with some Wolves I met on campus. They were part of a pack in town, and it was the first time I'd experienced anything like that." He sat up completely and draped my legs across his lap. I turned on my other side so that I could more easily see him, but he was staring forward, as if peering into his memories that he hadn't unlocked in a long, long time. "I told you that I studied under a master carpenter for a while. He was another member of the pack. For a few years, it was nice. I had a home, a group to run with where I felt accepted."

I propped up on my elbow, moving slowly so as to not interrupt, and after he took another few deep breaths, Orion continued. "I... met someone. The Pack Leader's daughter." My jaw clenched, and I felt a flash of rage and jealousy. Orion rubbed his hand over my calf in reassurance. "She... she made me feel loved. Or what I thought was love.

"And I let her convince me that I was strong. That I was to protect and lead not only her but the pack. That my own family's history in Antler Pointe was proof of that." He shook his head, as if trying to stop what happened next from playing out in his mind, but, of course, he kept going. His voice got rough with regret, anger. "So, when I challenged her father for Leader, I thought she would stand behind me no matter the outcome. When I lost, though, I was severely injured and exiled."

I stared in horror at what my Orion was telling me. To hear of the betrayal he'd experienced. "I'm glad now that the Pack Leader decided not to kill me. But at the time, when she—just turned her attention to another male in the pack, I wanted nothing more than to be dead."

My heart was breaking for this Orion, the one that'd been

beaten down before I met him, and I sat up, curling into his side. He accepted my touch and placed his arm around me. "My father passed away shortly before that. Perhaps his death was what made me so vulnerable to the manipulation. Because when I realized that she'd been hoping to align and mate herself to whoever took over as Leader, it was too late. That pack's leadership wasn't hereditary, and maybe she would've been chosen had she waited until it was time to select a new leader. But she was impatient and knew she wouldn't be able to win a fight against her father. When I lost, she looked at me… it wasn't as if I'd failed her. It was like I was nothing. And when I was given just a few days to lick my wounds and leave the territory, she was already slinking up to another male in the pack."

I kissed the base of Orion's neck and settled into the curve of muscle. My mate had been through so much, and while my anger was still very much present and simmering, so was the utter sadness for what he'd endured. I wanted to take the pain from him, to make him feel comfortable and settled.

"Mm," Orion hummed and rested his head atop mine. "That feels nice."

My lashes fluttered, brows furrowed. "What does?"

Orion rubbed his face on the top of my head and gave another contented grumble. "Whatever you're doing. It feels warm. Good." I concentrated again, on my desire for Orion to feel loved and rested, and I felt him nod against my scalp. "Yeah, that."

I kissed him again and petted the soft patch of hair on his chest. And while we sat, the tension in his body began to slip away. He relaxed back into the couch, his muscles molding into mine.

Our breaths seemed to sync, deepening until the jarring sound of the record skipping jolted me out of the sleep I was descending toward.

Orion slipped out from beside me, and I watched as he put the record in its sleeve and back on the shelf. He turned back around while he stretched his arms overhead, and I marveled the way his muscles ran over his form like water. There was something about the way he moved that wasn't human, like a smoothness that either I'd written off as him just being self-possessed or he'd previously held back.

Though my body was probably still done for the time being, I made no secret of my marveling of Orion's body. Tall and broad and lean with his almost white skin and hair, he was the essence of raw, otherworldly beauty. How anyone could reject this sweet, wonderful man, I'd never know. And selfishly, I was glad because it meant that he'd made it to me.

Ridiculous tears started to prickle in my eyes, and I blinked them away before he could become alarmed. But when my vision cleared, I saw him watching me with head tilted and nostrils flaring.

"What is it, mo ghrá?"

I cleared my throat to make sure it wasn't thick with tears. I smiled over at him, naked as the day he'd been born. "Just love you so much."

His eyes crinkled. "And I love you. Do you still want to see my full shift? I think I'll stay in wolf form while we sleep so that I can be more prepared in case they come back. My senses are sharper that way."

"Of course, baby," I whispered.

"Okay." Orion smirked before lowering his gaze. Again, he took a deep breath, and I didn't know what I had been expecting, but watching my mate's limbs contort and shorten and sprout fur was something I didn't think I'd ever be able to prepare for. There was no flash of light, but the thrum of *something* made my chest vibrate in kind. The popping of bones, thump of his arms—now front legs—hitting the wood floor made me wince if only in worry that it was painful. The whole process was fairly quick, but it felt like forever until finally I was faced with... a very large Wolf. I'd never seen one this close, but I was fairly certain that Orion's Wolf was bigger than non-shifter wolves.

The White Wolf, the mushrooms had called him.

Orion's green eyes were brighter than in his human form, but they were just as soft, just as light. His fur was the color of fresh snow, his nose as black as my hair. When his body was fully changed, he huffed and shook, and a giggle burst out of me at the action. He was cute.

He padded toward me, though the gap between the couch and coffee table was a bit snug for his body. I scooted closer to the edge and reached my hands out. Orion bumped his muzzle into my fingers, and I threaded them into his thick fur. It was soft and coarse, perfect for keeping warm in the cool air outside.

"My mate," I whispered and kissed him on the nose. It was cold and wet, and in return, he gave a long swipe of his tongue on my cheek. I gave a proper laugh now and peppered more kisses over his nose and beside his ears that seemed to be constantly moving. "Should we get ready for bed? We can watch a movie and fall asleep?"

He gave a little yip, and though I had absolutely no experience in wolf sounds and what they meant, I figured that it was a yes.

So I stood, and after bending forward to press a kiss on the top of his head, I set out to make sure all the doors were locked and turned the lights off. Orion kept by my side and used his nose and front paws to do half the work, which was a funny sight to see.

He sat in the doorway while I brushed my teeth and washed my face, and I chatted away about the things I'd been working on with Granna, about how Josie agreed to learn at my side.

We settled on the bed, and I set up my laptop to play one of my comfort movies. It was an old horror classic that was more campy than scary, and after I braided my hair and secured my silk scarf, I slid under the covers. In the dark, I sleepily watched the movie with Orion lying on top of the covers behind me. His head rested on the peak of my hip, and I petted him until I couldn't keep my eyes open any longer.

CHAPTER THIRTY-ONE

JASPER

"I understand all of your concerns, but we have all of this under control. You're dismissed." The pack meeting had *not* been going well. By the end, Graham all but spat the dismissal to everyone, and I saw multiple pack members bristle at the harsh command.

The full moon run was tomorrow, but several members requested an impromptu meeting to discuss a variety of pack matters. Some were petty squabbles, some logistical matters, and some were regarding pack membership. Monica requested an audience to hear about her desire to bring her mate into the pack. Some girl she met out of town who wasn't Wolf but another shifter. An Ocelot or something, which I thought was kinda cool. Come to think of it, I had never seen a non-shifter ocelot, never mind an ocelot shifter.

Graham immediately shot her down, stating that our pack was for wolf shifters and their human mates, and that bringing in other shifters was dangerous and too complicated. Some nodded agreement, some barely contained their disagreement, but I caught Ana, Declan, and I cutting glances toward one another.

Were they thinking what I was? Were they worried for whatever mates they might want to bring into the pack? In Monica's case, Graham agreed to the matehood but forbade Monica's future mate running with us. She would be mated, but her mate wouldn't be *pack*.

Had it always been like this? Mating between different shifter species was definitely rare, but not impossible. I had a Wolf buddy over in St. Paul who was mated to a true shape shifter. Now *that* was dangerous. Those Shifters were crazier than bed bugs, as my nanna would say.

"Declan, Ana, Jasper, stay back," Graham barked, and I was pulled out of my whirling thoughts. It'd been harder to focus these days. Lack of sleep was part of it, and Graham had me doubled up on my scouting. But the witch had stayed between campus, her new job at some witchy store downtown, her grandmother's house, and Orion's cabin. Over and over, day after day, I trailed behind her while keeping as far a distance as I could. It'd been nearly a month since she somehow reversed Graham's shift and pulled a knife on us, and things hadn't gotten any better.

I kicked at a thick fallen branch while we waited for Graham to finish talking to the two straggling members who asked for permission to run elsewhere or skip the run tomorrow altogether. That was a new thing, too. I remembered being a pup, when Chief was Leader, and a pack member skipping out on a full moon run at home was almost unheard of. If it happened, it raised a ton of alarms.

Not right not right not right, that familiar string of thoughts started running again, and my head throbbed with my trying to push it back. We were getting closer to the solstice, but none of us felt confident in trying to get her. After seeing what she did to Graham and feeling the waves of whatever the fuck she could do, who was to say we'd even be able to get our hands on her? We needed to take her alive and present her, but if we were all writhing messes on the ground, there wouldn't be any point to it.

The thick branch I'd been kicking at rolled over, and for a

second, it looked like a leg bone. It was about the same length and width. *So fucking stupid.* How in the hell we'd left behind a bone that she somehow happened to find was beyond me. But things got chaotic and messy each solstice. It was like a high, but different than the clear, energizing kind from running. It was frenzied, buzzy, and even now, my body was feeling dry and empty. Craving it.

"So, what's up Leader?" Dec spoke first, stuffing his hands in his pockets and holding his chin high, as if he hadn't been panicking and almost shitting his pants earlier.

"Man, this don't sound fucked up to you? My dad, Jas. What if he doesn't want us to stop? What if he gets a taste f-for pack mates or something—"

"She's not pack, and he isn't either," I tried to supply, but it felt lame.

"Yeah, but who's to say that it won't turn in to that, you know what I mean? Really, going after pack would be even easier, dude. We know how to cover our tracks, and the person would be easier to get. Oh, god." He made an agonized noise and shuddered into his hands.

Even I winced, the thought of harming a member of the pack when it wasn't a sanctioned challenge was unthinkable. We were family but deeper, and I wanted to say that would never happen, but the assurance got stuck on my tongue. Because when I thought of Leader, I wasn't sure how far he was willing to go. He was supposed to answer to us, and us to him and each other, but it was feeling more and more like he only answered to himself.

"I need a report on how scouting is going." Graham crossed his arms and stood tall. His Leader scent was like a thick, wet blanket. When had I grown to feel suffocated instead of loved?

"Same as before. Can't get too close to the houses 'cause of that barrier or the White One. But we know her routine."

Graham ran a thumb along his jaw, scratching at the stubble that was patchy and in need of a shave. "What about the other witches?"

Ana spoke up next. Her mouth was set in a tense line, her eyes warier than usual. "The old one leaves the house even less. When she does, it's shopping or lunch with the red-haired one."

Then Declan. "The new witch works from home. Her apartment's downtown. She's a little more varied. Spends the nights with other people sometimes. Usually not the same person twice. Other than that, she's at the witch house." He shrugged, but I wondered how much of him was still freaking out. By the split-second glance he gave me, I would guess that he was.

Graham didn't seem to notice, though. He was on edge and more paranoid about some things, but he hadn't picked up on the fact of our doubts. He knew that we would still follow him, and maybe that was the sickest thing of all.

Because after the high of the hunt and the sacrifice, the comedown was brutal. Not when we were still around each other or the cleanup afterward, but when we slunk back home and were alone.

"Jas, I still see her face. Every night," Ana confessed to me when we were setting out one day to scout the witches' house. Yeah, the last one had been sloppier than the others, what with Kara slipping away and starting to run. That was probably how we'd left evidence behind, but having the Chief as a member of the pack made us untouchable.

Our own guilt, however, was something that was getting harder and harder to cover up. I saw it every time I looked in the mirror, and I saw it on their faces, too.

River had been my best buddy as a kid. We drifted apart once we became teenagers, but the way he begged at the end was—

"Leader. Maybe..." Ana's face was pinched, and my insides clenched with something acidic. The sensation only got worse when I saw the way Graham's shoulders stiffened when he turned to face her.

"Speak," he commanded.

To give her credit, Ana didn't shy away from meeting his eyes.

We were loyal, and she'd known Graham since before he moved to Antler Pointe. They'd been friends before he took over the pack, but I didn't think she'd ever expected things to go this way. For Graham to pull us all into this and for us to grow addicted to it.

She seemed to decide on her course of action and squared her shoulders. "The witch is trouble. Her powers are unknown, and we could easily get someone else. He surely can't be that picky, can he? The others were just fine enough to allow him to come back." Though we'd been told more now that we were fucking in it, it was all so weird. After his first chance encounter last winter solstice, Graham agreed to provide for him each equinox, each solstice. So that he could stay longer and give us more each time.

I saw the corner of Graham's jaw tick, but otherwise, his face didn't change. I felt like I was going to break out in a sweat. "Ana, you are forgetting your place. He came to *us*. Recognized us as the rightful guardians of this—"

She interrupted him. "Yeah, b-but, we can't surely... we aren't at *war*."

Graham's fangs flashed in the firelight, his Leader scent overtaking us in thick, crashing waves. "Are you saying that you're ungrateful, Ana? That you don't feel more connected to the land? That your shifts aren't easier to control?"

Ana's resolve was proving even better than mine or Dec's could ever be. I shared a worried glance with him, but neither of us said anything. We just stood there. "I feel it, Graham. But do we *need* this? It—it can't be *worth* what we've done." Her voice cracked at the end, and if I hadn't heard it or smelled her grief and guilt, I wouldn't have been able to tell. Her eyes were still steely, her spine rod-straight.

Graham advanced a step, towering over her, even with several feet between them. "You need to mind your place, Ana." His voice was strong and dominant, but his eyes were bloodshot. I'd been around Leader enough to know that he was feeling it, but not the shame the three of us were drowning with.

One of my cousins down south had been an addict. For a long time, he was able to hide it from everyone—still going to work, still going to Nanna's for Sunday dinner. He was able to juggle it all, the fixes and the withdrawals. Until he wasn't.

Leader was strong. Leader had done a lot for us. We'd stopped the pack the next territory over from encroaching on our land. We had a better rein on the new pups and teaching them how to handle their shifts without needing to sequester for months on end until they could control themselves. Despite the blood on our hands, I couldn't deny that I was able to hear the land singing in a way that I never could before.

But I recognized the strain on Leader's face. The way it all melted away when we met with *him* and let his power take us over. Graham most of all. Christ, we were all fucking addicts.

"You were there the last time. You heard what he said and saw what he was able to do." I took a nervous gulp.

"Loyal pups, get the witch, and I can bestow on you more power than you've dreamt. Than you've already felt." The prospect of being bigger, stronger, and faster had sounded great at first. We'd all had tastes of it, but they'd mostly faded between each fix. Sylvie would allow him to give us more, he'd said.

Shit, what if I just left? What if I just left everything behind, maybe stayed with my buddy in St. Paul for a while? His pack welcomed his mate easily enough, maybe they'd take me in, too.

Mom and Dad's faces flashed in my mind, and I dropped the frantic hope. No, I wouldn't just leave them to this. We kept the others in the dark per Graham's assertion that the other's wouldn't understand.

Yeah, no shit, they wouldn't understand.

"Is there anything else we need to do, Leader?" I needed to get out of here. To run on my own to clear my head for a while. All I'd been doing in my wolf form was scouting for the solstice. I just wanted to be on four legs and not have to *think*.

Graham grunted, still staring Ana down. She finally averted

her eyes, but the hard look on her face remained. Leader turned to me and shook his head.

Usually I stayed back after the rest of us were dismissed, in case he needed anything or wanted to discuss something. But I was at my capacity, and if we spent any one-on-one time together, I might reveal my doubts that were growing bigger and bigger each day. Each hour, it felt like.

We were already out in the forest so that we could all speak freely and away from any non-pack human ears, so while the others went toward their cars or to catch up with some of the members that'd left, I stripped my clothes and left them in a haphazardly folded pile on a stump. I'd come back for them. Or not. It didn't really matter.

I ran through the trees, feeling the cold December air prickle my throat and electrify my lungs. I ran up hills, tumbled around the bends, and just pushed my legs as far as they'd go.

At some point, I found myself at the lake.

The moon was almost full, and its twin sat on the surface of the black water. It was one of my favorite places, ever since I was a pup.

The White One's father would let us run on the land freely. When all this territory was all of ours. He was Unpacked, but nice. Chief Thompson was kind to him.

Graham, though, wanted him gone. Out of the way so that there was no one else to question whether the land was ours.

I went closer to the water and sat. It moved softly with the other animals that lived within.

A howl made me flinch, and I hadn't realized I'd come out so far. Usually I tried to stay hidden when I ran to the lake, but I was out in the open. I could clearly see the White One's house, and I could see him and his female. She sat with a book and one hand on the White One who was shifted, baring his fangs, but coming no further. Protecting his mate instead of attacking me.

I howled back, telling him that I meant no harm. At least right now, it wasn't a lie.

I watched, and he kept watching. Waiting. But that was good.

Why had I submitted that day? My own body betrayed me—in that moment, my *Wolf* betrayed me. Because Graham was Pack Leader. This White One was nobody.

But he cared for his mate. Loved her like Dad loved Mom.

What would he do when we took her? What would he do once she was dead?

CHAPTER THIRTY-TWO

ORION

The light from my laptop was painfully bright, no matter how meticulously I'd configured the settings. Staring at it for hours on end was less than ideal, but it was a burden I had to bear at the end of each semester.

My headphones were even starting to press on my ears too much. I'd done a lot of research before purchasing them, and normally, the weight and pressure of them on my head, the nostalgic music I constantly played, and the way they significantly dulled everything around me helped make even the most unpleasant of tasks less difficult.

Grading the papers from my Introduction to Irish Literature class, though, was proving to be more taxing than I thought it would be. I had to put in tremendous effort to not glower and keep my face and words pleasant when I knew that most were just doing the bare minimum. It was one of the many courses students could take to fulfill their graduation requirements, and if I had things my way, I'd cease teaching it immediately.

But, as they were required to take it, I was required to teach it. I was on tenure-track, but not there yet.

I began typing up my comments on my tenth final analysis paper of the day, one that was riddled with grammatical errors almost too ridiculous to be real. My head was throbbing, but the faster I got through this, the faster I could relax and focus on other things.

Although the pack hadn't harassed Sylvie or myself since coming to my house, it felt like they were almost closing in. Their running on my land felt suffocating, and I trusted my Wolf too much to ignore the feeling of foreboding that'd come over me.

Though Antler Pointe was small, news of Sylvie's classmate's death had all but blown over. Hell, she had been in one of my classes, but even my students barely mentioned her. Let alone the other two that'd also gone missing this year. The more I thought about it, and the more Sylvie and I discussed it, the surer I was that the pack had something to do with all three disappearances. Sylvie always scoffed when I got overprotective, but I hadn't been able to get Graham's looks toward her out of my mind.

My eyes lifted from the screen, and my body turned toward my office door. A few seconds later, a soft knock came.

"Come in," I said, all irritation leaving me in a blink. The power this witch had over me would have been frightening if I didn't trust and love her more than anything.

It was still quite surreal that she knew about me being Wolf. That a few weeks ago, she'd let me knot and breed her without batting an eye.

I'd had two exes that were Wolf, so I knew what it was like to let that mask fall. To allow myself to half- or full-shift around another without really thinking about it. To talk about the other side of myself.

But I hadn't loved either of them. Well, I supposed that I felt a platonic sort of love toward Juno. Regardless, no one compared to my mate who quietly closed my office door with a sweet smile on her face.

Her hair was down and framing her face and shoulders with thick, black curls. Her skirt swished as she walked, and her scent was already taking over the room. I inhaled, greedy for her as always, and the atrocious paper was already forgotten.

"How's your day going, baby?" Sylvie let her tote bag fall to the floor and plopped down in the seat opposite my desk. It'd been a few days since she spent the night at my cabin, and having her in front of me almost left me panting. It was a stressful time of the year for both of us, but the reward of having her again kept me pushing through.

I pulled off my headphones and set them next to my laptop. "Shitty. And yours?" Though the head of the department was aware of our relationship, I hadn't wanted to make things uncomfortable for Sylvie. School was important to her, and I didn't want her last semesters to be difficult or awkward because she was with me. And I didn't trust the students or faculty besides Juno to treat her the same if they knew.

Her deep brown eyes were warm, and her smile didn't falter with my honesty. I didn't lie to her. Now that she knew I was a shifter, there was nothing else I would hide from my mate.

"Just got back from picking up my graded paper from Faust's office. You know that he required us to hand in hard copies? Who does that anymore?" Her bottom lip poked out, and a little furrow creased between her brows. Despite the irritation rolling off of her, I couldn't help but smirk. My Sylvie was sweet, she was kind, and she was strong. Those things I knew already.

This side of her, though, was another one of my favorites. Pouty, whining, even sometimes bratty. Like the flashes of her anger, these moods often receded quickly. And like the rest of her, I was absolutely smitten. Even when we bumped heads, which wasn't often, I couldn't help but catch myself adoring her all the same.

I shrugged, and she was already scoffing before I said anything. It made my own smile grow. "He's old school, but I can understand. I've been staring at this fucking screen all day and have only gotten halfway done." If I weren't sharply opposed to dealing with the inevitable complaints from my students, I'd do the same thing.

"Oh, so you're taking his side? I thought I was the one you loved."

I gave her a dry look, but I couldn't hide the lightness in my voice. "I wasn't aware there were sides. What am I supposed to do, anyway?"

"Wield your power as my mate or something? I don't know. I have to take another of his classes next year because of my schedule, and I'm already fucking dreading it."

My little witch even crossed her arms over her chest, keeping up this pouting thing. I knew I was taking the bait, but I couldn't resist. "You're complaining about having to print out and come pick up a paper, Sylvie. Because you haven't even mentioned your grade, I'm assuming you didn't do as well as you wanted."

Her lips twitched. "That's beside the point. His class is *boring*. And I worked really hard on that paper!" She ran her eyes over me, and I saw the glint of something else. Her scent started shifting in a way that made my heart pick up.

Though she'd come to visit my office a few times, even had lunch with me, we both tried to keep our relationship and time at school as separate as we could. Well, aside from the first time we'd had sex.

Sylvie stood, and I watched her as she rounded the side of my desk and leaned her hip against it. Her nails, always painted that deep red, caressed the side of my face, and the scent of her arousal almost made me shiver. She bent at her waist and placed a tender kiss to my forehead and leaned into my ear. "Can I convince you to help me, baby?"

Without waiting for an answer, she sank to her knees.

I'd be lying if I said that I hadn't imagined her doing this many times. Her sneaking away after a class and going to the next one with my cum dripping down her legs and the bruises from my grip on her hips. Why hadn't we done this before, again?

Her elegant hands rested on the tops of my thighs and rubbed them back and forth. When she looked up beneath her dark lashes, her eyes were round and wide. "Please, Dr. Gealach? I'll be good for you, I promise." My dick jumped in my lap, and my mouth was actually fucking watering. This was what I meant when I said she put spells on me. Her voice was melodic, her scent and appearance so sweet. Even though I knew she was being mischievous and trying to rile me up, I was past the point of caring. That look in her eye when she stood from the chair told of some other intention, but when she unzipped my jeans and palmed my cock, I knew I'd just let it be.

The old desk that'd been in my office when I moved in was large, probably too big for the room itself. But the wood was expertly crafted, so I couldn't bear getting rid of it. Plus, it would've been a hassle to get it out of the door.

I was more than grateful for it now, though, when Sylvie tucked herself right between my legs and all but hid under the thick wood. She pulled my hard cock out of my boxers and circled her hand around the base.

"I've wanted to suck your dick in here for so long. Will you help me and let me do this for you? Please?"

I groaned. She knew what she did to me when she asked like that. Sometimes it felt like I could keep my Wolf and human halves separate, and sometimes it felt like they collided into one another. When my mate scratched at this part of me that wanted to dominate, it was impossible for me to resist.

"Maybe. But only because you asked nicely." There was no way I was going to interfere in one of Sylvie's classes, but she knew this. And I was willing to play along. I looked down and was enraptured by the sight of her hand around my cock. The way our skin contrasted and the way her hand looked smaller like this. "Spit on it." My voice sounded like I'd been chewing on gravel, and it would probably only get deeper.

That glint flared again, and Sylvie sank her teeth into her bottom lip. Her brows turned upward as she nodded and did what I said. Watching her pucker her lips and spit over the head of my cock almost made me come immediately, but I was somehow able to hold it back while she began jerking and letting her spit slick my skin.

My head leaned back in my desk chair, and I sucked in air at the first laps of her tongue. She took the head of my dick in her beautiful mouth while continuing to move her hand along the shaft. With each suck and swirl of her tongue, I got closer and closer. At some point, my hand had made its way into her hair, and my hips were thrusting in time with her movements.

Just as my balls were tightened up toward the base of my cock, and I was groaning to Sylvie that I was close, she released me with a wet pop and dropped her hand.

I glared down at her and was met with a cheeky smirk.

Neither of us said anything, and after my breathing calmed, she started again. This time, taking all of me down her throat and swallowing so much that it made my toes curl. Right when I got to the edge, she stopped again and looked up at me with those innocent eyes.

The third time she stopped, I was about to pick her up and throw her over the desk, but we both froze at the sound of a round of knocks at my door. I'd been so close to coming down her throat that I hadn't been paying attention to anything outside of what she was doing to me.

When I looked down at Sylvie, so cutely hidden under my desk and her eyes now wide in surprise and panic, I gave her a reassuring smirk.

"Come in," I called and successfully suppressed my chuckle at the choked whimper Sylvie gave.

My desk was faced toward the door, and with the size of it, my mate was completely hidden from the view of the two students that walked into my office.

"Yes?" I asked and scooted my chair closer to Sylvie. At the same time, I opened my thighs a bit more and felt the tickle of her hair on my bare skin. I leaned back and cupped Sylvie's chin in my hand.

"Hey, Dr. Gealach. I know that you're still grading, but I was hoping to see whether you'd graded my final yet or not. I'll be out of the country, and it'll be harder for me to check my grade over the break." I kept my face blank but barely paid attention to what the first one was saying. Under the desk, Sylvie was holding still and holding her breath, but when I gave her a light scratch with my claws, I felt her tremble. With my hand now at the back of her neck, I felt the goosebumps that started running down her spine.

"And you?" I asked the other one who may have wanted something else or just been there for moral support. Though I'd never checked those professor rating sites, Sylvie once teased me that my reviews were neutral enough besides me having the reputation for being 'intimidating'. Just because I wasn't overly friendly and only talked as much as I needed to. Whatever.

While the other student stammered and started giving some sob story as to why their paper had been late and asked if I could please waive the points I took off for the late submission, I started pulling Sylvie closer to my dick that was still just as hard.

I obviously couldn't look down to see her expression, but her arousal had begun rising again. Good thing the two students were human and none the wiser.

If my mate had resisted, I would've just continued to pet her until my students left, but her scent revealed her decision before she made it.

"You expect me to believe that you'll be without internet to check your grades? And that your tardiness should get special consideration?" My questions sent the students into further arguing their cases, but now all my attention was turned to the kittenish lapping of Sylvie's little tongue at the slit of my cockhead. My body was already on a hair trigger, and it was taking the last bit of my sense to not start thrusting again.

The students were too absorbed into defending their cases, pulling up flight receipts and work schedules to show me, to notice the sharp, silent breath I took when Sylvie's mouth started suckling from my cock. The sweet, warm heat of her tongue and lips were close to driving me out of my mind.

I'd meant this as a little payback for her pouting and edging earlier, but it seemed that she was determined to kill me.

Sylvie swirled her tongue while she sucked, taking more of me into her mouth, and by some miracle, I was able to keep my words steady. Barely. "What class?"

"Intro to African-American Literature." The one who wanted to know their grade had indeed pulled up a plane ticket with their name on it as evidence. I hid my groan of pleasure behind an affirmative grunt and started pulling up the grades I'd already finished.

"I'm in your Irish Lit Two cl—"

"Not you. I won't be giving you points back," I said as I started blindly scrolling on my laptop. My brain kept unfocusing with all my faculties focused on the sweet witch on her knees.

Finally, I found the grades I'd already entered, and this student was one of them. Lucky for them that I was feeling generous. "I gave you an eighty, which put your final grade at an eighty-three." The one with the trip seemed placated enough, but the one I'd cut off was trying to further beg and explain their situation. At that point, I should've just told them to get out, but the release literally racing down my spine made it too hard to find my words.

With a sigh and a hand dragging over my face in feigned irritation, I tried to hide it as best as I could. They didn't seem to notice, not even really paying attention to me and completely unaware that I was shooting my cum down my mate's throat while she silently and greedily swallowed.

Shit, she was perfect.

When I still wouldn't budge, the two students left with only the faint scent of disappointment in their wake.

Once my door was closed, and I was alone with Sylvie once again, I rolled back my chair to finally see her.

She looked up at me with lids half-lowered and a sultry smile on her face. "So, will you help me?"

A low growl ripped from my throat, and I picked Sylvie up before she could even realize what happened. Her surprised little yelp when I sprawled her on the surface of my desk and tore through her panties was like music to my ears. "No, and I'm going to eat you out until you're a begging, panting mess. And I'm still not going to let you come."

She propped up on her elbows to look down at me. She was still aroused, but worry flashed on her face for the first time, and all pretense of her little game vanished. "Wait, baby, that's not f— oh, fuck." She flopped back down when I started flickering my tongue over her clit. Somehow she tasted even better than before, when she didn't know all of who I was. It wasn't just because the feeling of my shifted tongue drove her into near hysterics, the rougher texture adding another degree of friction that she loved.

It wasn't just the fact that she clung to the backs of my hands on her hips, unafraid and keeping the pressure of my claws on her skin.

She was my everything, and I could be completely myself with her. It was the greatest feeling in the world, and the little whines and squeals she made were just the icing on top.

I pulled back so that I could see her face, and it was flushed with her lips still swollen from sucking me off and her eyes clenched tight in bliss. "If you behave, I'll go easy on you when I see you tonight. But you'll be going to work without coming, Sylvie." Before she could answer, I went back to my meal with a smirk on my face.

CHAPTER THIRTY-THREE

SYLVIE

"**D**o you mind me coming over now? Work ended earlier than I thought it would." I spoke with Orion while I was already pulling up the long gravel driveway to his house.

"No," his voice sounded over the speakers in my car, "do you still have the key I gave you?"

I rolled my eyes. "Yes, of course. I'm not *that* forgetful, you know."

The telltale noise of his snicker made my heart patter excitedly. "I'm just finishing up entering the last grades but should be leaving in the next ten minutes or so. Will you be all right waiting for me?"

"Of course," I continued around the bend, the cabin and lake coming into view. Though I felt completely at home and comfortable at Granna's, Orion's house settled something greater within me. Maybe it was just the fact that it was strongly associated with *him*. With the moments we had together and my feelings for him that were deepening every day.

Not to mention that I'd been railed in every room of that place.

My body was practically vibrating with anticipation, and just to heighten it even more, I asked, much lower, "How do you want me when you come home?"

There was a pause and faint rustling of papers before he spoke, lust in his voice palpable through the phone. "Naked."

I huffed a laugh and barely suppressed the 'duh' that I wanted to respond with. I pulled up in front of the house, in a spot that was feeling more and more like mine, and cut the car off. I put the phone up to my ear. "And what if I'm not?"

The resounding growl left my mouth dry, and I felt the telltale flutter in my gut. "You *will* be naked, waiting on the bed."

"Well, I'm already at your house." My eyes traced over its facade. The sun was almost completely set, and the kitchen light Orion left on shone through the shutters. Just to torment him a little, I said, "S'pose I could do that and just keep busy while I wait for you."

Another growl, this one deeper, and his deceptively calm tone made me grin. "If I get home and discover that you've made yourself come before I arrived, I'm going to be very upset."

"Even if I stay on the phone with you while I do?"

I could practically hear his teeth creaking with the clenching of his jaw. Though I'd take my Wolf any way that he was, all facets of him, I particularly loved when he let himself go. The memories of the past few times, where his body half-shifted in the height of our love making, ran through my mind, and I couldn't stop my grin. Despite Orion leaving me frustrated the other day after I taunted him in his office, he'd more than delivered once I met up with him that evening.

As if he knew exactly what I was thinking, Orion grumbled, "Behave, Sylvie."

I shifted in my seat. "But what if I'm impatient?" I pouted, knowing he'd be able to sense it. Sure, I could heed his request —well, demand. But the image of me spurring him on to his absolute limits and the way he'd fucked me last night on the living room floor, so that all I could do was take it, kept playing in my mind. How his claws had dug into my skin. I wanted *that*.

"Where are you."

I grinned and chewed the edge of a fingernail. "Sitting in your driveway. Thinking about whether I'm going to wait in the living room, the bedroom, or the dining room. And touch myself while I think of you. I still have my vibrator over here, I think."

A moment passed, and his voice was laced with a growl. "Touch yourself all you want, Sylvie, but you *will* stop before you come."

My chuckle was far deeper than I'd intended. "I don't think you can control that, baby. I'm already halfway there with you growling like that." And that wasn't a lie. I could already feel the wetness pooling between my legs, and my nipples felt sharp and sensitive beneath my dress.

"Then you'll have me to deal with later. Consider thoroughly if you want to go several more hours without me letting you come again."

"You okay, baby? You sound like you're wound up a little tight."

There was another moment, but then Orion spoke, voice steady and deceivingly calm. "Naked. On the bed. And if I find you're not, I will be very fucking upset."

I grinned down toward the phone. *Oh, this will be a fun night*, I thought to myself. "Yes, sir."

His answering growl made me laugh out loud, and just as I reached into the passenger seat to grab my purse and overnight bag, the shifting of light before me caught my attention.

My body froze, utterly shocked when the front door of the cabin opened, light from inside spilling out into the quickly darkening yard.

And then I felt utterly cold when a—woman stepped out onto the front porch.

I blinked a few times, wondering if my eyes were playing a trick on me, but she didn't go away. In fact, she walked closer, stopping to rest her arms on the wooden railing near the front steps.

She was looking right at me.

It took me a long time to figure out what to say with her staring with an expectant brow raised. Finally, I pried my mouth open to croak, "Orion..."

"I'm packing up my things now, so you better—"

"Why is there a woman at your house?" I bit out the words, anger creeping up. There was a strange woman. In my mate's house. And the way she was looking was as if she was challenging me. Conveying with her eyes that she'd already staked her claim.

"What?"

"Why. Is there. A woman. At your house." I seethed. Wrath. I wanted to march up to the porch and rip her throat out then wait for him to get back and claw at his face.

"I don't know what you're talking ab—what does she look like?"

My eyes were burning, but I gritted to him, debating on just turning around and going home before I did something that would surely get me arrested. "Blonde. Tall. Pale." Was that how he liked his women? Her coloring was like his, and mine was the complete opposite. Her perfectly straight hair was neatly parted on the side, and though it was harder to see with the light coming from behind her, I could tell that she was thin, her jeans and blouse clinging to her lithe frame.

Was this the woman from the pack he'd left those years ago? Did he lie and go off to see her when he took that time away to 'camp'? In that moment, I realized that I was far more capable of murder than I ever thought before. My rational mind would have reasoned that my anger was most likely misplaced on her rather than him, but at the moment, I didn't care. She was here, still staring at me, and—was she *smirking*?

I reached for the door, but Orion's curse made me pause. "Stay in the car. I'll be there in fifteen minutes." He sounded just as angry as I felt, and I supposed most men did get that way when they got caught. I couldn't believe it. Orion never, *ever* gave me an indication that he would do something like this. Underneath the rage, I knew that my heart was breaking. And once I throttled this woman and gave him a piece of my mind, I knew that I would have to feel it.

"Who is she, Orion."

His voice echoed over the phone, and I heard the air whip past him as he was probably bolting out of the English Department. "Fuck. What the *fuck*."

"*Who, Orion.*"

And then, the woman grinned. And the tilt of her lips made her look an awful lot like… like him?

The sound of a metal door opening and closing made me jump, and I heard the slaps of Orion's boots on asphalt as he made his way to the parking lot. The woman kept staring, kept grinning, and I felt my brows tighten in confusion. My call with Orion shifted, his phone hooking up to the car speakers, just before I heard the click of his seatbelt.

"My mother."

ORION

What the *fuck* was my mother doing *in my home*. And how did she get a fucking key?

I cursed aloud at the traffic that was slowing me down. It was a busier time, what with people starting to go out for dinner or whatever evening plans they had, and I narrowly avoided getting into three different accidents as I weaved between lanes, testing fate that I wouldn't get pulled over for speeding.

"Sylvie, listen to me. Stay in the car until I get there. I'm just a few minutes away." Though I'd now exited campus and could see the edges of town coming upon me, the racing in my heart and dread settling over my mind felt like it was going to make me explode.

"I—is she dangerous?" Sylvie's tone shifted from harsh to something wary.

I'd heard her speak like that enough now, and I cursed myself again for making her anxious. "No—she's not." I took a deep breath and pressed harder on the gas when I reached the road that led out to my land. There were luckily no cars about, and I let mine hit ninety miles per hour, trying to shave off as much time as possible. "She's just," I struggled to find the word, "complicated at best. Unpleasant at worst."

And then there was a surprised squawk. "What, Sylvie?"

"There's someone else here. Another woman with dark hair, skin a little lighter than mine." She didn't sound angry at all anymore.

Once again, I cursed to myself, *What the fuck*. "Must be Ramona." I was coming up on the turn off to my private road, tires shifting over gravel now.

"Y-your sister?" Sylvie whispered.

I gritted my teeth. "Yes. I'm pulling up now, Sylvie. Just wait for me to get there, please." I tried my best to soften my voice but knew that I was doing a shit job.

Surprisingly, though, I heard her snort something close to a laugh. "I just waved to them, and your mom waved back. Your sister is just staring at her phone. I'm gonna get out of the car."

"No, Syl—" But the call cut off. Did she *hang up on me*? If I weren't so furious about my mother and sister popping up unannounced, helping themselves to *my home*, I would've been dreaming up more ways I would be teaching my little witch a lesson when I got home. But no, now I would have to deal with Meredith and Ramona. Horror made my stomach clench. Were they expecting to... spend the night? "Fuck, fuck, fuck," I was chanting as the house finally came into view.

All three of them were standing on the porch now, and I homed in on Sylvie's nervous fidgeting but warm smile pulling across her face. I had hoped that Sylvie and Meredith would never meet, or at least, not for a long while, but it seemed as though I wouldn't be getting my way in this.

My car screeched to a halt, releasing a puff of gravel dust and dirt, and I'd barely put it into park and turned it off before I was darting toward them.

"… and your flight went smoothly?" My nostrils were flaring, taking in the scents of Meredith and Ramona, but focusing in on Sylvie's cool cherry to ground me. The sourness of her anxiety was spiking, but there was no fear.

Meredith was surely enjoying it nonetheless.

I leapt up the steps, and Sylvie turned to gift me with one of her bright smiles as I wound a hand around her back, gripping her waist. She relaxed into my touch, and I pulled her closer.

"Hey, O, what took you so long," Ramona droned without looking up from her phone, and I just grunted.

"Yes, son, we've been waiting for quite awhile." Meredith gave me a mocking glance while displaying perfect calm in the face of my shivering rage, adrenaline still pumping. Her nostrils flared, and her smile grew wider.

I didn't attempt to hide the rumble in my voice. "You didn't tell me that you were coming to visit."

"Hard to let you know when you don't pick up the phone." Ramona sank into one of the rocking chairs Sylvie had gifted me.

Meredith flicked her hair behind her back, almost as pale as mine. "Your sister's right. I tried to call you many times," she shrugged, "so, what were we to do?"

"A text message. A voicemail." They both knew that I abhorred talking on the phone. Well, with anyone but Sylvie. Especially when I got to listen to her little teasing earlier. I bit the inside of my cheek—to think, I'd been planning on which surfaces to take her on throughout the night. And now, this.

Meredith rolled her eyes that were a pale blue instead of my green, "Oh, well, it's too late for any of that, son. Your sister and I are here to visit with you. We haven't come since you moved away, so it's long overdue."

"Meredith—"

She scoffed. "So disrespectful," like I hadn't called her by her name since I was a child, "and you never even mentioned that you were seeing someone." She gestured to Sylvie, whose scent shifted with discomfort and whispers of hurt.

The growl that rumbled from my chest was far louder than I would have intended had I done it consciously. But Sylvie didn't stiffen at the outburst. Though I would never be able to claim her like I would another Wolf, I had in every other way. The dress she wore displayed my mark proudly, and the fabric of my shirt shifted over the one she'd given me, reminding always of its presence.

My protective instincts were surging at the threat their visit posed. Ramona was fine, but my mother brought her own sort of danger. She'd never laid a finger on me, and I didn't fear for Sylvie's physical safety. But I knew how her words could hurt. And how my anxious mate could possibly react to her barbs.

Though Sylvie was growing used to and was blessedly unafraid of all parts of me, the same could not be said for my mother. She was between Sylvie and I height-wise, and though she appeared slender and self-possessed, my mother's appearance often belied her true nature underneath.

Meredith's answering growl, one meant to put me in check for my outburst, *did* make Sylvie stiffen. To her, it was undoubtedly unexpected.

"Oh, calm down you two," Ramona called over, disinterested in our confrontation. She'd seen us descend to this place many times before.

Meredith straightened and smoothed a hand down her blouse. Her scent was simmering with irritation, probably with Ramona and I both not bristling at her show of dominance. But she hadn't had that over me for a long while. "Forgive us, Sierra. My son and I admittedly have quite the tempers, don't we?"

My claws and fangs drew instinctually, rage at my mother's slight fueling me. I'd had all my life to learn when her seemingly innocent words were merely veiled insults. When her passive expression contrasted with the vindictiveness in her scent. "You will *not* come into my home and disrespect my mate. Apologize to her. Now."

"It's okay, baby, I don't think she—"

"No," I met Meredith's eyes to make my threat abundantly clear, "she intentionally insulted you. You will apologize to my mate. Or leave."

Meredith's eyes and scent flashed with challenge before she scoffed and cut her gaze away, backing down. I belatedly realized that I'd been clutching Sylvie's side very tightly, nearly ripping the fabric of her dress. I fought to loosen my hold, and I felt my fangs begin to retract. "My apologies, sweetie. I didn't mean to get you or my ungrateful son in a tizzy."

"It's fine, really," Sylvie said sweetly. She looked up at me, and I tore my eyes away from my mother. "I can go back home and let you all catch up?"

"No," Meredith and I said at the same time, but I kept my eyes on Sylvie. She was so kind, so sweet. Selfishly, I wanted to keep her here, even with my mother and her vicious words. Not that I didn't think she would protect herself if needed. But I knew that she would hold herself back in a show of respect because she cared about *me*.

Just like I thought, her lips tugged downward in a slight frown. "But this is family time. They deserve all your attention."

Pride for my mate swelled in my chest. I was sure my mother, though she'd told Sylvie to stay, would like my focus to be solely on whatever she came here for. Ramona probably couldn't care less, which was fine with me. "You are my family. Stay, please."

Though her face was still pulled down in that slight frown, her scent became deeper, sweeter. It made me want to cover us both in blankets and hold her close. To shut the world out and just be with each other. I enjoyed my solitude immensely, but now, I wanted Sylvie included in that.

I was about to tell Meredith and Ramona to leave, right then and there, but my sister's dry voice broke the silence. "Yes, please. You're already way more interesting than him."

I kissed Sylvie's brow then cut my eyes toward my little sister. Or, not so little anymore, it seemed. She'd grown since I'd last seen her, and she smelled… more settled? Like her being had begun to solidify with adulthood drawing nearer. As if she could feel my gaze on her, Ramona lifted her head from her phone, and I parsed through her features. We shared some from our mother, but our noses and eyes we clearly got from our fathers. Her honey brown eyes and wider nose looked just like Sean's.

"So, are we going back inside or continuing to stand out here for no reason?" She bent back down to whatever she was scrolling through.

"You're sitting," I said.

She just huffed and stood, walking toward the door. The rest of us followed, and I stiffened at the cacophony of scents that hit me. Meredith and my sister had been here for a few hours, at least, and it was aggravating how much their scents were already tainting the mix of mine and Sylvie's.

Ramona plopped down onto the couch, putting her feet up on the coffee table, and Meredith perched on the arm of one of the chairs near the fireplace. I felt heat rise on my face, anger flaring again. Though I'd made renovations and added to the cabin, this was the home Da and I built together. Where he'd lived until the day he died. It felt like a betrayal to have her within its walls. The urge to tell her just that was throbbing in my mind, but the reassuring rubbing of Sylvie's hand on my lower back calmed me and let me swallow the words.

"I need to speak with Sylvie," I said while I was already grabbing her hand and pulling her toward our bedroom down the hall. Meredith would surely be able to hear what we were talking about, but at this point, I didn't give a fuck.

I tried my best to not zero in on the *suitcases* propped against the doorways of the spare bedrooms and closed Sylvie and I in the room, our room. She flipped on the switch that turned on the lamps, and at least in here, it just smelled of us.

Immediately, she reached her hands up to my chest, rubbing again in calming circles and intentionally pressing on the mark above my left pectoral. I leaned in until my nose was pressing against her scalp. I inhaled past all of the aromas of herbs and fragrances that were still clinging from her work earlier today and felt *her*. My mate.

"Rion, are you okay?"

I exhaled through my nose. "No."

She chuckled, but continued to rub, continued to soothe. "You sure you want me to stay? I don't want to add to your stress."

My arms circled around her and pulled her even closer. "Yes. If you're alright with that. I'm sorry that this is happening."

Sylvie rested her cheek on my chest. "No need to be sorry. It's just unexpected, is all. But I'm excited to meet them."

I pulled back to see her face, even though I could sense that she was being sincere. "Really."

"Wow, yes, really. I can already see the resemblance." When I surely showed my confusion, she rolled her eyes and poked at my sternum. "You and your mom look so much alike. I can't *believe* I thought you were cheating on—"

Another involuntary growl left my chest. Was *that* why she sounded so upset on the phone? I raised my palms to her cheeks, meeting her eyes and holding them. "Sylvie. You are my mate. There is no one else. There will be no one else, ever. I am yours for as long as you'll have me." The last bit of lingering tension in her shoulders released, and her lips pulled back in a bright, glorious grin.

I searched her face and blurted what had been simmering in my mind. "Does that scare you? Does all of this—everything— frighten you?"

Her grin softened to a smaller smile, and I internally cursed myself for saying anything at all. "No, Orion. You couldn't scare me. Do you annoy me sometimes with your smart-alecky bullshit? Yes. But I also love that about you, so it's okay." She rose on her toes to kiss me, and when she made to pull away, I just followed, deepening the kiss. For a moment, she was surprised, but then she sank into it, into me. I prodded her lips open with my tongue, and she welcomed me in immediately.

There was nothing better than this. To have Sylvie's love and understanding and to hold her in my arms. After Da died, I'd felt without true family and mistakenly sought it out in a pack only to find that they were worse than my mother could ever be.

And then my little witch came in to save me. To offer me the magic of her kindness. Though I was sure she knew this already, I would die for her.

Our kiss quickly turned from affection to heat, and I was about to lift up her dress and bend her over the bed, my mother and sister in the other room be damned, when she gentled her lips against mine with a frustrated moan and pulled back.

"We can't have sex with your mom and sister right down the hall."

"Why not?"

Sylvie scoffed, and I nuzzled my nose against hers. She did the same back. "Because I'm trying to make a good impression, you animal."

I gently captured her lip with my teeth, nibbling and swiping it with my tongue before dropping my hands. Sylvie's lust spiked before turning to frustration, and I snorted. I dropped down to sit at the foot of my bed. Now, much closer to Sylvie's breasts, I couldn't help but pull her back to me.

She was like a fucking magnet.

My hands rubbed over the silky fabric of her dress, first over her full hips, then up to her nipples that were pebbling under the thin fabric. She rested her hands, tipped in long, dark red nails, on my shoulders. I pinched her nipples at the same time, and her gasp made me smirk.

"Orion," Sylvie whined, and I relented, trailing down her waist and back to her hips. My thumbs caressed the sides of her belly, and I wondered what she would look like swelled with our child. Would she want that? We hadn't yet discussed our relationship getting to that point. Was it too early for couples to be having that conversation?

Instead, I said, "You still have some consequences to contend with, my little witch. I came home to find you fully clothed."

Her breath hitched, and I relished the waves of her desire enveloping me. I was completely hard in my jeans, now, and I once again couldn't care less about my mother and sister being in the house. As many times as I heard unwanted conversations or Meredith and her husband fucking over the years—I'd never developed a sense of embarrassment about these things.

But I knew that Sylvie didn't share the same sentiments. I didn't have the heart to tell her, also, that Meredith certainly heard everything we'd talked about earlier.

To cool us both down, I moved my elbows to rest on my knees and resisted the urge to lean into her. She rustled the back of my head, giving me a shivering scrape of her fingernails before pulling back completely.

"Okay, okay, so we should probably go back out there," she said more to herself than me.

"Most likely. Though, they were uninvited, so we don't owe them anything."

Sylvie gave me a weak shove. "Rion, they're your family. And I did want to meet them, remember? You can get your revenge on me later."

I cocked a brow. "Promise?"

She gave a long-suffering sigh. "*Yes.*"

"Then I'll look forward to that to help me get through this."

Sylvie turned toward the door, and I stood to follow. "Then come on, Dr. Gealach. Introduce me properly to your family."

CHAPTER THIRTY-FOUR

SYLVIE

It was tripping me out how similar Orion, his mother, and sister were. Though they had different fathers, Orion and Ramona almost looked like full siblings. And now, up close, I could see that he and his mother shared more than just their fair coloring. Orion looked very much like his father, at least, from the photos I'd seen, but when he spoke, his expressions pulled in ways that mimicked his mom's. Not to mention that the air of *more* that surrounded both of them was the same.

And Ramona, with darker hair and skin than her mother and brother, was just as dry yet perceptive as Orion. "*Love* what you've done with the house, O," she said while her thumbs were tapping furiously over her phone screen. We'd all settled around the dining table after Orion begrudgingly offered to make everyone dinner. I knew that he was warring with the discomfort of a shift in our plans, the groceries he'd bought earlier that day for the two of us now having to stretch for four. But he swallowed any protest and just gave noncommittal grunts to his sister's jabs as if they were their version of exchanging pleasantries.

When Orion described his father, I pictured warmth, gentle

guidance, and ease. His mother, on the other hand, was… intense. "So, is it against some sort of policy for you two to be engaging romantically? You know, with you being his student." She sipped from a very full glass of wine and watched me with piercing, icy eyes.

I blinked widely at the accusation and noticed Ramona finally lifting her attention to the conversation. "I'm not—"

"Sylvie isn't my student, Meredith." Orion's body went still while he was chopping away in the kitchen, and if he threw the knife at his mother's head, I wouldn't have been surprised.

His mother pursed her lips and gave me another once-over. Her head cocked to the side, and my heart quickened. I hadn't been bullied when I was in school, but I knew what it felt like to be in the crosshairs. That a cut was sure to follow. "And you wear my son's mark. Are you sure that's something you can handle?"

My shoulders bristled, and though I had the urge to slap a hand over the mark, I fought to keep both in my lap. Orion's growl wasn't helping to relieve the tension in the room, but I managed to take a deep breath and steel my spine. "I love your son, and though I'm not like you two, I accept and embrace *all* parts of him. Who he is and all that comes with it. So, yeah, I'm sure." I picked up my wine glass and felt proud of myself for the steadiness of my hand.

Ramona put her elbows on the table, resting her chin the cradle of her palms, and looked between us with the largest show of expression that I'd seen from her yet. "She told *you*, Mom."

And then the anxiety creeped up again. Had that crossed the line? Was it a disrespectful thing to say? I shot a worried glance to Orion who had stopped chopping again to stare at me with an intense gaze that made me fidget.

His mother broke the trance he was pulling me into. "Well, congratulations are in order, I believe. I would ask if you were pregnant, but I scent that that's not the case. I am glad that my son has someone in this big, lonely house."

"Don't, Meredith." Orion was wearing the apron I'd bought

him a few weekends ago and holding a delicate-looking spatula, but his glare toward her was no less menacing.

"Hey, didn't your dad build this place?" Ramona called over her shoulder, and I cringed.

"What did you do with that old trailer, anyway?" Meredith asked nonchalantly, and I tried to imagine this woman living out here with Orion and his father. When I'd asked him of his childhood, the juxtaposition between his life at his mom's house and that at his dad's was stark. Where he'd lived in cold luxury with Meredith and her husband, my mate undoubtedly preferred the adventures and care with his father who barely made ends meet.

The image I had of Orion and his dad's life didn't fit at all with this prim and manicured woman. Her expensive perfume and designer clothes were out of place in the cozy cabin, but I would wager that she couldn't be bothered to care.

Orion just grunted at his mother, but I saw the stiffness in his shoulders as he began frying on the stove. Soon the aroma of our cooking dinner loosened the conversation, and Meredith asked Ramona superficial questions about school and her friends. The teenager gave bored answers while going back to scrolling on her phone, and I made myself busy by meandering to the record player in the living room and putting on a Minnie Riperton record to hopefully put Orion and I more at ease.

He made dinner quickly and efficiently, as always, and after I helped him set the table, we all sat, with Orion and me on one side and Ramona and Meredith on the other. The music made the silence of the initial bites of the meal only marginally less awkward. I caught myself hooking my socked foot around Orion's ankle for some sort of grounding, and he leaned into the touch.

"This is great, O." Ramona had started eating by making delicate cuts into her chicken and taking small bites of the arugula salad on her plate but quickly descended into taking larger, inhaling mouthfuls. Her black hair was pulled into a thick and shiny braid that fell over her shoulder. Though her oversized shirt and pants looked comfortable, I guessed that they were just as expensive as her mother's clothes.

"Is that a compliment? You're losing your edge, Mona." Orion punctuated his words with a large bite of chicken, and I tried my best to hide my rising smile. His mother most certainly made him uneasy, but I could tell that he loved his sister.

Ramona rolled her light brown eyes. "Don't push it, Casper."

I almost spit out my wine. Meredith had been watching her children's exchange with cool observation, her plate looking barely touched. But when I caught her eye across the table while I took a calming gulp of water, I saw her smirk before she threw it back with her drink.

"So, how long are you in town for?" I piped up. It seemed like a safe enough topic, and I tried to inject my voice with as much cheer and excitement as possible. Though Orion wasn't close with his family, I *was* going to make a good impression on them, dammit.

Meredith just shrugged, but Ramona added, "Just the long weekend. We knew you probably wouldn't come by for Christmas."

"And what if we were out of town? What would you have done?" Orion added shortly. I fidgeted in my seat, worried about the direction this was looking to be headed, but they seemed to be running with it.

Meredith shrugged again, her almost-white hair slipping across her silk blouse. "Gotten a hotel, shown Ramona around town."

"*You* would have shown her?" My eyes drew in confusion.

"Yes," Meredith looked between Orion and I, "I did grow up here. Not much seems to have changed."

I fought to keep my gaze forward instead of running a questioning glance Orion's way. Had he told me that? My mind raced over the information he'd shared with me about his parents, but he'd mentioned so little about her.

And then another thought sprang in the forefront of my mind. "Did you know my mother?"

Meredith raised her napkin to pat the corner of her lips and threw it on her half-full plate. I knew that Orion would be irritated by the gesture, but my focus was on his mother's face. She gave me an assessing once-over, and if I hadn't been used to my mate's tendencies at this point, I would have been taken aback when she leaned slightly forward and sniffed toward me. Ramona was looking between all three of us but remained quiet.

"Caley?"

My body immediately rose in my seat, my heart hammering in my chest. "Yes!" I glanced at Orion and found him already looking down towards me, smiling softly. He nudged his foot closer to mine.

"Hm, not sure why I didn't see it before. Yes, she and I went to school together, actually." Meredith seemed to soften a little bit with this knowledge. After a moment, she added, "I was sorry to hear about the accident. I went to her funeral. Though you were probably too young to remember my being there."

Orion put an arm around the back of my chair, but the mention of my mother's funeral didn't make me feel upset or sad. My head tilted, and I tried to wrack my brain for memories of that day. Though, I was only two at the time, and any images I had could have easily been conjured due to stories I'd been told.

Meredith continued on, "I actually tried to bring this one with me," she pointed to Orion, and my brows flew to my hairline. "He fought me all the way, and his father was not on my side on the matter. I eventually gave up and went alone."

Orion cleared his throat. "I've never been too good in crowds... especially back then."

He placed a kiss on my temple, and I muttered, "It's okay, baby, I understand." I turned back to Meredith. "Were you friends? I don't know much about who she was outside of being my mother."

Meredith shrugged and her face tightened, almost as if she

were trying to furrow her brow but couldn't. "I remember her being very… kind. Children can be quite cruel, as I'm sure you're aware. But she never was. The least I could do was go pay my respects when she passed." And then she stood up and drifted toward the kitchen. "Son, where's the rest of the wine. I know this couldn't have been the only bottle." She picked up the empty and waved it around for emphasis.

I deflated a bit at her redirection but tried my best to keep the smile on my face. Meredith was busy looking in all of the cabinets, and Ramona had gone back to her phone. But my Orion noticed. His finger caught my chin and turned my face towards him. His kiss was chaste and soft, and though I was committed to play the welcome hostess, I wanted nothing more in that moment than to be alone with him. To digest the connection our mothers had, something I suspected Meredith didn't want to discuss further for some reason, and to curl up into him like I'd planned.

A crashing shift of something in the kitchen made him flinch, and I chuckled before lunging to give him two more quick pecks. Orion nuzzled his nose against mine and said quietly, "I love you," before standing up to go assess his mother's damage.

My eyes followed his retreating form, marveling the way his ass shifted in his jeans all the while, until I caught Ramona giving me a knowing look. Heat rose on my cheeks, and the smile I gave her was almost in apology for ogling her brother in front of her.

"You two are cute," she said with an upward tilt as if it were a surprise.

"Um, thank you?"

"Mom was worried that you were a gold digger or something when we first got here." I blinked with wide eyes at her, though her words had less of a bite than Meredith's did.

"And, do you think that?"

Ramona shrugged and started gathering her and her mother's plates. "Wouldn't make a difference if you were. Mom is, so like, it's not like she can judge."

Cleaning the kitchen and dining area should have taken far

less time with double the people, but Meredith promptly settled in the living room with her wine once Orion refilled her glass. And though Ramona tried to help, her questions of how to use the dishwasher and which soap was for the dishes left Orion shooing her out of the way with an exasperated grumble.

I wiped down the table and countertops while he tackled the dishes, which was a routine we easily sunk into. However, someone had cut off the record player while we were bustling around, and the television blaring instead was a small but palpable interruption in our usual calm.

While his mother and sister were debating on which movie to turn on, I ran a calming touch over Orion's back, knowing I would find the muscles tense beneath his shirt. After starting the dishwasher, he straightened and leaned his back against the counter. Orion closed his eyes and inhaled toward the high ceiling, and his fingers tapped in a rhythm I'd seen many times. I found myself breathing in time with him, and it *did* make me feel calmer. Perhaps there was something to breathing exercises.

Without opening his eyes, Orion opened his arms, and I immediately stepped forward into his embrace. He smelled like the forest and coffee, and the strengthened calm I felt with him was worth everything and more. His shirt was soft, and I kissed the area just above my mark at the same time he kissed the top of my head.

After a few moments of holding each other, Orion bent to whisper in my ear, "Thank you."

I hummed. "For what? You're the one who cooked."

His big shoulders shrugged, slightly nudging my face at the same time. "For just being yourself." I knew that he could feel my smile with my face pressed to his chest like this, and I could feel his pressed against my hair.

And then his sister's voice behind us made me jump. "Hey, O, do you have any—oh, gross."

Orion's growl was halfhearted, like he felt he needed to do it. "*What*, Mona?"

"I was just trying to see if you had any popcorn, but if you just want to make out in peace, I'll leave you to it."

Orion gave a long-suffering sigh, and gently maneuvered around me. After reaching in the pantry, he retrieved a glass container filled with popcorn kernels and shook it a few times in his hand. He pulled out a saucepan and set it on the stove. "Here."

Ramona looked almost horrified, her eyes wide. "What the hell am I supposed to do with that?"

"I can show you," I volunteered and offered an encouraging smile. I waved her over, and she dragged her feet all the way to stand beside me at the stove. "Go spend time with your mom." I gave Orion a gentle shove on his side, and after a few tries, I got him to get moving.

"Don't think I'm done with you. You've got promises to keep," he muttered on his way out, and I caught his cheeky smirk just before he disappeared around the corner.

CHAPTER THIRTY-FIVE

ORION

With my mother and sister sleeping in the two guest rooms, I had to delay my plans for Sylvie and I. Instead of savoring and caring for her, I was waiting on my mother and sister. Instead of ramping the both of us up all night and morning, bringing Sylvie to the edge again and again, we settled for hushed lovemaking underneath the covers.

I tried to tell her that the volume with which we did it made no difference—Meredith would know with scent alone. But I also had no reason before to get the bedrooms soundproofed, so she would hear anything we did as well. When you had hearing as sensitive as ours, you learned to live with unwanted noises very early on.

Sylvie still felt uncomfortable with me fucking her fast and hard into the mattress. Instead, our brows were stuck together, connected like magnets, while I thrust into her as deeply as I could go. Her legs were wrapped around my naked waist, my boxers kicked off as soon as our hands fumbled for each other under the comforter. She'd discarded her usual oversized t-shirt as well, and I reveled in the feeling of her flesh against mine. To be with my mate was the closest I would get to a religious experience. Closer even than those moments I ran free in my wolf form.

Nothing would compare to the feeling of sinking into her warmth. Of letting myself become trapped in her grounding eyes that were gazing at me like I was her salvation.

"I love you," she whispered, cried, and I groaned the words back to her. Even that, though, couldn't encompass all that I felt for her. Or all that she was to me. So, with my body, I gave her more, all that I had left to give.

Sylvie's inner walls constricted on me, almost making me come right then and there, and I trapped her scream underneath my palm. I wanted so badly to let her pleasure be known. Both the human and Wolf in me wanted to hear how much our connection affected her, but I heeded her wishes and made sure to keep this moment between us as private as possible.

I watched as a worshipper at her feet as my mate became overcome with another wave, and I held my own back to give her as many as possible. The way she was handling my family's unexpected visit made me even more proud, more in love with her. I wanted to give her everything.

Sylvie groaned around my palm, but I understood her words perfectly. "Come in me, *please.*"

That was enough to snap my restraints. Ever since I was able to experience locking into my mate, knotting and breeding her, I couldn't resist in the slightest when she asked for it.

My hips slammed harder into her, stinging of her nails digging into my back sweet and distant, until my own release flashed like lightning behind my eyes. Though I was able to muffle Sylvie's exclamations, I hadn't the wherewithal to do the same with my own. And by the glazed look in her eyes, Sylvie barely noticed my long, sustained growl as my knot began to swell and lock us together. My thrusts stuttered, now trapped in Sylvie's body that so graciously accepted this unnatural treatment.

Sylvie dug her own claws into my back while I painted the

inside of her, filling her with my cum and knotted cock plugging her up.

Stuck inside, I did my best to hold my weight off of her, even when my body felt a thousand pounds. My shoulders were heaving with sated panting, and my mate kissed over my brow and temple while we both trembled.

With another groan, I shifted us onto our sides, face-to-face, and she slung her leg over my hip. "I love you," I whispered again, voice drowsy and rough.

"And I love you, Orion. This is nice," she said and petted my hair, smoothing the unruly curls that were certainly a mess after a night's sleep and what we just did.

"Being trapped on my dick and held hostage with my morning breath."

Sylvie chuckled, and then we both moaned at the wave of pleasure it sent through us. My hips began moving, chasing that feeling, and we both somehow came again, albeit on a smaller scale than we had before.

She gave a sated sigh. "I can't believe you were depriving me of this before. Morning breath and all."

"Well, it is an awkward thing to bring up, if you admit. It's a very non-human feature of my anatomy that is very explicitly for child-making and nothing else." I gestured a hand to where we were joined.

Sylvie ran her soft touch over my side, and I scooted my head back on the pillow to better see her. I hardly monitored her scent during these moments anymore. I just took the shifts and swells as they came, enjoying my mate without worrying unless there was cause.

But, did she truly enjoy this time? The extra skin contact was pleasant, absolutely, but did the realities of what it meant make her uncomfortable? She was on birth control now, but would she want to be forever? What if it failed?

She must've seen these questions on my face, because her caresses just continued, lengthened. Her scent turned sweeter but clouded with anxiety, too. It was how she smelled when she was hesitating to tell me something, wanting to broach a topic she wasn't sure how I would take.

"What is it?" I asked instead of letting my mind run with further worry.

She bit at her lip for a few more seconds, her toe tickling the back of my calf, and I waited. "Do you want that? To have kids, I mean. With me."

My heart picked up, wanting to scream the answer, but my mind hesitated. What if she didn't? What if begging for me to come in her while we fucked was all it was—lust pushing her to say words that didn't mean anything else? Would I scare her away if I told her that I did?

I took a deep breath. "Yes," I said because I was done keeping things from her.

Some of her anxiety cleared, and I relaxed a bit more. "When?"

"When what?"

She kept stroking my side, her fingernails giving light scratches. "When would you want to? Have kids."

I blinked, eyes unfocusing to think through her question. To be frank, I hadn't thought about it in those terms. At some point in my early adulthood, I worked through my fear of repeating the mistakes of my parents and realized that I did long for a family. A connection that was similar but deeper than a pack. I wasn't sure when the idea of Sylvie being the one to have a family with began to take shape. Perhaps it'd been the back of my mind since I'd realized that I wanted her.

Our relationship was less than half a year old, and yet, in some ways, it felt like it had always been. The before didn't matter anymore, and the only thing that drove my worries for the future was the fear of her no longer being in it.

"I hadn't thought about a 'when,' really. Just that I want that with you. Do you want that?"

Her eyes were wide and open, something I always admired about my mate. "Yeah, but…" I held still, willing myself to remain calm. My fingers started tapping and flicking, though, and she noticed. She moved her hand to my shoulder, holding it over my mark. "I just meant that I didn't want a baby right now. Maybe not for a while, though I'm not sure how long. Is that okay?"

I relaxed once again. "Of course, mo ghrá. I'm not in a rush."

She sank further into her pillow. I hadn't even realized how tense she'd gotten. "Okay. Sorry, I was worried that you'd want to start right away. I know you're more established and a few years older than me, so—"

"Are you calling me old?"

My teasing had the desired effect, and she smiled. "Well, you *are* five years my senior."

"So you *are* calling me old. Should I be offended?"

Sylvie leaned forward to press a kiss to my lips. Her body shifting sent another shock of pleasure between us, and we both sucked in short breaths. I was still hard and trapped inside her, and most likely stuck for at least twenty minutes more.

I rolled over, bringing her on top of me. The morning light was flooding our bedroom with golden rays, but I was fully focused on my mate and not the sight of the land around us. Her breasts hung plump and round above me, and I cupped them in my palms. She brought her hands to hold my wrists, and her hips began to move.

This was also the danger of knotting inside my mate. Being held together so often turned to us wanting each other again before we could separate. I rolled her nipples between my fingers, mouth watering and wanting to flick over them with my tongue. But watching her grind on top of me, and listening to her pleasured yet frustrated moans, was its own kind of bliss.

"You want to have my pups, Sylvie? Let me fuck and fill you so you can have my baby?" Her eyes rolled back then clenched shut as she started to rise and fall in a shortened rhythm. She was even tighter like this, where we still couldn't move much, but it was more than enough to leave me growling and thrusting up into her.

She reached for the headboard, nodding frantically. I could tell that she was trying to be quiet with the way she held her lips closed. She trembled above me, brows turning up and whines coming through her nose. I clutched her jaw and tilted it down for her to look at me. "Tell me."

My claws had come out at some point, and I rejoiced in the shivers their prickling incited in her. Why had I been so afraid of her reaction to my Wolf? My mate embraced both parts of me, and I felt the luckiest in all of the world to have my little witch who loved me like I loved her.

I flicked out my tongue, now longer and flatter with my half-shift, and licked one of her nipples that dangled over my head. "Fuck, I want to have your baby," she cried, and I sucked her breast into my mouth, let my fangs graze the sensitive skin.

Sylvie came apart over me, body constricting so much that I was unable to move inside her at all anymore. The silky friction nearly made my eyes cross, and my release shot down my body. More cum filled Sylvie, building the pressure between us. She landed on my chest, panting and trembling, and I wasn't much better. It was blissfully uncomfortable, and I let the scrape of my claws on her back soothe us both.

Once our labored breaths turned to deep, calm ones, Sylvie shifted her head on my shoulder, and said sleepily, "Hey, it snowed."

I turned to look and was met with the sight of twinkling white covering the land around the lake. The trees were frosted with snow that must've collected all night like I'd thought it would. A sense of loss threatened to pop the bubble of my content in this moment. I loved running in the snow.

But I couldn't do that without risking Sylvie's safety or us going out of town. And Meredith and Ramona probably didn't want to leave on an impromptu camping trip. I wasn't even sure my mother shifted all that much anymore. I shuddered internally at the thought. Being as limited as I was now was torture. I couldn't imagine doing it on purpose.

Sylvie began to sit up, and though I missed her pleasant weight on my chest, we were still trapped together for a little while. She untied the scarf on her head and began to take her hair out of the two braids she put it in last night. My claws traced delicate lines back and forth on her lower stomach, where the pressure of me and my cum inside her created a little roundness that hadn't been there before.

It wasn't the same as a pup, but it made me even more excited for when the time would eventually come. She was always beautiful, but I knew that when she *was* pregnant, her beauty would have another layer entirely. I would happily bear months of her bemoaning my helicopter caring. I was already protective of her as it was.

"So, what would you like to do with your mom and sister today?" She fluffed out her hair, releasing a downpour of her scent that I drank up greedily.

The question of what to do with my mother and sister was enough to halt my daydreaming entirely. If I'd known that my ignoring Meredith's phone calls would result in a surprise visit from her and my sister, I would've answered every time her name popped up on my screen.

I'd long ago learned that my mother wasn't going to change. The biting comments, the controlling behavior. All of it hurt when I was a child, and as an adult, the wounds were raised, bumpy scars. But the point of staying away was to ensure that they stayed healed.

"Hey," Sylvie said quietly, "what's the matter?" Her fingernail scraped the edge of my jaw, and the hair that'd already begun to sprout overnight prickled against her touch. The noise was sharp and soothing.

Her other hand rested beside me on the mattress, and I searched the high ceiling above while she did the same to my face. I felt her dark, hickory colored eyes on me, smelled her concern. "Having her here brings up a lot of old feelings." Too many to keep straight, but I knew for certain that they were unpleasant. I was already on edge after dealing with final grades I had to enter and the inevitable pleas from students who should have been doing more earlier in the semester. Not to mention the Antler Pointe Pack members constantly being around. No more was it just a few passing through the forest, taking advantage of running on my land. Now, they sat and watched. Waiting for me to do something out of line.

With my mother here, I felt again the confused pup that didn't understand the world or the people around him, and his mother's pushing and snapping and embarrassment just making it that much more overwhelming.

"What can I do to make it easier for you?"

I sighed and tried to give Sylvie a reassuring smile, but it was weak at best. "Nothing, mo ghrá. Just being with me." I paused, but added, "Driving the conversation with her, maybe."

"I can absolutely do that, baby. But, um, is this a situation where I shouldn't be nice to her? It seems like she really hurt you, and I don't want to be kind to someone that was unkind to you."

My face heated, and the backs of my eyes itched. I blinked the sensation away at the same time I brought Sylvie back to my chest. I'd never had the urge to touch and be touched by someone as much as I did with my mate. With her it was never wrong or uncomfortable.

"Thank you. And," I cleared the thickness in my throat, "I want you to be yourself. Having a child on the spectrum was something my mother didn't know how to handle well. Still doesn't. I'm not sure if I've forgiven her, but I've accepted it."

Sylvie and I laid together, breathing and whispering about what we could do for the day. Meredith and Ramona woke up at some point, and the sounds of electric toothbrushes and the shower going buzzed in my ears.

My mate was a comforting weight on my chest that kept the boyish anxieties from making me float away all together. She spoke of her new job and how much she enjoyed it, especially compared to her last one.

It was an… uncomfortable conversation Sylvie and I had nearly a month ago, now. How I had to admit to her of my defeat. That I'd been too arrogant to just keep my head down and ignore the pack members following me. Da used to shake his head and say that I had too much of a Leader's instinct for my own good. Because despite my lack of social awareness sometimes, I also felt the need to take charge.

That was how my old packmate ended up convincing me to challenge her father. I was a mess after Da died, but I already had the desire in me. The knowledge that I was far more observant, paying attention to the rest of the pack in a way that no one else did. It was a gift and a curse, and on the night of my challenge and the night Sylvie found me, I'd been bested.

Sylvie didn't realize at the time that I was so injured and clinging to my human form so tightly that the rest of my right mind was buried far too deep. It was still no excuse for endangering her, but… I was glad things turned out the way that they had.

Without my own misstep, turning behind the downtown buildings to fight off Graham's thugs tailing me, I might've never met my mate.

Sylvie trailed her fingernail in the dip of my shoulder and circled my mark. She talked about the plot of her next story, of her final assignments and her graduate program application. She framed it as a whim—just applying to APC with the expectation that she wouldn't get in and continue to work at the shop and on her witch studies.

I'd already resigned myself not to interfere, but there was no doubt in my mind that she would be accepted. She was a talented writer, and her ability to juggle work, her writing, and growing her power made me want to puff up my chest and show her off to everyone and also lock her in the house to keep her preciousness safe. The possessiveness, I at least had in check. Most of the time.

Sylvie and I emerged from the bedroom in fresh clothes, but she did me the grace of not showering after she had last night before bed. Having our scents all over each other made me feel more at ease.

We started our morning routine, which helped even more, and it was almost like my mother's and sister's presence couldn't touch me with an Otis Redding record filling the house with rich crooning and a skillet sizzling in my grip.

Luckily, I had enough in the fridge to make breakfast for everyone, and I just finished plating the eggs and bacon at the same time Sylvie finished setting the table and plucking the last pieces of toast from the toaster.

The aroma of food was its own bell, and Ramona padded into the room. Despite having been up for at least a half hour, she looked exhausted and hadn't changed out of her baggy pajamas. Her hair was in a messy heap, and she just grunted at Sylvie and I as she slid into a barstool.

I grunted back, thankful that she didn't seem in the mood to speak, but Sylvie didn't have trouble being sociable. "Morning, Ramona. Did you sleep okay?" She put a cup of coffee in front of my sister who clutched it like Sylvie would threaten to take it back. At the same time, my sister wrinkled her nose, and I caught the mischievous glint in her eye. Oh, no.

"Fine, until I was woken up the *strangest* noise this morning."

"Mona," I gritted, Sylvie's embarrassment mixing with my own irritation. Ramona was a little shit, and my mate didn't deserve to be teased for us enjoying each other.

Ramona spun in her seat to face me. "What, big brother of mine? Don't be mad that the walls are thin here."

Before I could snap a retort, my mother came breezing in, already dressed for the day in a dark blue sweater and jeans. Her hair was neat, and her makeup was clearly done. When she rounded the corner and took in Ramona's disheveled presence, she ran her narrowed eyes up and down my sister's form. "Would it kill you to not look a mess, Ramona? Your lack of consideration for your appearance is off-putting."

My sister blanched, glancing quickly at Sylvie, then me, then the floor before rolling her eyes. "We're not in public, *Mother*. I just woke up."

Meredith just threw her hair over her shoulder and sat at the table. "Calm that rat's nest, Ramona."

I felt the flare of my sister's own embarrassment and aggravation, but she didn't have some sort of witty comeback for our mother. Instead, she sat as far away from Meredith as possible when we all convened at the table.

The unspoken expectation for me to contribute to the conversation was an anvil on my shoulders, but Sylvie did as she'd promised. Any time there was a lull, or my mother looked to me as if she was going to ask a question or take a jab, Sylvie swooped in.

As soon as everyone slowed down eating, I shot up from my seat and proceeded to clear the table. What I didn't expect was for Ramona to do the same. Before Sylvie could start helping, Ramona took her plate and empty mug, along with her own, and joined me in the kitchen.

Her shoulders were high, the tension in her back telling. Ramona and I were unalike in many ways, and I'd had enough time around her to pair her expressions and body movements to the truth of her emotions in her scent.

I didn't say anything, because I knew that when she got like this, it would only make it worse. So, I cleaned and kept half of my attention on Sylvie who was discussing the day's plans with my mother. Instead of giving into Meredith's skepticism, Sylvie trudged forward, being her kind and sweet self. Gods, how much I loved her.

"Where do you want me to put this?" I focused back in on Ramona, finding her holding a half-dirty skillet in the air with suds still clinging to the back of it. My dry comment was on the tip of my tongue, riding along with the distress at the *thought* of her letting the dirty dishes touch the clean cupboards.

But, the vulnerable uncertainty in her eye made me stop, and I just sighed. Teaching my sixteen-year-old sister how to properly wash dishes should have been ridiculous, but she clearly didn't know what she was doing. I supposed having a chef in the home all one's life would do that to you.

I pointed out the proper dish towel for drying and the cupboard where the skillets went before slowly washing the dish. I didn't chastise or outwardly correct, just let her see the process and what I was doing. Making a show of checking for any stray pieces of food before giving it a final rinse. After drying and putting the skillet away, I snuck a glance and saw Ramona taking extra time to carefully wash a platter. She was a little heavy-handed with the dish soap, but I was proud of myself for fighting the urge to inspect every dish she washed.

And if I made a mental note of where she put everything to take a look when she wasn't in the room, that was my prerogative.

Our rhythm was far clumsier than mine and Sylvie's, but we were eventually able to get the kitchen clean enough for my standards. When Ramona turned around, her sleep shirt was absolutely soaked, but the tension in her shoulders was gone.

"Son, do you have a lighter?" My mother barged in as if she could sense the ease between my sister and I. She was digging around in a handbag, unlit cigarette sticking out of her mouth.

Without a word, I opened a drawer in the kitchen and offered her one. It was the kind for lighting candles, but it would do.

My mother eyed it suspiciously, but was obviously too in need for a nicotine fix to put up a fight. She took the lighter and tried to offer me a cigarette in exchange.

Meredith had smoked all my life, and it was the one habit I'd picked up from her. Our runs together and our cigarette breaks were the only times we were amicable with one another. Where my mother didn't cut. I remembered the years she was pregnant and then breastfeeding my sister being particularly difficult because I lost both reprieves for a while.

I shook my head, and it took Meredith a few awkward moments to realize that I really wasn't going to smoke with her.

Sitting in the biting air with a cigarette and a cup of coffee sounded almost like the best thing in the world.

Almost.

After looking quite perplexed, Meredith shrugged and headed toward the front door. Over her shoulder, she called, "Sylvie suggested we see where you work then walk around downtown until lunch. I'm ready to go whenever you all are."

With her outside, the three of us stood in the kitchen for a moment, breathing in the looser air that my mother had been taking up without trying at all. Sylvie set the tea kettle on the stove and took down our travel mugs without a word. "You want some hot chocolate for the road, Ramona? Or tea?"

"Um, yeah. Whichever." My sister twisted the damp towel she was still holding, and I watched her curiously. I rarely ever saw her nervous. Irritated, yes. Snide, often. But we both seemed to have inherited our mother's arrogance, because I wasn't used to the scent coming off of her. "And…" She huffed and threw the towel down on the counter, and I couldn't help swooping in to drape it evenly on the drying rack where it belonged. "I'm sorry. About poking fun at you earlier. Sylvie."

My brows threatened to fly to the back of my head, which was probably the wrong thing to do, because my sister took one look at my face, huffed again, and said, "Whatever," before she stomped back toward the guest rooms.

Sylvie and I turned toward each other, and her face mimicked mine. It was going to be a long weekend.

CHAPTER THIRTY-SIX

SYLVIE

Ramona stuck by my side while we walked through downtown, admiring the holiday lights lining and hanging over the streets. Decorations were bright, and there were a few performers on the corners playing holiday music while vendor booths lined the blocked-off road.

The holiday market was a tradition I hadn't been able to partake in before, and it hadn't really been on my radar until I frantically searched for things to do in town to keep Orion's family occupied. Thankfully, it was their last night, and we were set to take them to the airport tomorrow.

Orion clutched my hand, and I sent calm through our twined fingers. I still didn't know what the hell I was doing in terms of soothing others in this way. Even Granna wasn't able to provide specific guidance about this particular ability. It was a strange realization that her knowledge had limits, and I could tell that it frustrated the both of us.

Whatever it was, it seemed to be working, because Orion was at least able to remain cordial with his mother, which was the true litmus test of his mood. The sights and sounds were overstimulating to me, so I couldn't imagine how he was feeling.

Meredith seemed perfectly comfortable, waving and talking pleasantly with people she hadn't seen in decades. I could tell she was eating up the attention and appreciation for how great she looked. And she did—far younger than she was and impeccably dressed and coiffed.

Ramona's moods, on the other hand, were up and down. With the lack of relationship between Orion and Meredith, I'd assumed that Ramona would be close with their mother. Through the long weekend with them, I now wasn't really sure that was the case.

"So, when do you two plan on making it official, Sylvie?" Meredith appeared while we were slowly browsing a tent that had vintage clothes and trinkets. She wrinkled her nose, presumably because of the dusty smell that clung to everything in here.

"Ah… what—we're exclusive and…" I tried and failed to form a concise answer with her piercing blues pinning me where I stood. Though she seemed to have gotten used to the idea of me being around, Meredith had an uncanny ability to literally flay you alive with just a glance. A few words, and you'd be frozen over.

When it was directed toward Orion, I had no trouble coming in and engaging her in conversation, but when it was directed toward me, I floundered. And my patience was wearing thin. We were hosting, but I'd never been around someone who just *expected* to be waited on like Orion's mother.

"How long have you been together, again?" Meredith picked up a glass vase, turned it around in her manicured grip, and set it back down.

"Two and a half months, Meredith," Orion supplied shortly. His eyes were tight and unseeing while he flipped over an old record.

At last, I found something to say. "We're taking things as they come. But I'm committed to your son, as you know." I didn't meant to sound curt, but this woman was so tiresome. If anything,

I would argue that a mating mark was as 'official' as a marriage proposal. But, maybe she just wanted to plan a wedding.

Meredith fished around in her Prada handbag, and after checking her phone, she produced a cigarette and a lighter that Orion bought her that first full day of their visit. "Oh, I've never known my son to just 'take things as they come'. He has far too much trouble with a lack of rigidity. Certainly you're old enough to shack up, as they used to say, but why would you?"

"Didn't you get knocked up in high school, Mom?" Ramona shot, and the daggers Meredith shot back would have made me burst into a flurry of ice shards. But Ramona stood her ground, even raising a brow and taking a sip from her styrofoam cup of cider.

Meredith looked like she was going to say something else but decided not to, and she instead turned out of the tent, muttering something about "disrespectful fucking children."

Orion's lips on my forehead brought me back, and I let my calm flow again. How funny was it that making it for him was easy? It was the giving it to myself that was next to impossible. "I do intend to give you a ring. If you're worried about that." He had bags under his eyes, which, through all of our time together, I'd never seen before. We hadn't been able to talk much about our other troubles, like the murders and the pack and Granna's slips getting worse, but they were all wearing on us.

I pressed up on my toes to give him a kiss on the cheek and joined Ramona while she flipped through a rack of denim jackets. "I wasn't worried, baby." I sent him a smile and let him sink into his search through the boxes of records. We'd been shopping a couple of times at the record store in town—enough for me to know that the laser focus he went into was comforting and most beneficial to him when he had no interruptions. Orion muttered to himself, fingers tapping on his chin while he considered which ones to purchase.

Ramona and I browsed in silence for a while, navigating the thin space between clothing racks. I'd gotten quite used to taking space with others without speaking—Orion and Granna were both very fond of it, and I'd grown to enjoy it as well—but I noticed Ramona's fidgeting. I wondered what her life was like, living in a big house with everything she needed, but all under her mother's thumb. Or was it just when they were around others? At home, was Ramona left to her own devices? With the rate she seemed to be texting whoever when she first arrived, I chalked it up to a multitude of friends, but with each hour, she brought her phone out less and less. I wasn't even sure I saw her on it at all today.

We kept moving through the clothes, and I found a black dress with lace appliqué on the sleeve hems. I plucked it off the rack and held it up to my front, trying to judge if it would fit. A throat clearing made me take notice that Ramona was now on the same aisle as me, fingers testing the feel of a thick sweater. "Do you really want to marry my brother?" We both glanced at Orion who was still fully fixated in his browsing, and I watched him shake his head to himself and stuff a record back into one of the boxes. I couldn't help but smile fondly.

"Yeah, I do. Though, I'm already mated to him."

Ramona got a weird look on her face, some mixture of discomfort, longing, and sadness. "Mom's not mated to Dad."

I nodded and tried to imagine being with someone so long without truly knowing them. Since he'd revealed his Wolf to me, I realized how large a part of Orion I'd been missing. I still hadn't really told him how much it'd hurt to not have his trust earlier, but the more he told me about his life and from what I'd seen firsthand, I understood. But to truly see him relax with me was better than anything I ever imagined. It made me do the same.

I chose to be honest with Ramona. "I couldn't imagine not being mated to your brother. Not knowing about who he is. I love him so much."

Now it was Ramona's turn to nod, and she turned to hunt through the rack behind us. Her face was very noticeably hidden from my view this way. "Well, obviously, if you hurt him, I'll have to kill you."

Her words took me so far aback, I didn't realize I was cackling until my laughter was already echoing loudly through the space. Neither Ramona nor Orion turned to me, but I could see the very edge of her face and the little tilt in her lips. "Obviously. And I wouldn't blame you."

"And... I know that he and Mom don't really... vibe, but. If you guys have a wedding, or whatever, I'd wanna be there. If that's cool."

Though a wedding was pretty low on my list of things to think about at the current moment, the sudden talk of a ring and tying myself to Orion in that way made me feel lighter. It was something to look forward to amidst all that was still difficult.

I draped the dress I was going to buy over my arm. "Absolutely. I doubt we'd do anything big, but you're definitely invited." Ramona nodded along, not looking at me. I caught sight of Orion starting to make his way over. "And," I added as nonchalantly as I could, "if you ever wanted to come visit. We'd be happy to have you. I know he likes having you here." She laughed off what I said, but I decided not to push.

Instead, I turned my attention to Orion who was clutching at least ten records to his chest and his free hand tapping quickly down at his side. "Wow, you must've hit the jackpot." I pointed to his haul.

His eyes crinkled, and he launched into a detailed explanation of his spoils. A few special editions he'd been hunting for a while, some random ones that he found interesting. I worried for a moment that there was no room on the shelves at the cabin for more, but I was sure he'd find the space. The thought of curling up on the couch with Orion, reading beside each other with a record playing, made me feel antsy. Just a few more hours and we'd be alone again.

We paid the owner of the little shop on our way out, and Ramona snickered. "Jeez, O, you could've left some for other—"

She cut off mid-sentence at the same time Orion's head snapped up and over to the left. We emerged back out into the throws of the festival, but it took me a second to figure out what Orion and Ramona were looking at.

My pulse quickened in a mixture of dread and anger, and when I looked up at Orion, he was already moving forward and starting to pull me with him. Ramona was clearly confused but followed us unquestioningly, and the closer we got, the easier it was to hear.

Meredith held her cigarette between two elegant fingers, and her face was pinched in haughty indignation at Graham looming over her. Ana and Jasper stood behind him, but they blanched when they saw Orion and I heading toward them. "… and if you think for a second that I give a shit about who you are, you're sorely mistaken." For good measure, Meredith blew smoke in their faces.

The joy my mate had been experiencing thirty seconds ago completely evaporated, and that fact made me more upset than anything. The records he bought were in a paper bag clutched at his side, but his posture was rigid. The softness in his eyes hardened in an instant, and I felt the energy around him start to churn.

"You come to my territory without asking permission? I think my pack and I have been quite hospitable in letting it go this long." Graham spoke low enough to obscure his words from the festival goers wandering around. But he was growing more brazen.

"Get away from us, Graham, and take your followers with you." Orion's voice was beginning to rumble, but when Graham's attention directed to me, he let loose a full out growl. Passersby looked around, certainly hearing something but unsure of where the noise came from with no animals around. I wondered how in the hell all of this was kept a secret from most people. How it'd been kept secret from *me* for so long.

I pushed forward, despite Orion trying to keep me shielded

behind him. "Don't make me keep good on my promise. Leave all of us alone."

"As if I give a fuck about you or your little threats." Graham sneered, and that was it.

I lurched forward. *Hurthurthurthurt,* was a constant string blaring between my ears, but I was thrown behind a wall of comfort and restraining protection. Orion's arms circled around me, holding my shaking body.

I had just enough sense to not start swiping at him, but I was seething, looking for any other way to get at Graham, to get at his throat, to scratch deep lines in his arrogant face. To make him pay for bothering us. To make him hurt. "Baby, you need to let me go. Let me go let me go let me go." My hands were down at my side, opening and clenching at nothing. Orion, though, was strong enough to keep me immobile.

"Mo ghrá." His voice was strained, stiff. "I will handle it. Please let me take care of you."

"Orion," I jerked in his arms, but it just made him hold me tighter and kiss my temple, "I love you, but get the fuck off of me, I will fuck him up—" I flailed and thrashed, but he held on tight.

His words were a mixture of sweet and harsh. "*Sylvie,* stop. I know you can take care of yourself, but we are in public, and I don't want you to do anything you'll regret. You let *me* handle this." He placed another kiss on my temple, took a deep breath, and held it for a few moments. He exhaled, then started on another inhale, and I found myself mimicking the action.

Orion still wasn't letting me go, but the breaths were helping. I was feeling less and less like my skin was too tight on my bones. Like I wasn't going to search for the nearest thing I could use as a weapon.

"*Your* threats and posturing are completely asinine, and how my son hasn't taken his rightful place as Leader is beyond me. But what I *do* know, is that I have no time for someone who's decided to make his daddy issues everyone else's problem. Now, get away from us before I remind you how to respect your elders."

"Get your—"

"Hey, okay, let's all just calm down!" A new voice rang out between everyone—Jasper. The murmuring of humans around us was coming more into focus, and Orion must've sensed my calming down because his arms loosened enough for me to turn my head. My cheek was still smooshed into his chest, but I saw Ramona's wide eyes going between us, her mom, and the pack members we were facing.

"Graham, now is not the time. My mother has done nothing wrong, and your resorting to accosting those connected to me when I'm not around just shows you to be weak. Unless you want me to shift and blow up all of this shit right here and now, I suggest you leave." Buried in my loose hair, Orion's claws scratched soothingly at my scalp.

"Fine. Next time, it's you and me, White One." And the smile he gave, instead of making the rage flare again, chilled me to my core. He didn't spare any of us or his pack members another glance before turning and walking further into the holiday market.

The people that'd been lingering around to eavesdrop eventually started to dissipate, unaware that the simple brawl they'd expected could've gone a completely different way.

Meredith dropped her cigarette butt to the ground and crushed it beneath her heeled boot. Her shoulders were thrown back gracefully, but when she looked up at Orion and I, I saw the dimming glow at the edges of her eyes.

The four of us stood for a moment until Ramona broke the silence, "So, would anyone care to tell me what the fuck that was?"

Orion grunted, but the sound was strained and not the usual resounding response he'd been giving his sister. His body loosened further around me, and I let him tug me by the hand toward a bench close by. His steps were not his usual smooth gait, and he all but collapsed onto the cold metal. Orion pulled me into his lap and latched himself onto my neck. My hands automatically went around him, even with the thicker layers we wore making it a bit more difficult. He breathed and scented at my throat, snuffled in my hair.

Now that I'd calmed down, the pack members no longer in sight, I noticed the faint tremors wracking Orion's body. If I didn't know any better, I would've assumed he was shivering from the cold. But I knew that he didn't ever really get cold, his Wolf nature making his body equipped for harsh winters.

"Baby? Are you okay?" I tilted his chin so that I could see his face. The dark circles under his eyes were even darker on his pale skin. His was looking off to the right, but he left his face open for me to examine.

He gave a wan smirk, and at least his eyes looked as clear and bright as usual. "Yeah. Just need a second."

"Why?" Ramona and I asked at the same time. I glanced toward Meredith whose face was now pinched in concern, even with her standing a few paces away.

Orion brought his lips to mine, and I accepted the nuzzling of his nose. Even with the tenderness, he winced and breathed between us, "You're very strong, my little witch," and then louder and meant for his sister and mother, "just give us a minute." I pulled back in horror, reading the true meaning behind his words.

Meredith started murmuring to Ramona, explaining the requirement of some packs for shifters visiting the area to notify the local Pack Leader, but I only caught bits and pieces while I continued to search Orion's drained face.

"Orion… did I hurt you?" Tears started to well and, despite my better efforts to blink them away, fall. My skin was still flushed from our encounter with Graham, but the tears felt cool in the winter air.

I brought my hands to his face and felt the clench in his jaw. He was trying to figure out what to say to me, and that was enough confirmation on its own. More tears fell, but I pushed past my shame for something far more pressing. I thought of calm, of delightful rest after a long day, and sent the feeling through my touch to him. His white lashes closed over his eyes, and the rumbling purr he let loose was low and content.

Orion stopped shaking, and his breathing deepened. Soon, he grasped my wrists and gently pulled them off his face. He placed sweet kisses on my wrists, one by one, and this time he met my eyes. His lids were lowered a bit, but it made him look peaceful, maybe sleepy. Orion smiled at me. "I love you, Sylvie."

I bit at my lip and shook my head, trying to clear my shame. Orion wasn't upset with me, but it was hard to not be upset with myself. I hadn't realized I'd been doing anything to him in my desperate attempt to inflict harm on Graham. Selfishly, I wasn't ready to ask him just how I'd made him feel. "I love you, too. I'm sorry."

He looked away. "Don't be. You were trying to help. I just want you to know that *I'll* keep you safe."

"I know that, baby. I…" How could I explain that the urge this time wasn't to protect us but a deep, undeniable need to do damage for the sake of it? The slight was just the permission—the trigger.

Meredith cleared her throat behind me, and both Orion and I swiveled our attention to her. "Son, I think it's time to go. I've grown too tired of all the noise and lights."

I felt Orion breathe a sigh of relief, and he gently placed me on my feet before standing. His movements were more fluid, but not as smooth as usual, and he started us toward the car.

What did I do to him? The worry kept circling round and round in my head. My responses to Ramona's quips were half-hearted at best, and the only force grounding me to what was going on was Orion's hand holding mine tightly, like he knew how much I wanted to pull away and hide myself.

It took a frustratingly long time to reach his car, and Orion opened the doors for each of us before sliding in the driver's seat.

Despite his protests, I slid in the back with Ramona and gave his mother the passenger seat. She walked up to the front each time, anyway.

Pulling out of the parking lot was a stop-and-start kind of affair, and I knew by the tension in the back of his neck that Orion was growing more and more irritated by the lack of system to get everyone out in a timely manner.

He turned up the dial on his favorite driving playlist, but his mother quickly followed with turning it back down. "Son, you didn't tell me that the pack was bothering you. When your father and I lived here, the Leader let us be. His son needs to learn some respect—"

"Meredith—"

"Your father's family started that pack. Just because your great-great-grandmother abdicated doesn't mean that they can treat you this way. Obviously, with their history of picking shit Leaders even all the way back then, they could use you. You're a smart man with a Leader's instinct."

I saw Orion's fingers start to tap rapidly on the steering wheel, no longer following the music but his own internal beat. Meredith reached out and placed her hand over his to stop the movement, but Orion recoiled and shoved away her touch. He resumed stimming and bit out his words. "I'm not fighting for Leader, Meredith. I won't endanger myself or Sylvie."

"Orion, your father—"

"*No.*" Orion's shoulders moved with his breathing exercise, and I found myself joining him. We turned out of the lot and started to leave downtown. Christmas lights flashed past, and despite his firm word, Orion wove us fluidly in and out of traffic. "You don't get to speak on Da or how I live my life, including my relationship. You are my mother, and I respect you for that, but you aren't owed anything else. Is that clear?"

I expected Meredith to growl again. Maybe posture and try to assert her dominance as his mother. By the flinch she gave and the ticking in her slender jaw, I thought she would. But after a beat, she huffed and looked defiantly out the window. It was probably the best Orion would get.

Orion turned the music back up, and we continued out of town toward his cabin. What was I going to say to him once we were alone? I wanted to both melt into his arms and stay as far away as possible. When I'd lashed out at Graham and stopped his shift, it didn't seem like I'd *hurt* him, necessarily. What would I have done if Orion hadn't held me back?

"Well, besides you all almost shifting in front of the whole goddamn town, I'd say that was a pretty cool festival. The cider was good." Ramona leaned forward in her seat. "What records did you get again, O?" Despite the tension between him and his mother, my mate couldn't resist the opening, and he started running through the list of his haul. When Ramona asked follow up questions about his reasonings for choosing each, he relaxed with every word. Ramona nodded along to what he was saying, and when we were finally pulling up the cabin, the two of them had begun to debate on what records he recommended she start her own collection with.

The sight of the cabin and the lake behind it was supremely comforting. The trees stood like a dark veil around everything, but I could feel the humming of life woven throughout. To feel connected and part of the rawness of the world around me was something I'd been missing for many years. And here, at Orion's house, I felt it in my blood, through every fiber.

The air even tasted clearer when Orion opened my door and helped me out. Instead of walking me to the front door, he tossed his keys to Ramona with encouragement to head inside and start the kettle for some hot chocolate. She and his mother proceeded toward the house while Orion held me to him. I accepted his embrace, despite what I'd done. He kissed the top of my head and rubbed his cheek on my scalp. "Are you okay?"

I bit the inside of my cheek until I tasted blood, but it helped keep the tears away. I shook my head.

"Please tell me what's wrong, Sylvie. I want to understand." His voice was back to the husky caress I'd fallen in love with from the first time he spoke.

I kept my face tucked into the curve of his neck. "I feel so bad for hurting you. And I don't even know how—I just," I took a breath, trying to steady the quivering in my voice, "I just don't ever want to hurt you again. I'm so sorry, Orion."

Orion titled my face up toward his, and his eyes shone brightly, reflecting the light from the house. "Please don't be, Sylvie. I'm all right. And proud of how strong my mate is. You are a gift to me." He looked away, but I didn't miss the pink spreading on his cheeks, "And… I'm trying to find a way to make this land safe for us. I don't want to fight. But I'd do it for you. I'd die for you, mo ghrá. If it ever came to that."

The tears won the battle and ran in a near flood down my cheeks. Our breaths fogged the air between us while I fought for something to say. That I'd do the same for him. That I'd kill for him.

A kiss was all I could muster through the flood of emotions, and Orion readily accepted it. I hoped he understood. If not, I would explain.

My arms circled behind his neck, and our kiss deepened. Orion held me closer, and the kiss heated to a warm burn. His tongue tasted like apple cider and explored my mouth lazily. I did the same with his, letting this kiss be a reset.

My phone ringing and vibrating in my back pocket snagged my attention, but my mouth was much slower in pulling away from Orion's. I gentled my lips, and he moved his to my cheek, then to my neck. My skin heated under his touch, and my mind started turning fuzzy. He nudged his nose past the collar of my coat and painted kisses up and down and around my mark.

I managed to pull my phone out and saw that it was Roz calling. My thumb was less than steady swhen I answered, "Hello?"

"Hey, sweetie, ah, I'm sorry to bother you, but I think you should come on home."

Orion stilled and pulled back, listening along to the call. "Yeah, what—what's wrong?" In the background, I heard a bustling, then a crash of glass.

"I—your granna's having a hard night, and I'm not sure... I think it would help if you came home."

CHAPTER THIRTY-SEVEN

SYLVIE

I found another few shards of glass under the corner of the fridge and swept them into the dustpan. Screaming and a heavy guitar solo filled my ears, but I swore I could still hear the tinkling of the remnants of the pitcher Granna threw on the floor. Well, to hear her tell it, she'd dropped it. That Roz was overreacting. She was just stressed out, was all.

When Roz had turned to leave, thinking she'd been the trigger for the episode, Granna surprised us both by giving her a hard hug. Granna held her best friend for a long time and told her that she loved her. That she was the best friend she'd ever had.

Granna had quickly pulled away, tears in her eyes, but said nothing else to either of us before trudging outside to tend to her garden. In the dark.

I'd turned on the lights that lit that side of the house so that she'd at least be able to see what she was doing, and she stayed out there for a long time. I knew that her garden gave her such joy, but it was also very cold, especially for someone that threatened to freeze in the slightest draft. But when I urged her to come inside for some tea and time reading on the couch, her usual nighttime routine, she refused.

I'd kept one ear out of my headphones while I cleaned the kitchen that was... a mess. My usually tidy grandmother had cooked large pots of her Samhain stew and other random dishes and set out on a personal project to label everything in the kitchen. Roz had caught her mid-organization, she'd asserted. That she was almost done and would clean everything up, but she got frustrated, then mad, and then the pitcher had just slipped out of her hands.

When I asked her why she'd made all that food, she said that she needed enough for everyone.

I dumped the contents of the dustpan into the trash while my music changed to a poppy indie song. My head bopped along while I wiped down the counters again and waited for the water to boil for some tea.

It was the middle of the day, but by the creaking in the floor I'd heard earlier, Granna was just now waking up. She'd been despondent last night, apologizing to me before retreating into her bedroom, but when she finally made her way downstairs now, her eyes widened at the sight of the clean kitchen before she immediately collected herself.

Granna was dressed in a simple turtleneck sweater and jeans, and her hair was brushed smooth and loose down her back. She'd grown paler with the colder months, but her brown skin was still warm against the cool gray of her hair and the green of her sweater.

I shoved my headphones to my neck, and cleared my throat. "Um, I was wondering if you'd want to finish decorating for Yule? Josie will be over in a few hours, Orion a little while after that, and then we can all have some of the stew you made?"

Granna looked at me. Really looked. She worried at her bottom lip while running her eyes over my face, down to my feet.

And then she started crying.

In any other situation, I would've immediately started crying and rushed to the other person. Granna had always said that I had a sensitive heart—like it was something to love and pity because it would leave me feeling raw from other people's emotions just as much as my own.

But I'd never seen Granna cry. Not when she talked about my mother, not when I was sad, not even when we watched sad movies.

"Sweetheart, I—" she roughly swatted at her cheeks to clear the tears "—I have very much enjoyed having you here. Being your grandmother has been the joy of my life. You've grown to be more amazing than any of us hoped." She took a deep breath that turned into a gasp before smoothing out. "Your mother would be so, so proud. And I know that you'll go on to do and be so much more. I love you more than I ever thought possible." By the end, her words were little more than a hoarse whisper. She wiped at her eyes again, and I realized that I was tearing up, too.

Unease. Panic. Dread. They were churning so fast in my chest, that I felt like I couldn't breathe. This and the hug with Roz all felt like... a goodbye.

"I love you too, Granna."

"Oh, sweetheart, I didn't mean to make you upset." She walked to me, and I somehow managed to collapse into her much smaller frame. She sniffed. "I just wanted to make sure you knew. I'd been so flustered when you called asking to move in." She chuckled thickly. "I nearly told you to just visit a spell and go back, but I'm so glad I couldn't do it. These past few months have been marvelous. All because of you."

Another torrent of tears spilled down my face and soaked into her sweater. "Granna... I'm so glad to be here with you. And I'm so sorry for all the years I wasn't. All the times I visited only to hang out with friends or go off on my own, I—"

"Shh, sweetheart," she patted my back, "none of that. I've never been upset with you for living your life. Because I've always... I've always lived mine. If anyone needs to forgive anyone, it's you."

I pulled back and frantically searched her face. Even lined with years, I saw the origin of mine and my mother's. My eye color was hers, as was the shape of my jaw and brows. But where my eyes and lips were round, hers were more angular. Her nose was sharp where mine wasn't. For a second, I got caught up imagining what my grandfather must've looked like. How many of my features were his?

But I mustered up the courage to ask the thing that I needed to. It felt like black sludge on my tongue, but I finally croaked, "Granna... are you going to hurt yourself?" She'd been doing so well. The slips in memories were normal for people her age, but the sentimental words for someone who, all her life, had been decidedly unsentimental, wasn't just jarring. A thousand alarm bells were going off in my head.

Her head cocked into a confused tilt, but I saw the moment my meaning dawned on her. The rest of her tears cleared, and she smiled. "No, sweetheart. I'm sorry again for scaring you. I just needed you to know all of this. To let you know that no matter what happens, I have loved you with all of my heart. And that I hope you'll one day... forgive this old lady for her mistakes."

If she wanted me to believe that she wasn't giving deathbed confessions, she was doing a shit job. I didn't say that, though. Maybe I was too scared by the possibility of her leaving, so I just took her assertion that she wasn't going to hurt herself because it felt safer.

Before I could say anything else, she ran a hand over my curls and asked. "How about we start decorating? That was a good idea." And she looked almost back to normal. Enough to at least placate my cracking heart. I nodded. A cozy night in with my favorite people sounded like just what I needed.

. . . . .) . . . . .

"Dude, I don't know how you're wearing that. It's cold as *my* tit out here. Ha! Get it?" Josie laughed at her own lame joke while we crunched through the snow. It wasn't a terribly thick layer under the cover of the trees, but it was enough where our progress was slowed.

I shrugged and stuck my hands into the convenient pockets of my new dress. My trusty knife was a comforting weight beside my hand, even if we were using garden shears for our foraging instead. My coat over it wasn't nearly as thick as Josie's, but I was more than warm enough with it and the boots on my feet.

Granna had suggested we go out to find more evergreen branches with juniper berries for decoration and treats, and after hesitating to leave her alone, Josie convinced me to give her some space while we went quickly to fill the bag I'd brought.

The sun was just set, but I found I could see just fine while Josie's phone's flashlight was arcing and bobbing with her every step.

My feet carried us a little further than I typically went, past the marker I usually stayed behind, but the walking felt nice. The biting air energized my muscles, and my head felt clearer. Eventually, we happened upon a thick cluster of evergreen trees, and I directed Josie in taking clippings. She chatted away about work and her newest fling.

"Okay, and *then*, he wanted to do it, but I could tell that he was trying so hard to pretend that it was 'just okay', but yeah, right, and—" I'd never had the sensation of the hair at the back of my neck raising so strongly, though I'd written it in stories plenty of times. That feeling when you know that someone is right on you.

It was more uncomfortable than I thought it would be. But instead of freezing and listening, my body pivoted around, garden shears at the ready and already plunging toward the threat my conscious mind hadn't even yet registered.

Josie yelped, and so did whatever I'd just stabbed with the sharp gardening tool.

Next thing I knew, I was on my back with the snow wetting

my coat and hair. Rough, hairy hands held my wrists and ankles, and another one clamped over my mouth to muffle my screams. I flailed and bucked, and for a split second, the hold on me loosened, but before I could scramble to my feet, I was slammed back down. I bit at the palm over my mouth and tasted my attacker's blood. But they held on.

"Hey, Sylvie." I opened my eyes to find green eyes over mine. But they weren't soft and bright. They were cruel and half-shifted already and wrong, wrong, wrong.

☾

ORION

The drive back into town was long and annoying, but having my mother and sister gone made me more relaxed than I'd been in days. It was easy to assume the role of silent host and chauffeur when I was around my mother, but it was also taxing to be at her beck and call. Saying goodbye to my little sister was always harder, especially after she'd grown older and not been the sullen, irritating child she once was.

I passed the sign welcoming me to Antler Pointe, and I started toward Sylvie's grandmother's home. My Yule gifts were in the trunk, and I fidgeted in my seat, wondering if Sylvie would like hers.

After consulting with Juno, I decided it was best not to get her an engagement ring so soon. Though Meredith's questioning of when we'd 'make it official' had me rethinking the decision at first, I decided to stand my ground.

It didn't stop my planning, though. I would need to figure out a way to find out what kind of ring she would like. Maybe I could talk to Josie? To be frank, Sylvie's friend was a bit too boisterous for me, but she was certainly the person closest to my mate. And I needed to ask her grandmother for her blessing to propose.

Maybe I could do that tonight. Just so that she would know my intentions and secure that important piece before I made any other plans. She would probably have quite a bit of information to aid in ring consideration as well.

I arrived at the little white house a half hour or so after sunset, feeling much lighter than when I had left town. I piled my simply wrapped gifts into my arms and made my way to the front door. My weight shifted from side to side, and my nose picked up something strange. I craned my head to look at the driveway and yard surrounding, and I detected Sylvie's scent leading toward the forest.

Before I could think more of it, the door opened, and I smiled distractedly at Sylvie's grandmother.

Instead of calm and polite and slightly snarky, as she'd always been with me, she stepped back without a word and closed the door behind her.

"Where's Sylvie?" I asked. "I smelled that she went outside with Josie." My skin was itching, needing to get to my mate. She wandered the wood often, to the point that she should've known her way around, but I didn't want to put anything to chance with the pack watching us closely these days.

Sylvie's grandmother furrowed her brow, as if she hadn't considered Sylvie's absence until now. "She and Josie went out to gather some branches for decorations..." She frowned. "They should be back now, though."

I thought that getting Sylvie's phone call when she found that girl's body was the feeling of true fear, but this was far, far worse. With my last bit of sense, I lowered the gifts to the floor, right at her grandmother's feet, and ran out of the door.

My steps punched through the snow, and trees whipped past while I followed Sylvie's scent. I could imagine she and Josie walking leisurely, collecting and chatting, but at a copse of evergreen trees, I skidded to a stop.

A growl ripped through my chest, because now it wasn't just my mate and her friend, but the scent of *them*. I sunk down to my hands and knees, sniffing at the ground at a body-sized impression in the snow.

I gave a long, high-pitched whine because they'd hurt my mate. Though it was outrage instead of fear twined with her scent, I smelled blood, too. If they'd gotten her to the point that she was down and fighting, it wasn't good.

With shaking hands, I pulled my phone out of my pocket. I'd been avoiding fighting Graham, not wanting to repeat history and potentially perish in the process this time. But in trying and failing to find another way, I endangered my mate anyway.

"Hey, what's up?" Juno answered the phone on the third ring.

My voice was already twisting and changing, and I pulled a lock of Sylvie's black hair that'd fallen against the white snow. I brought it to my nose, but it did little to comfort me. "I need your help. They took her, and I'm going after them."

I knew that I wouldn't be able to take on the whole pack by myself, and judging from the at least three other Wolves that were just here, I would be facing more than just Graham himself.

I gave Juno the general direction where the scents were heading, and they were already running out of their house. We hung up, and I didn't bother changing out of my clothes. The constriction of fabric and subsequent rip let me feel like I was destroying something. But it wasn't enough.

My shift, though only taking a minute at most, felt unbearably long. As Wolf, the absence of my mate felt even worse, and another whine escaped while I bounded off on the trail of Sylvie's scent.

I would get her and tear down any that got in my way. I'd promised and promised to keep Sylvie safe, and I'd failed again. Despite my instincts to protect, they still took her.

CHAPTER THIRTY-EIGHT

JASPER

Any time one of us got close enough to knock her out and carry her, Sylvie lashed out with whatever it was that she could do. The first time, she'd nearly knocked Declan unconscious, and the second, she forced Ana back from her half-shift. So, we had to resort to using Josie as incentive to keep Sylvie walking with us to the meeting place.

My old friend bobbed, unconscious, in my arms while Sylvie walked behind Graham in his wolf form. We were less connected this way, and I was thankful for it. We'd been planning to take her for a while, obviously, but actually doing it felt too real.

The first time, with Wes, we'd blindly followed Graham to the spot. I didn't know what I'd been expecting, but Wesley Bowers bound and gagged in the middle of a forest clearing was not it.

Ana, Dec, and I had proven ourselves loyal enough to be in Graham's inner circle and had been given more responsibility in the pack for a while. It mostly entailed acting on his behalf in settling disputes between pack members, lending an extra hand where it was needed, and keeping our ears open to any information that would be helpful for him in leading us all.

I didn't know Wes very well, so maybe that was why I didn't immediately turn and run away. What we did as pack was different than human laws and customs, and we settled our scores our own way. So, at first, I'd thought Graham brought him out there to scare him or something. Maybe he'd insulted him or another senior member of the pack, and, yeah, I was down for that. Respect was one of the most important things, and though we didn't outnumber the Antler Pointe humans, this was *our* home.

The blood had been rushing in my ears, drowning out Graham's explanation of exactly what the fuck was going on, and when *he* stepped out of the brush, I almost passed the fuck out.

But the high, writhing around on the ground, feeling *everything* like bubbles and the best candy in the world was worth it. In it, the forest spoke to us. I *saw* it. Felt it. The land claiming that it was ours and our job to protect.

But what does that mean? How long are we gonna keep doing this? I didn't even try shaking the thoughts away this time. They always came back, anyway.

Watching Sylvie's back and her head swiveling, obviously trying to figure out how she could get out of this, I wanted to shout. To warn her. Graham had always been the one to draw first blood. To slit their throats and carve into their chests, being careful of the hearts.

He wanted them alive for it.

I'd tried to tell Dad about all of this once. Gotten pretty close, but at the last minute, I chickened out. Because what could he do? What could any of us do? Graham was the final authority, and *he* was more powerful than all of us.

"Got two for one!" Graham had laughed when we stumbled upon Sylvie and Josie in the forest. They'd stopped close the invisible barrier, and I'd expected them to turn around, as Sylvie always did.

And then they just... stepped right through it.

My blood had run cold, realizing that this was it, and my mouth watered at the prospect of another fix.

You're pathetic, I'd thought, and I didn't even try to argue. This was wrong, this was awful, but the scariest part was that I knew I couldn't stop. That none of us could. Was it even about being the guardians of this land anymore? When was the last time we'd run just for the fun of it? Felt the earth, untainted by what we were doing?

Would I ever wash the blood off of my hands?

Sylvie glanced back at Josie in my arms, and the look she gave me made me want to curl into myself. She'd always been kind. Nice. So had Wes, River, and Kara.

But *he* wanted her specifically, and that had never happened before. How could we refuse, and how could I explain that to Sylvie who was eyeing me in a way that made me wonder why I wasn't already dead?

Her voice wasn't cold. It was hot—vicious. "You should have listened to my warning."

I wanted to scream that I'd wanted to. That I didn't want to hurt anyone and just wanted to go back to the way things used to be. Before Kara, before River, before Wes... and before Graham became Leader.

He'd been so charismatic, talking about all the ways he could strengthen the pack. How Chief Thompson was out of touch. How the older generation didn't understand the current needs, and that we would do better. I was nearly thirty, stuck working with my dad like I'd started doing when I was old enough to stock shelves, and I'd fallen for it hook, line, and sinker.

And fuck, I'd *killed* people. To placate some god that made us high for a few hours, only to disappear when we had to clean up the mess.

I didn't realize my feet had been slowing to a stop until Declan bumped into my back. I needed to say something. I needed to stop this and figure out a way to get Sylvie and Josie out of here. Even if it angered *him* and Graham.

I turned to look at Declan, who was in wolf form like Graham, only to see that... we were here.

SYLVIE

My head felt like it was going to explode. I want to tear my skin off to relieve the burning I felt from being forced into submission because I didn't want them to hurt Josie. At some point while I'd been trying to fight them off, they'd knocked her out, and it was Graham's triumphant grin informing me of that fact that made me stop.

His Wolf was burly and a dusty brown color. Another Wolf trailed behind our procession, leaving three of us walking between them and Josie in Jasper's arms.

I was still trying to streamline my thoughts to figure out how to get the both of us away. Would I be able to carry her if it came down to it? Josie was shorter than me, but if she remained unconscious, would I be able to sprint away with her dead weight in my arms or over my shoulder?

Would I be able to fight them all off or create some kind of distraction that lasted long enough to get us both away?

I glanced back at Jasper behind me, and my rage flared to the forefront again. "You should have listened to my warning," I seethed. None of them spoke of what their plans were for us, but I had to imagine that we weren't supposed to survive this. Just like Kara hadn't. And maybe Wesley and River, too.

They'd all looked happy and bright in the photos their families supplied to the news stations, and I refused to end up like that. To never see Orion or Granna again.

Jasper looked like he was about to puke, and I imagined driving my knife into his stupid face. If he was having regrets now, it was far too late.

While I was imagining who I'd take out first, feeling the weight in the concealed pocket of my dress, Graham stopped us in a darkened clearing that made all of my hair stand up on end. We'd come in a completely different direction, but I recognized one of the fallen trees and cluster of mushrooms. Where I'd last seen a thigh bone and blue hair clip. If I started running east, I'd eventually reach Vinny's.

There was no shred of a doubt that they'd murdered Kara. Chased her down and killed her. Had they intended this for me all along?

Graham's body began to contort, his fur and claws shrinking back. My stomach churned, and I looked away. Watching Orion shift felt magical. Graham's shift, on the other hand, was almost grotesque. I heard the thumping of his muscles twisting and the pops of his joints reworking.

Once he was on two feet and in human form, he walked to a pile of rope that'd been placed at the base of one of the large trees that lined the clearing.

Naked and dick swinging, he walked over to Ana. "Tie up and set the other one over here." He pointed to the ground at his feet. She did as she was told without a word, and I fought to remain quiet as she took my best friend from Jasper's arms and got to binding her wrists and ankles.

Graham stepped up to me, smug smile on his lips and hair standing on end. I refused to break our eye contact, to back down.

Up close, I saw the redness of his eyes and the strain bracketing his brows. He called to the others, "You all shift. It's almost time."

I wanted to spit at him again, maybe have it land in the middle of his face. But I refrained. "Time for what?"

He chuckled. "You'll see. Gonna be a big show." He looked to the other Wolves. "Dec, you and Jas make sure she doesn't run." The two of them crept up on either side of me and my fingers itched. Which one first?

They hadn't bound my hands for some unknown, stupid

reason, and just before I reached into the pocket obscured by the draping skirt of my dress, a rustling of leaves and breaking of twigs made all the Wolves' ears perk and their bodies stand at attention.

My own started buzzing in a way I'd never felt before, and my gaze darted frantically in the direction they were looking. What the fuck was happening?

In my moment's hesitation, a… man—figure—crept out of the black of the forest.

Over seven feet tall, they walked out of the depths of the wood, clad only in dark leather trousers. Their skin was textured, almost like the bark of a tree but a lighter, golden pine color. Loose, red and brown leaves and vines hung from their head like hair, and sprouting from their temples were large horns like those you'd see on an elk.

And their eyes, in the dim light of the fire, were an unnaturally sparkling gold.

Hunched and even more grotesque than Graham's contorting shift, they took one look around, and their face split into an impossibly wide grin. My stomach threatened to literally fall out of my asshole as I stared in horror at the large pointed teeth that jutted out of their mouth.

"Good work, loyal pups." Despite their distorted, lanky body and hunched spine, their voice was smooth and deep. Had I not been staring right at this… thing, I would've marked the voice as pleasant.

Graham jerked forward, still in human form, and I noted his body twitching even more now. He wasn't at all hesitant as he neared the unnatural being with relief and excitement in his half-crazed eyes.

With unnaturally long fingers and knuckles like the bends of tree roots, the being offered their empty palm. Graham reached out expectantly as a bright, white light flashed.

As it faded, a golden dagger appeared, and Graham took it in a firm grasp.

Well, fuck this, I thought to myself not a second before my fist closed around the knife hidden in my pocket.

I'd never used it for self-defense, but it was familiar enough in my grip, and I flipped open the blade just before I buried it in one of the Wolves' neck. With no finesse, just wild anger and the need to survive, I jerked my arm back and wrenched the blade through their throat. Hot blood spurted and splattered on my face, but I barely felt it.

The Wolf dropped to the cold, snowy ground, and I started backing away from the other to give myself room. I wouldn't have the element of surprise anymore, so I needed to be smart about this. Bargain for Josie's safety, maybe?

The other Wolves startled and started toward their fallen pack-mate who was breathing shallowly on the ground, pool of nearly black blood growing beneath them. I held my knife at the ready, closed fist and blade pointed outward. I wouldn't leave my friend, but who was I kidding? Whatever that thing was, looking at me with disdain while Graham barked orders at the whining Wolves, would probably have no trouble finishing me off.

I'd go down fighting in every possible way.

Josie was still lying in the snow, arms and legs bound, and her hands were turning blue. She didn't deserve to get dragged into this. Kara, Wes, and River hadn't deserved to be part of whatever sick ritual this was, but I was no longer under any illusions that I wouldn't fall to the same fate. I wasn't going to leave Josie, and unless a miracle happened, these were my last few minutes.

What would it feel like to be a ghost?

I sent a silent apology to Orion, to Granna, and readied myself for Graham who was stalking forward with his much larger weapon. Why the tree monster wasn't just finishing me off, I didn't know, but just as I readied my body and all the power I could muster, my ears picked up the steady beat of feet running through snow. My mark warmed, and my heart picked up even more, adrenaline pumping and hope rising.

Graham raised the dagger, and I swore I almost saw my reflection in the gilded blade before his body was thrown to the side by a white blur. An arc of blood danced in the air, and my own shout of surprise was drowned by the thud of bodies hitting the snow. My hand shook with unplaced rage and fear, but it felt like I couldn't move.

Snarls rang out in the dead of the night, and I tried to keep my eyes on the three different spots of chaos.

A large, lean Wolf with reddish-brown fur stood before Josie, baring its fangs and snapping at Graham's Wolves who were doing the same.

To my right, Graham's pink flesh grappled with the white Wolf that I knew and loved so much.

And directly across the snow-covered ground stood the being that gave Graham the dagger. Presumably, the one who wanted me dead. They looked on the whole scene with detached, disappointed eyes and didn't move at all to help the 'loyal pups' that'd brought me to them.

A deep bellow followed by a piercing yelp brought my attention back to where Orion fought Graham, and my feet finally moved me forward. They kept going at each other, crimson blood and snarls flying up from the scuffle of teeth and golden blade.

I didn't know how to get in the middle without accidentally injuring Orion, and as far as I knew, my powers required me to touch to do anything useful.

Graham's two Wolves, Ana and Jasper, were still facing off with... Dr. Vanders. A cold breeze brought a flurry of snowflakes and their familiar scent over to me, and tears spilled down my cheeks. They stood over my friend, protecting her, and my mate was protecting me while I was standing and doing nothing.

I took a deep breath, trying to steady the buzzing of my awareness that had only grown in intensity, but before I could exhale, an agonized whine shattered all clearing of my mind.

Another spatter of blood curled in the frigid air, painting the snow and side of my face red. Two bodies sank into the snow, and a phantom, stabbing pain in my chest made tears spring to my eyes.

The gold-hilted blade was still in Graham's half-shifted grip while he lay on the ground, gasping up toward the sky like a fish out of water. Transparent steam trailed up from a gaping wound in his throat, but I barely registered it as I sank to my knees beside Orion.

Air whistled out of his black nose, and his snout was covered in red and tissue. He struggled for a moment to get his legs under him, but he collapsed again, sending up tufts of bloody snow.

I dropped my knife at the sight of the blooming wound at his chest. There were scrapes and slashes elsewhere, but this one was darkening so fast, the red spreading across his fur with every breath. My hands hovered over the wound, and I... I could feel it. The cold lethality of the dagger's strike.

My mate was dying.

Even as I pressed my hands to the stab wound, trying to stop the bleeding, I knew that it was doing nothing. His bright green eye blinked up at me, and through a flood of tears and blubbering and pleas, I sent calm through my hands. Because it was all I knew how to consciously do that could help, and I hated myself, even cursed Granna for never teaching me substantial healing magic.

Orion's eyelids were taking longer pauses, blinking more slowly while watching me all the way. "I can't do this baby, I can't do this, please don't leave me, please."

He huffed a gust of air through his nose and just looked. His body relaxed under my touch, but the blood kept coming.

It wasn't fair, it was *bullshit*, and I raised my gaze to see the being still watching us with those detached eyes and distorted body. I felt like I could breathe flames, that I could decimate entire cities with how much rage I had, but it all just came out in one long, agonized scream. The veins at my temples bulged with my cry, cursing this being for doing this in the only language I could muster.

They had no reaction to my outburst, of course. Just looked down at Graham in disappointment and then back at me like I was a mere annoyance. They weren't even trying to get me. Dr. Vanders was doing their best to take snaps of their teeth at Ana and Jasper who were even more aggressive now that Graham was down.

I looked back down at Orion and blinked the tears out of my eyes while his blood squelched under my hands that were pressing, pressing to no avail. We'd barely had any time together, and all I kept thinking about were his promises to keep me safe and the life Josie said she'd seen for us.

He'd kept his promise, saved me from Graham, but it seemed as though our future was going to be cut short. I started hyperventilating, feeling the life within my mate dim like it was my own, and I was so preoccupied with holding his stare for as long as I could that I didn't notice the heavy, crunching footsteps until they were right on me.

"Amnes." A new, deeper voice boomed through the trees and rattled my bones in a soothing way. I flinched when the earth literally shook beneath me, and out of the corner of my eye, I saw the others startle and face the other being that charged from the darkness.

They were like the one who'd given Graham the dagger, but their bark skin was a deep brown. Their hair, instead of red and brown, hung in blacks and greens.

Whoever they were, instead of disappointed or indifferent, their sharp teeth were drawn in outrage. They charged at the other whose face broke to reveal true fear before trying to retreat.

The other was already on them, though, and I struggled to focus when they started to move faster than my eyes were physically capable of tracking. Their long fingers were tipped in claws that swiped, and their fight sent them crashing into trees, breaking them like twigs. Luckily, none landed on any of us, but I curled over Orion, keeping my calming touch on him and trying to protect him from any more pain.

A loud, wet ripping followed by a thudding crack rang through the air before the ground shook again.

The red-haired being was lying face up in the snow, mouth sneering as they stared up at the other. Held in their dripping, dark hand was an unnaturally red heart.

The second monster spoke in a language that at first sounded unfamiliar, but I then felt the meaning of the words in my blood. Like that of the fungi and spiders.

"Your attempts at hurting her are pathetic, Amnes. Drawing sacrifices to come outside of this day that nature allows us. Toying with the mortals of this world and tricking our own descendants to do what you were too cowardly to do, lest I be able to smell your hand on the killing blow. You die a fool, cousin." The black- and green-haired monster sank its long, sharp teeth into the beating heart in their hand and… ate it while making the other one watch.

When they'd swallowed every morsel, and the one at their feet ceased breathing, the tree-skinned monster lifted their gaze to me, and instead of the golden reflection that my sweet mate's eyes sometimes gave, this being's glittered between their bright white sclera and large, pitch black pupil.

This time, in deeply accented English, the monster spoke to me. Blood dripped in thick drops from their mouth, but they didn't bother to wipe it away. "Your mate is almost gone—"

There was no reason for me to believe they could, but the words blurted out of my mouth before I thought it through. "Can you save him? Please." Because whatever the fuck these things were, maybe… maybe they knew how to help.

Instead of hunger or disdain or predatory wrath, the monster's round eyes softened along with the rest of their face. They glanced at Graham who lay a few feet away, still staring up at the sky. They pointed a long, twisted finger. "That one barely hangs on. A life for a life. If you wish."

I didn't need to think about it. "Yes. Please. Do it now."

A set of growls reached my ears, but the being just raised their hand, and I watched Jasper, Ana, and Dr. Vanders all fall to their sides. I flinched, and witnessing their still-breathing chests only made me feel marginally less horrified.

It may have been my raw, swollen eyes, but I thought for a moment that I saw the monster give a slight, gentle smile before starting towards Orion and I. Though they'd just killed the other one—their cousin, apparently—and knocked out the other Wolves with just a wave of their hand, my body didn't even stiffen at their approach.

They stopped between where I hovered over Orion, whose breaths were barely there, and where Graham lay in a similar condition. They spoke no words, said no spell, but my head became light with the rush of energy that circled around us like a tornado. My chest heaved, feeling at once like there was too much air and not enough—like I could disappear on its current—and I watched through heavy eyes as it pulled something from Graham's open mouth.

It wasn't a physical thing, just a shimmering tawny light that once removed, left a pale, cold body.

The being turned toward Orion and me, and like a wet pebble tumbling out of one's hand, they crouched over us and let the ball of light fall.

Uncaring that I was still covering half of his body, the light found and landed just between Orion's unblinking eyes and disappeared.

I held my breath as I felt—something. An energetic stirring under his skin that preceded a heavier thump of his heart, and instead of the shallow pants he'd been taking, my mate's chest swelled with a larger breath.

And then another. And another, and then his spring green eye met mine again, saw me, and he gave a raspy cough.

I tightened my arms over Orion, sending all the love and comfort and rest I could until my head throbbed and my muscles trembled. But it was helping, he was breathing even deeper, and I could hear his heartbeat strengthen and even out.

I whimpered into his fur that was slowly shrinking into

smooth skin. Where paws and claws had once been, I felt his warm, strong hands grasping at my arms. He was here, he was alive, it was okay—

"Sylvana."

I froze. No one ever used my real name. To avoid confusion, my family had called me Sylvie from the day I was born, and there was no mistaking what the being said in that deep, smooth voice. How did it know my name?

I looked up at the monster that'd saved me and Josie and my mate, but they weren't looking at us. I followed their gaze, where they were grinning with blood dripping out of their mouth.

At Granna.

CHAPTER THIRTY-NINE

SYLVANA

"**S**ylvana."

That voice was like honey, and sudden tears fell from my eyes. Another year had passed, but he looked the same as he always did.

There was blood dripping from his hands, his grinning mouth, and he was the most beautiful thing I'd ever seen. His hair hung long and loose like vines, and tall, proud antlers extended from his temples. His deep brown skin was textured like bark. Otherworldly.

Mine.

I went forward, boots falling through the snow and chaos frozen around us, but I couldn't bring myself to care. He was here, and no matter how difficult today already was, I felt as light and young as the first time we met.

My granddaughter and her Wolf kept their eyes on him. Which was smart, since he was strong enough to easily dispose of the creature that lay lifeless in the snow. Over the fifty-five years he'd been visiting me, some creatures from his realm were able to slip through the portal. Especially those whose powers relished the night and cold like his.

I stepped around the body of a Wolf, poor thing, and he met me. He pulled me into his bare chest, and it smelled like pine needles and cold nights and hearth fires. His fingers, long and thin, twined in my hair. Cozy warmth, calm, spread throughout my body, and the rest of my nerves settled.

"My mate." He spoke over me, and I began to weep, like I did every time we were reunited. It was like I saved up my tears all year for them to spill at the first glimpse of him. Fifty-five years with only a long, beautiful night between the other three-hundred and sixty-four.

I craned my head to look up at him, so tall that I barely reached the middle of his chest when he was in this form. The blood was smeared on his lower face and neck, and his teeth were stained with it. Gold, shimmering eyes gazed down at me like I was the most precious thing in the world. Even wrinkled and old, I believed it when he told me every time.

I couldn't help but smile at him. My life here was simple and happy. My garden and my home were my safe places, Roz was the best friend I'd never deserved, and Sylvie was the light of my life.

With my mate, though, I felt alive. Complete and whole like my soul was singing. These past few weeks, when my decision became more and more *real*, it was a struggle to not let guilt overtake me completely. But seeing him now, I stood even firmer in my choice. He'd found a way, and we would be together. Always.

"I've missed you," I said, and he grinned, sharp teeth like perfect points. This was how he'd been the first time I invited a portal to open in my backyard. *Summoning an Elemental Sprit* in The Book, I'd found, didn't summon a specific entity but invited whatever curious creature who happened to be nearby. In the dead of winter, I spent all my nights studying, and in a thirst for more knowledge, I'd thought I would learn from something otherworldly. When my mate stepped out of the shimmering ripple within my circle, I'd been taken aback, excited, and a little afraid.

My mate ran a finger around the edge of my face and bent down to give a featherlight kiss to my lips. I wrapped my arms around his slim waist, felt the tickle of his long, black and moss-green hair on my cheek. "My sun, how I've missed you, too. No more will we be apart." He gave another kiss to my forehead, and I shuddered with more weeping.

It was in these moments that I wanted nothing more than to have Caley here.

"G-Granna?" I clenched my eyes shut, working up the nerve to turn around. There was no avoiding this anymore. Though Sylvie meeting him had always been a possibility, I... was afraid. For her to see all the ways I'd failed. To see the mistakes and hard decisions I made.

I twisted within his arms, and then we were both looking at my sweet granddaughter. She was crouched over her own mate that was slowly gaining consciousness. When he registered my mate's attention on them, he curled an arm over Sylvie, protecting her even when he had just been on the brink of death. I smiled at them both. I had been right. He would be here for her.

"Hi, sweetheart." I winced. Every word felt inadequate with my granddaughter's wide eyes looking at me and her grandfather with wary confusion. There was so much I had to explain.

"Hello, Sylvie," my mate greeted. "And hello, again, Snow Pup." Somehow the boy was able to get even paler, blinking wide at my mate. At one of our visits, my mate spoke of a young white Wolf that he stumbled upon while hunting for us. How the pup had been unafraid but trying to hunt alone.

My own grandmother was a seer, which was how I was able to recognize it in Josie all those years ago, and the older I got, some of my own premonitions popped up. Like dreams during the day. I was delighted to see that as far as my granddaughter and her mate were concerned, they'd been correct.

"Um, Granna... who-who's this?" By the way she drew out the

question, she already had an inkling. But I couldn't blame her for being hesitant. We'd decided to keep the truth of us for her safety. To keep what happened to Caley from happening to Sylvie and encouraging Michael to take her to live near his family. I couldn't bring myself to stifle her interests when she came to visit, but the barrier my mate put around the house kept her shielded from those that wanted her.

Apparently, though, it made them resort to soliciting the pack to do their bidding. Graham was a stupid boy, and if he weren't already dead, I would have slapped him.

After a baleful look where Graham's body lay next to his 'god', I straightened my spine. Sylvie deserved an explanation. "Sweetheart, this… is my mate."

"You may call me Coill," he added, and I smiled gratefully up at him. They were the same words he'd greeted me with when we first met. Since then, he'd given me his true name, part of my mating gift and a true show of his trust in me. With it, I could get him to do anything, he'd said. I held the secret close to my heart.

"Your… mate." Sylvie's eyes flitted between us, then up and down his body. I probably didn't want to know some of the questions that were forming in her mind, and thank goddess she didn't voice any except, "For how long?"

I chewed at my lip and took a breath. "Fifty-five years."

"I… why didn't you tell me?" Her voice cracked, and I went to her. Coill stayed where he was, but I felt his support surrounding me.

I sank to my knees in the snow, the cold barely permeating my awareness. Orion sat up and shifted to wrap his arm around Sylvie's back. I looked into her eyes, the ones she'd inherited from me. So often I'd felt like I was interacting with my younger self.

I prayed that she'd be able to forgive me. Us. "I'm so sorry, sweetheart. I couldn't. Things are… dangerous. We feared so much things turning out like they had with your mother." I took a shaky breath. It was like tearing open a wound each time I spoke of her.

"What are you talking about? She died in a car accident." Sylvie and Orion bristled, and a tentative crunching of snow rang behind me. I craned my neck to find my mate sinking down to sit beside me. Even with their trepidation, Sylvie and Orion didn't back away, which made my face hot once again. We didn't need their approval, but dammit, did I long for it.

Coill ran a hand over my hair, petting the grey strands that used to be almost black. When he spoke to Sylvie, his voice was low, soft, and filled with sorrow. "Your mother did not. She was killed." We'd both grieved in our own way and together when we could. For me, the years had been long, but with time working so differently between our realms, he'd missed so much. To mate one year, then meet his three-month-old child the next. He was immortal, but the years hadn't made him immune to emotions. We tried to make the most of our fleeting moments together, but we always made time to talk of her. To look at pictures of Caley and share stories and memories. The sight of a lone tear running down his cheek now made me start crying all over again.

"Why? How?" Though her eye color was like mine, the round, emotive shape was all his. All Coill's.

He kept running his fingers through my hair, giving me calm even when he was feeling sadness. "It is... frowned upon by many where I am from. Our matehood. My family," he gestured toward the body that was quickly decomposing and becoming a husk of dust, "had been suspicious, but I didn't think—" He shuddered, and I placed a hand over his thigh. "To keep you away and unaware as much as we could was to keep you safe. Do not be upset with your grandmother. Please."

Sylvie frowned and glanced at Orion before looking back to Coill. "I'm not upset. Exactly. Just... confused. And hurt."

He nodded, vines shifting and elk-like horns cutting through the air. "I understand. This has not been easy, but most of all for your grandmother."

"And... and you are my grandfather?" she whispered and leaned closer into Orion's bare chest.

Coill smiled warmly and nodded once again. "Yes, Sylvie. I have watched you from afar, but I am so pleased to be speaking with you now."

Sylvie hesitated for just a moment before reaching out a hand. Coill held out his, and when their palms touched, they both sucked in surprised gasps. Like with like, I could feel magic stirring around them. Cool and alive, it sparkled.

How long had I imagined this? Every time Sylvie asked questions about her grandfather and the answer sat like a rock in my stomach. And when she'd stopped asking all together, it felt even worse.

"So, what now?" Orion whispered, eyes on me. He was perceptive, Sylvie's mate, and I wanted to laugh if all this hadn't felt so bittersweet.

Because I was leaving.

I gave Orion a long look, and by the grim purse of lips and subsequent glance at Sylvie who was still gazing at Coill, he'd deduced the answer to his question.

Fifty-five years, and I was finally going to be leaving with my mate. Going to his realm to truly begin our lives. To do so, though, I'd be giving up this one.

"You're leaving, aren't you?" Sylvie's question made me jump, but I really shouldn't have been surprised. With each passing day, while she honed and came into her powers, she was far more aware than either of us were used to.

Admittedly, I'd been a wreck for a while. The guilt and nerves had been eating away at me while the excitement left me at risk of floating through the days. When I met her stare, no words came out. But my nod was enough, and Sylvie's simple one in return was a kindness and a dagger to my heart all at once. I didn't deserve her, because even though I could see the grief already creeping over her, I was going to leave anyway.

We all sat in silence for a while, leaning into the cold wind and the creaking of the wood. Just as she'd finally met her grandfather, he would be leaving.

Though he was powerful, his body wasn't stable in this realm. My blood made it possible for Caley and Sylvie to live here, but each minute diminished his strength. It was probably why the other one, now just a pile of dust stirring in the winter wind, had solicited the pack to supply sacrifices. Hearts.

And when the opportunity came for them to exact some rite of twisted honor by keeping their bloodline free of mixed blood, they solicited the pack to take out Sylvie. Just as his family had gotten another to kill my Caley. After Coill returned and slaughtered those that had a hand in Caley's death, they took care to leave us alone. Until now, apparently.

My consolation that we'd hopefully be able to visit next winter solstice felt cheap, so I held it back. Sylvie had already lost so much, and I felt a right villain for adding to it.

But then there was him. My mate's hold tightened around me, and another wash of calm softened the negative emotions swirling in my mind. With him, my heart was so, so full.

Coill broke the silence. "I know that I have no right to ask you both of anything, but I hope that you will continue to watch over her. To know you are her mate warms my heart, Snow Pup."

Though his face was blank, Orion's eyes were sharp. Assessing. "I will. Always."

"Hey, because I'm part..." Sylvie waved her hand, unsure of what to call him. A strong pull of fondness made me want to wrap her in my arms. Despite her anxious spirit, when actually faced with danger or world-shattering information, Sylvie was able to find her footing so easily. I was almost loath to admit that I'd been more rigid the first time Coill and I met. How silly my skepticism felt, now.

"Fae," Coill supplied.

"Fae. Since I'm part Fae, can I be turned? By a shifter bite."

Coill frowned like the question didn't make sense, but then his expression smoothed with understanding. "No. Shifters are descendent from those of us Fae that are able to change forms. With my blood, you are immune."

Sylvie turned and shared an excited grin with Orion who offered a much more guarded, but just as excited, smirk in return. I had an idea about what they were looking forward to, and I was happy for her.

When she turned back to us, her head tilted like it so often did during our lessons. How I would miss those. "You can change forms? Is this what you really look like? Or just in this world? Can I change forms?"

Coill still had blood on his face, but his grin at her didn't look menacing in the slightest. My mate was vicious when it was needed but also so kind and sweet.

Without a word, golden light began to shimmer around him. Though I was certainly biased, I appreciated this shift as opposed to the contorting way the shifters of our world did it. Coill's features slid and changed within the golden light, his body shrinking to a height similar to Orion's. His horns were still present, but his skin released the bark camouflage and smoothed. The lankiness disappeared to reveal strong, bulkier limbs. His thighs pressed against his leather trousers, filling them out where they'd before been loose. Instead of a back hunched to reach our line of sight, his spine was straight and noble. Royal.

His hair was no longer green vines and leaves but tumbling waves of black, and I saw the moment true recognition dawned on Sylvie. She'd gotten some features from her father, but her likeness to Coill's true form was undeniable. He was hard and delicate at the same time. The pointed taper of his ears, I knew, were sensitive and left him a chuckling mess when tickled, but his lengthened canine teeth were their own vicious weapons.

How many times had I caught Sylvie out of the corner of my eye and thought, for a split second, that it was him?

Coill gestured to himself. "This is my true form. The other is easier to assume in this world. For protection and to blend into the wood. In my world, on the other side of the veil, is the wood that our family calls home." Some of his smile faded. "Though you have inherited many gifts from Sylvana and I, I do not sense an ability to shift. I am sorry."

But Sylvie took it in stride. She just nodded and looked, cataloguing the features of her grandfather and adjusting all of this into her model of the world around her. She was so good about that. All of this.

"And... is that where you're going to go?" She looked at me. "Where you're both going to go?" I remembered her as a little girl. Being worried about her father or when she realized for the first time that I lived alone. Her worries grew along with her and the understanding of the complexities of the world, but when actually faced with danger or something difficult, she slipped into another place. Another sense where even at a young age, she squared her shoulders and faced it head on.

She was looking at me like that, now, and I drew my own courage to match hers. "Not the forest, exactly. But—yes."

Her lip wobbled, but she shook her head. Her eyes shimmered with the threat of more tears. "Now?"

For that answer, I looked to Coill. To cross the veil, to become Fae enough to live amongst him was complex magic that had taken him all this time to figure out. Since the day Caley was killed, he'd taken it upon himself to find a way to bring me over so that we could be together. So that he could protect me himself, instead of relying on the veil to separate me from those that wanted to drive us apart.

Coill always called me his sun, but looking into his eyes was like being under the warmest sunshine. With the way he crossed from his world into ours, time was different and twisted, but the love between us was constant. I was scared to leave Sylvie, if only to say goodbye to what we'd have if I decided to stay, but I was done being apart from my mate. "I would like to seal the portals. To prevent any more from coming over tonight and reprimand all that knew of Amnes's plans. And more importantly, I have found a way for us. Our home is prepared for you, my mate. I am ready whenever you are."

"Will," I cleared my throat, "will we be able to come and visit? Like you've visited me each year?"

He ran his thumb across my cheekbone. "Of course. We will be careful."

I looked around the clearing, though it was all dirty and bloody snow, dead and unconscious bodies, and us. I would never sleep in my bed again. Work in my garden again.

I turned back to Sylvie. She was the most important, and despite the new tears that were dripping into her lap, she offered me an encouraging smile. A nod.

I rushed forward and threw my arms around her. "I love you so much, sweetheart. Thank you for being understanding, and I'm so sorry that I had to keep things from you. You are truly, truly, the light of my life."

She wept, chest heaving, and I sobbed with her. "Thank you for everything, Granna. I'm glad that you're able to be with your mate finally. I couldn't imagine being apart from Orion like you have had to endure. You deserve to have this happiness."

I kissed her wet cheek and held her head in my hands. "Thank you, sweetheart." I glanced at Orion. "You take care of my granddaughter, you hear me? I can always come back and zap some sense into you if you forget."

He didn't pick up on my joke and instead grimaced and shuddered at the memory of my striking him. "There will be no need, I assure you." He began to stand, and the three of us followed suit. Sylvie and I gave each other one last embrace before pulling away from each other.

Sylvie turned to my mate. "And you, ah… grandfather. Coill." She fidgeted for a second before launching forward and bringing him in for a hug. I saw him stiffen for half a breath before he melted, wrapping his arms around her. He whispered something in her ear that made her cry harder, then frantically nod her head that was still wet from the snow and sticking out from fighting. When they pulled apart, the blood spatters on their faces were like an intentional pair.

She looked up at him one last time, took a step back. "Make Granna's sacrifices worthwhile. She's been waiting a long time for this."

He took my hand at the same time he bowed to Sylvie. From what I understood, lowering one's horns for another was a sign of deep respect. By the surprised expression on Sylvie's face, she felt the gravity of that and his words. "I swear it, Sylvie." Orion stepped forward and put his arm around her, and my granddaughter let herself be held.

I turned to my mate, but there was nothing left to say. I was ready.

Coill pulled me back into his chest, and I settled my face onto his warm skin. "Take a deep breath, my sun. We will be home when you finish it." With one last look at Sylvie who just cried and grinned, I did just that and felt my old life fall away.

CHAPTER FORTY

SYLVIE

Orion unlocked and held open the front door for me. Though we kept the house cooler than most, it was still far warmer than the frigid February air. We stomped our boots on the welcome mat and started on our coming home routine.

Home.

After Granna left with my grandfather, whatever spell he cast to put the others to sleep immediately broke. To their credit, Dr. Vanders and Josie took what happened in stride. Once they realized that Orion was alive and okay, they didn't blanch in the slightest at the sight of the bodies on the ground. Josie, after gaping at the Wolves that turned into naked people, took a breath and kept it moving. Jasper and Ana, on the other hand, had been a weird shade of resignation.

Seeing Granna so happy and finally meeting Coill left me feeling far better than I probably would have been, but Orion still tightened his grip around my arm when I'd started forward toward the two of them. Their Leader was dead, but they were just as responsible.

With clenched teeth, I spat at them, "You are horrible. Grieving a murderer instead of those you've killed. Or even apologizing for trying to do the same to me. For nothing!" At least they'd had the decency to flinch and cast a regretful look at us.

Jasper, with eyes sunken and naked body curling into itself, looked pathetic. "You're right. I—I'm sorry." His blue eyes were cast downward at our feet, but I didn't feel a hint of satisfaction at his supplication.

Ana, nude but back straight, gave a clipped nod. "You are right. Though, I know my apology probably means shit." I snorted, and she continued, "There's no excuse for us getting swept up into this. It was far from worth it."

Josie piped up, and I hadn't noticed until then that she was leaning into Dr. Vanders's side. Their arm was slung around her shoulders. "And you're just going to—what? Walk away and not answer to anyone for what you've done?"

I looked to Orion, and saw his sharp eyes taking in the other two Wolves. With mine on the firm set of his jaw, I felt some of my anger retreat.

Ana's mouth was pressed into a flat line, and she gave a shake of her head. Jasper flitted his gaze up to us, but when he looked at my mate, he curled into himself even more. What a coward.

"We will be honest with the pack. They were kept from all of this, but they deserve to know. And we will accept whatever punishment they see fit." Her face took on a deeper, grimmer tint, and I wondered if death was among those that were acceptable pack punishments. She took a shaky inhale and deeply bowed her head. Her blonde hair shifted over her shoulders and partially hid her face in shame. "We are sorry, White One. Sylvie. All of you. For all that we have done."

Both Ana and Jasper remained bowed in an unmistakably submissive posture, and I looked up at Orion. He was already searching my face, silently asking me what I thought. Certainly, I hadn't forgiven them. I wasn't sure I ever would. But, the fact remained that the Chief would most likely prevent any legal repercussions—that would put shifter identities at risk. And as much as I now knew that I had the capacity to kill, *my rage was quelled enough to feel no desire to physically harm Ana or Jasper. There had been enough death.*

Orion read whatever expression was on my face, then turned to Josie and Dr. Vanders. No words were exchanged between them, but they gave him enough to turn back to the two contrite Wolves.

Orion's pale skin and hair blended so beautifully with the snow around us, a few errant flakes falling into his hair. He stepped forward to stand over them.

His broad shoulders were strong, and I watched while he bent his head to Ana's neck. Orion's fangs were out, and a swell of satisfaction and pride rushed through me as he growled threateningly over her.

Ana hunched further, animalistic whine coming through her nose as she sank all the way to the ground. She planted her face into the dirty snow, and a humorless smile spread across my face.

My mate then stepped to Jasper, who lasted less than two seconds with Orion growling at his throat before joining Ana on the ground.

In human form, aside from his fangs and claws, Orion's voice even made my body tremble. "You will keep your promise to tell your pack of all you've done and honor their judgement. You will never bother us, or my mate and I will not be merciful again. You don't even deserve this." The two of them nodded, faces smashed into the snow.

Orion didn't tell them to get up, but his turning back to us was a dismissal in of itself. His face was blank, but when he took my hand in his, I felt something under his skin. It wasn't magic, but it was strong. Like power.

The four of us didn't spare the other Wolves another glance or word, and we left the clearing.

What my mate and I didn't expect, however, was to be invited to a pack meeting not a week later.

We'd met Dr. Vanders in town for coffee and were sitting outside in the cool sunshine. After wallowing for a few days, I let Orion pull me out of bed when Dr. Vanders invited us, and I was reminded again of a world that existed beyond the safety of my mate and the cabin.

Chief Thompson had a new air of grief about him that was very different from mine. His son had not been a good person, but I could tell that he genuinely mourned him still. Orion and Dr. Vanders stiffened at his approach but relaxed once he extended the invitation to the both of them.

"We're still working things out, but I wanted to extend an apology on behalf of the pack and from me personally. Ana and Jasper told us... everything. We're meeting on Saturday to discuss where we're going from here and what their punishment will be. We felt it was only right to have you all there. There's no pressure, but we agreed that we want to move forward and make amends."

I could tell that Orion had been too flustered to make a decision right then and there, and Dr. Vanders and I decided without discussion to not push him to talk about it. But I knew my mate, and if he truly didn't want to be involved with the pack, he would've flat out refused. Instead, he'd listened to Chief Thompson, and after a few days, he requested my input, stating that he wouldn't meet if I was against it.

Even with the prospect of seeing Ana and Jasper again, I swallowed my resentment and encouraged Orion to hear them out. I wanted to see for my own eyes how the pack was going to handle it.

But where I'd half expected them to make excuses for their murderous packmates or admonish us for our causing Graham and Declan's deaths, they all extended apologies.

Led by Chief Thompson, we observed their meeting in a stretch of woods I hadn't been in before. I recognized each and every member of the pack, but where I'd wanted to feel rage, it didn't rise. Most of them looked betrayed when Chief Thompson grimly reiterated what his own son had led the three Wolves to do.

When Jasper and Ana presented themselves, nude and kneeling before the pack, I watched with cold eyes as they voted to prohibit them from running with any pack members or sharing in their meals for five years. My brow furrowed, but when I looked at Orion and Dr. Vanders, they nodded along with the verdict. It wasn't death, and it wasn't exile, but by the haunted looks on Jasper and Ana's faces, the punishment was more severe than they'd hoped. Good.

After that initial meeting, we continued to attend. At first, it was to clarify our new relationship with the pack now that Graham and his poison no longer led them. When I haltingly explained the predicament about how to handle Granna's disappearance, Chief Thompson offered to help with a death certificate and any other legalities I needed. Thankfully, Granna had left a packet containing account information that reflected her signing over all her assets, including the house, to me over a year prior. And I accepted the Chief's help so that I could move forward in this way.

The pack met weekly, it turned out, and each time we went, Orion and I both relaxed into the tentative embrace of the other Wolves. Those that'd been around for a while even spoke highly of my mate's family as the founders of the pack and expressed their excitement to have us around. Dr. Vanders was still torn, what with them being a member of their family pack and unwilling to yet tie themselves to another, but they came with us more often than not.

"How do you feel, baby?" I asked through my yawn while I emerged from the bedroom in my Freddy Krueger t-shirt and slippers. Tonight had been our initiation into the pack.

It'd taken my mate all of these weeks to process his complex feelings surrounding Antler Pointe Pack as well as the lingering effects from his past experiences. But tonight, under the full moon, we both stood before the pack. Orion stated his oath to support and respect them, and they all vowed to do the same for him. My own vow, as his mate, followed, and the subsequent pack run was more than magical.

The shifter members stripped their clothes and changed, all together under the full moon, and we set off. Every time he shifted, I was so in awe of my mate, and tonight, with a new family around us, I could see how happy it made his Wolf.

He was still his quiet, observant self, keeping me in eyesight at all times, but after a while, he yipped and wove through the trees with the others. Dr. Vanders hadn't taken the vow but was allowed to run with the pack tonight, and all the Wolves' playing and good spirits were infectious. Those of us non-shifters that were present stuck together and chatted. They all knew my hand in Declan's and Graham's deaths, but I didn't detect an ounce of animosity from them. Though Declan's grieving parents were somber, they were as accepting as they could be.

Now, months after what happened, I felt lucky to not only have found my witch family with Josie, but a pack family as well.

Orion was already putting the kettle on the stove and pulling packets of hot chocolate from the cupboard when I made my way into the kitchen. My mate was picky and often physically cringed when he described the food his da would prepare for them during his visits, but powdered hot chocolate was, for some reason, something he loved. "I feel good." He turned to me, and I took in the lack of under eye bags and exhaustion on his face. The semester was starting to pick up, and we were still waiting to hear whether I got into the MFA program or not, but I didn't think Orion realized how much he'd been worried about the pack until the issue was settled.

I still missed Granna—sometimes the grief would overtake me and leave me gasping for breath. But, then I would breathe, remember the exercise Orion taught me, and think about her and Coill finally living together. If I'd been her, waiting each year for a night with Orion, I would have made the same decision.

Though I'd moved all of my things into the cabin and began to pack away Granna's, I still kept the house and had no intention of selling it. These days, when I wasn't working, at school, or at home, I wrote in the sun room and attended the garden. Josie, it turned out, was better than me with the plants and flowers, and we tried our best to care for them. Neither of us had Granna's touch, but we were managing, even with cold working against us.

Orion leaned against the counter, and I brought my hands to his chest. "Did you enjoy the run?" he asked.

I took in the hard and soft lines of his face, the swooping curl of his eyelashes. The light over the stove brought out the flecks of gold in his irises, and, under my palms, I felt the vibration of his fingers tapping rapidly at his sides. "I did. Everyone was so nice, and I loved watching you all play." It was nice to have confirmed that without Graham, the pack was a welcoming group. Nothing was perfect, and there were some that were standoffish, including Jasper and Ana, but all of them treated us with respect and voted in favor for us to join.

Like always, I was drawn to Orion's mark, and my finger had already started tracing little circles around the brown scar. My own throbbed in recognition, though it still felt incomplete.

Orion still hadn't bitten me, even with Coill's confirmation that it wouldn't harm or turn me. At first, I knew it'd been to let me rest and adjust to Granna's leaving. After that, it was a mutual decision to make a statement when joining the pack. For me to be accepted as a mate without the bite. Graham's assertion that unbitten mates were unclaimed was apparently a sentiment that a handful of others held, despite there being pack mates in the same exact position.

For me to be accepted, mated and unbitten, was our last 'fuck you' to Graham and all his destruction.

Now, there was no more reason to wait. "So, is there some kind of formal way to claim a mate through a bite?"

Orion had been looking off in the direction of the dining area behind me, but he turned his gaze to me. Though his voice stayed steady, his expression unchanging, his pupils widened. "Not necessarily. Some just do it. Some construct a sort of intimate cere-mony around it. Some engage in a chase where the bite is the inevitable reward." He shrugged and slid his eyes away again. I kissed the little dip in his chin, unable to keep my lips from curling at the idea forming in my mind.

Orion looked down at me, face tilted and eyes narrowed, undoubtedly catching the shift in my scent. The kettle hadn't yet started whistling, but I pulled it off of the burner and turned off the stove.

Without a word, I left him in the kitchen, walked to the back door, and unlocked it.

The sight of the lake and the moon above always made me pause. Even after all these nights eating or working on the porch or walking alongside my mate in his wolf form. After a pause to take in the black water and white moon above and on the surface, I toed off my slippers and began backing down the porch steps.

By now, Orion was standing in the doorway and watching me. His hair was still a bit windswept from the pack run, but it was the wildness of his face that left me grinning. Instead of uncomfortable, the cold left me feeling invigorated, excited, and the dead grass prickled beneath my feet. I reached up and tugged my hair loose from its topknot and shook out my curls.

Orion started to follow me, body almost vibrating with want, but he immediately halted when I put up a hand. I heard his grumble of frustration, even across the space between us, and I giggled. "Give me at least five minute's head start, Dr. Gealach."

He eyed me up and down, and my lower belly lurched. His pink tongue swiped against his bottom lip, and I could've sworn his fangs were already coming out. "You get three. Run now, my little witch."

With another laugh, I turned and sprinted into the trees.

It hadn't snowed in a week or so, which was a blessing because the sight of it still brought on triggering memories.

In the light of the moon, I flew through the forest, running around trees in a nonsensical pattern to try and confuse Orion as best as I could. I rubbed up on the bark of an oak tree and pet the gills of a cluster of fungus on a nearby fallen log before taking off in the opposite direction. Deeper and deeper I went, this time trying my best to touch as little as possible. I had no experience with something like this, but hopefully his lust and my distractions would buy me some time.

Just as I slowed to a creep through the brush, a piercing howl through the air made my heart pound even harder in my chest. Through the quiet of the night, I heard Orion begin his search. His steps were far smoother than my excited stumbling, and I strained my hearing to keep track of where he was.

That was another thing that'd changed. I didn't have Coill here to walk me through all the parts of me that were Fae, but in his goodbye, he left me a piece of myself I hadn't known was missing.

"My granddaughter, child of my Caley, I love you more than words can express. You hold the best pieces of her, of me, and of my Sylvana. You are my heir and the namesake of my mate. Your mother chose your true name, and I give it back to you, Ta Sylvana'a eu Eulaliat Ravanian. Keep it close, for it can be used against you. But it is also who you are. Of this world and mine. Embrace it. I will see you soon."

Both sides of my powers continued to sharpen, though I was certain it was my Fae part that allowed me to see and hear far better than I used to. It was like after being exposed to Coill, something clicked into place, and I felt steadier. Less uncertain.

And I heard the moment Orion changed directions, right before he let loose another howl. When I'd decided to start this chase, I envisioned drawing out this game and trying my damnedest to outsmart my mate, but I picked up running again and didn't even attempt to disguise the noise.

I knew how this was going to end, but the primal part of my brain, the one concerned with survival no matter the reality of the situation, made me startle and run faster at the knowledge that Orion was eating up the distance between us.

Twigs and hard, frozen earth beat against the soles of my feet, but I kept moving. Thickets scraped against my legs, but I didn't even feel the sting while cold air filled me with gleeful fear.

I took a sharp turn around a giant evergreen and saw a flash of white out of the corner of my eye. In the snow, my mate was able to blend in quite well, but in the blacks, browns, and greens of the bare, winter wood, he stood out.

The trees suddenly broke to reveal the lake and the yellow light from the cabin, now far on the other side of the water. But before I could turn back under the cover of the woods, Orion emerged.

He was naked and hard, pale skin bare and fur that'd already begun to sprout on his arms and legs. His almond-shaped eyes slipped between the bright green and a solid gold, reflecting the light around them. Orion's cock was flushed pink and already dripping, curving slightly toward his belly, and my mouth began to water. Chest heaving, he continued toward me while I stood, frozen.

His fingers and toes were each tipped with light brown claws, and his fangs were as white as the moon.

Orion growled in an impossible bass that made my legs quiver and a pathetic whimper escape my lips. That just made him do it again, almost on me now, and I turned to run away, but tripped over a thick tree root.

Instead of slamming into frozen earth, though, my descent was broken by warmth that lowered me the rest of the way. I yelped in surprise and squirmed against his hold, instinct and lust warring inside of me.

Orion pushed my thighs open, and the pressure from his claws was on the sweet line of pleasure and pain. The black sky above was sprinkled with stars, but it was my mate's hungry face that had all of my attention. He lowered himself until our noses were almost touching, and I brought my legs around his waist. Orion was fully straddling both of his selves, neither wolf nor man, and I could've cried with how much joy I felt. We still had so many things to figure out, but I wasn't afraid or anxious or worried. I knew that I could do it, and with my mate, I knew that we would thrive.

ORION

My mate.

Mine.

When she'd started running from me, it took every ounce of my strength to not leap on her right then and there. I'd agreed to give her a head start, and when I'd finished my count, half-shift already complete, I followed her sweet cherry scent through my homeland. The pack run had been far better than I'd anticipated, but *this*, to run after my mate and have her under me, welcoming me, was the best.

My wonderful, beautiful, unique, and powerful mate who'd once saved me before even knowing me. Who gifted me kindness and understanding with every breath, even in her darkest hours. I would do anything for her and spend my life giving her everything.

"Sweet little witch." She groaned and pulled me closer to her. "Mine." Tears fell from her eyes, and I dragged my tongue across her cheeks to catch them. "Say it."

Her sharp nails dug into my back, making me even harder than I already was. "Yours. Always." Before I could rip her shirt right down the middle, Sylvie tugged it up and off, throwing it to the side. With one sharp motion, I tore through her panties and left her bare beneath me.

I wanted so badly to thrust into her, but instead, I took her nipple into my mouth. She cried out, nearly a scream, and I growled around her sensitive, soft skin. I sucked and circled my tongue, let her feel the roughness and the prickles of my fangs.

My claws dug into the earth on either side of her, clinging to the last bit of control that I had until she was a begging mess beneath me.

Sylvie trembled and panted and moaned, and I moved to the other side. My mate enjoyed the danger my sharpness brought, knowing that she was always safe with me. When she threaded her fingers through my hair and traced the point of my ear, though, I couldn't hold back any longer.

The moment I took her in one long, harsh thrust, I sank my fangs through her neck, and I was lost.

She was my mate regardless, but the intense locking of our connection was almost too much. She sobbed and cursed and rejoiced underneath me, and I let my hips retract and snap. Claiming her.

With one hand cradling the back of her head, and the other holding the curve of her waist, I fucked Sylvie into the earth beneath us. I mated her on the land that was ours, and her screams of ecstasy only made me hold on tighter, move deeper and harder.

As her inner walls tightened again around me, my knot began to swell until I couldn't move anymore, and my own release broke through.

I filled and knotted her, my mate now claimed in every possible way.

When I finally released her throat, Sylvie caught my mouth in a deep, lazy kiss. She licked her blood off of my lips and tongue. I was flying, drunk on her and our bond that was somehow even stronger than before. Like we were always meant to find each other.

I pulled away to gaze down at her, but I didn't need to see her face to know how she felt. Her scent sang of a deep peace, and as if an extension of myself, I felt it in my heart beside my own.

"I love you, Sylvie."

Her sleepy grin with lips stained red made my heart feel like it was going to spill over. "I love you, too, Orion."

We lay there, under the dark sky, until our bodies ceased trembling from pleasure and adrenaline. "Are you ready to go to bed, mo ghrá?" I traced the outline of the fresh mark with my claw and felt an accompanying warmth in my healed mark from her.

"Yeah, although, I don't know how—" She let loose a little squeak and tightened her arms and legs around me as I began to stand. There was no pulling out of her for a while yet, and though the cold didn't much bother either of us, I wanted to clean our bodies and get my mate sleeping in my arms.

Sylvie clung to me, trusting me to take care of us. "Let's go." My arms easily supported her weight, and I turned us back toward the cabin after scooping up her fallen shirt. The shifting of our bodies sent ripples of pleasure between us.

I nuzzled my nose against Sylvie's and felt the tickle of her curls against my face as I started into the forest. The trees swayed and the sky overhead began to lighten while we made our way home.

EPILOGUE
FIVE YEARS LATER

"Auntie!" My niece ran around the side of the dark green house, and, for the first time in weeks—*months*—my face split into a grin. I crouched down, letting my bags fall to the ground, and swept my arms open wide.

The little girl slammed into my chest with more force than was right for any four-year-old, but I managed to hold my own. I held her close and breathed in the cold and wild smell of her, of my family. I swayed with her in my arms, kissing her pale, rusty curls, and felt my eyes threaten to burst with tears.

This was already so different than what was waiting for me at home. Here, there was warmth. People who cared.

"Mona?" My brother's voice reached my ears over my niece's squealing, and I loosened my hold, just a bit, so that I could look over her little head.

"S'up, O?" I schooled my voice to flatness and just barely succeeded. My brother looked much the same, but he always seemed more settled now, since he'd found his mate. And his three years as Pack Leader made him even surer of himself.

Never one for my deflections or shenanigans, Orion just grunted and crossed his arms over his bare chest. I knew my brother had a full sleeve of tattoos, but they'd apparently spread to encompass his right shoulder and part of his chest, now. His jeans had a series of stains on them, and I could see the dirt caked under his fingernails.

"Auntie Mona, you're here!" My niece squealed again, and she disentangled her arms from our embrace to run around the front yard of my brother's home. She was a Wolf pup through and through—she squealed, fuzzy braids bouncing around her, and I marveled at her dexterity as she leapt repeatedly in the air. She had far more dirt stains on her clothes than my brother had on his, and her cheeks smelled like tomato juice, as if she'd snuck one to eat while tending Sylvie's garden.

"Ramona?" A softer, smoother voice came from the same direction my brother and niece had, and my eyes landed on my sister-in-law who cradled my nephew in her arms.

"Jesus, Sylvie, your tits are out." I scoffed and held a hand to shield her bare breasts from my view. My sister-in-law was wearing a pair of loose, draw-string shorts and not a stitch of clothing as her top. Instead, she held her youngest at her breast, and he sleepily fed from her, eyes closed and completely unbothered by his sister's outbursts.

Sylvie pushed her sunglasses up to the crown of her head and rolled her eyes. "Well, we weren't expecting any company. It's hot out, and it's just easier with him." She waved a hand toward the baby who wore only a cloth diaper and had a little fist curled against the plump curve of her breast.

"What is it, Mona? Did something happen?" my brother interrupted, always cutting to the chase.

"What do you mean?" I straightened and dusted off my jeans. Now that she was mentioning it, I was starting to sweat under my sweatshirt. From all my time inside lately, I'd barely registered the rapidly warming spring weather, and it was even warmer here than back home.

"What do you mean, 'what do I mean'? You've shown up at our home with bags packed like you're running away. Are you in trouble?" My brother's gruff pressing made me flinch, an unforgivable crack in my facade.

By the widening of Sylvie's eyes, she immediately noticed the shift in my expression. A moment later, Orion's head cocked, certainly catching the change in my emotional scent, or some shit like that. I'd learned to school it around Mom, but I was so, so tired now.

Sylvie stepped forward, my nephew still suckling on her, and she brought her hand to cup my chin and raise my gaze to hers.

I felt the power coursing within her touch, her influence making my eyelids droop and my back relax. Held by her earth-brown eyes, my shoulders dropped and released much of the tension I'd been carrying since New York.

The tears that'd been collecting since then sprang and spilled down my cheeks. But I didn't even have enough energy to sob.

I'd visited my brother and sister-in-law more and more over the years, becoming addicted to how different their home was to my parents'. To any that I could hope to forge on my own.

Sylvie's black brows, as dark as mine, drew in knowing concern. "Oh, honey," she whispered and held my cheek under her warm palm. I closed my eyes, basking in the simple gesture, and my lip trembled like a child's. There was no telling what Sylvie was able to discern from me in this moment. Her powers were weird, but I'd never thought to question when she would see me upset and give me this.

"Mommy, why is Auntie Mona crying?"

I blinked, wet eyelashes clumping and sticking together, and Sylvie called down to her daughter without moving her eyes from my face. "Dahlia, would you get Auntie Mona some of the lemonade I made for you?"

Before the little girl could disappear into the house, I brought myself to snark, "And a shirt for your mommy."

Sylvie didn't drop her hand like I'd hoped, however. She pursed her lips and ran her thumb over my cheekbone. The sweet warmth that she was pushing into my body felt so nice, like hot apple cider for my cold, shivering mind, but I was afraid of growing too accustomed to the feeling.

"I don't need a shirt, sweetheart, your auntie is teasing." Sylvie finally let her hand fall, but she didn't look any less concerned. I knew the bags under my eyes were heavy, that my clothes were rumpled and musty from my day of packing and travels.

Dahlia giggled and pointed at her mother. "Mommy's boobies are out to feed Ollie!" Sylvie rolled her eyes toward the sky then to the side, where my brother was now absently touching his son's fat little toes while he looked at me with a mixture of confusion and wariness.

When he met the eyes of his mate, though, he smirked, almost as if to convey—ew. That he liked Sylvie's decision to go out shirtless.

Sylvie flashed a grin at him, and I looked away, already entirely uncomfortable by the intimacy they had together.

They turned their attention back to the wiggling girl at their feet, and Sylvie answered her daughter's exclamation. "That's right, sweetheart. Now, you remember what I asked you to get for your Auntie Mona?" Dahlia nodded happily, practically bouncing out of her baggy little dungarees. "Okay, and do you need Daddy's help?" The little girl was already grabbing Orion's hand with both of hers before Sylvie finished her question.

While the two of them disappeared through the front door to get lemonade, I reached out my hands, desperation creeping into my voice. "Can I hold him?" Ollie'd quit drinking at some point, and he was beginning to squirm in Sylvie's arms.

"Sure." She transferred my nephew and a cloth from her back pocket to me just in case. I threw the towel over my shoulder and settled the baby in my arms.

After Dahlia had been born, I'd felt like I was going to break her, convinced I was holding her wrong and going to snap her neck or something. But multiple visits and many hours of practice had me feeling an expert by the time they had Ollie three years later.

He was a shade or so paler than Dahlia and I, and his soft, black curls were the same pattern as my brother's. A sweet and hefty boy, he was much quieter than his rambunctious sister. I bounced and pat his back, waiting for the belches to come.

Sylvie crossed her arms over her naked chest, and her own curls were springing out of her loose topknot. My brother seemed to be uncomfortable with any emotions that didn't come from his mate or children, but Sylvie held no such reservations. While it terrified me, it was part of the reason I'd come here, right?

I tried to look everywhere but in her eyes, but, just like my brother, Sylvie cut to the chase. "We'll have to tidy up Ollie's room for you and put sheets on the guest bed, but you're obviously welcome to stay for as long as you need. Do you want to talk about it?"

I ran a hand over my frizzy hair and wiped away the beads of sweat prickling along my temple. Ollie let loose a hearty burp, and I gave the top of his head a quick kiss. "Not really anything to talk about. But thanks."

Sylvie smiled at the baby who'd twisted in my arms to get a look at his mother. "I hope you can stand the chaos. The cabin is not nearly as quiet and clean as you're probably used to back home." I shrugged and turned Ollie around in my arms so that he was fully facing Sylvie now. He gurgled and giggled at the funny faces she was making for him.

Sylvie and my brother had only visited Mom and Dad's once while Sylvie was newly pregnant with Dahlia. They came to see me at least once each school year after I went away to college, but I much preferred visiting them here in Antler Pointe. "I like it here."

Before Sylvie could say another word, Dahlia and Orion came back out with glasses of lemonade in each of their hands. My brother walked slowly behind Dahlia, watching her intently and proudly as she balanced both large glasses in her little hands.

They both made it down the stairs and to us without incident, which made Dahlia beam up at her mother, then me. I accepted the glass she offered my way and took a giant gulp. The tangy sweet was another one of my favorite things when I came to visit in the warmer months, and it at least made me feel a little less like I was melting.

Orion took Ollie from my arms, and even though his weight was making my muscles ache and my chest sweat, I immediately missed him.

"Will you help me get Ollie's room ready for Ramona, baby? Then, I think it'll be nap time for you guys." She directed her statement to Dahlia, who'd snuggled up to her thigh and was silently drinking lemonade while staring up at me.

Her big, green eyes made me feel so seen. So large and noticeable, which was as uncomfortable as it was exactly what I'd longed for at the same time. When I'd packed two bags and left my apartment and school behind without a word to anyone, I hadn't really planned on anything but getting away.

A two week stay in the hospital would do that to a person.

I tugged at my sleeves before downing the last of the lemonade. "I can put the sheets on. And. Obviously, I don't want for you guys to just wait on me while I'm here. I know you have work and stuff, so I want to help around the house and with the kids and all." The words weren't necessarily vulnerable, but they made me feel further opened for scrutiny. I'd learned a lot living on my own and when I'd visited in the past. Every time I thought back to the first day of Mom's and my surprise visit, I wanted to shrink into myself.

Orion shrugged and let his son slobber all over the teething necklace he'd put on at some point while he and Dahlia were inside. "It would be the least you could do. The kids go to Montessori most days, but there's more than enough to keep occupied. When are you leaving?"

"Baby—" Sylvie tried to gently interrupt, but I wasn't offended. The exhaustion and relief was most prominent for me right now. And besides, I was more than familiar with the way my brother communicated.

"It's okay, Sylvie. Though, I don't know how you stay in the pack's good graces sometimes, O." He grunted, but I had a suspicion that he knew exactly what he was doing—that him acting any differently toward me would send me over the edge. Which wasn't wrong. "I can take them to school, watch them so you guys have more free time, help around the house and the garden, anything. And... I don't know how long I'll be here." Honesty was best with my brother, and that was as transparent as I was willing to be right now.

Orion finished his lemonade and let Ollie inspect the cool, still-sweating glass. My brother kept his eyes on his son but spoke toward me. "That's good timing, then. Sylvie's working through drafting and revisions right now, and I'll have final papers to grade coming up. Once school is out for the summer, your help with the kids would be nice."

I nodded quickly. Anything to occupy my time. Anything that allowed me to stay with my brother and his family was good with me. "Sure. Thanks."

I hadn't realized how worried I'd been about getting my brother's permission until he gave it like it was nothing. Like my being here wasn't too much of a wrench in his routine. Every other visit, I made sure to text and give notice far in advance. I'd gone along with Mom's plan to surprise him that one time, and after seeing his reaction on the porch, I vowed to never do it again.

Until now, I guess. Shit, if I were him, I'd have probably reacted far worse than he did. Maybe having kids just forced you to learn to roll with everything.

Dahlia gave a big yawn and pushed her glass up toward Sylvie who took it from the little girl. "Okay, nap time. Let's get out of the heat."

Breathing another sigh of relief, I picked up my bags, refusing my brother's offer to get them, and followed everyone inside.

Dahlia bopped her head and wiggled her legs to the beat of the music while we rode into town. To celebrate my visit, they let me pick what we were all going to have for dinner. Though I pretty much loved anything my brother made, I didn't want to make him cook. Especially after he'd spent all day working in the garden and keeping his children entertained.

I wasn't a shifter like my mother or brother, but my hearing was advanced enough that the stomach grumbles increasing in intensity were starting to bother even me. And when I offered to go pick up the food, Dahlia specifically requested a 'girls' trip,' so the three of us piled in the car while my brother stayed behind to finish cleaning and watch Ollie.

I craned my neck to smile over at Dahlia, wiggling happily in her car seat. She smiled back, bright and easy and in a clean pair of overalls. Sylvie and I chatted about her newest book, which sounded super depressing but in a good way.

I remembered watching her walk across the graduation stage, both for her undergraduate and graduate degrees, and now she was a successful author. For each ceremony, my brother had been sitting amongst the faculty in their regalia, but instead of looking pained, I could feel his pride all the way across the auditorium. When Sylvie had graduated from the MFA program, the college even let him and a months-old Dahlia be the ones to present Sylvie with her diploma.

Since then, I'd religiously ordered her first four novels, and I had already preordered the upcoming one she was working on. I'd never been a reader like Sylvie, Orion, or Mom, but my sister-in-law was a great writer.

Sylvie asked me what I thought about her most recent release, and I shrugged. "It was good."

When we finally parked at the restaurant downtown, I could already hear the neon red sign buzzing. Sylvie killed the engine, and I hopped out to get Dahlia out of her seat. We'd ordered online for the food, but my brother was staunchly particular in his distrust of delivery. Despite living so in the middle of nowhere that driving into and back out of town was a hassle and a half. Something about inflated wait times and his food sitting with a stranger.

I pulled the glass door open for all of us, and the smell of grease and pizza made my stomach give a hearty growl which in turn gave Dahlia the giggles.

Vinny's didn't look like much, but the pizza was one of my favorite things I'd tried in Antler Pointe. My brother and sister-in-law seemed indifferent to it, but Dahlia had been enthusiastic at my suggestion for some greasy pizza and breadsticks.

The outdated dining area was completely empty, but I could hear a few voices going back and forth in the kitchen amongst the fryers popping and some rock music playing.

As soon as we made our way to the register, the owner of one of said voices sauntered out of the kitchen.

"Hey, what can I get you?" He spoke around a sucker that he had in his mouth and prowled to the tablet before us.

Sylvie and I both stood without saying anything. I wasn't sure what she was able to notice, but this guy's scent was... like nothing I'd ever encountered before. His white apron was splattered with flour and red sauce, and underneath, he was wearing a red shirt with *Vinny's* written in cursive across the front. His light brown skin had a smattering of tattoos, and he even had quite a few on his knuckles and backs of his hands.

His face was angular, and the piercings only made him look more severe. The silver snake bites matched the rings in his septum and left nostril, while his brow and ears were a mixture of black jewelry. His long black hair was up in a messy bun, and the back and sides just above his ears were shaved close to his scalp.

And he was staring right back at us. While my mother and brother and his children smelled like snow and the richness of the woods, this guy was like... humid nights and spice.

What they all had in common, though, was the wildness that tagged along with all shifters.

Sylvie broke the loaded silence with a clearing of her throat. "We ordered online. Should be under the name Orion."

The guy tore his eyes away from us to scroll through the tablet. When he found our order, he retreated into the kitchen. Sylvie and I shared a glance that spoke of our intention to discuss this later, and then the guy was coming back out with two pizza boxes and a bag of breadsticks. His mouth was set in a firm line, but when he saw Dahlia eying a little cup on the counter filled with suckers, he plucked one out and offered it to her.

She took it and mumbled a happy 'thank you' before putting it in the ridiculously large pocket at the front of her overalls.

"Thanks," Sylvie said while I reached for the stack of food. He transferred the warm boxes to me, and just before we turned to leave, I locked with his eyes that were the darkest I'd ever seen. Black instead of dark brown like Sylvie's or Ollie's.

We got everything into the car, but when Sylvie backed us out and started to pull out of the parking lot, I caught him watching us through the large window. He pulled the sucker out of his mouth, and I saw that his tongue was stained blue.

I lifted the backs of my fingers to my nose, where his had brushed mine for just a second before pulling away. His fresh scent lingered on my skin, and my mind automatically conjured dense brush, warm water, and high branches to sleep in.

Most shifters I encountered, especially in this region, were Wolves.

"Never met a… jaguar shifter before."

Sylvie bit at the tip of a long, red fingernail. "Me neither. We're gonna have to tell Rion about this. And the pack."

ACKNOWLEDGMENTS

In the Light of the Moon is my second novel, but it is just as much a grassroots operation as my first. Without these people, I would have literally scrapped this book. Without them, there wouldn't be a whole new series in the works.

To Alexia and Darcy, thank you once again for being my sounding boards, my ideal readers, and the ones who have helped me shape my books into what they are today. Your willingness to help me is invaluable, and I couldn't do this without you.

To my sister, thank you for all your help with your attention to detail on this book's first cover I have the upmost trust in your keen eye, and this story and its design would be nothing without you. You are the best sister I could've ever asked for.

To the indie authors I've interacted with this year, thank you for your guidance and encouragement.

And to my husband, thank you for being my steadying force that keeps me going. Thank you for being my light in the dark.

And you, dear reader, thank you.

AFTERWORD

I hope you enjoyed this sweet and weird little book. While traveling to North Carolina, I had the idea for a sweet witch that worked at a pizza restaurant and a gruff, white wolf that relied on scents to navigate social situations. What started as a project to give me a break from *Twin Blades* sequel plotting turned into a full on novel that is the start of a whole new series.

A Light in the Dark is a series of interconnected standalone novels, all with a guaranteed happily ever after. You can read Ramona's story in book two, *Scars of the Sun*, and learn more about a sweet side-character couple in *Bloom in Darkness*.

And, if you're interested in a bonus chapter filled with more Sylvie and Orion sweetness, you can subscribe to my newsletter for a free download.

ABOUT THE AUTHOR

Noelle Upton is an indie author and lover of fantasy, romance, and dark tales. When she's not writing or reading, Noelle enjoys dancing, chatting with friends over good food, and laughing with her husband. Her three series, *Twin Blades*, *A Light in the Dark*, and *Demons & Cryptids* are ongoing, and *In the Light of the Moon* is her second novel.

www.noelleupton.com

ALSO BY NOELLE UPTON

Twin Blades

The Warrior Queen, the Protector of Innocents… fights in seedy taverns and picks pockets for the highest bidder.

But her people have been rebuilding from near eradication. And after a century of running, Meline returns home at the request of the only family she has left. They've built a kingdom from ashes and connected with other leaders to give them all a fresh start, but they are still under attack with the threat of another slaughter on the rise.

So, to atone for her sins, Meline agrees to travel to faraway lands and persuade more to her family's cause. Even if the agreement demands she take a personal guard. But not all is as it seems, and her Shadow is hiding a secret of his own.

Through homecoming and redemption, Meline finds herself leaning on her companion as they face tense negotiations, assassins, and the mysterious powers of a dark Goddess. But will it be enough to confront the person she once was and conquer Death? Or will it lead to the ruin of those she loves most and the future of her people?

Shadows & Flames

He is blessed with Fire.

She is cursed with Death.

After years apart, a new contract brings Meline and Elián face to face with both each other and a mysterious new enemy, more powerful than these immortal assassins could imagine. While they travel to a new world, the spark between them burns even brighter, and back in their realm, an old foe has been stoking the flames of war.

Shadows and Flames follows two immortals with Goddess-given powers as they rebuild what was broken between them, rescue a dear friend, and shed light on secrets that could break them all over again. It is the second installment of the Twin Blades series.

Tyler Lee has the weight of his family's hopes on his shoulders. After moving away from Antler Pointe in the seventies, he returns as a jaded vampire and takes over his family's funeral home so that his elderly parents can finally retire. Now back in the town his younger self was so determined to escape, he's mentoring his nephew, managing his brother's recovery, and counting down the days until he can live for himself again. That is, until he sees a sweet boy with golden hair and pure soul through the crowd and can't resist spending a night with him.

One night turns into more, and Delaney and Tyler form a bond that feels a little too much like fate. Even still, Tyler worries that his darkness is too much for his boy, and Delaney's past threatens to rip them apart.

Bloom in Darkness is a standalone novel featuring characters from the *A Light in the Dark* series. Prior knowledge from *Scars of the Sun* (ALD #2) is recommended.

Love Always, From Antler Pointe

Welcome back to Antler Pointe, a town filled with humans, shifters, vampires, and faeries. This time, we catch up with Sylvie and Orion for a special moment, Río and Ramona as he tries to make up for some oversights, and Tyler and Delaney as the former showers his mate with an unexpected surprise.

After their own celebrations, the Antler Pointe couples convene for an "Intimate Palentine's Day Extravaganza." Hosted by one very excited Jaguar and his mate who would do anything to keep that goofy smile on his face.

This Valentine's Day novelette is filled with a few spicy moments, a lot of sweet ones, and a special night for this found, supernatural family.

Prior knowledge of the previous *A Light in the Dark* series books is recommended before reading this story.

Wicked is the Night

Xiomara is the head enforcer of the Serafim Group, the best shifter family business in the world. She gets called in to collect heads or make sure people get with the program, but this new assignment is different. When her father tasks her with taking down their biggest rival from the inside out, Xiomara is all too eager to sign the marriage contract. Her husband turns out to be a stupid workaholic, but the job gets harder the longer she's out from under her father's thumb.

Boone isn't new to this. At one hundred and twenty-five years old, he's been in the business since he was running moonshine in the North Georgia mountains. Benicio Serafim has been a thorn in his side for the last few decades, and when the opportunity arises to get close enough to stab him in the back, Boone doesn't hesitate. His new wife is a ball of chaos, claws, and hidden knives, but he slowly grows used to his kitten.

Will Xiomara be able to end Boone Albright when the time is right? Will Boone be able to take down the Serafim Family? And who the hell is stealing from them all?

Wicked is the Night is a paranormal romance standalone novel and is book three of the A Light in the Dark series. Prior knowledge from the previous books is helpful but not required.

How I Became a Succubus's Pet

Daniel, a college junior who somehow found his way in a History of the Occult class, is trying to keep his scholarship. With a degree he may not even want hanging in the balance, he decides to go all-out for this extra credit paper. But conducting a ritual from an old, forgotten textbook isn't one of his brightest ideas.

Not when it ends up being real.

After summoning a succubus and accidentally binding his soul to hers, Daniel is dragged to Hell where he waits for his demon to find a solution. He works in her shop, meets new friends, and builds a new life for himself while Feronia's allure grows by the day. One that asks him to submit.

www.ingramcontent.com/pod-product-compliance
Lightning Source LLC
Chambersburg PA
CBHW010732310726

48971CB00010B/2810